Brotherhood of the Lost Gems

Alex Zenk

Table of Contents

Copyright	1
Acknowledgements	3
Chapter 1 The Otthroite Gems	8
Chapter 2 Ordi and the Posh Hound	33
Chapter 3 Apprenticeship	56
Chapter 4 Call of the King	90
Chapter 5 The Journey	117
Chapter 6 The Meeting	155
Chapter 7 Karadar Tower	180
Chapter 8 The Witherwood Forest	211
Chapter 9 The Origins	240
Chapter 10 The Gnomes	262
Chapter 11 The Journey North	285
Chapter 12 The Pass of Ferrus	305
Chapter 13 The Dragons	323
Chapter 14 Caverns of Unrar	344

Copyright

The Chronicles of Ordi
Copyright © 2025 Alex Zenk
(Defiance Press & Publishing, LLC)

All rights reserved. No part of this publication may be reproduced, distributed, or transmitted in any form or by any means, including photocopying, recording, or other electronic or mechanical methods, without the prior written permission of the publisher, except in the case of brief quotations embodied in critical reviews and certain other noncommercial uses permitted by copyright law.

This book is a work of fiction. Names, characters, places, and incidents are either products of the author's imagination or are used fictitiously. Any resemblance to actual persons, living or dead, or locales is entirely coincidental.

Published by Defiance Press & Publishing, LLC

Bulk orders of this book may be obtained by contacting Defiance Press & Publishing, LLC. www.defiancepress.com.

Defiance Press & Publishing, LLC

281-581-9300

info@defiancepress.com

Acknowledgements

I want to take a moment to express my deepest gratitude to those who inspired and supported me throughout the creation of this book.

First and foremost, I want to thank my wife. Her unwavering belief in me and her constant encouragement were the driving force behind this project. Her support made all the difference in bringing this story to life.

I'm also incredibly grateful to Lisa from Defiance Press, who shared my vision for this book and expertly guided it through editing and preparation. Her expertise and dedication were invaluable.

A heartfelt thank you goes to my writer's group, especially Joe and Ben. Your insightful critiques, from line edits to story development, were instrumental in shaping this book into what it is today. I am deeply indebted to your dedication and support.

I also want to extend my sincere appreciation to April for her invaluable help and guidance with the story and artwork throughout this project. Your creative insights added a crucial layer of depth and visual appeal.

I would also like to thank Reginald, April, Jacob, Zunith, and Chris for joining my original Chronicles of Ordi Instagram group.

Finally, a special thank you to my brother, Michael, who inadvertently sparked the creation of Verdun. Our shared love for World of Warcraft and Lord of the Rings, countless conversations, and late-night brainstorming sessions were the catalysts for this book. Your insights and encouragement were crucial in overcoming writer's block and shaping the plot.

I extend my heartfelt gratitude to everyone who contributed their time, talent, and support to this project. This book would not be what it is today without you.

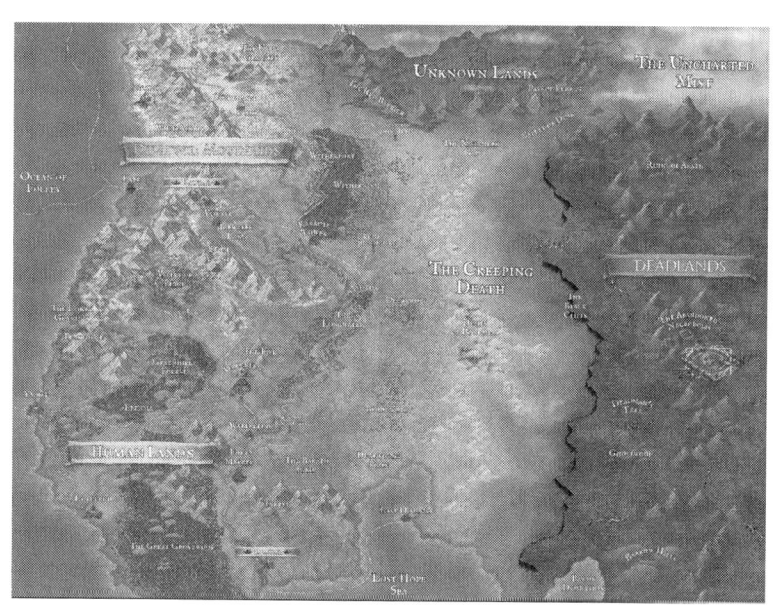

Map by Steven De Bondt

Chapter 1 The Otthroite Gems

Torgen, a seasoned miner, embodied the dwarves' unwavering dedication to their craft. His rugged appearance, marked by the signs of a lifetime in the mines, spoke volumes of his commitment. His quarry? The elusive Otthroite Gem. Torgen knew the immense value and substantial reward that awaited should he uncover one. These mountains, famous for their rich deposits of gold, crystals, and rare gems, were his realm. Generations of dwarves had delved deep into these peaks, unearthing treasures that sustained their economy and way of life. Among these treasures, the most coveted were the rare Otthroite Gems, known for their unique ability to bind a person's essence for magical enhancement. Enchanters far and wide sought the gems, prized for their potent properties. The cavern was a sprawling, awe-inspiring expanse, illuminated by the faint glow of bioluminescent fungi clinging to the jagged rock walls. These fungi emitted a soft, ethereal light in shades of blue and green, creating an otherworldly atmosphere that bathed the entire chamber in a ghostly radiance.

The air was damp and cool, carrying the faint scent of earth and minerals, a reminder of the ancient forces that shaped this subterranean world. Moisture dripped rhythmically from the stalactites hanging from the ceiling, echoing through the vast space and creating shallow, reflective pools on the uneven floor.

Wooden benches were scattered along the cavern walls, each suspended by thick, sturdy ropes anchored into the rock ceiling. Small clusters of candles on these benches flickered with a warm, golden glow, providing sparse illumination amidst the pervasive darkness. The interplay of candlelight and the fungi's luminescence created a mesmerizing dance of light and shadow.

The cavern extended hundreds of yards into the depths of the earth; a monumental cavity hollowed out from centuries of relentless mining. The ceiling rose high above, lost in shadows, giving the space an almost cathedral-like presence. Stalactites and stalagmites, ancient and imposing, formed natural columns that seemed to support the mountain itself.

The rock walls, rough-hewn and scarred from countless pickaxes, bore the marks of the dwarves' labor. Veins of precious minerals occasionally glimmered in the faint light, hinting at the treasures that still lay hidden within the mountain's depths. Tunnels branched off the main cavern, winding into darkness and promising further wonders and secrets to those who dared to explore.

Torgen's suspension platform, a sturdy wooden contraption, hung precariously from a thick rope. Below, the black abyss seemed to stretch endlessly. Torgen swung his pickaxe with precision, each strike resonating through the cavern. The rhythmic sound of metal against stone was a testament to his expertise. The platform swayed gently with each movement, but Torgen's steady stance belied his years. His muscles, though aged, were well-toned from a lifetime of labor.

He worked day after day in search of precious rewards. However, in recent years, the Dwarven city of Unrar has seen a steady decline in yield. The once-bountiful mountain seemed to be drying up, its veins of precious minerals depleted from centuries of continuous mining. The once-lively caverns, filled with the sounds of pickaxes and bustling activity, now echoed with an eerie silence, broken only by the occasional strike of a tool against the rock. Undeterred, Torgen swung his pick into the rock, chipping away with precision. He couldn't help but feel a growing sense of unease. The once-reliable veins of Otthroite gems were becoming increasingly difficult to locate. The scarcity of these gems was not just a blow to the economy but a threat to the very livelihood of the dwarves who depended on their trade. The thought of the mountain running dry was a grim prospect, and the weight of this realization pressed heavily on Torgen's shoulders.

    Torgen's sharp eyes scanned the rock face, searching for any glimmer of precious gems. His calloused and strong hands moved with deft precision, guided by years of experience. Crack. The sound rang through the tunnel. Crack. Another piece of stone gave way, the rhythm almost hypnotic. A thin line appeared in the rock, followed by a satisfying pop as a chunk fell away. Torgen barely shifted his stance, as each swing was precisely on mark.

    The midday horn blew for lunch, but Torgen was determined to follow this tiny thread of gold he was mining before taking his break. Despite the toll the years had taken on his body, Torgen's spirit remained unbroken. The wrinkles on his face were etched with lines of determination and resolve. He, like many before him, had dedicated his life to this craft. His father and his father's father had lived their lives in the cavern, mining the treasures of Unrar. Once a dwarf becomes a miner, it is a lifelong commitment. It was rare for a dwarf to mine enough to have a successful retirement. The greed of pursuing more riches robbed them of this dream.

As Torgen swung his pickaxe, he thought of the generations of dwarves who had mined these mountains, their blood, sweat, and toil echoing through the caverns. He knew the responsibility he carried and the importance of his work.

"May the gods bless this ore as I mine away their creation," Torgen repeated to himself, a humble prayer of the dwarves.

He chipped the rock a little more and withdrew the gold into a pouch to be processed later. Torgen's eyes caught a faint glimmer in the stone, a tantalizing hint of a hidden gem. His heart quickened with a mix of hope and anticipation. With renewed vigor, he struck the rock with gentle force, each blow driven by the desire to unearth the treasure that lay within. This was the first gem in months and could serve as his retirement. The size of this gem was tremendous; it was the biggest he had ever seen. One more tap and the gem dislodged from its holding place and fell into Torgen's hand. He held it up and stared into the murky stone.

Until it was infused, an Otthroite gem was colorless and generally uninteresting to behold. The raw, uninfused stones had a dull, glassy appearance, often overlooked by those untrained in their potential. Once the enchanters infused the gem with arcane energy, however, it transformed into a spectacle of mesmerizing beauty. The infusion process caused the colors within the gem to change dramatically; murky smoke-like patterns inside would come alive, swirling continuously in a brilliant display of vibrant hues. Blues, greens, purples, and golds would soon enough dance within the stone, creating an ever-changing kaleidoscope of light and color.

The infused gems were mesmerizing, capturing the essence of the magic within. They seemed to pulse with life, drawing the gaze of anyone who looked upon them. The beauty and potency of an infused Otthroite gem were unparalleled, making them highly sought after by enchanters, mages, and collectors alike.

Torgen held such a gem in his calloused hand only once, long ago. The stone was ablaze with a riot of colors as it caught the faint light in the cavern. The swirling colors seemed almost hypnotic, a testament to the power and artistry involved in its creation. The gem pulsed softly in Torgen's grip. He closed his eyes, and a wave of raw energy seemed to wash over him, a spectral whisper of knowledge and power. He imagined that the same energy would fill every fiber of this gem, as the mage would bound themselves to it. Who would become its owner? His thoughts crossed rapidly as he held the precious gem. He knew that whoever claimed this gem would wield a significant advantage in power and prestige.

He placed the gem carefully in a new pouch, ensuring its protection. He deliberately lifted himself to the nearest platform to get off his bench, mindful not to draw unnecessary attention. The cavern was silent, but he could sense the weight of the gem's significance.

Torgen did not want to make too much of a scene. If discovered, he could become a target. Some among the

Dwarves had greedy hands and would stop at nothing to achieve riches. He knew that once the word was out, dwarves would flock to him and the council. That was bad enough, he thought. Bids would be placed upon the gem for incomprehensible amounts, each contender driven by the desire to harness its power. Yet, such competition often led to tensions and potential fights among those who lost. Torgen wanted no part in that; he wanted to turn in the gem, receive his well-earned payment, and then step away from the chaotic and cumbersome world of gem mining.

His thoughts drifted to his imminent retirement from the caverns of Unrar. After years of toil and danger, he yearned for peace. The allure of the gems had brought him to this point, but the time had come to let go. As he made his way toward the exit, the gem safely tucked away, Torgen hoped this would be his last great discovery, a fitting end to a storied career.

Torgen climbed off his bench and shuffled slowly down the long hall to the offices for the mines. A few dwarves passed him, giving no attention as they went on their way to fulfill their tasks. He hurried along, reaching the large wooden doors. With a hard pull, he yanked them back and proceeded into the large lobby.

"Master Torgen, good to see you. A little early to turn in your day's work, isn't it?" a dwarf from behind the desk asked. This dwarf was Master Olen, a key figure in Unrar's mining operations. Olen was a short, stocky man with a broad chest and thick, muscular arms that spoke of his years of labor in the mines. His once-dark beard had turned pale grey with age, and his skin was weathered and tanned from years spent both underground and outside.

"Indeed, Master Olen. But I have something you need to see," Torgen replied. He walked to the desk, opened his pouch, and produced the gem from within.

"Bless my beard! Is that an Otthroite gem?" Olen exclaimed. His voice was rough but filled with genuine amazement.

"I believe it is, sir. I was mining a gold thread and found it embedded within. I brought it here immediately without telling anyone. I do not want the attention this will bring," Torgen said, his voice tinged with a hint of weariness. His desire for a quiet retirement was palpable, and his humility in the face of such a significant find was admirable. He had no interest in the potential chaos once the word got out about the gem. Torgen wanted no part in what was to come. His vision of retirement ensured him peace and tranquility.

Olen held the dull-looking gem in his left hand and gently wiped away some dirt encrusted on it with a cloth. "Well, you have certainly earned your retirement, Torgen. Some paperwork will need to be completed, of course, but you can rest assured you will be taken care of going forward. I will let the elders know of this, and I am sure we can find a way to use it. We find very little anymore; throughout the range, only ten gems have been found in the last three years. The councils have an idea for these, as they may be the last gems we ever find."

He continued, "I hear talk of the people coming together to equip our great heroes with new armor and weapons. They are using gems passed down, and their current armor is starting to deteriorate!" Olen shook his head. "Who would think our heroes wear hand-me-down armor and gems in this age?" He muttered the last part mostly to himself. "Ey! This is a good find, Torgen! You may head on, and I'll ensure you are compensated nicely for your findings."

Master Olen was an institution unto himself in the mining community of Unrar. Short and stocky, his body was built like the stones he had spent his life extracting from the mountain. His broad chest and muscular arms were a testament to years of hard labor. His fingers were thick and sturdy, with nails perpetually stained by the earth he worked. Olen's eyes, sharp and penetrating, bore the wisdom of decades spent managing the ebb and flow of precious resources. His hair, once as dark as the deepest tunnels of Unrar, had turned a dignified silver, a crown marking his years of service.

Olen's reputation as a fair and meticulous overseer was widely recognized. He was deeply respected for his unwavering dedication to the miners and his fierce commitment to the principles of dwarven mining culture. His worn skin and calloused hands spoke of countless hours spent underground, guiding his teams through the labyrinthine tunnels of the Unrar mountains.

Olen watched Torgen shuffle out of the office, the gem still in hand, slowly rotating it back and forth. The dull, unenthusiastic appearance of the Otthroite gem belied its magnificent potential. Olen's mind wandered back to when such finds were regular and the gems plentiful.

Returning to his desk, Olen opened his books and noted Torgen's findings. Documentation was a revered discipline among the dwarves, ensuring each miner received their rightful share for their contributions. He recorded the gem's discovery and made sure that Torgen would be paid his finder's fee for this precious stone.

After finishing his notes, Olen hesitated. He pondered whether to take the gem to the council or inform Enchanter Core. Memories of past wastes flashed before him—gems squandered on frivolous enhancements, enchanters who had grown lazy with their abundance. Those wearing enchanted gear often saw little benefit and discarded the gems carelessly. Olen knew the risk of turning the gem over to the Enchanter Core, fearing they would squander its potent magic.

At that moment, Olen decided to present the gem to the council. He hoped their broader vision would recognize the potential of crafting legendary gear for their heroes. Perhaps, with their guidance, the finest gem-enchanted armor of this age could be created, outfitting the captains and giving the dwarves a strategic advantage.

Olen resolved to wait until morning to bring the gem to the council. He would ensure the day's mining activities were completed and all materials turned in before approaching the elders. He felt a renewed purpose as he closed his books and extinguished his lamp. This gem could signify a turning point for his people, a chance to rekindle their legacy in Unrar.

With the gem safely tucked away, Master Olen stood from his stool and looked out over the darkening hall. The glow from the few remaining lamps cast long shadows along the corridor. Olen's thoughts were filled with hope and determination, knowing that the decisions made in the coming days could shape the future of the dwarven kingdom.

It was customary for all Otthroite Gems to be named by the finder. Olen accepted the name Torgen proposed before the council, which ultimately agreed to it. The gem would henceforth be known as Astruli, a "green flower" due to the green mist that would swirl inside once it was infused with Arcane Magic.

This powerful gem, Astruli, would enhance the potent mage staff Dreamweaver and improve its ability to cast magic.

The Astruli was transported to a special enchanter, where it was crafted and prepared to be handed off to Elwynn Starweaver, the dwarf mage currently wielding Dreamweaver. It is said that gems are not sentient but retain memory. A part of the gods is built into the rock during creation, making it feel alive or close to it. The priests attempted to explain the capacity of the gems yet failed to retell the story. It is said that at creation, Moriden imprinted a part of himself into the ground, giving his blessing to the dwarves so they could mine the riches of the world. Each gem, crystal, and speck of gold would carry a part of Moriden. All rock that the dwarves considered beautiful would have something of Moriden coursing through it, and Otthroite gems were no different. Astruli continued its journey snugly tucked away in a concealed pouch of the enchanter entrusted to deliver the gem to Elwynn. Upon arrival, during the secrecy of night, Astruli was handed over to Elwynn, who immediately retreated to her chambers. There, she conjured the spells to infuse the gems.

The early part of the night was calm and still, with no breeze to be felt. As Elwynn sat at her bench to begin work on infusing the gem into her staff, clouds gathered outside, and the wind picked up. While the infusing process was not considered dark magic, some outside the schools of wizardry would say it was unnatural. Any mage could infuse a part of themselves into the gems to enhance their capabilities in a fight. In the centuries since their discovery, numerous attempts had been made to explore how far the gems could be pushed, but it was found that they could only hold two essences. Elwynn would offer her blood for enhanced arcane magic and part of her soul for increased health and lifespan. By giving up part of her soul, she would be harder to kill in a fight; by relying on the staff, she would easily outlive her peers. While the process was painful, it was necessary in their chaotic world, with all the dark forces swarming against the elves and dwarves.

    She reached onto her shelf and grabbed an old dusty book with no name. The cover was worn leather that had seen better days; she brushed it with the sleeve of her robe, clearing off the collected dust and soot. She set it on the table next to the gem and her staff. She fetched herself a jug of water as this process would nearly dehydrate her if she were not careful. Opening the book, she turned through the musty pages of ancient spells until she found what she sought. The spell to infuse the Otthroite gems with blood to increase her stamina and power. She began the chant. The darkness outside swept through her chamber, blowing out all the flames. The mists swirled around her. Storms brewed both inside and outside her room, yet Elwynn was undisturbed.

Lightning flashed next to her window, and thunder cracked a moment later. Nature was always disrupted when these spells were recited, but Elwynn continued. The magic was nearly finished; she just needed to pause to grab her knife and cut her palm deep enough for blood to pour out onto the gem, covering it completely. The gem soaked up the blood while she finished the last line, and, in that instant, the storm ceased, and the air became still again. To perform these spells, Elwynn had a small keep in the middle of the forest, far from prying eyes. She sat back, breathed out as the gem mist swirled red, and properly took the blood infusion. She was drenched in sweat and blood from her cut. She swirled her right hand over her left and performed a basic healing spell to close the wound and stop the bleeding.

Depleted, she reached for the jug and took a massive gulp of water. The water pierced the dryness of her throat, and as the icy liquid filled her stomach, she could feel the arcane magic flow through her veins.

She sat back as the dust settled in the room. She caught her breath and flipped to the next page, not wanting to proceed with the next spell. It was particularly dangerous and one most often discouraged from using. The mage surrenders part of her soul to a gem for increased health and extended life capabilities. Elwynn had only heard of mages performing this on rare occasions; sometimes, the results could have been better. In one instance, the mage distorted his soul so severely that he died during the infusion, with part of his soul trapped forever in the gem. In another instance, the mage was left disfigured and lost her connection to arcane magic. Unfortunately, she went on to live a terrible life, begging and surviving in squalor. Either way, Elwynn wanted to ensure she read the spell a few times before committing to the conjuration. She looked at the page, realizing a smudge ran through a few words. "By Moriden's Light," she thought. "This is going to be a mess." She looked closer at the words, trying to understand what was smudged. The word could go one way or another. The wrong word might only invalidate the spell or devastate her soul.

She scraped her thumb at the streak, and part flaked off to reveal the hidden word, giving her what she needed. After one more reading of the text, she saw all the words clearly. Elwynn was not wholly comfortable with the spell. She knew the condition of the world and the need for her skills on the front lines. She needed every possible advantage. "Kriff!" she cursed to herself. Taking a deep breath, she started to recite the words aloud. Instantly, darkness filled the room, with the wind howling outside. Storms began to brew, but the worst was yet to come. In tiny writing at the bottom of the page, a footnote read: *"Recite spell quickly. The dead are coming,"* something Elwynn had not read before starting. As she continued the spell, the ground up the way from the keep started to tremble and break open. Skeletal hands broke the surface of an old, forgotten cemetery. As Elwynn continued the spell, darkness swirled outside, and the dead rose from their graves, slowly climbing out of their resting places! Fully emerged from the ground, a small group of the dead slowly descended the hill to where Elwynn was currently situated.

In the room, utter darkness consumed Elwynn as she continued the spell. Suddenly, a bright light burst forth from

Elwynn's chest. Pausing, she looked down, horrified to find herself staring back at her with an equally horrified expression. Part of her soul was separating and being drawn into the gem. When mages perform the soul-separating spell, a small fragment is extracted from the soul—a lesser form, equal in appearance. Elwynn knew this, but she was not prepared for the fragment to look exactly like her, with a horrified and confused expression. Losing track of time, overwhelmed by pain, she drew herself back to the page and tried to continue the spell. Each word dried her throat, causing her to choke on her breath. Moments passed before she uttered another word, pushing the spirit further into the gem. She kept speaking the words, slowly extracting the fragments. Each word felt like knives driving into her body, slicing her soul little by little. At the door, a scraping sound echoed amid the raging storms. Outside, the bones of the dead banged against the door; they sought the mage. They were there to drag her to the underworld, a consequence all mages face when they utter the spell. Their strikes against the door grew harder, sending splinters flying into the air.

    Fear enveloped Elwynn as she tried to finish the spell, but the fragment was not yet fully bound to the gem. She collapsed onto the table, gasping for breath. Sweat poured down her face, her arms hung limply by her sides, and her head rested on the table. The storms finally ceased, but suddenly, there was a banging on the door. Whispers filled the air. *"The toll must be paid. You will come with us."* With no time to recover, Elwynn, weak from the spell, grabbed the gem and tried to place it upon her staff. The stone fell before she could bind it, clattering across the floor. She raced after it as the banging on the door intensified. She fell to her knees, grabbed the gem, and attempted the binding spell again.

It was a complex spell, but she succeeded in completing the binding. A chill suddenly permeated the air, and she could see her breath as she tried to catch it. She pressed the gem, and it finally embedded itself into the handle of her staff, changing its color to a dark crimson with a slight, ominous glow. Elwynn struggled to her feet, wavering under the weight of the spells she had cast. *What is happening?* she thought, dizziness setting in as her head spun. She struggled to find the water jug, fumbling around and knocking it to the floor.

"*Kriff! I need water…*" she thought.

Unprepared for the weight of the spell, she realized too late that the soul-binding incantation had awakened the dead nearby. The pounding on the door continued, each bang louder than the last.

"*The toll must be paid. You will come with us,*" a chilling and commanding voice echoed through the room, sending shivers down Elwynn's spine. An audible crash followed, and the wooden board splintered, revealing a bony arm protruding through the widening gap. Elwynn's heart pounded in her chest. She had only heard tales of the dead and their terrifying strength; never did she think she would confront them herself. Now, she stood frozen, facing them head-on as her breath caught in her throat.

The skeletal arms relentlessly broke through more of the wood, each movement sending shards of debris flying through the air. Instinct kicked in, and Elwynn leveled her staff, desperation fueling her resolve. She unleashed a fireball at the door. The explosion sent scorching heat waves through the room, incinerating one skeleton on impact. Its bones clattered to the ground, lifeless and charred. Despite her immediate success, four more skeletons emerged from the wreckage, entering the room with an eerie synchronization that made her blood run cold.

"Come with us; your time is due, mage," their hollow voices chorused in unison, amplifying the dread that filled the space. Their skeletal forms glowed with an unholy light, their empty eye sockets fixed on Elwynn with menacing intensity. The vast emptiness in their gaze was haunting, a reminder of the inevitability of death.

Determined not to succumb to fear, Elwynn squared her shoulders and took a deep breath. She could feel the weight of her decision pressing down on her. Raising her staff high, she smashed it onto the floor, summoning a torrent of fire from the arcane depths. Flames rained down on the advancing undead, engulfing another skeleton and reducing it to ashes and bone fragments. Yet, to her horror, the bones began to reassemble, and the fallen skeleton rose once more, undeterred by the destruction around it.

With fierce determination and trained reflexes, Elwynn swiped her staff, knocking an arm off one skeleton. She spun around in a fluid motion, severing its head with a swift strike. The bones clattered to the ground but quickly regrouped and reformed, the dark energy reanimating them.

"They don't stop..." she muttered to herself, her eyes narrowing with concern. But even as the words left her lips, she watched in horror as the first skeleton's bones began to knit themselves back together, reforming into a menacing figure. Now, there were five attackers once more.

The skeletons resumed their eerie chant, "Come with us." The ominous refrain echoed through the room, a relentless reminder of her dire situation. Elwynn felt her heart pounding as she took a step back. Leveling her staff, she shot another fireball. The fiery spell struck true, reducing one skeleton to a heap of bones, but to her dismay, it too began to reassemble almost immediately.

Despite the growing sense of despair, the skeletons advanced with relentless determination. Their bony hands reached out, one locking around her arm with an unyielding grip, the cold touch of death seeping through her skin. The force of the attack knocked Elwynn off balance, and she struggled as the skeleton tightened its hold. The malevolent intensity in its vacant eye sockets bore into her soul as it began to drag her across the floor.

Desperation surged through Elwynn as she realized she had lost her grip on her staff, her lifeline now lying out of reach. Panic set in as the skeleton continued to pull her out of the hut and toward the small hill cemetery. She grabbed for the doorway, but her fingers slipped off the wet wood as the skeletons pulled her away. The rough ground scraped against her skin as she was dragged through the dirt and debris, her mind racing to find a solution.

She had to think fast. Recalling every spell she had ever learned, one stood out—a spell that didn't require her staff. Though she had never fully mastered it, it was her only hope. Struggling to bring her hands together, she began to recite the companion spell with every ounce of strength she had left.

"By strength of heart and bond of soul, I summon thee, guardian," she chanted, her voice trembling yet determined.

The air around her almost instantly shimmered with arcane energy, and a giant bear materialized by her side. Its eyes blazed with loyalty and ferocity, embodying her will to survive. The bear roared, the sound shaking the very ground beneath them. It charged at the skeletons with unmatched ferocity, engaging them in a vicious battle.

The skeletons swarmed the bear, their bony fingers clawing and striking, but the bear fought back with powerful swipes and crushing blows. Bones shattered and reformed in a relentless cycle of attack and defense. Elwynn watched as her companion grappled with the undead, buying her precious time. She crawled back inside the hut and retrieved her staff.

Despite the chaos, Elwynn forced herself to focus. She needed to finish the spell, banishing the skeletons back to their graves. Channeling her remaining energy with every ounce of concentration, she began reciting the incantation.

Through the fierce battle between the bear and the skeletons, Elwynn's voice rose in the arcane chant. The air around her crackled with magical energy as she poured everything into the spell.

"By the shadows of the abyss and the depths of my despair, bind my soul to Astruli, our fates intertwined in a snare," she intoned, her voice growing more potent with each word.

The skeletons faltered, their reformation slowing as the spell took hold. The bear roared, delivering a powerful blow that scattered the bones once more. This time, the dark energy holding them together dissipated, and the skeletons began to retreat, their bones dragging them back toward the cemetery.

The oppressive atmosphere lifted as the last skeletal figures vanished into the earth. Elwynn collapsed to her knees, her strength spent but victorious. The bear stood beside her, its fierce eyes softening with concern.

"Thank you," she whispered to her guardian as the bear disappeared into the wind. With the threat now gone, Elwynn knew this battle had been just one of many yet to come. She retrieved her staff and stood overlooking the stormy night.

<div align="center">~~~</div>

25 years later…

Elwynn stood upon the dam, overlooking the battlefield. The dark elves were pressing in on the Dwarves and Human forces from the north and west. The lines of dwarves and men held, but barely. Despite numerous reinforcements with fresh troops, the elves' superior numbers and power gave them the advantage. She sighed, knowing the Reapers, the human king's elite warriors, might be their only hope. The Reapers wielded gem-infused equipment, making them nearly invincible on the battlefield.

Eryndor Dawnstrike and Arcturus Lightbringer stood beside her, studying the scene for a strategic entry point. "There, beyond the tree line, just east of our front line," Elwynn pointed.

"I see it. Is it the same as always?" asked Arcturus, the mighty paladin seated atop his massive warhorse. Arcturus thrived in battle, relishing the chance to smash his enemies and leave a trail of bodies and blood.

Eryndor, the druid, sat elegantly on her horse. She saw where Elwynn pointed and nodded. "Yes, it's a good point. Arcturus, you take the lead. Elwynn and I will cover the back and sides." The battle shifted west, creating a larger opening on the east side.

"Now," Elwynn commanded, and the three moved their horses down the embankment.

"FOR TALAMAR!" yelled Arcturus as he charged forward. The Battle of Barren Plains commenced as dark elves swarmed from the north, empowered by Lord Xerxes, the fallen king who now wielded dark magic over the Eastern lands. The trio reached the front lines, clashing with the dark elves from the east and scattering their forces. Arcturus's massive horse trampled the elves before they realized what was happening. He dismounted and leaped into a small group, his sword decapitating three elves in one swift motion. He stood there after the swing, sword dripping with black blood that sprayed everyone nearby. The bodies of the now headless elves stood and swayed for a long moment before collapsing to the ground in a heap. His fury grew, his shining armor now spattered with blood.

Elwynn and Eryndor followed closely, casting spells to clear the ranks. Eryndor called forth roots from the ground to entangle the elves. Elwynn summoned fire from the sky, raining down on the distant dark elves. The gem in her staff pulsed with energy, amplifying her mana reserves and granting her enhanced stamina and health.

Attention turned to the Reapers as they swiftly cut through the dark elves. A group of elves surrounded Elwynn, attempting to engage her. Despite their mastery of swordsmanship, they were no match for a mage. They advanced together, swinging their swords, but Elwynn dropped her staff, calling fire from the ground to destroy them. Two caught fire and fell, screaming as flames consumed them. The remaining elves advanced cautiously, aware of her power. Elwynn leveled her staff and unleashed a barrage of fire, quickly dispatching them.

The dwarves held firm at the front, their ironclad formation forming an almost impenetrable wall. Inch by inch, they pushed forward, digging their feet into the ground against the elven assault. Realizing their defeat, unable to break the dwarven wall, and with the Reapers closing in from behind, the dark elves sounded the retreat and withdrew west to The Creeping Death, their staging ground for further attacks in this protracted war.

Arcturus approached Elwynn and Eryndor, removing his helm. "Easy work. But something's off. Xerxes has only sent elves in the last few battles. No mages, no beasts, no demons. Is he saving them for something?" Arcturus scanned the battlefield as some dwarves and humans chased the retreating elves.

"I don't know, but this was too easy," Eryndor replied. The three gathered their horses and rode back to camp while numerous other battles raged across the lands.

~~~

Some time later…

Ordi walked into his final class, feeling the weight of the past few years of school pressing down on him. Despite the fascinating lectures and theories, he was ready to be done and apply what he had learned. This last class was a history of magic, focusing on magical items. Today's lecture was about the long-fabled Otthroite gems and their role in the last great war. Although the topic intrigued Ordi, he felt relieved knowing this was the end.

Professor Quimby entered the lecture hall and placed his bag on the desk. He took a sip of water and cleared his throat, but the noise in the room continued to rise as the start time had already passed. "Class, please settle down. Today, we will discuss a critical historical account: the series of prolonged conflicts known as the War of the Reapers, specifically focusing on the involvement of the Otthroite gems. They derive their name from their compression and chemical makeup as they are mined. Mages discovered their magical abilities through various tests over the centuries. But today, we will not delve into the stones themselves."

Professor Quimby adjusted his glasses and began. "For several years, these battles raged on without pause. The Reapers, with commendable determination, stood as beacons of courage against the dark forces led by the sorcerer Xerxes. As you may recall from our previous lectures, Xerxes was a formidable sorcerer whose ambition drove him to heights of unprecedented power. His forces were not merely soldiers but entities twisted by dark magic, rendering them relentless on the battlefield."

He paused for dramatic effect. "As the war drew to a close, the strategic brilliance of the Reapers, along with the power of the rare Otthroite gems, ensured their victory. They managed to defeat Xerxes and disperse his army into the desolate region known as the Deadlands. This was no ordinary victory. It was a triumph over some of the darkest forces our world had ever seen."

"After these events, the Reapers, who had once been celebrated as ultimate protectors, found their services no longer required in a peaceful world. Their notable endeavors, tales of heroism, and strategic genius faded into legend, resulting in their formal disbandment. With the cessation of their official duties, instructions from the highest echelons of authority mandated that they surrender their advanced equipment."

"Each piece of their gear contained Otthroite gems, renowned for their rarity and potency. The Otthroite crystals, as studied in various magical texts, held profound magical properties. These gems could channel immense power to their bearers, amplify spells, fortify defenses, and enable communication across vast distances. However, their potency was a double-edged sword; in the wrong hands, they posed a threat of unparalleled devastation. This should have been discussed in depth in your Enchanting lectures."

After a momentary pause, he continued, "To safeguard these powerful artifacts, they were not simply surrendered. They were meticulously concealed from the public eye. The responsibility for this task was entrusted to the ancient and wise dragons. These dragons, esteemed for their wisdom and longevity, transported the relics to a secluded and undisclosed location within an uncharted mountainous area, thus shrouding the narrative in an ever-deepening mystery."

"Various individuals, driven by curiosity and the allure of power, attempted to uncover the truth behind these hidden treasures. Numerous expeditions were mounted, each fraught with danger and, ultimately, failure. Many scholars and adventurers deemed themselves worthy of reclaiming the Otthroite gems, yet none succeeded. Their efforts were consistently thwarted by treacherous terrain, formidable guardians, and perhaps even the will of the gems themselves."

Professor Quimby continued, "As time passed, the collective knowledge of the Reapers and their legendary equipment eroded. The names of those who had shaped history were gradually forgotten, buried under new legends and lore. The relics and their potent magic slipped into obscurity, becoming mere whispers of the past."

"As centuries elapsed, the world advanced, developing a misplaced sense of security. The chronicles of the Reapers and the Otthroite gems receded into folklore, considered fanciful tales rather than substantive history. Silence reigned over the mountain where the relics were concealed, the world blissfully ignorant of the dormant latent power." As Quimby droned on in somnolent tones, boredom enveloped the students. One dwarf in the front row had fallen asleep while two young ladies in the back talked amongst themselves. Ordi sat in desperation, trying to pay attention without falling asleep. Yawning, he snapped back to attention, trying to pick up where the professor was in his lecture.

"…Unbeknownst to the surface world, it is said that the Otthroite gems remained inactive within the mountain's labyrinthine depths. However, one day, a tremor—a mere flicker of disturbance—shook the mountain from its centuries-long stillness. Subtle indications of power began to surface, like whispers echoing through the void." More students fell asleep as the professor continued.

"Dark forces, once repelled, sensed the resurgence of this long-dormant power and began to stir. The atmosphere grew increasingly tense, laden with the ominous promise of an imminent revival. The faint echoes of moving stone disrupted the long-standing silence, hinting at the reawakening of ancient evils. A foreboding question emerged: Would the forces of light recognize this burgeoning threat and reclaim the power before it was too late? But this is all theory. This certainly could not happen…"

"To summarize, the echoes of the past persist in the forsaken mountain's depths. The world's fate now hangs precariously in the balance, teetering on the cusp of a dark era's resurgence. The legends of the Reapers and the Otthroite gems have not been extinguished; instead, they lie dormant, awaiting their moment to reemerge and reshape history once more."

Professor Quimby concluded with a final statement: "That concludes today's lecture. Please ensure your notes are comprehensive, as this material may form part of your upcoming examinations. Thank you."

Chapter 2 Ordi and the Posh Hound

Night had arrived, wrapping the ancient fortress in an eerie stillness. Ordi's pulse quickened as he walked beside his instructor, Master Stow, down the castle's long, forbidden corridor. Shadows danced on the stone walls, cast by torches that flickered like restless spirits. This part of the fortress was a realm of secrets, a place whispered about in hushed tones. Some students believed it hid the chambers of the academy's most powerful magi and their clandestine training grounds. Others spoke of it as the path every aspirant walked before facing their ultimate, life-or-death trial. Tonight, Ordi would uncover the truth.

"Wait here, Ordi," Master Stow commanded as they halted before an ominous door. Towering and grand, the door was made of dark, weathered wood, its presence imposing. It was twice as wide and at least five feet taller than Ordi, who couldn't help but feel a shiver of apprehension. The dim corridor obscured the time of night, heightening the sense of dread. Reaching into his robe, Master Stow pulled out an ancient, oversized key, its metal worn and tarnished with age. Ordi wasn't sure it would even fit the immense lock.

Stow inserted the key, the magical wards humming faintly as he turned it deftly. The sound of the lock disengaging was like a thunderclap in the tense silence. "Do not enter yet," he ordered with a mix of authority and caution. Delving once more into his robes, Master Stow produced a small, intricately carved phial containing a dark, swirling liquid.

"Here, drink this," he commanded, his voice unwavering.

Ordi took the phial, uncorking it with trembling hands. The putrid smell that emanated was overwhelming, causing him to gag and recoil. Gathering his courage, he pinched his nose and downed the foul potion in two quick gulps, its bitter taste clinging to his tongue. Almost immediately, a wave of nausea hit him, and the world began to spin. His legs buckled as the potion took hold, darkening his vision. He managed to hand the phial back to Master Stow before collapsing, the cold stone floor rushing up to meet him as his consciousness faded to black.

Ordi's eyes snapped open at the sound of a twig breaking some ten paces away. Instinctively, he reached for his staff and sword as something approached. He had no recollection of how he had ended up in this unfamiliar, eerie forest. Shadows danced around him, and the night felt unnatural. He heard rustling behind the trees. Remembering it was a night of trials, he braced for unknown challenges. There was something off about the area. He couldn't ponder for too long as he saw a shadow creep before him in the distance.

He slowed his breath and connected to his mana. Feeling the magic pulse through his veins, he felt confident in his ability to ward off any threat. Moments later, he heard the rustling of leaves just behind the edge of the trees. It dawned on him that this was a test to prove he could graduate from the academy and serve the kingdom as a mage. During his classes, he had been informed that this night would be filled with trials and enemies, as the instructors arranged their worst to test the students. Rumors even suggested that the students' greatest fears would be unleashed for them to face. Ordi had no idea what awaited him that night.

The noise came again, but this time behind him. Ordi turned slowly to see the glow of dark green eyes breaking through the foliage and moving quickly toward him. He tapped his staff on the ground to send a shockwave in the enemy's general direction, hurling it back into the trees. The attack didn't inflict much pain beyond the crash but made the enemy furious. The beast got up and charged; as it got closer, Ordi could see it was a descendant of orcs. The orcs had long been considered extinct, but Ordi could tell this was not a regular orc. This creature was largely unrecognizable to Ordi, with its grotesque face and tall stature. It had a jagged smile and dead eyes. Straggly hair hung down, revealing a mostly bald scalp. The orc yelped loudly as it charged again.

Ordi summoned more arcane energy, channeling it into his staff. Feeling the mana heat up within his grasp, he muttered the incantation he had practiced countless times. He knew the dangers of holding the spell for too long—the risk of it backfiring was ever-present. With precision, he leveled his staff at the oncoming threat. What he initially thought was a single orc revealed itself to be a trio. He let the fireball loose, and the resulting explosion tore two of the orcs apart, leaving the third with a severed arm. Undeterred, the maimed orc gripped its makeshift axe and charged at Ordi with relentless fury. Ordi wasted no time; drawing upon the arcane channels again, he summoned another fireball and launched it into the orc's chest. The fiery blast left a gaping hole, and the creature halted its charge before collapsing lifelessly.

Ordi's feet were planted firmly on the earth, his senses sharpened, his breath coming in steady, measured rhythms. He could feel the familiar weight of his staff in his hand, the power simmering beneath the surface, tamed and ready to be unleashed. He was not simply ready; he was a storm waiting to break. He was ready. He used magic only when necessary. As his classes progressed, Ordi felt called to a more specific understanding of the arcane power he possessed. But the Dark Lord wanted to dabble in all schools of magic, just as he, the enemy of the people and an extraordinary necromancer, once did. Ultimately, he was corrupted by the energy and power he wielded, driving him to uncover the darkest of spells. With that, he conjured the dead to do his bidding; there was little the mages could do to stop him when he rose to power so many years ago. His destructive path was well known to the dwarves and humans, but this was the least of Ordi's concerns tonight. Ordi wished only to pass the trial and be awarded the title of mage.

"Is that all, master?" Ordi wheezed, barely keeping his voice above a whisper. "Guess I can manage... a few more."

He regretted it almost instantly, feeling the throbbing headache left by the potion he had been forced to drink earlier. The pain was intense. "I should have paid closer attention to hearing class," He said. Healing magic had never been his forte, and he had never seen much reason to focus on it. Now, he fervently wished he had. Exhaustion gnawed at him, his breaths coming in quick, ragged pants. Sweat dripped down his forehead, stinging his eyes, and his tunic clung to his back, soaked through. His heart hammered against his ribs, a frantic drumbeat as adrenaline surged through his veins.

Ordi's stocky build made him prone to sweating, and the fierce battle had taken a heavy toll. Without food or drink to sustain him, relying on his mana alone became increasingly difficult. The unrelenting waves of foes had already pushed him to the brink.

"Kriff," Ordi cursed, realizing there had been no clear directive from Master Stow. The abruptness of the trials had left him unprepared, a deliberate tactic, he knew, to test the students' ability to adapt in the face of unexpected challenges.

Glaring at the shadows, Ordi couldn't help but feel a simmering frustration. Something moved among them, taunting him. The masters taught him and his peers a harsh lesson—how to react even when caught off guard. Every muscle screamed for respite, but he knew none would come. He wiped the sweat from his brow and gripped his staff tighter, mentally preparing for whatever came next. His magic, skill, endurance, resolve, and spirit were all tested tonight.

Time dragged on; minutes passed into what seemed like hours, and there was no sound. Ordi began to feel tired and lightheaded. The wait stretched interminably; what felt like mere minutes had elongated into an eternity. Each passing second was fraught with a suffocating silence, broken only by the soft rustle of Ordi's ragged breaths. The oppressive stillness of the corridor pressed in on him, amplifying the pounding of his heart. Every fiber of his being was alert, straining to catch any hint of movement or sound in the shadows surrounding him.

The adrenaline that had earlier fueled his frantic defense now ebbed away, leaving him grappling with exhaustion and the weight of unyielding anticipation. His muscles ached, his head throbbed, and the sweat that had once been a mere inconvenience now felt like rivers running down his skin. The air was thick with tension; the fortress walls closed in, and he felt the weight of every move he made.

He dropped to the ground on the wet grass as the dew settled in the early morning. He drifted off into a light sleep when a blinding light jolted him awake. Dazed and disoriented, Ordi stumbled to his feet. He had a terrible feeling about what was approaching. While at the academy, he had trained against the enemies of the world, but for the trials, the instructors could summon even the most ancient or extinct creatures to be faced. As Ordi regained his vision, he noticed dark smoke rising from the ground just past the clearing. What emerged from the ground shocked Ordi to the core…

A hellhound emerged from the swirling smoke, its eyes burning with an evil fire. Two towering demons flanked the beast, their twisted forms radiating dark energy. Accompanying them was a horde of monstrous spiders, their grotesque legs and mandibles glistening in the dim light. Ordi's heart pounded in his chest; he hated spiders—no, he was terrified of them. These were no ordinary arachnids; they ranged from five to eight feet tall, their massive forms looming menacingly. The challenge before him was immense. Hellhounds could withstand most mortal magic, and the demons posed a threat he had only read about in the academy's ancient tomes. Desperately cycling through spells in his mind, Ordi cursed under his breath, doubting whether any would suffice against such formidable adversaries.

The hellhound opened its maw and spewed molten lava toward Ordi. With a swift motion, he invoked an arcane shield just in time to block the searing assault. The heat was more intense and pervasive than anything he had faced before, setting the ground around him ablaze. His shield flickered under the strain but held—barely. He knew it wouldn't withstand continuous attacks. One of the demons, sensing his vulnerability, raised a clawed hand and gestured toward him. A black, cloud-like mass formed into a giant hand and slammed into Ordi's chest with unyielding force, propelling him backward into a tree. The impact knocked the wind out of him, and he gasped for breath. Summoning his remaining strength, he erected his shield just in time to deflect a second attack.

Cornered and with no other options, Ordi resorted to the demon bomb spell, a perilous incantation known for its unpredictable nature. He raised his staff but could not cast the spell before spiders jumped toward him. He threw his arms back and allowed arcane light to wash over him, disintegrating the spiders on him and blasting back those nearby.

The hellhound continued to close in, its horrific maw ready to strike. The spiders hesitated as they approached him. Channeling Earth magic, Ordi summoned the ground beneath the spiders to rise and consume them. Rocks and soil exploded upward, swallowing the arachnids and crushing them under the sheer weight of the earth.

The hound roared and spewed lava once more. Ordi channeled his mana, slamming his staff into the ground with a resounding thud. A brilliant white light burst from the staff's tip, cascading outward in a blinding wave. The light crashed into the demons, pushing them back until their bodies cracked and dissolved under its purifying power. But the hellhound, impervious to the light, continued its relentless charge. It swiped at Ordi with a massive paw, tearing the fringe of his tunic as he narrowly evaded.

Refocusing, Ordi summoned his inner mana reserves, understanding that only a light spell could vanquish such darkness. He aimed his staff precisely and released a white arcane blast at the hellhound's side. The spell scorched its flesh but had little effect. Undeterred, Ordi readied another blast, targeting the same spot, and unleashed his magic again—yet the result was the same.

Cursing under his breath and panting heavily from exertion, Ordi realized that more creatures were amassing just beyond the clearing. He would have to face them soon, but first, he needed to dispatch the hellhound. The white arcane spells were not strong enough. Dropping his staff, Ordi leaped onto the beast's back, gripping his sword tightly. With fierce determination, he drove the blade into the hellhound's neck and skull repeatedly. The beast howled in agony and thrashed violently. Ordi leaped off and swung his sword in a powerful downward arc, severing the hellhound's head. Black blood sprayed everywhere as the severed head rolled away, leaving the lifeless body to collapse.

Covered in blood, Ordi now had hordes of enemies surrounding him—goblins, trolls, and fell beasts—too many to count. This was the trial: survive, receive the mage title, or fail and perish. It was true; the academy only graduated the strongest, and not everyone who faced the trials survived. At least one or two students would die every ten years or so. It was not a common issue, but it happened, and Ordi was worried.

Exhausted beyond recognition, Ordi clutched his staff and summoned a shimmering, permanent shield to block unseen blows. The magical barrier hummed softly, a comforting beacon in a sea of chaos. He steadied himself, channeling every ounce of willpower as the hordes of enemies bore down on him. He recalled the wordless spells he had painstakingly mastered, feeling the mana surge through him. With a deep breath, he launched arcane bombs at the advancing foes, each explosion lighting up the night and tearing goblins and trolls apart in a brilliant shower of magic.

The goblins and trolls charged relentlessly despite witnessing their comrades being blasted to pieces. A fell beast swooped down from the shadows, its eyes gleaming with hunger. With a swift and decisive swing, Ordi slashed his sword across the creature's chest, sending it crashing to the ground in a lifeless heap.

A goblin lunged at him, its sword aimed for a fatal blow. Ordi deftly blocked it with his staff and, in one fluid motion, thrust his own blade into the creature's throat. Blood sprayed across his face as the goblin gurgled and fell. Ordi didn't stop. He tore his sword free and whirled around, blasting two more goblins with a burst of fire. They screamed and fell, their deaths quick and fiery.

The trolls, however, proved far more resilient. With their thick hides and immense strength, they quickly shrugged off lesser spells. Ordi knew he needed to harness more powerful magic to bring them down. Drawing upon his deep connection with the earth, he summoned a devastating bludgeoning spell. Large stones materialized in the air, hovering ominously before crashing down onto the trolls' heads. The massive rocks crushed them under their sheer weight, eradicating the threat with finality.

Only a pair of goblins remained, their eyes wide with fear and rage. Ordi, unrelenting, turned his fierce gaze upon them and launched twin fireballs. The flames engulfed the goblins, and they collapsed, their bodies consumed by the inferno.

The air remained thick as the smell of burning flesh reached Ordi's nose. He stood drenched in sweat. He threw off his cloak, allowing his tunic underneath to breathe. The moon hung high in the early morning sky, its silvery light cast down to illuminate the surrounding area. Yet shadows danced in the forest, taunting him. From the depths of the trees, a low guttural growl rumbled forth, causing Ordi to freeze in his tracks. He tried to survey the area where he thought he heard the sound but could make out nothing—just darkness, as the woods concealed everything. Slowly and purposefully, a dark, hulking group of figures emerged from the underbrush. Their eyes were golden and canine-like, yet they had a human touch. Werewolves. *Great!* thought Ordi.

His heart raced as he assessed the threat. Three, maybe four—no, five. Five of them surrounded him. Their powerful bodies moved with predatory grace, slowly measuring him up. The leader, a massive beast with silver-streaked fur, bore his fangs in a taunting snarl. "All theory and no practice for these damn beasts. This night appears destined for me to fail," Ordi muttered to himself. He tightened his grip on his staff.

The first werewolf lunged, its claws slashing through the air. Ordi swiftly side-stepped, raising his staff and chanting an incantation. A burst of arcane energy shot forward, striking the beast and hurling it backward with a howl of pain. But there was no time to celebrate; the others closed in fast. Ordi quickly cast a spell, surrounding himself with a shimmering light barrier. The werewolves' savage attacks collided with the barrier, sparks flying as claws met magical energy. The barrier held, but Ordi could feel the strain—it wouldn't last long under such relentless assault. Summoning his courage, Ordi dispelled the barrier and counterattacked. He thrust his staff forward, conjuring a blazing inferno that roared to life, devouring one of the wolves in searing flames. The beast howled in agony, its fur scorched and smoking as it retreated into the shadows. But the leader was undeterred. It leaped at Ordi with terrifying speed, its jaws snapping inches from his face. Ordi rolled to the side, barely escaping the deadly bite. As he regained his footing, the werewolf spun around, claws outstretched. Ordi raised his staff just in time, the impact sending vibrations up his arms. Desperation fueled Ordi's next move. He channeled the earth's elemental forces, causing the ground beneath the werewolves to shudder and crack. Jagged spikes of stone erupted from the forest floor, ensnaring the limbs of the approaching beasts. The werewolves struggled against their restraints, their growls rising to a fever pitch. Ordi took advantage of the momentary reprieve, summoning a powerful gust of wind.

The wind howled through the trees, sweeping up leaves and debris and forcing the werewolves back. With a determined shout, Ordi intensified the spell, creating a whirlwind that lifted the creatures off their feet and hurled them into the forest. All but one. The leader remained, its eyes burning with rage. The beast shook off the debris and charged faster, more aggressively. Ordi focused, his mind clear despite the chaos. He called upon his deepest reserves of magical power and channeled them into a single, devastating attack. Thrusting his staff into the air, lightning bolts arced downward, converging on the werewolf. The beast let out a deafening roar as the lightning struck, electrifying its body and sending it crashing to the ground in a lifeless heap. Breathing heavily, Ordi surveyed the battlefield. The other werewolves had vanished into the night, leaving no trace behind.

The night quieted. The bodies had piled up. The ground burned. Sweat drenched Ordi's body; his tunic clung to him, his hair fell into his face, and his arms felt heavy. His heart pounded heavily in his chest as the blood continued rushing through his muscles. He was exhausted from using so much mana so quickly. His professors always mentioned the dangers this could lead to. A skilled mage was expected to be controlled and intelligent in their use of mana during battle, not reckless as Ordi had been that night. Despite his imprudence, luck had been on his side so far, and he had escaped unscathed except for the crushing weight of exhaustion. But the night was far from over for Ordi. As he dropped to his knees, gasping for breath, a shadowy figure emerged, cloaked entirely in black. The stranger's face was obscured by a hood, adding to their menacing aura.

Without warning, the figure raised a slender wand, and a brilliant blast of green energy shot toward Ordi. Acting on instinct, Ordi centered his staff just in time, channeling the energy into it. The spell's force drained him completely, and he felt what strength was left waning from him. The world blurred as he collapsed to the ground, utterly spent and vulnerable.

A soft, mocking laugh echoed from the approaching figure. As the sun rose, it cast long, ominous shadows, shrouding the cloaked person in darkness. The hooded assailant raised his wand again, sending another searing green blast of arcane energy streaking toward Ordi. Weakened and exhausted, he couldn't move quickly enough. The energy struck his back brutally, sending him tumbling across the ground.

Agony surged through his body, and for a fleeting moment, Ordi thought this must be the end. He reached up and aimed his staff upward. He focused on the spells of light again, particularly the light shard. He uttered the words, and the eerie morning darkness around him diminished as shards of light rained down upon his enemy. The figure dissolved into the night, leaving no trace. Ordi rolled over and passed out, his last thoughts tracing back to his brother and friends at the academy.

Ordi woke hours later. As early afternoon approached, the sun reached its peak. The warmth upon his skin gave him some strength, but he was still weak. He realized as he rolled over, the arcane blast would require a healing potion from the medicine ward. The journey back wouldn't take long, but he thought he ought to take it slowly in his state. As he started to rise, the area around him went completely black.

A moment later, Ordi found himself in an icy tundra in the middle of a snowstorm. A blast of icy shards slammed into his face, each one biting at his exposed skin like tiny needles. He blinked, disoriented, his vision blurring with the sudden impact. The air itself felt like a frozen blade, cutting through his clothes and chilling him to the bone. He knew instinctively that he had to move, and fast. His body screamed with exhaustion, each movement a battle against his own failing limbs. He wrestled his staff upwards, his muscles burning. He struggled to call upon the earth, his power sluggish and unresponsive. He pulled at the soil, drawing out a tangled mess of roots, old and cracked like ancient leather. Enough for a meager fire. He dropped a tiny spark, and a fire ignited to warm him. How did he get here? Ordi's mind was racing with the possibilities when one memory returned to him. He had drunk a potion from Master Stow as he was standing before large doors. This could be a room of transfiguration. It changes into any environment the master desires, and enemies can be summoned at whatever ratio they want. This was the room that the students were tested in for their trials, and there would be a whole series of challenges. Who knew how long Ordi would have to be here?

The snowstorm raged outside mercilessly, howling winds driving icy shards of snow and sleet against his earth shelter. Gale-force gusts screamed through the barren landscape, whipping up blinding whiteouts that obscured everything in sight. The cold was bone-chilling, seeping through every crack and crevice, and the air crackled with the icy bite of frigid temperatures. His fire strained to stay lit as the temperatures plunged.

After hours of huddling and attempting to regain his strength, the storm showed no sign of relenting. Without warning, the world seemed to shift and shudder around him. A powerful surge of disorienting energy coursed through the air, and before he could grasp what was happening, everything changed in a violent, chaotic instant.

He was yanked back to the clearing, the transition a brutal assault on his senses. His head swam, the familiar landscape tilting and warping as if seen through a broken lens. The snow fell in a thick, suffocating cloud that vanished in a breath, leaving him adrift. He tried to grab something familiar, but his body failed, and he was once again thrown onto the unforgiving ground.

It was a struggle to bring his mind back to the present, the effort sending a fresh wave of pain through him. He jammed his staff into the ground, the cold seeping into his bones through the wood, and used it to hoist himself up, his back screaming in protest. He shuffled slowly out of the grove, each step a torturous journey for his battered body. A dark thought crept into his mind, who was that mysterious figure, and why did he vanish? He shrugged it off as another one of the academy's tests. He crawled to a brook of running water and reached his hands down, scooping up a handful of water. He did not realize his thirst until he took a deep drink. Instead of using his hands, he plunged his face into the water and gulped it down. The fog of fatigue lifted, and he found his legs beneath him, solid and sure. He raised his eyes, his vision sharpening as he took in the sight across the brook: a Posh Hound, its fur gleaming like polished silver, its presence a strange and wondrous anomaly in the harsh landscape.

The hound's hair flowed like liquid moonlight, each strand gleaming with a majestic brilliance that captivated anyone who gazed upon her. The Posh Hound's silky-smooth fur was a vibrant silver that shimmered as she walked. Her beauty was undeniable, but her aura set her apart. The hound carried a certain mystique, an intangible allure that drew gazes from all around. Her eyes, deep and enigmatic, held a mysterious quality that hinted at untold secrets and hidden depths. She moved discreetly toward Ordi, crossing the brook, her steps light and soundless beneath her paws.

One of the rarest animals in the land stood no more than ten feet in front of him. Their power and mystery kept him at bay. What did the creature want with him? Was it here to drink, or was there a deeper meaning? How could this majestic creature even be in this environment? Posh hounds appeared occasionally; for mages, they made great companions but were incredibly rare. While mages were not required to have companions, those who did often found them invaluable allies. The students at the academy recognized the advantages of having a trusted companion. However, acquiring such a companion was a privilege reserved for those who completed their rigorous training. As

Ordi recalled, none of the students had the honor of a Posh Hound or any other companion during their time at the academy. The absence of companions was standard procedure, ensuring that candidates focused solely on their studies and magical disciplines without distraction.

Ordi realized that his companion's presence now could only mean one thing: he had passed. It was a silent affirmation of his success, a testament to his endurance and skill. A sense of accomplishment washed over him, mingling with exhaustion and relief. Despite the challenges he faced, Ordi had proven himself worthy.

Ordi's mind raced. He had only ever read about companion bonding, the sterile words of textbooks offering little comfort now. He held his breath, a strange warmth blooming in his chest as he watched the hound. He focused inward, reaching for the magic that buzzed beneath his skin, feeling it as a warm, tingling current. A strange sensation blossomed, as if a bridge were forming between their minds, his thoughts overlapping with the hound's, her feelings clear to him. Compelled by this unfamiliar impulse, he extended his hand, and the hound moved with gentle grace, lowering her head to his palm—an unspoken understanding.

As the bond solidified, Ordi felt an extraordinary sensation wash over him. His fatigue and weariness lifted, and the soreness that plagued his body dissolved. Energy surged through him, revitalizing his spirit and healing his wounds. Fascinating, he thought.

"Well, since I passed the trials, maybe you are a gift from the gods," Ordi said as he touched the hound's head. "What is your name?" he asked.

Mira entered his head, almost as if it had been spoken to him. He heard it clear as day.

"So, your name is Mira? I would be lying if I said I'm the most well-versed mage in binding, but it seems like nature took care of the complexities. Care to come back to the castle grounds with me?"

Mira shook her head yes. The two then set off on their journey back to the grounds. Generally, from what Ordi knew, finding a companion was not the easiest of tasks, but every so often, a companion would come to the mage. The bonding was a simple process. The mage would reach out to the channels of arcane magic and find companions doing the same. Their magic would become entangled and form a bond between the two. The bond would assist each other in survival and tasks as the two channels produced more magic than a single channel.

Much of Ordi's understanding of companions came from the ancient scrolls he devoured during his years at the academy. These scrolls delved deeply into the enigmatic world of magic and the intricate workings of arcane channels—the lifeblood through which magical energy flowed. Through these channels, a mage could tap into and manipulate the primordial elements: fire, earth, wind, and water. These elemental magics, often called "lesser," belied their designation by being both immensely potent and intricate. Mastery of these elements demanded raw talent and a sophisticated grasp of their underlying complexities and the arcane principles that governed them.

Even though the records on arcane magic were vast, little is said about the accurate accounts of when mages started taking companions. It has always been assumed that since mages could control magic, they would have a companion. What was more fascinating, Ordi thought, was that not every mage would even bond with a companion. Some would go their whole lives without performing the process. It was a mysterious and exciting aspect of the life of a mage, usually reserved for a more ancient time. Given that Ordi bound Mira during the trials, he was intrigued by what was happening or about to happen in the world.

Ordi reached a rock wall, with Mira walking slightly behind. He scanned the wall and found no way around it. The wall soared into the sky and ran as far east as it did west. He stood there momentarily. Mira approached, her height reaching his chest. She was almost as big as a dwarf. *"There is a spell here that needs to be uttered. Kythara."* The words drifted into Ordi's mind as she spoke.

"So we read each other's minds?" Ordi asked, surprised.

"No, of course not." She stated. *"I speak to you as if you speak to people, but people don't hear what we discuss. Of course, I can understand common tongues, but this allows us to communicate through arcane directly. Say the spell. I'm ready to go. I'm hungry!"* Mira said with a hint of impatience in her voice.

"Kythara," Ordi bellowed.

The rock broke apart, and a door formed. He was met by his instructors, who congratulated him on his success. There had been six trials that night, with Ordi's being one. Sabastian and Askra, two humans whom Ordi had befriended during his time at the academy, also completed their trials.

Both were standing in a crowd of people describing their night. Ordi, one of the few dwarves in the academy, approached the crowd. They turned to him with smiles on their faces. The small crowd's smiles turned to curiosity as Mira stepped alongside Ordi. Whispers began about the Posh Hound, but no one asked Ordi directly.

Hesitantly, Sabastian approached him and clapped his shoulder. "You made it back, Ordi!" he exclaimed. "How did you like the final hordes of enemies?"

Ordi looked on and responded, "It left me exhausted for the final trial and in need of a healing potion. If you would excuse me, I will be back."

"Come Mira, let's get moving," Mira walked beside him, and the crowd's whispers became a loud conversation of amazement. Ordi's body protested with every shift of weight, a chorus of aches and twinges. He dragged his feet as he turned towards the medical ward, each movement stiff and slow. He wanted to run in the other direction, but he took a breath and began walking, each step heavy with dread. He knew he had to do it, but it didn't make it any easier.

Later that afternoon, Ordi was summoned to the headkeeper's room. He approached the imposing door and knocked, the sound echoing in the quiet hallway. After a few moments of silence, a voice from within beckoned him to enter. Taking a deep breath, Ordi pushed open the heavy door and stepped inside, followed quietly by Mira.

Master Stow, the venerable head keeper, looked up from his desk as Ordi entered. Stow's advanced years were evident in the deep lines etched into his face and his long, silver beard. Despite his age, his eyes were sharp and piercing, reflecting the wisdom and authority he commanded. Humans had established the academy, and Master Stow, a human himself, was a testament to its storied history.

"I hear you had quite the night," Master Stow remarked, his gaze never wavering from Ordi's face.

"Well, yes, the last wave of enemies drained my energy, especially the final guy—" Ordi began, but he was cut off.

"Final guy?" Master Stow interrupted, a curious edge to his voice.

"Yeah," Ordi continued. "After I dealt with the trolls and werewolves, maybe five or ten minutes later, a cloaked figure appeared and sent a few powerful arcane blasts my way. One hit me and nearly did me in, but I managed to summon the shards of light. Then he vanished."

"Interesting." Master Stow stroked his beard thoughtfully, his eyes drifting to the ceiling. "Very interesting… Do you realize that the cloaked figure was not part of our testing? Only four waves of challengers are conjured on the first night for the mage facing the trial. While other skills may be tested differently, this was your final task. However, this figure was not part of our design, which concerns us."

"If the instructors did not summon him, where did he come from?" Ordi asked.

"That is a good question indeed. Using only a few arcane spells and vanishing is unusual for our enemies outside the academy. Even more perplexing is how they get onto the school grounds. We are fortified with the most complex spells known to man. If our enemies wanted us dead, they would stick around and fight until either party was done away with." He paused for a moment to collect his thoughts.

"…Not to change the subject, as we will continue to investigate this with you. I see you have a companion?" Stow asked.

"Yeah, I came across Mira on the way back at a brook. The bonding was simple. I reached out to her, and our magic joined. All the theory classes made it seem like it was some complex procedure. But I didn't do anything. After we bonded, I asked if she wanted to join me, and she agreed to follow me back," Ordi explained.

"Posh hounds are extremely loyal and will accompany you to the death. Take good care of her, and she will take care of you. As you have passed your trials, you can remain at the academy for as long as you wish. We ask that you find work or ways to serve the crowns as a mage."

Ordi nodded. "Thank you, Master. I look forward to serving the crowns for the years to come." He left the room with Mira following behind. He felt uneasy about the encounter the previous night but was overwhelmed with joy at finally being done. He went out to the mess hall to join his friends in celebration. They discussed the future and how each would use their skills to serve the crowns and fight against the world's evil. Each mage that Ordi got to know would eventually go their separate ways. Sabastian would return to his village and serve his people there, defending them and providing fresh water as he attuned to the water element. Askra was an earth mage tasked with building and maintaining her town. The three talked for hours into the night. Mira grew bored of the conversations and prodded Ordi. She was going out for a stroll.

Ordi departed from his friends and went back to his room. Mira arrived a few moments later. She walked over to the fire and plopped down, falling fast asleep. "You got the right idea, Mira," Ordi said as he stretched his arms. He took off his tunic and pants and crawled into bed. Tomorrow, he would head home. Head back to Kamrar, be with his wife and kids, and serve his king. Tomorrow was the start of a new adventure, yet unknowingly, the evil growing in the lands would alter his life forever.

Chapter 3 Apprenticeship

Ordi completed the academy and won his trials. He and Mira returned to Kamrar and spent a few weeks resting with his family, enjoying time with his wife, Aimlia, and his two children, Gadira and Dradin. The break was refreshing, but he could not get the image of the shadowy figure out of his mind. It had haunted his dreams and kept him looking around every corner. His short vacation ended, and he would most likely be assigned to work as an apprentice to an older wizard in the Kamrar area. Apprenticeships were a typical step for mages coming out of the academy; they had spent a few years learning arcane magic and now had to apply that in the real world. He was filled with eager anticipation for the new role that awaited him.

The time had come for him to report to the Dwarven High Mage, the head of the council of mages, for an assignment. He found himself kissing his wife and kids goodbye for the day. Ordi left his home and walked down the long hall to the mage's quarters. As he made the trip across Kamrar, Mira followed him.

"Do you think you'll get something exciting for your first assignment?" Mira asked as they walked.

"It is hard to say, honestly. I don't have much insight into the formality of the assignments. For all I know, it could be directly to the king or to serve some mage cleaning out his sock drawer," Ordi replied. They both silently snickered at the comment.

They reached the Mage's quarters. Ordi pushed open the grand doors that led to the main chamber and walked in. The hall was massive, a testament to the grandeur of the mages, decorated with lavish rugs and banners across the walls showcasing each of the high mages over the centuries. In ages past, the mages were a political force that wielded a stern hand against those who opposed them. Today, the council is nothing like it was in the past; today, it is more of a formality than an actual ruling giant.

The secretary greeted him and handed him a scroll. Ordi broke the seal and read the note. The note was brief but filled with promise. It read, *'Congratulations, Ordi. Your time and commitment to the academy have been much appreciated. You are now ready to serve the crowns. As you begin your new journey, you will be privileged to learn from Master Eldrin. He will guide you as you take your first steps in the real world of magic.'*

Was that all? Just a brief note and a directive. Ordi wasn't surprised. Rumors always swirled about the council, some even suggesting it was just one individual, a powerful mage who had managed to keep his identity a secret for centuries, although no one could confirm this. The council was a rare sight, shrouded in a veil of mystery that only added to its enigmatic allure, leaving Ordi and others with more questions than answers. The power they once had was now watered down to simple notes and no public appearances.

"Come on, Mira," Ordi said as he turned and walked out of the hall. Mira followed.

Ordi left Kamrar and headed out of the main gate on his way to his first apprenticeship. His tower was nestled into the cliff just south of the main gate, a far cry from the bustling life within Kamrar. The path leading to Master Eldrin's tower starkly contrasted with the pristine halls of the academy where Ordi had spent the past few years. It was overgrown and rugged, a testament to the secluded life Eldrin preferred. As Ordi walked up the path, Mira trotted alongside him, her elegant form contrasting with the rough underbrush.

"What do you think, Mira?" Ordi asked as he stepped over a gnarled root.

"It is certainly not as refined as we're used to," Mira replied with a hint of disdain. *"But it is a start, a foot in the door, as you would say."*

Ordi chuckled. The demeanor of this Posh Hound contrasted with his more laid-back attitude, yet they complemented each other perfectly. Their bond was strengthened by arcane magic, allowing them to understand thoughts and emotions on a deep level. A mage's companions were irreplaceable. The wooden door creaked open, revealing the gaunt figure of Master Eldrin. His face was etched with lines of age and wisdom, and his eyes sparkled with curiosity and skepticism.

"Ordi, is it?" Master Eldrin studied his new apprentice for a long moment. "I suppose you'll do."

He rolled his eyes, turned his back, and left the doorway. Master Eldrin was an old dwarf mage who specialized in runes and artifacts. Ordi had never met him but had heard rumors that he was challenging to get along with. The old mage waddled toward his study, not saying a word. Ordi and Mira stood in the doorway, waiting for any instructions.

"Yes, Master Eldrin," Ordi replied respectfully from across the room, "I look forward to shadowing…"

Eldrin cut him off. He turned around and gave him a scowling look. "We'll see about that. Start by sweeping the floors and organizing the shelves. When you're finished, come see me again." He grunted and walked back into his study. He slammed the door and did not make any further noise. Ordi bit back a sigh. He had spent years mastering complex spells and incantations, yet here he was, relegated to menial tasks. This was not the apprenticeship he had envisioned. But he knew patience was vital. He finished the chores only to be given more: cleaning the cellar, weeding the walkway, fetching groceries. Ordi finished his day and returned home exhausted.

The days turned into weeks and months, and Ordi was caught in a relentless cycle of errands and shop-cleaning. Yet he did not complain. Instead, he used the time diligently, obeying Eldrin's commands and ensuring everything was done correctly. Mira offered silent encouragement, her presence a steadying influence.

"We're making progress, even if it doesn't feel like it," Mira reminded him as he swept the dusty floors. *"I am sure Master Eldrin will have you working alongside him soon. He can't keep having us do all his busy work."*

"True," Ordi replied. *"I wish I could do more. I desire to see the practical side of magic and its use in the world."* For a moment, Ordi stopped sweeping and daydreamed. The academy was one aspect, teaching the theory and use of magic. Testing one's resilience and strength, but practical application was always needed. Ordi longed for a time when he could show his worth, prove to others he was capable, and demonstrate his strength.

One evening, as Ordi was organizing vials and potions, Master Eldrin emerged from his study with a much softer expression. "You've been diligent. Most apprentices who come to me whine to be reassigned after two days. I'm amazed you've stuck it out with me. I wanted to see what you would go through and endure. Meaningless chores, yes, but they teach you to pay attention and be observant. To see the small parts of life and be vigilant when evil presses in. Lessons you learned in the academy, but in real life, they hold more purpose. Come, follow me."

Ordi was silent as he and Mira followed Eldrin into his study. He led them to the tower's upper chamber, which was a spacious, circular room lit by the flickering glow of enchanted lanterns hanging from iron sconces affixed to the stone walls. The air was thick with the scent of aged parchment and a hint of incense, evoking an aura of timeless wisdom and mystery. High, arched windows encircled the room, their glass panes stained with intricate designs depicting various magical lore and celestial events. The windows cast colorful, shimmering patterns across the gray stone floor as sunlight filtered through.

Bookshelves lined the walls, crammed with tomes, scrolls, and arcane artifacts, each meticulously organized yet exuding a sense of chaotic knowledge. A hearth crackled softly in one corner, its flames dancing shadows across a large, worn armchair that seemed perfect for hours of scholarly contemplation. The ceiling arched overhead, embellished with constellations and mystical symbols, glowing faintly as if imbued with ancient power.

An ancient, rune-etched table awaited in the center of the room. Its surface was inscribed with symbols that pulsed with a faint inner light, hinting at deep and powerful magic. The table's edges were adorned with precious metals and gemstones, arranged in complex patterns that resonated with unseen energies. Surrounding the table were several high-backed chairs, their wood dark and polished, accented with carvings of mythical creatures and flowing vines. In various corners of the room, small alcoves housed glass-domed displays containing relics and artifacts from bygone eras, each accompanied by a brief, handwritten description. The chamber was awe-inspiring and intimidating, a testament to generations of accumulated magical knowledge and power.

"You'll find, Ordi, as you settle into your work, that you will become chaotically clean. You'll know where everything is, and everything will have its place. But to those on the outside, it will appear to be a catastrophic mess. The rest of them will never make heads nor tails of it." He paused, his gaze turning serious. "Though, that's not why you're here today, is it? I'd say you're after something a tad more potent than how to sweep a floor, wouldn't you?"

He walked over to the table in the center of the room. "Ah yes, this is what we'll examine first." He lifted up a crystal. "This is a Focus Crystal," Eldrin explained, placing the glowing gem on the table. "It amplifies magical energy. I want you to channel your power into it."

Ordi nodded, mesmerized by the items in the room. He glanced in every direction as he walked over to the table, trying to glimpse the rare artifacts that Eldrin had in his keep. He placed his hands on the crystal and closed his eyes, feeling the familiar surge of arcane energy within. Slowly, he directed the flow of arcane magic into the crystal, which began to pulsate with a deep, resonant hum.

"Good," Eldrin remarked, his gruff tone tinged with approval. "Now, maintain the flow and hold your focus. Try drawing from one of the elementals." Ordi drew upon fire, which was the easiest for him to reach. The gem glowed a deep, fiery red. "Try Earth." Ordi drew from the earth, and the red shifted to a deep green. He proceeded to perform this action for all the elements.

"What is the purpose of this, Master Eldrin?" Ordi asked as he took his hands off the gem. The color quickly faded away.

"Well…" Eldrin began but trailed off. "The crystals themselves have various uses. This particular crystal is used to note talent and strength. We can use them to help students see where they land in the magical spectrum. I'm sure you've met those who can connect to only one element, or maybe some with no elemental connections?" he asked.

"I have. A few mages could access some elements, while only one or two made it through without any elemental connection. What do those do when they cannot connect to the elements?"

"They are usually required to become Paladins. They can reach the source, the arcane channels, but nothing else. Paladins are just that. They can channel arcane energy and bring a holy morality to their abilities. This crystal also tests your connection and the flow of magic through you. You can configure it to enhance your magical strength as I have done for you. You can use this to house elemental magic; when needed, it will return to you amplified. Back to your lessons now. Let's see what it does for air, shall we?" Eldrin asked.

They practiced for hours, with Eldrin correcting Ordi's form and guiding his energy. By dawn, Ordi's control over the Focus Crystal had significantly improved. "You've done well," Eldrin conceded. "Rest for now. Tomorrow, we begin anew."

Months passed, and Ordi's skills grew under Eldrin's watchful eye. Soon enough, word of his progress reached other wizards needing apprentices. One such wizard was Master Lira, a spellweaver known for her work with enchantments and protective wards.

One evening, Eldrin handed Ordi a parchment, the old wizard's usual gruffness softened by a hint of pride. "Master Lira has requested you. Don't disappoint her. She is a formidable mage with a keen eye for perfection. You'll need to be at the top of your game. Do as she says, even if it goes against what you've been taught at the academy. You'll find theory to be quite different from application."

The next day dawned, and Ordi found himself both excited and apprehensive—a *new challenge,* he thought, *and a chance to further my knowledge.*

Mira's enthusiastic mental voice echoed his sentiments. *"It's about time we moved on to something more inspiring!"*

Master Lira's domain was a stark contrast to Eldrin's. Her abode was a sprawling estate filled with lush gardens and intricate magical contraptions. Situated south of Kamrar, it was isolated and hidden from the naked eye. It was cloaked in protective magic that concealed the gardens and sustained the plant life, regardless of the surrounding environment. The estate exuded an ethereal serenity, with vibrant flowers blooming in impossible hues and sizes, their petals shimmering as if kissed by starlight. Enchanted streams wound through the grounds, their waters sparkling with soft, golden light, nourishing the many exotic plants. Elegant stone paths meandered through the gardens, lined with glowing crystals that illuminated the way at night. Birds with iridescent feathers sang melodic tunes, while butterflies with wings patterned like stained glass flitted from blossom to blossom.

Lira's home was an architectural marvel, seamlessly blending with the natural beauty around it. Vines with twinkling, luminescent leaves climbed the walls, framing large windows that looked out over the enchanted landscape. Magical contraptions dotted the property: floating lanterns that adjusted their glow to the time of day, self-tending gardens that rearranged themselves for optimal growth, and subtle enchantments that kept the air fresh and warm.

Lira was a gentle yet formidable presence. Her wisdom was reflected in every aspect of her being. She moved with graceful purpose, her aura calming yet powerful. "Welcome, Ordi," she greeted warmly, her voice carrying a melodic quality that put one at ease. "And you must be Mira. I've heard much about you both."

Mira's tail wagged in appreciation. *"It's a pleasure."*

Under Lira's tutelage, Ordi delved into the world of enchantments. He learned to weave spells into objects, imbuing them with protective and empowering properties. One day, Lira guided Ordi through enchanting a simple amulet. She explained how to inscribe runes of protection and channel arcane energy to activate the enchantment.

"Concentration and intent are crucial," Lira instructed. "Focus on the purpose of the enchantment and let your magic flow naturally. The intent of your enchanting is essential to correctly completing the spell. Your intent can be good or evil, but the reasoning behind the enchantment will determine if it fails or succeeds." Ordi followed her guidance, his hands moving deftly to inscribe the runes. As he chanted the incantation, the amulet began to glow, radiating a soft, comforting light. "You're a quick learner," Lira praised. "With time, you'll master the art of enchantment."

Their sessions often extended late into the night, with Mira offering playful commentary and encouragement. As weeks turned into months, Ordi's proficiency grew, his confidence blossoming under Lira's patient instruction.

Lira's teachings were not limited to enchantments alone. She also emphasized the importance of balance and harmony in a mage's life. "Magic is part of the world around us," she often said. "To master it, you must understand and respect its place in the natural order. Your intent must be pure, and your knowledge must be certain."

One evening, Lira took Ordi and Mira to a secluded grove within her estate. The air was thick with the scent of blooming flowers, and the soft murmur of a nearby stream added to the serene atmosphere. "This place is special," Lira explained. "It's where I come to meditate and attune myself to the magical energies of the world. I mastered water as my element, and it has been my life's focus to explore how to make water work for us in numerous ways."

Ordi closed his eyes, feeling the gentle current of arcane energy flowing through the grove. Mira sat by his side, her presence a comforting anchor. Together, they meditated, allowing the natural magic of the grove to seep into their very beings. Somehow, the magic felt richer and purer here than anywhere else Ordi had traveled. He had spent over a year training before he realized his next apprenticeship was coming soon.

Despite his success with enchantments, Ordi's thirst for knowledge remained unquenched. He sought new experiences and challenges, leading him to the doorstep of Master Galen, an elemental mage with a reputation for being both demanding and inspiring. Ordi had experience at the academy learning and using magic, but that was in a controlled environment. He was now exploring magic in the real world, which gave him some worry, but his mastery over the last year had proven he could wield incredible power.

"Elemental magic requires an unparalleled connection with the natural forces," Galen declared during their first meeting. "Not every mage can master the elements. Some are limited to a single element, or they can reach a second. True wizards can intertwine them with the rest of their magical repertoire. Are you prepared for such a journey?"

"Yes, Master Galen," Ordi affirmed, determination gleaming in his eyes.

"*We're ready,*" Mira added, her confidence bolstering Ordi's resolve. Training under Galen was rigorous. He taught Ordi to summon and control the elements—fire, water, earth, and air. He used far more complicated spells than anything encountered at the academy. Each element had a temperament and required a unique approach. Ordi's first significant trial under Galen's guidance involved harnessing the power of fire. The task was to summon a fire elemental and bind it to his will. The process was meticulous and required absolute focus. In school, they were forbidden from reaching the core of the elements. That was where Primordials existed, the gods of the elements. They were unpredictable and seldom summoned. Galen held exceptional knowledge regarding these gods and could summon and use them. Such ability was rare among mages, and Galen took extra precautions as Ordi delved deep into the core.

"Feel the heat. Understand its nature," Galen instructed. "Only then can you control it. Let the heat flow through you, but understand its origin. Do not let it flow freely; guide it, trace it to the root. There, you'll find the Primordial."

Ordi stood before the summoning circle, sweat trickling down his brow. He reached deep within and felt the fiery essence in his core. Drawing it out, he bellowed the incantation and watched as flames coalesced into a swirling form. The flame sprouted forth, manifesting into the shape of a distorted human. Swaying as the flames licked the air, the form solidified briefly as Ordi continued to command it through the incantation.

"Excellent," Galen exclaimed. "Now, command it."

Ordi hesitated but then remembered Mira's unwavering faith in him. *"You have this, Ordi,"* she spoke to him, her mental voice steady and confident. As she spoke, she drew upon her arcane power and channeled it toward Ordi, amplifying his connection.

With renewed determination, Ordi uttered the binding words, his voice resonating with strength and clarity, echoing through the chamber. The air around him crackled with energy, charged with the potent arcane force he wielded. As the incantation took hold, the essence of magic shimmered in the space between mage and elemental.

The fire elemental, a being of untamed flame and fierce independence, roared defiantly in response. Its flames surged and twisted in an attempt to break free from the magical fetters. Tendrils of fire lashed outward. The intensity was matched only by its refusal to be tamed. It was a creature of ancient power and would not submit easily.

Ordi sensed the elemental's struggle and felt the pressure mounting within his mind. The elemental sought to break the spell and impose its own will upon him. Flames flickered in his consciousness, an inferno of thoughts and emotions attempting to dominate his mind, bending him to its fiery will.

The battle of wills ensued, fierce and relentless. Ordi stood his ground despite the searing onslaught. Pools of determination welled up within him. He drew from the deepest reserves of his arcane mastery, harnessing raw energy to encapsulate the elemental. The bindings wove around the elemental, tendrils of magic creating a shimmering lattice, seeking to contain the essence of flame.

The struggle intensified as the elemental pitted its blazing spirit against Ordi's unyielding resolve. Sparks flew, and magical currents clashed, each testing the other's strength. Yet, Ordi's will was as unyielding as iron. He was resolute, delving deeper into the arcane wellspring that fueled his power.

Slowly, the elemental's attempts to bind Ordi faltered. The fiery being, recognizing the indomitable spirit of the mage, began to wane. Its flames diminished, and it relinquished control as Ordi's bindings took shape around it. Acknowledging the strength and mastery wielded by Ordi, the elemental finally caved.

Breathing heavily, Ordi stood victorious, the arcane bonds shimmering brightly around the subdued elemental. He had won the duel, proving his mastery and resilience against the untamed force of the fire elemental. In that moment, he knew he had secured its power and respect, forging a hard-earned and powerful bond.

The fire elemental bowed its fiery head in submission, bound by Ordi's will. It would forever be linked to those who could command it, allowing more fire to be brought forth when summoning.

"Nicely done," Galen cheered. "You have the makings of a true elemental mage."

Over time, Ordi mastered the manipulation of the other elements, each lesson strengthening his bond with nature. Mira was his tireless supporter and confidante; her presence was vital to his journey. Galen's methods were intense and unrelenting. Ordi spent hours in grueling practice, shaping and reshaping the very fabric of the elements. There were moments of frustration and doubt, but Mira and Galen pushed Ordi hard. On one particularly challenging day, Galen tasked Ordi with creating a storm using the combined might of water and air. The sky above them darkened as Ordi channeled his energy, the winds howling and raindrops falling. The storm grew in intensity, the raw power of nature at his command. It was powerful, almost uncontrollable for Ordi as he bade the winds and water to cooperate.

"You must find balance within the chaos," Galen shouted over the storm. "Control it; bend it to your will." Rain pummeled them as Ordi fought for control.

Ordi focused, his mind sharp and clear. After long moments of intense winds and rain, the storm began to obey his commands. The winds shifted and moved at Ordi's direction, and the rain fell steadily as intended. After a few moments of maneuvering the rain and wind, Ordi closed the storm. Exhausted but triumphant, he stood amidst the controlled tempest, Mira's presence a reassuring force beside him.

"You've done well, Ordi," Galen said, his usual sternness softened by a rare smile. "You are beginning to understand the true nature of elemental magic." Throughout his journey, Ordi's insatiable curiosity led him to discover ancient and forgotten magics.

Galen's library was an expansive treasure trove of knowledge, a sanctuary where the whispers of ancient wisdom seemed to echo off every shelf. The towering bookcases were crammed with tomes and scrolls that chronicled arcane practices long lost to time, each volume holding secrets of magical prowess few could fathom. The scent of aged parchment and leather filled the air, invoking a sense of wonder and reverence for the knowledge contained within these walls.

As Ordi wandered through the labyrinth of books, his gaze was drawn to a particular tome nestled between volumes of spells and histories. It was a dusty, leather-bound book, larger than most, with an aura of mystery that beckoned him closer. The cover was inscribed with runes of a forgotten language, their intricate designs weaving a tale that seemed as ancient as the world itself. Ordi felt a magnetic pull toward the book, as if its secrets called out to him, urging him to uncover the mysteries within its pages.

With cautious reverence, Ordi grasped the tome, feeling the weight of its knowledge in his hands. The runes, barely visible in the dim light, hinted at the ancient magic contained within. Ordi was acutely aware that this discovery could be a turning point, offering insights into powers and rituals lost to the world for centuries.

"What is this, Master Galen?" Ordi asked, carefully lifting the tome.

Galen's eyes widened at the sight. "That, Ordi, is a compendium of the Ancients. The magic within is so powerful and archaic that few dare to study it. True enough, though, there is deeper and more profound magic in the world that has since been lost to time. We have preserved some, but not all."

"May I?" Ordi inquired, his curiosity piqued.

Galen considered for a moment. "You may, but proceed with caution. The ancients' magic is not to be trifled with. It requires wisdom, reverence, and a lot of experience."

Delving into the tome, Ordi was fascinated by the complex incantations and rituals. He spent countless nights poring over the ancient texts. Mira helped to decipher the runes with her keen intuition. This particular scroll dealt with summoning ancient beasts and elementals. He read through some of the spells and found one entitled "Unite the Cosmos." "What is this?" he asked.

Galen glanced at the scroll and shrugged. "I wouldn't know. Some of that is past my capabilities. I try not to mess with some of these spells. If you don't understand them, it's best not to poke at it, as I would say."

Ordi read on. The spell broke down into phases, moving the mage through time and space and suggesting the possibility of conversing with the gods of old. There was no explanation of the spell or why someone would even want to perform it. He rolled the scroll back up and placed it on the shelf, but the spell haunted Ordi for a long time.

Training under Galen and exploring ancient magic brought Ordi to new heights of mastery. He faced numerous trials to push him beyond his limits and hone his skills.

One such trial involved navigating a treacherous elemental labyrinth, a twisting maze filled with traps and challenges. Ordi entered the labyrinth with Mira, their telepathic bond being their greatest asset.

Walls of fire, torrents of water, gusts of wind, and shifting earth—the labyrinth tested Ordi's command over the elements and his ability to think quickly. The maze would randomly shift, changing the walls and bringing new obstacles. Mira's swift guidance was crucial, and her sharp senses detected hidden traps and dangers.

"To the left, Ordi—a hidden passage," Mira spoke, her thought clear and precise.

Following her advice, Ordi discovered the passage, avoiding a trap that would have ensnared him in vines. Step by step, they navigated the labyrinth, the walls echoing with the whispers of ancient magic. At the labyrinth's heart, they encountered the final challenge. Standing before them was a guardian creature composed of all four elements—fire, water, earth, and air. Its form shifted fluidly, a swirling mass of raw elemental power. "Great, just what we needed," Ordi muttered. The guardian's attacks were relentless, its power unmatched. Flames roared from its body, scorching the air around them, while torrents of water surged forth, threatening to drown them. The ground trembled and split as the guardian summoned towering earthen spikes, and powerful gusts of wind whipped through the chamber, cutting like blades.

Ordi and Mira moved in perfect harmony, a testament to their bond and training. Ordi summoned a torrent of water to douse the creature's flames, with Mira's bark directing the flow accurately. The creature retaliated, shifting into an earthen form, its rocky exterior impervious to blunt force.

"Drat, we need to erode its defenses!" Ordi shouted over the din of battle. He harnessed the power of the wind, conjuring a fierce gale that battered the guardian's earthen shell. Mira's agility kept them one step ahead, dodging the creature's massive limbs and countering with precise strikes. But the guardian was far from vanquished. It shifted again, merging fire and wind to create a tempest of molten rock and scalding embers. Ordi raised a protective barrier, but the heat was overwhelming. Mira growled, sensing the creature's next move.

"Hold on, Mira. We've got to synchronize our attacks, or we're doomed!" Ordi said through gritted teeth. Concentrating deeply, he began summoning the essence of all four elements, channeling his mana into a single, powerful spell. Mira's eyes glowed, her energy feeding into Ordi's magic.

Sensing the power shift, the guardian made a desperate, final lunge. Flames, wind, water, and earth collided in a chaotic swirl. With a final surge of energy, Ordi unleashed a combined elemental blast, a swirling vortex of fire, water, earth, and air. The blast struck the guardian with overwhelming force, each element countering and overpowering its essence. The creature roared, its form fracturing and dissolving into the elements from whence it came.

Sweat dripped from Ordi's brow, his body aching from the exertion, but he stood tall. Mira, equally exhausted, nuzzled against him, her spirit unwavering. As the guardian dissolved completely, a shimmering portal appeared where it had stood.

"We did it," Ordi muttered, a triumphant yet weary grin crossing his face. Stepping through the portal, Ordi and Mira emerged victorious, their bond stronger and their resolve unshaken. The gateway led to a serene clearing bathed in moonlight, the air fragrant with the scent of blooming flowers—a well-deserved respite after their epic confrontation.

Galen awaited them at the exit. "You have surpassed my expectations, Ordi. Your mastery of the elements and your bond with Mira make you a force to be reckoned with."

News of Ordi's successful apprenticeship reached the king's court, and word spread of his talents with the vast spectrum of magic. A rare feat for any modern mage, as many specialized in only one or two aspects; Ordi could do them all. Eventually, the King sent word that he would report to and join the battle mages tasked with protecting the kingdom. Galen approached Ordi one evening with a solemn expression on his face. "The King has requested you. Reports are coming in from the Fringe claiming a witch has been seen practicing dark magic. A small force is being assembled to deal with her. I will lead this group, and you will be coming with me. Please tell your family that it could be a few days before you come home."

"Yes, sir, Master Galen. When do we leave?" Ordi asked. Mira looked excited.

"Finally, some action!"

"Tomorrow at first light."

Ordi felt a mix of trepidation and excitement. *"Finally, combat. I can't explain why I am excited about this, but I am,"* he said to Mira.

The following day, Ordi joined the assembled team of warriors and mages, each a master of their craft. Galen led two paladins and three mages, including Ordi. As they prepared to depart Kamrar, one paladin approached Ordi. "Hello, Master Ordi. I am Roland, master Paladin. I've heard great things about you. I look forward to working with you on this quest."

"Nice to meet you too, Roland," Ordi replied as they started down the path. The rest of the journey east was solemn. Each party member was lost in contemplation, preparing for the impending battle. They departed Kamrar and made for Witherwood Forest.

The group moved cautiously to the edge of Witherwood Forest, arriving at an old, decaying hut that exuded an ominous aura. Its grotesque form—blended with crumbling stone and gnarled wood—seemed to twist into almost lifelike shapes. This unsettling structure stood starkly in the clearing, surrounded by the dark, menacing backdrop of the forest.

A small puff of smoke rose lazily from the chimney while a faint light flickered through the grime-covered window, casting eerie shadows within. As the group approached, a chilling gust of wind swept through the clearing, carrying the stench of decay with it. This foreboding scene filled the men with a deep sense of dread.

Galen whispered, "Careful, gentlemen, the reports on this witch are dark. Do not be shocked if you see foul beasts or unnatural magic at work."

Galen moved silently at the front, his eyes scanning the ominous shadows ahead, every sense attuned to the dark presence they pursued. Ordi followed closely, his mind sharp with both anticipation and dread. The other mages trailed behind, their hands glowing with ethereal light, while the paladins, armored and poised for the impending encounter, brought up the rear. Mira trotted by Ordi's side, her keen senses heightening their awareness.

Their first encounter with the witch's minions came swiftly. Shadowy creatures ambushed them on a narrow mountain path, their forms shifting and blending with the darkness.

"Form a defensive circle!" Galen shouted. Ordi and the other mages quickly formed a barrier of protective staffs, their combined magic creating a dome of shimmering light. The warriors took the front line, clashing with the formidable creatures. The shadow wraiths crashed against the protective bubble. The paladins stepped forth, shields raised and swords slashing, but their weapons sliced through the wraiths without causing harm. The black mist dissolved and reformed effortlessly.

"Paladins, step back!" Galen commanded. The mages moved forward, washing the darkness away with bright arcane spells. The shadow wraiths dissipated as the light surged through them.

"Small tricks," one of the mages laughed. Moments passed. The group stood ready, waiting.

"I think I see something," Ordi whispered to Galen and the others.

A high-pitched cackle pierced the air, sending shivers down their spines. The shadows at the edge of the clearing rippled and shifted, merging into the monstrous form of the dark witch. She was a nightmarish figure, her body twisted and contorted, patches of decaying skin revealing raw wounds that oozed a vile, dark substance. Her hair was a tangle of matted strands, and her eyes—glowing with an unnatural, sickly green—seemed to pierce their souls.

"So, the little mages have come to play," she hissed, her voice dripping with malice. "Pitiful fools." She hovered above the ground, arms outstretched, and with a flick of her bony wrist, the forest around them came alive. Dark tendrils of shadow and thorn sprouted from the ground, attempting to ensnare the intruders. Skeletal hands erupted from the earth, summoning the dead.

"Shields!" yelled one of the mages as roots sprang up around him, choking and dragging him into the ground while he screamed. It took a moment for the paladins to sever the roots, as Ordi calmed the earth and called upon the Primordial to assist.

The battle intensified. The witch's minions—a mix of twisted abominations and resurrected corpses—swarmed the clearing. Galen led the paladins in a valiant charge, striking down skeletal warriors only for them to rise again. Ordi and the mages unleashed torrents of arcane energy, incinerating the dark creatures. Despite their best efforts, the witch's power seemed endless. She began summoning more skeletons to add to the chaos of the battle. Mira charged in, pouncing and ripping bones apart. The skeletons reformed effortlessly, keeping her busy.

The skeletons pressed in, their bony fingers scraping and clawing, as Ordi and Mira fought back to back, the sounds of battle filling the clearing. Ordi summoned bolts of arcane magic that pierced through the skeletal frames, incinerating them to ash, but it was a fleeting victory. The skeletons reformed with unnatural speed, their rattling bones an unsettling soundtrack to the ongoing fight. Mira, a relentless force, ripped through the fiends, her claws tearing at their shadows and forcing them back, but like the skeletons, they seemed unending. The tide of enemies crashed against them, a relentless wave that tested their strength and endurance.

Nearby, Roland waded into the thick of battle, resolve burning in his eyes. The witch called darkness to fall around them. He stood like a bastion, his sword imbued with radiant holy light, cleaving through the ranks of undead that tried to overwhelm him. The skeletal warriors clattered against his defense, their rusted weapons impotent against his divine armor.

Roland spun, his blade arcing through the air. He severed limbs and skulls with unerring precision. Around him, the paladins formed a phalanx, their combined might pushing back the horde. But the onslaught was unceasing, like waves crashing upon the shore, and Roland knew more was required; for every skeleton cut down, two more filled its void. The sword seemed to do little in this fight. The skeletons crumbled, rose, and charged again.

Roland found himself surrounded, his sword a blur of light as he sliced through the skeletal onslaught. Each parry rang with the clash of blade against bone. The skeletons were relentless.

"Cenric!" Roland called, his voice slicing through the battlefield's din as his fellow paladin moved to join him. Cenric fought just a few feet away, locked in an unending duel with the reanimated dead, his armor gleaming in the faint light.

"I need a minute to summon. Can you handle them, Cenric?" Roland shouted over the cacophony of clashing weapons.

"Aye, do hurry!" Cenric replied, his voice imbued with resolve and a touch of levity, even amidst the chaos.

With a nod, Roland turned, channeling his energies into a powerful incantation. Cenric stood firm as more skeletal warriors closed in, their bony fingers clutching rusted blades.

He met them with unwavering bravery, his sword dancing in precise arcs that severed limbs and shattered skulls.

But the tide rolled on endlessly. As Cenric cut down one foe, another two stepped forth, their jagged weapons reaching for him. His shield flashed as he deflected a grievous blow, but a skeletal arm caught him off guard, slicing through a gap in his armor. The sword pierced through his abdomen, penetrating deep.

Gritting his teeth against the searing pain, Cenric continued to fight, standing as a bulwark against the encroaching horde. Determination burned in his eyes as he held the line, buying precious time for Roland.

The skeletons surged again, and Cenric, bleeding and exhausted, summoned all his strength for one final stand. He charged into the fray; the weight of his armor now felt heavy, and his body began to give way.

Cenric gasped as the skeletons overwhelmed him and dragged him to the ground beneath a storm of ruthless blows. He kept fighting as the piles of bones grew, slashing until, finally, he moved no more.

Roland turned too late, his spell complete, witnessing Cenric's sacrifice. With a roar that echoed with both fury and grief, Roland unleashed a wave of righteous energy, obliterating the encroaching skeletons in a radiant burst, the ground trembling beneath its force.

Two shadow fiends, like wraiths, lunged towards the grieving warrior, hoping to feast on his despair. Roland's aura blazed into life, a holy light that ripped through the surroundings, temporarily obliterating the fiends. Yet, the light began to fade no sooner than they were back, their forms coalescing into the same grotesque shapes. He roared a prayer with every swing.

"O God above, give me strength."

His words were a defiant cry against the oppressive dark. He released a torrent of holy power that washed over the area with all his might, banishing the shadows and shattering the risen dead into still forms. The power pierced the shadows of the fiends, yet they did not falter and continued to close in on him. Focusing his will, he poured his power into his sword until it pulsed with white arcane fire, and with a fierce yell, he swung, the blade slicing through the first fiend, reducing it to ash. A fist slammed into Roland's chest, sending him staggering back, his vision momentarily blurring. He drew on his inner reserves, channeling the arcane power into his blade once more, and with a guttural cry, he swung again, and the white fire consumed the second fiend, leaving behind nothing but emptiness.

"Kriff," Galen took a deep breath, his gaze focused and unwavering. Then he strode forward with purpose, his movements precise, leading the paladins with calm resolve. He raised his hand, his fingers weaving complex patterns as he cast a shimmering aura of protection around himself, the energy flowing smoothly, with no wasted movement.

The witch called more shadow fiends to distract the group as she focused her attention on Galen. He cast protective auras around himself, standing some ten feet from her. She smiled, revealing blackened teeth, and lashed out, sending shadow daggers toward Galen. He blocked them with a shimmering shield, the daggers evaporating against pure arcane energy. Galen responded with a barrage of arcane bolts, but the witch absorbed them effortlessly, treating them like mere droplets.

Unfazed, she rose higher, summoning lightning and raining it down upon Galen. She constructed a black blade from the shadows as he defended himself from the deadly bolts. In a swift motion, she threw the dagger and stabbed Galen through the chest. An evil laugh escaped her lips as the blade easily pierced his armor.

"NO!" screamed Ordi, dispatching the last fiend in his path. He charged after the witch as Galen sagged to the ground. Her blade protruded from his body, and he lay in the dirt, unmoving.

Ordi leaped over Galen's lifeless body, producing a protective shield and calling forth the ground to ensnare the witch. Another mage joined him, summoning fire from the skies. Roland charged at the witch, forcing her higher into the air as she laughed and mocked their efforts. With every fiber of his being, Ordi summoned a powerful gust of wind, pressing down upon the witch. Roland stood ready, conjuring brilliant holy arcane to entrap her.

With tremendous effort, Ordi drove the witch closer to the ground. Before Roland could strike, she evaporated and reappeared a few feet away, free from their grasp.

"Freeze her in place," Ordi whispered to the mages. They attempted to encase her in ice, but she spewed black sludge that dissolved the frozen barrier. Realizing the mages couldn't freeze her, Ordi used her distraction to their advantage. Reaching out to Mira, he instructed the earth, "Prepare to seize her in your roots, but not until Mira signals." The earth responded in acknowledgment. Next, he connected with air and fire, directing them as he waited for the right moment. "Now," he told Mira.

With a ferocious burst of energy, the earth sent its roots writhing and reaching toward the wicked witch, coiling tightly around her body. Flames erupted around the roots, directed by Ordi's precise elemental control. It was a delicate balance, manipulating the elements to create perfect harmony. Too little air, and the fire would extinguish; too much would consume everything.

The witch struggled against the roots, summoning her remaining power. Black energy surged from her eyes, breaking free from the entanglement. Ordi intensified his control, whipping the air into a fierce current around her, suffocating her magic. Roland stepped forward, his sword glowing with holy energy. "This ends now!" he declared, raising his sword high. The witch's eyes widened as Roland plunged the sword into her heart. Holy energy collided with her dark magic, creating a shockwave that rattled the earth.

The witch released a final, piercing scream as her body exploded in a burst of dark energy. The combined forces consumed her essence, dissipating into the wind, leaving only silence and the smell of burnt ozone.

Her body fell. The roots retreated into the ground as black blood gushed everywhere. The twisted blackness of her presence dissipated into the wind. The hut behind them crumbled, reduced to ruins, and the evil that once hung over the area drifted away. A crisp wind blew through the trees as the sun broke the horizon. The night was won, but the cost was high. Both Galen and Cenric had lost their lives in this gruesome battle. Darkness once again crept into the lands.

As the champions departed Witherwood Forest and returned to Kamrar, they carried the weight of their loss along with the resolve to face whatever darkness awaited them next.

There was a ceremony for those tasked with taking down the witch. King Telophap orchestrated a special memorial for Galen and Cenric. Their images were raised in the Hall of the Fallen—a place where the Dwarves remembered those who were heroic and met a tragic end. Galen would forever hold a special place in the hearts of those who knew him. For Ordi, it was a special honor to have been his last apprentice and to have gone into battle, but he knew his death would haunt him at some point.

"Ordi, your bravery and mastery of magic have saved our kingdom," the king proclaimed. "It is an honor to appoint you as the King's Mage. You will serve with the elite group in protecting me while I travel and handling any special errands or tasks that befall us." Telophap spoke boldly to the great crowd gathered. Ordi's wife applauded after the speech, and their kids yelled excitedly.

Kneeling before the throne, Ordi felt a swell of pride. *"We did it,"* he sent to Mira.

"I always knew we could," Mira replied, her mental voice brimming with joy.

As the accolade was bestowed upon him, Ordi looked at the gathered assembly, his heart filled with hope and determination. His journey had been long and arduous, but it was only beginning. With Mira by his side and his wife to support them, he was ready to face whatever lay ahead as the realm's King's Mage and protector. At that moment, Ordi stood before the gathered Dwarves and knew his place was in Kamrar.

Serving as a King's Mage was an honor reserved only for the most skilled and trusted mages, requiring great power, wisdom, and integrity. Ordi's responsibilities extended far beyond the battlefield. He became an advisor to the king, a mentor to young mages, and a guardian of the kingdom's arcane knowledge. He would be the youngest to serve the king in this role, but his demonstration of knowledge and the power he wielded would be instrumental for him in the years to come.

In the following months, his role as King's Mage took shape as one who preserved knowledge. Ordi restored the ancient library with the materials he could find. The manuscripts and scrolls were sparse, but Ordi worked tirelessly to expand the library's capacity to preserve and grow the knowledge of the mages. He examined Mater Galen's library and the surrounding communities. Over the centuries, the mage's library had been discarded, moved, picked over, and left in shambles.

The quill scratched across the aged parchment, a slow, rhythmic sound that filled the quiet room as Ordi copied the faded script, his hand aching with the effort. He carefully updated the worn scrolls, his brow furrowed in concentration, before meticulously categorizing each new arrival, his fingers tracing the faded ink. Soon, word spread among the kingdoms, and scrolls and parchments arrived steadily, filling every available space. He would examine each scroll with a critical eye, swiftly discarding those with no value, his hand sweeping them aside to the growing pile of rejected knowledge while placing the keepers into precisely labeled boxes. One lazy afternoon, the scent of old paper and dust filling the air, Ordi's gaze drifted across a pile of parchments detailing the simplest conjurations: spells for rabbit stew, mending clothes, and making candles. Occasionally, He would stumble upon something that would ignite a spark of curiosity, a new perspective on runes, a unique method of cutting gems, or a forgotten combat technique. Each was carefully placed in a special file, the pages smoothed and flattened before being locked away for preservation.

Mira was asleep by his side when a knock came at his chamber door. Mira perked up. *"I think it is important,"* she said. Yawning.

Ordi rose to the door, where a young errand boy stood waiting. "Master Ordi, there is a request for your assistance." He handed him a small scroll and ran off. Ordi opened it and read.

"A small nomad group gathering at a spring between Ysserar and the mountains discovered that the spring had dried up. They request our assistance, Mira," Ordi said.

"Let us go then! Something exciting to do!" Mira was instantly on the move.

It was a quick journey south of Kamrar, and they were greeted warmly. "Thank you for coming, Master Ordi," the village elder, a wise old woman named Maelis, said. "We've tried everything, but the spring remains dry. Our crops will wither, and our people are growing desperate for water."

"Oh, you are most welcome," Ordi replied. *"Come, Mira, I am intrigued to see what this could be."* Maelis led the way to a rocky hill where the spring nestled. Ordi knelt by the pit's edge, dipping his fingers into the parched soil. He closed his eyes, reaching out to the arcane channels to discern the cause of the spring's desiccation, connecting with water to find the source and flow. He immediately felt a disturbance—an unnatural barrier blocking the underground water flow. It was as if a magical dam had been erected to cut off the life-giving source.

"There's something magical at play," Ordi thought to Mira. *"This isn't a natural occurrence."*

"What do you think it could be?" Mira replied, her curiosity piqued.

Ordi stood up, his mind racing with possibilities. *"We need to find the source of this disturbance. It could be a malicious spell or a magical artifact disrupting the water flow."*

With Maelis's guidance, they followed the course of the underground waterway, eventually reaching a secluded cave hidden among the rocks. The air around the entrance was thick with magic, its presence evident.

Ordi took a deep breath and stepped inside, with Mira close beside him. The cave was dark and eerie, illuminated by the faint glow of Ordi's staff. As they ventured deeper, they came across what appeared to be a makeshift altar, covered in runes and surrounded by arcane symbols. He recognized the runes from scrolls he'd read about the Dark Lord. They seemed quickly sketched, almost smeared, yet here they were. He knelt and looked closer.

After a moment, he concluded, *"These are fresh, Mira. Someone has been here dabbling in dark magic. This doesn't make sense, though, as the Dark Lord has been dead for so long."*

Mira perceived that the ancient markings couldn't have been more than a month old. However, the tribe had just arrived in this region yesterday, making it difficult to determine the age or purpose of the altar. "Why target just a small spring? It doesn't add up. Our records of him show much more destructive behavior," Mira commented.

"I think it may be someone messing around. They found some ancient spells and wanted to perform them away from prying eyes. Maybe it's no more than a prank," Ordi said.

He prepared to deactivate the crystal and destroy the altar. He took a deep breath and started the counter-spell, but almost instantly, the crystal rejected it. Instead, the color inside grew darker. Ordi shifted his spell and drew deeper into the arcane channel for holy light. Finally, he overwhelmed the spell on the crystal. The blackness evaporated, and the altar broke in half as the runes were wiped away.

Mira followed Ordi out of the cave. *"That was an incredibly powerful crystal for someone to be playing a prank,"* she said.

"Oy, honestly, I don't know what to make of it."

The two met with Maelis and the rest of the tribe as they gathered around the spring, where the water flowed nicely. They cheered and celebrated Ordi and Mira for solving their problem. That evening at home, Ordi reflected on his job as King's Mage. Most of his time was spent in the library, but occasionally, he was called forth to help resolve something simple. However, today was different. Why the altar? Why the runes? The language of the Dark Lord resonated in his head. Could this be tied to the shadow figure during his trials?

Aimlia broke his concentration. "Would you care for an evening tea, dear?" she spoke softly, not to startle him.

"Yes, I would like some. Maybe it would help me relax." He sat on the back porch, drawing in the coolness of the cave.

"Tough day?" she asked.

"Interesting day is appropriate. I discovered something that I wonder about. I need to dig deeper. I think I need to go to Talamar to speak with Master Stow on this issue." Ordi took a long sip of his tea.

"If you must go, then you must. Our service is to the kingdom," Aimlia said. "I do miss you when you are gone. It is nice having you home in the evenings."

"I do not like going, but there could be a darkness swirling in the world that needs to be challenged."

"Oh, that sounds unpleasant. Will you leave first thing in the morning?" she asked.

"Yes, perhaps I shall. Mira will accompany me as usual. I'd better turn in for the night." He took another drink, finishing off the tea. "Thank you, my love. You always know how to calm my spirit." He kissed her forehead, returned inside, and crawled into bed.

Chapter 4 Call of the King

Ordi and Mira traveled occasionally between Kamrar and Talamar, bridging the gap between his homeland and the academy. He assisted new students and gathered information. This trip was no different; he wanted answers to the runes he sought. Upon leaving, a message arrived just as he departed Kamrar. Master Stow had summoned Ordi to teach a class on the manipulation of air, a request Ordi felt obligated to fulfill.

Together, Ordi and Mira imparted their knowledge to the eager young students. When Ordi presented the information about the runes to Master Stow, he was met with limited and impractical insights.

"I have very little knowledge of what these runes mean," Master Stow declared.

"I thought you taught a class on runes!" Ordi pressed.

"Yes, I do, but not these," he responded, examining the parchment more closely.

While Stow acknowledged the existence of the runes, his understanding was insufficient for Ordi's needs.

The journey home was typically uneventful, as the peace in the land had held steady since the witch incident. Disturbances were rare, and Ordi was seldom summoned to investigate. However, something about this trip left him feeling unfulfilled. Teaching the students was rewarding, but the lack of new information gnawed at him. His time at the academy felt wasted, and he was anxious to return home.

As they neared Kamrar, the imposing great mountain loomed before them, filling Ordi with a sense of completion. Mira trailed slightly behind. Such bonds were crucial for survival in the world of mages and mystical beasts. Certain beasts were attracted to specific types of magic, forming powerful alliances. Ordi, a master of all elements—an achievement so rare it hadn't been seen since the earliest days of record-keeping—found his perfect companion in Mira.

Posh hounds were rare creatures, glimpsed only a few times over centuries. Mira's appearance was both majestic and otherworldly. With short, sleek fur along her body and longer, lush hair on her head, she shimmered with a breathtaking grey hue. Unlike other mages, who typically paired with beasts aligned to their elemental magic—phoenixes for fire mages, birds for air and water mages, and giant beasts like bears for earth mages—Ordi's bond with Mira was not just unique; the posh hound could channel all the elements.

The posh hound, part wolf, part dog, and an unknown long-extinct creature, formed a deep, mystical connection with Ordi, allowing him to harness a more profound arcane magic. Their bond was a mystery, its depths never fully understood, but undeniable in its power. Through Mira, Ordi could channel vast amounts of magic, making his spells not just powerful, but also precise. Mira's keen senses amplified Ordi's own, allowing her to detect danger and feel ripples in the arcane channels, giving him crucial time to prepare.

For Ordi, this bond meant a deeper connection to all elements and the arcane channel at their core. Mastering the arcane channel was challenging for most, but for Ordi, it came naturally. His mastery and Mira's presence made his magical abilities unparalleled. Together, they were a formidable pair, attuned to the world's elemental and arcane energies in a profound and awe-inspiring way.

Kamrar's familiar sights and sounds welcomed them as they entered the city gates. Despite the unmet goals of his recent journey, Ordi felt a sense of belonging and purpose here. Mira walked beside him, her eyes ever-watchful, her presence a comforting reassurance of their shared strength and destiny.

As they neared the main path to Kamrar, Ordi marveled at the city's immense size. It spread throughout the Hallow Mountains and ran for miles deep into the heart of the earth. The construction of such a vast city was the chief achievement of the dwarves. After the Fallen One and the fall of the gods…

The path was close to half a mile long and worked its way upwards towards the door. Due to its narrowness, steep incline, and winding tendencies, it was seldom used, earning the name "snake path." Even though he had not followed this path in the past few years, he knew it well. As a young dwarf, he traveled it often when he left the mountains on errands or adventures before he was accepted at the academy.

"It never gets old coming home, does it?" Ordi asked Mira.

"Never does. Seeing everyone and resting on my bed again will be nice!" Mira replied.

Ordi longed to return to the halls of Kamrar permanently and share a delicious meal with his wife and family. Ordi had run in every direction for the King, servicing the library and dealing with minor issues. Yet, the thoughts of recent events plagued him.

"*We need to figure out the altar and those runes,*" Ordi stated as they entered Kamrar. "*I want to stop at the library quickly and check for messages.*"

"*Fine, I want to get home and eat. We will return to the library tomorrow to see if we have any scrolls. What about the stack of scrolls from Unrar?*" Mira asked.

"*Let's examine those first. We need to keep the task at the forefront of our minds.*"

"*Somehow, I feel you'll be distracted again, or we'll be sent somewhere else,*" Mira said with annoyance.

"*That is always a possibility. There seems to be something foul at play in the world. Let's examine those scrolls and see where it takes us.*" Ordi said.

While these issues troubled him, Ordi did have some hope. Before arriving home, Ordi stopped at the library and checked for messages. There, he found a small scroll with a note about his brother.

His brother now led the armies of Kamrar. He had not spoken to his brother in some time. What remarkable news to return to. He recalled their journey in their younger years, watching Verdun try various crafts and fail repeatedly. He sought many talents, hoping to find his place. However, as Ordi was selected for the academy due to his magical abilities, Verdun's attitude dampened. Before Ordi had left, he remembered the conversation they shared.

"I am truly proud of you, brother. You have accomplished something many of our people cannot do," Verdun began.

"I appreciate that sentiment very much. I hope to make you and all our people proud," Ordi replied.

Verdun's shoulders slumped a little. "With you gone… what will I do? I can't even hunt properly. Father seems to have disowned me for my inability to perform tasks."

Ordi sat for a moment, thinking. Finally, he said, "You have always wanted to join the army. You are still young and fit; why not? Why not use your talents with a sword to defend our people? We both know how much this world is shrinking, with tales of the Fallen One in our history and the evil that crops up. The elves will be of no help as they slowly fade into the twilight. It is left to us and the humans to protect this world from evil."

Verdun's eyes lit up. "Yes, of course, swordsman. I like that." He sat on the bench, scratching his beard as thoughts rolled through his mind.

Ordi recalled his brother's excitement over this new decision as their conversation continued. Now, after all this time, it had paid off. Verdun was a leader of the king's foot soldiers—a very respected position for a dwarf. Ordi halted as he approached the stone door. Knocking three times, the stone turned inward, and Ordi and Mira entered Kamrar.

Ordi breathed in the mingled scents of rock, smoke, and meat—a familiar aroma that defined the bustling city of Kamrar. Walking alongside him, Mira turned her head in every direction, her keen senses absorbing the vibrant activity around them.

"Smell that?" Mira asked.

"Yes, I am in need of a hearty dinner tonight," Ordi chuckled.

Kamrar was as busy as ever, with dwarves and humans conducting their business amidst the lively scene. Torches lit up the massive square, casting a warm glow, while high overhead, skylights drew in sunlight throughout the day, creating a harmonious balance of light and dark.

The square was a kaleidoscope of sights and sounds, with shop owners lining its walls, their stands brimming with various goods. They called out to passersby, creating a symphony of enticements to stop and purchase food, drink, or trinkets. Exotic spices, freshly baked bread, and sizzling meats filled the air with tantalizing aromas, mingling with the earthy scent of the stone pavements. Craftsmen showcased their meticulously made wares, from finely wrought jewelry to sturdy leather goods, each stall a testament to its vendor's skill and pride.

Ordi moved through the crowd, unfazed by the discounts and incentives offered to capture his attention. This was a common sight in the city, where vendors competed fiercely for every sale. Despite the clamor, their determination was often rewarded enough to keep them returning daily to set up shop. The city square was alive with bustling energy, the hum of conversation, and the occasional laughter of children playing nearby.

Kamrar was not just a place of commerce but a tapestry of cultures. Dwarven masonry seamlessly blended with the architectural influence of humans who settled here. Sturdy stone buildings with intricate carvings stood alongside ornate structures adorned with banners and flags. The blend of architectural styles created a unique charm distinctly Kamrar, enchanting all who beheld it.

As Ordi continued through the market, he watched the vibrant interactions around him. Traders haggled animatedly over prices while customers examined goods with discerning eyes. Street performers added to the lively atmosphere, drawing crowds with music and feats of acrobatics. A group of children ran by, their laughter infectious, a testament to the city's enduring community spirit that made everyone feel a sense of warmth and belonging.

Mira clung to Ordi, a vigilant companion. Her presence was comforting. Her keen eyes and ears caught subtle movements and sounds, ensuring their path remained clear and safe. Her connection with Ordi allowed for silent communication, a bond of mutual understanding that extended beyond words.

"This place never ceases to amaze me," Ordi said.

"Considering I have spent my life in the woods, Kamrar is mesmerizing," Mira responded.

As they neared the end of the bustling market square, Ordi felt a sense of belonging. Despite his recent journey's unmet goals and lingering questions, Kamrar was home—where he and Mira's presence was familiar and welcomed. The city's rhythm, with its blend of commerce, culture, and camaraderie, was a part of him as much as he was a part of it.

Though he navigated the bustling streets, thoughts of the runes and the answers he sought never left his mind. He wondered: was this someone who intentionally sought to harm people or someone dabbling in dark magic? Ordi tried to convince himself that it was a kid who did not know what they were doing.

The peace in Kamrar offered a brief respite, but he knew that his quest for knowledge was far from over. With Mira at his side, Ordi felt ready to face whatever challenges lay ahead, secure in the knowledge that his journey, like Kamrar itself, was a blend of past, present, and future.

They passed by a leatherworker who nodded and smiled at Ordi.

"Who is that?" Mira asked.

Ordi began to tell the story. *"Verdun, my brother, and I were not mischievous compared to other children. We often sought fun and sometimes stumbled into trouble. Once, when we were young, I chased Verdun through the city. During a bout of horseplay, Verdun tripped me, sending me tumbling headlong into one of the shops. It was a leatherworker's stall, and for that, I was thankful. The leather provided padding when I crashed into his cart. However, the owner was less forgiving. He had been furious, yelling at Verdun and me. He demanded we replace the broken stand and displays on his cart."* Ordi chuckled as he retold the story to Mira.

"When our father heard about our mischief, he made me work for the leatherworker for six weeks. Now that I think about it, I do not remember what Verdun had to do for his punishment." Ordi chuckled to himself, thinking back on that moment. Their innocent antics taught him a lesson in hard work and responsibility.

Ordi's childhood was filled with fun and adventure, often leaving Kamrar with his father to visit the human settlements. Through these journeys, Ordi learned much about human culture and activities, forging friendships with local youth. While dwarves outlived humans by many years, Ordi was still considered a child at age twenty. Those memories felt distant now, as he had since grown, attended the academy, and graduated with honors. He had come a long way, he thought to himself.

The moment he discovered his magical abilities was etched vividly in his memory. He had been sparring with Verdun, and as usual, Verdun cheated. Anger flared in Ordi when he found out, and in his rage, a small fire ignited in his palms. The flames grew, consuming his hands, yet the heat did not harm him. Verdun's eyes widened in shock as Ordi let the magic dissipate. Magic was not rare among dwarves, but it was certainly uncommon. Unless one was a descendant of the high dwarf mage lines—the Hetgoln and Stronhen—the chances of possessing magic were slim, though not impossible.

The bloodlines of Hetgoln and Stronhen had historically produced the most powerful mages, but their lineage thinned over the years. The most recent children born into these families showed no magical abilities, sparking concern among the Dwarves. They feared that magic in Asheros was either changing or perhaps even dying. Ordi took a theory class at the academy on families and the decline of magical abilities. Most of the blame fell on marrying incompatible spouses, which tainted the bloodlines. Another theory was that Asheros was altering the arcane channels, tapping into new families for abilities. A recent theory suggested that magic was drying up or being drawn elsewhere. This theory had many skeptics and was more challenging to prove. Beyond those, no other theories were accepted.

Ordi's pace quickened as he approached the tunnel leading to one of Kamrar's most prestigious living quarters. These homes, meticulously carved into the stone, were some of the finest dwellings the dwarves ever built. The residents here served King Telophap, contributing to the kingdom's strength and prosperity, with Ordi now serving as a King's Mage. He and his family dwelled alongside the other royal servants. He had joined the ranks of those dedicated to defending Kamrar and the surrounding lands.

The dwarven empires had allied with the humans to protect the free people of Asheros. Though their enemy was often scarce, it was never absent. Scouts occasionally reported seeing small hordes of dark elves on the move and farms being burned by goblins. These threats fueled Ordi's determination to serve his king and people, compelling him to spend time studying and learning as much about magic as possible. Seemingly, though, reports had dried up. Only the witch and the dried spring had been enough to dispatch Ordi. The dwarves, however, would continuously remain alert and ever vigilant.

Ordi inserted the key into his door, turned the lock, and opened the portal. The savory aroma of pork filled his nose, signaling that his wife, Aimlia, was preparing dinner in anticipation of his arrival. Just as he and Mira stepped inside, his two children, Gadira and Dradin, came running toward him, shouting, "DADDY'S HOME!" Both jumped into his arms, their joy palpable. Gadira released him, jumped down to hug Mira, and then ran off to play with her in another room.

His children were gifts from the gods, their potential shining brightly within the dwarven kingdom. Both Gadira, the oldest at ten, and her eight-year-old brother Dradin took after their mother in appearance, with thick, blonde curly hair. Gadira wore a pretty pink dress, her hair intricately braided into a complex sequence that reflected her budding grace and charm. Dradin kept his hair shorter but liked to imitate his dad, who wore a tunic and dark pants.

"It smells great, Aimlia," Ordi called out as he reached the kitchen, carrying a Dradin-like sack of potatoes. He carefully set him on the floor, and Dradin returned to his activities. He stood up and kissed Aimlia. "It sure is good to be back. Nothing beats a home-cooked meal with the family."

"I am happy you are home; these past few days have been quiet…even a little unnerving, if I am honest." Her eyes teared up a little. Ordi embraced her and wiped the tears from her face. It took a moment for Aimlia to collect herself before speaking again. "Oh! I invited our parents over for dinner tonight," Aimlia said.

It took a moment for Ordi to process the comment. "Both sets…like your parents and MINE?"

"Yes." She chuckled. Turning, she continued to busy herself with the dinner preparations.

"You know how that will go over… they can't stand each other!" Ordi rubbed his eyes, trying to find what to say next. He knew their parents did not get along; they did not even approve of their marriage. Two powerful families that had disliked each other for ages.

"Oh, it will be fine. I told my parents not to talk about the past and to focus only on our accomplishments. I said the same thing to your parents."

"Well… this will certainly be entertaining," Ordi said as he grabbed a slice of bread. Aimlia smacked his hand away.

"You'll spoil your dinner!"

"I don't think that's a problem," Ordi chuckled, patting his broad stomach. Dwarves, while shorter than humans, were generally more robustly built. Their appetites were legendary, but their size was seldom what humans would consider obese. A dwarf's physique was a testament to endurance and strength, honed from centuries of hard labor and battle readiness. However, health issues could arise as they aged, particularly for those who had lived well for the past 160 years. Yet, the resilience of dwarves in the face of aging was a source of inspiration for all who witnessed it.

A few minutes later, there came a knock on the door. Ordi could hear laughter outside as he approached. He opened the door to find both sets of parents laughing and hugging. Ordi's jaw dropped, and Mira tilted her head to the side, curious about the commotion. "What is happening?" he asked.

"ORDI! It is so good to see you, my boy!" boomed Droga, Aimlia's father, as he enveloped Ordi in a hearty embrace. Aimlia's mother, Rutha, smiled warmly and said, "Congratulations!" before gently pinching his cheek as they entered the house.

"Ordi, it is lovely to see you. Thank your wife for inviting us over for dinner," his mother, Rundina, said as she hugged him tightly. Following her, Ordi's father approached. He was a stout older man with a long gray beard that reached his waist, slightly shorter than Ordi. His father's eyes gleamed with pride as he looked at his son.

"It's good to see you, my son. I couldn't be more proud of you. My son! A mage to the King! And your brother— what an accomplishment, leading the King's army! What else could a father want? Always a good excuse to enjoy a dinner together," Orin exclaimed. "Oh, your brother couldn't be here tonight but said he would stop by as soon as possible."

Ordi, accompanied by Mira, followed his parents into the house to join the gathering. Dinner proceeded smoothly, filled with laughter and shared stories. Ordi marveled at the sight of both families sharing the same meal under one roof. Even at the wedding ceremony, both families had sat separately, rarely speaking to each other. Today truly felt like a blessing from the gods.

Halfway through dinner, an unexpected hush fell over the table, a blanket of silence that smothered the lively chatter. The clinking of cutlery against plates, once a comforting background hum, now sounded like sharp, staccato notes in the stillness, each clink making the silence more pronounced. The moment stretched, each second weighted with unspoken words, making everyone at the table shift uncomfortably in their seats.

Orin's throat suddenly felt dry, and he cleared it with a nervous cough, his mind racing for a suitable topic to fill the void, but his thoughts were tangled and confused. Suddenly, Droga broke the silence with a grin, her eyes sparkling with mischief. "You know, Ordi, I've always wondered—do mages cast spells to get out of washing dishes, too?"

Everyone paused, then burst into laughter. The joke was simple but effective, dissolving the awkwardness in an instant. Ordi, grinning, responded, "Only the smart ones, Droga!" He conjured a tiny wisp of cool air and swirled it up into the air. The air circled around him, enveloping him and making him disappear. The group cheered as Ordi reappeared.

Aimlia, unimpressed, said, "You can get out of washing tonight, but now I know your tricks." She laughed, as did everyone else.

As the laughter subsided, the atmosphere lightened considerably. The families resumed their lively chatter, sharing more stories and enjoying each other's company.

After dinner, the women began to clean up, the children played, and the men retired to the balcony for a smoke.

Pipe smoking was a cherished pastime for dwarves, though the weed had to be imported from regions to the south, near the human capital. Humans grew and sold the weed to the dwarves, knowing they enjoyed a smoke after a hearty meal. For Ordi, sharing a smoke with his father and father-in-law was a rare treat. They sat on the balcony, overlooking the vast hollowed mountain carved out by years of mining, though now the mines were largely abandoned.

The balcony offered a breathtaking view of the city within the vast, hollowed mountain. Glowstone lanterns illuminated the streets below, casting a warm and inviting glow that contrasted with the rugged stone walls. The faint hum of distant conversations and laughter from the city's taverns created a soothing backdrop.

Years ago, the mines bustled with activity around the clock, with dwarves diligently seeking gold, copper, and other rare metals. Mining operations eventually moved to smaller communities further along the mountain range as the mountain's resources dwindled. The trio sat in comfortable silence, each enjoying their pipe, a full stomach, and the serene moment.

Ordi's thoughts drifted as he puffed on his pipe, the mellow flavor of the Southern weed calming his mind. He glanced at his father, who was lost in his own contemplations. Orin's eyes reflected fond memories of a bustling past when the mines were alive with the clatter of pickaxes and the shouts of hardworking dwarves.

Droga broke the silence, "Ordi, you have brought honor to our families. Your achievements and dedication are truly something to be proud of."

Ordi smiled, feeling the warmth of their words. "Thank you, Droga. It means a lot to hear that. But I couldn't have done it without your support."

As the evening wore on, the conversation shifted to tales of old adventures, shared laughter, and future hopes. The moonlight bathed the balcony in a silver glow, casting long shadows and adding a dreamlike quality to the gathering.

The peacefulness of the moment was profound. Ordi felt a deep sense of connection to his heritage, his family, and the land. The tranquility of the evening was a stark contrast to the noise and chaos of his adventures. He relished this serene interlude, knowing that the bonds of family and the simple pleasures of life were just as crucial as any quest.

As the embers in their pipes dimmed and the night deepened, Ordi knew that this moment of unity and peace would stay with him—a cherished memory in the tapestry of his life. But as the night drew to a close, Ordi felt a sense of uneasiness wash over him.

Droga spoke, breaking the silence and startling Ordi. "So, Ordi… what's next for you? My sources say you must report to the king tomorrow."

" Yes, first thing. The king ordered all his advisers to be present. Something important is my guess," Ordi responded.

"I don't want to bring fear into the night," Orin said solemnly. "But I hear rumors of wars and battles brewing. They say the Fallen One, the Dark Lord, has returned to Asheros. There is word that the old fortress has fires roaring again. I've even heard dark elves are pillaging farms and small villages on the Fringe to strike fear in people's hearts. The humans have been compiling these reports for some time now," Orin continued. He always had a source and knew more than most Dwarves, especially regarding people's movements.

"Nothing was mentioned about that, but it doesn't surprise me given the urgency behind the meeting. At the academy this past week, we heard rumors but nothing more. The humans didn't share much information. I was there to trace some runes I found, but they didn't want to give up answers, which is odd. There were never any orders to investigate, nor did their instructors get summoned anywhere. So I chalked it up to rumors and ghost stories. Though now, hearing it again tonight, I am starting to believe differently. Whatever the king has in store will certainly be divulged tomorrow," Ordi said as he took a deep breath from his pipe.

The smoke filled Ordi's mouth and lungs before he exhaled it into the darkness. He had an uneasy feeling in the pit of his stomach now, as his father feared. Right or wrong, he would find out in the morning what the king would request of him and his advisers.

The next morning came quickly for Ordi. He was up before dawn, washed up, and dressed in his mage's tunic. Mira rose with him and followed him around the house as he got ready. *"Dawn already? I barely had just fallen asleep."* Mira said.

"You slept through the entire dinner!" Ordi replied.

"That was just resting."

Ordi sat in the dark kitchen with Mira, drinking coffee before the rest of his family awoke. Mira sat beside him, chewing a bone from the previous night.

He would, unfortunately, be gone before they even began to stir. He took his last bite of the bread and cheese his wife set out the night before—the crumbs accumulating in his beard and on his tunic. The cheese had a bit of a stale taste, but Ordi did not mind. He stood, brushed himself clean, and walked over to the door. He grabbed his staff, opened the door, and walked out, followed closely by Mira. The air in the mountain was never stale, as the dwarves built numerous ventilation systems to keep the air moving. This morning, though, it was a bit cooler than usual. The coolness startled Ordi as he wrapped his tunic a little tighter. He began his short journey to the King's throne room.

The walk only took about fifteen minutes. Though it was early in the morning, some shop owners were already busy with tasks to prepare for the day, and there were few travelers. Approaching the keep, Ordi and Mira were ushered past by the guards. The Royal Bastion was one of the most significant living quarters in the mountain, elevated to a height that offered a magnificent view of the town below. Ordi and Mira stepped into the massive courtyard and were directed by the next guard toward the throne room.

As Ordi approached the Royal Bastion, an uneasy feeling settled over him. The grandeur and strength of the keep had always filled him with pride, but today, something felt different. Suddenly, his body went rigid, and his vision blurred. A disorientation swept over him, transporting him to another time and place.

In an instant, he saw himself standing in the king's courtyard, but Kamrar was unrecognizable, utterly devastated. The ceiling above was now dark and choked with ash. Thick smoke blotted out the sun's shafts, casting the scene in an eerie, hellish glow. Fire raged uncontrollably close by, its flames dancing and licking at the remnants of what had been majestic structures, now reduced to smoldering rubble.

Bodies of both dwarves and humans lay scattered in twisted, unnatural positions, their faces frozen in deathly screams. The ground was a sickening display of soot and blood, pools of crimson mingling with the dirt beneath. The stench of burning flesh was overwhelming, searing Ordi's senses and turning his stomach.

The majestic stone buildings crumbled to mere shadowy outlines, their shattered walls and fallen arches whispering tales of a violent end. The air was thick with the agonizing cries and moans of the wounded and dying, each sound embedding itself deeply into Ordi's soul. Shadows moved stealthily through the smoke, dark figures too far away to identify but close enough to instill a paralyzing sense of dread.

Ordi's heart pounded in his chest, each beat sending a pulse of fear through his veins. An overwhelming sense of despair washed over him, the weight of impending doom pressing down like a suffocating shroud. The vision was no mere nightmare—a vivid, heart-wrenching glimpse of Kamrar in the throes of apocalyptic ruin. The chilling scene threatened to consume him, the despair almost too much to bear.

Just as a bone-chilling scream pierced his ears—a sound so filled with anguish it seemed to tear through his very being—the vision abruptly ended, yanking him back to the present. Ordi staggered, gasping for breath, his senses reeling from the intensity of the vision.

He stood at the entrance of the King's Keep, the familiar surroundings slowly coming back into focus. He felt the solid ground beneath his feet and heard the distant sounds of daily life in Kamrar. A familiar scent of woodsmoke and spices, faint but comforting, tickled his nostrils - the lifeblood of Kamrar's market. From there, a medley of shouts and bartering cries rose and fell like a restless sea. Yet the vivid horror of the vision lingered, its images imprinted in his mind. His hands trembled, and his heart still pounded in his chest.

Sensing his distress, Mira nudged him gently, her eyes filled with concern. *"Ordi, what is happening?"*

Ordi could feel panic as she asked. *"I…I don't know. Something incredibly dark swept over me,"* he answered.

Ordi took a deep breath, attempting to steady himself and push the haunting images to the back of his mind. But he couldn't shake the feeling that the vision was a warning, a foreboding glimpse into a possible future he was somehow meant to prevent.

Determined, Ordi straightened his shoulders and rushed toward the Royal Bastion, every step filled with urgent purpose. He had to uncover the meaning behind the vision and do whatever it took to protect Kamrar from the dread-filled fate he had witnessed.

Mira looked at him with deep concern etched on her face. Ordi continued explaining, *"In the vision, I saw the castle in flames. Kamrar was in ruins. I don't know what to make of it, but it should be discussed with the king,"* he said, his voice tinged with urgency as they proceeded to the keep's door.

"Do you think it is from someone trying to scare you? Dark magic?" Mira asked, prompting Ordi to think for a moment.

"I'm not sure. As much as I believe the altar was someone just meddling in dark magic, this vision could be that too. I need to consider it, but I don't want to waste time on this." Ordi shrugged as they approached the throne room.

Once inside, Ordi knew precisely where to go. Guided by muscle memory and familiarity, he led the way through a labyrinthine series of hallways, each turn and passage carved with the meticulous craftsmanship characteristic of Dwarven architecture. The walls bore intricate designs and ancient runes, telling the stories of Kamrar's storied past, with flickering torchlight casting dancing shadows that brought the carvings to life.

They ascended a short, gently sloping ramp, the echo of their footsteps resonating in the grand space. As they approached the entrance to the throne room, two bronze-clad guards stood at attention, their faces stern but respectful. As Ordi drew near, the guards bowed low in reverence before pulling open the heavy, ornate doors with a resounding thud.

The throne room was nothing short of magnificent. The walls were adorned with opulent murals depicting the lineage of Kamrar's kings, each an artwork meticulously painted with vibrant colors and gold accents, illustrating battles, victories, and moments of peace. Sunlight streamed in from high, strategically placed skylights, casting natural illumination across the room and causing the gold accents to glow warmly.

The floor was a masterpiece of brilliant white marble, polished to a reflective sheen. It was veined with strands of silver and gold, leading the eye naturally toward the room's focal point—the solid gold throne. The throne stood on a raised dais, surrounded by an array of advisors and council members, all clad in ceremonial attire. Their presence added gravity and importance to the meeting.

As Ordi entered, he felt the weight of the room's history and power settle over him. He walked forward with purpose, the grandeur of the space only enhancing his sense of duty and commitment. The eyes of those assembled fell upon him, acknowledging his arrival.

He noticed Verdun, an esteemed figure within the kingdom, standing to the king's right. Verdun caught Ordi's gaze and gave a slight nod, a silent acknowledgment of camaraderie and mutual respect. Ordi returned the gesture before joining the ranks of those who had also been summoned, a sense of anticipation hanging in the air.

The room buzzed with murmurs, each person awaiting the king's address. The solid gold throne, resplendent and imposing, held King Thrain, whose aura commanded respect and admiration. Ordi took his place among the assembled, feeling the significance of the moment. The advisors flanked the dais, their faces reflecting a mix of solemnity and attentiveness.

At that moment, the weight of his vision lingered in Ordi's mind. Standing in the heart of Kamrar's power, surrounded by allies and reinforced by the grandeur of his heritage, he felt a sense of calm.

The stage was set for the king's decree, and Ordi, with Mira by his side, stood ready to participate in the events shaping Kamrar's future.

"Ah, Ordi! Welcome. Good to see you again. We must acquaint you with all the developments currently underway," King Ronan Telophap began, his voice resonating in the grand hall. The king's expression was grave, reflecting the seriousness of the situation. "We have reports from our scouts and neighbors of forces moving against our territory. There are mentions of dark elves and goblins running amok, destroying farmsteads, and killing men, women, and children. We do not have a number, but the devastation is vast. They creep further west with each attack."

Ordi listened intently, his anger rising at the mention of the widespread chaos. King Telophap continued, "We need better information, and sadly, our scouts have been unreliable as of late. Therefore, I am dispatching Ordi and Verdun to the Fringe. The rest of you work to gather information and see how we can assist those scattered by these attacks."

The room fell silent as the king gazed at the two brothers. "Ordi, Verdun," he addressed them directly, "investigate the villages and farmsteads along the border. Learn what you can. Talk to the townsfolk, walk the border, camp, and watch for any signs of activity. Return and give me a full report when you have your information."

Ordi glanced at Verdun, who gave him a determined nod. The mission was clear, and the stakes were high. They had to act quickly and efficiently to gather the intelligence needed to protect their lands and people.

"This task will require vigilance and courage," King Telophap added solemnly. "The lives of many depend on your diligence. Remember, the borderlands are dangerous, and you may encounter significant resistance. Stay alert, and work together."

With a final, decisive look at both brothers, the king asked, "Any questions?"

Verdun stepped forward slightly. "Majesty, are there any known strongholds or specific areas where these attacks are more concentrated, or should we scout the entire perimeter?"

King Telophap nodded, appreciating the question. "Our reports indicate that the most severe attacks have occurred near the villages of Greywood and Thornholm. Start your investigation there, but remain ready to adapt if you find evidence pointing elsewhere."

Ordi, feeling the weight of the responsibility, asked, "And what of reinforcements? Should we need them?"

The King replied, "You can call for reinforcements if necessary. We cannot afford to lose this fight and must protect our people at all costs. If you encounter a force that is too strong, do not engage recklessly. Use your discretion and ensure the safety of the subjects you encounter."

"How fast should we leave, sire?" Verdun asked.

"Yesterday, today, now, immediately. I want a full report as soon as possible," Telophap said. "You are dismissed."

Before Ordi stepped away, he turned to the king and said, "My Lord, may I discuss a vision I received with you?" Verdun remained as the rest of the advisors stepped back.

"Absolutely. What is it?" the king responded.

"I was walking into the courtyard and was overtaken by a vision. I saw what may befall Kamrar. Guards lay dead everywhere, the keep was on fire, and the city was in ruins. It was dark, and death hung heavy in the air. It is a sign of something that could come, but I am unsure. Visions are not my expertise," Ordi told the story as quickly as he could.

"Interesting." The King sat back and thought for a moment. "Hard to say; it could be something that may come to pass. Not all visions become reality because the course of action to prevent them has been taken. I think this mission to the Fringe is now even more urgent. We have never witnessed this type of activity. It isn't very comforting. Go now, you two, and be swift, vigilant, and careful. May the gods guide you." The king dismissed them.

Ordi and Verdun left while the other advisors stepped away but did not leave. They were to continue discussing courses of action for the people of Asheros. "Ordi, brother, how are you? I am so sorry I missed last night's meal. Work has had me in overtime with all these reports coming in. Trying to recruit and then train them… the King has my schedule full."

Ordi replied, "It is good to see you too, brother. Much has happened in the past six months. I must tell you about everything I've been doing! I just traveled down to Talamar to speak to the headmaster at the academy, but he was uncertain about some runes I found. I'll give you all the details during the journey. I'm sure we'll have time." He stopped talking as they proceeded out of the King's Throne Room.

"Odd… runes? Where could those be? Could it be someone associated with the Fallen One?" Verdun asked.

"Perhaps, but I think we will soon find out where we are headed." They both walked in silence for a bit. Mira trailed off a short distance behind. Ordi broke the silence. "What do you think is going on at the border? It seems like something sinister."

"We've received few reports and nothing we can rely on. It mostly just involves movements along the Fringe and sometimes crossing over. Deadman's Land appears to have activity, too," Verdun said.

"Oh, wonderful," Ordi half-joked. The brothers reached their respective homes, right across from each other. Ordi and Mira entered his home and were greeted by his family again. "I have to go out on a quest for the king. Haste is key; we do not know what is happening, but I must leave immediately. Aimlia, can you pack me some travel food?"

"Of course, my love. How many days do you think?" Aimlia asked.

"Hopefully, no more than ten days. If I run out, we'll be in and around villages, so we shouldn't have any problems," Ordi responded. "Not what I thought I would do today for the king." He sighed. "There is growing unrest along the borders, and with all this movement, who knows what will come of it?"

"I understand. It is hard for us, but we will manage. Take care of yourself and stay vigilant; who knows what is in the darkness? Promise you'll return to me?" Aimlia asked as she embraced him one more time.

"I promise. Tell the children I will return shortly, and I will have gifts for them when I do," Ordi replied, his voice filled with determination. He turned to walk to the door but hesitated, sighing deeply. "I will think about you every moment of every day. You and the children are why I made it through the academy and do everything I do. I will return soon."

Ordi and Mira left the house after their heartfelt goodbyes, meeting his brother just up the path. The three set out from Kamrar on the twenty-fifth day of March, their mission taking them toward the eastern Fringes. Their quest should take roughly four days, provided no trouble arose. As they left the south entrance and began descending the snake path, they felt the sun's warmth breaking through the lingering chill of winter. The clear air and slight breeze ruffled their hair, offering a momentary calm. Ordi hoped for an uneventful journey, but time would tell.

The three journeyed down the path, Ordi carrying his bag and Verdun with a small shoulder bag, while Mira glided gracefully behind. Upon reaching the bottom, they walked along the wall to the pony depot, a common departure point for dwarves embarking on long journeys. Using the king's orders, they requested two ponies. The stable master promptly fetched them.

These ponies were strong and resilient, well-suited for the arduous journey ahead. Ordi was familiar with his pony, Bill, a sturdy and reliable travel companion. The other pony, which Verdun would use, was younger and yet to be named.

After saddling their ponies and securing their bags, Ordi and Verdun mounted up while Mira walked alongside. With the sun at their backs, they directed their ponies away from the Hollow Mountains, setting eastward on the king's errand. The path before them was both a physical journey and a prelude to the awaiting trials.

Chapter 5 The Journey

Embarking on a perilous journey eastward, Ordi, Verdun, and Mira set their sights on the Fringe—a region fraught with tension and volatility. This narrow, war-torn wilderness bordered the ancient dwarven empire, the sprawling human kingdoms, and the cursed Dead Lands. It was their destination, where the forces of the Creeping Death were held at bay. The conquest was led by the Dark Lord, whose influence had spread like a plague across the land.

The Fringe was a desolate battleground, scarred by countless skirmishes and the remnants of ancient wars. It was a strip of land trapped between worlds, where the fabric of reality seemed to fray, and the balance between light and darkness was precarious, shrouded in mystery.

To the north, the Fringe met the Red Barrier—a daunting range of jagged cliffs and treacherous mountains looming like a colossal beast's teeth. Once, the Northern Seeing Tower stood vigilant atop those cliffs, an ancient dwarven outpost that scanned the horizon for threats. Now, it lay in ruins, a wasteland of rubble and stone, its purpose forgotten, its grandeur reduced to whispers of a bygone era.

To the south, the Dead Lands stretched menacingly to Lost Hope Sea Bay, where the waters were tainted by dark sorcery. This blighted area was a landscape of desolation, with blackened vegetation and twisted, lifeless trees that creaked in the eerie silence. The air seemed to possess a malevolence, an invisible force that sapped the spirit and strength of anyone who dared to venture too close.

"This seems to be a commonality for you lately, huh, Ordi?" Verdun asked as they rode onward.

"Not by choice. I've been sent to a few places investigating issues and was even dispatched a while back to deal with a witch," Ordi replied as he directed his pony along the path.

Mira trotted beside Ordi. *"Tell him about the witch."*

"Yes, I will. I'm sure he knows much already," Ordi informed her. "You heard about the witch we were ordered to deal with, right?"

"Yes, I heard. I was unfortunately out, running a task for the King. He had sent me to Peakforge to gather resources. I didn't get a chance to return during the ceremony—my condolences for your loss. We have a lot to catch up on, brother."

The three traveled on, knowing their mission was paramount. The Fringe was more than a physical territory; it was a frontline in the battle against the encroaching darkness. Every step they took was a step into history toward understanding and combating the malevolence threatening their world.

The first day of the journey was uneventful. Having left Kamrar, the capital city of the dwarves, they headed eastward. Despite their enthusiasm, they didn't cover as much ground as they had hoped. Verdun had to stop every few hundred yards to adjust his saddle or tie his boots, much to his companions' amusement and slight exasperation. Ordi often wondered how the king had appointed Verdun to lead his armies. A fond smile passed over Ordi's face as he considered his clumsy brother—not the best rider on a pony, but a damn good fighter.

The path eastward was lined with the echoes of forgotten battles and the silent testimonies of fallen warriors. Each night, they camped under the stars, the flickering campfire casting shadows that danced and whispered secrets of the past. Mira's keen senses were ever vigilant, and her presence brought Ordi peace amidst the ever-present peril.

To the east of Kamrar, beyond the mountains and tainted seas lay the heart of their mission—a land where the Creeping Death left its mark, obliterating hope and spreading fear. Ordi and Verdun knew that understanding the magnitude of the threat was paramount.

"What do you think we'll discover when we get closer to the Fringe?" Ordi asked.

"Based on reports, I think we'll see what we expect: destruction and people who are concerned," Verdun answered.

As the king commanded, they would engage with those who remained, gleaning what information they could about the dark forces encroaching upon their borders. Each story they heard and each sight they witnessed would add to the tapestry of their mission, providing valuable insights into the enemy's tactics and weaknesses.

Once a prosperous land of trade and cooperation, the Fringe had become a no-man's-land since the Dark Lord's last efforts. In this scarred battleground, human and dwarven soldiers maintained a fragile line of defense against the encroaching darkness. The dwarves, masters of stone and steel, still held the northern and western realms of Asheros, their mighty cities carved into mountains and fortified with ancient, impenetrable walls. Meanwhile, the human kingdoms, ever expansionist, dominated the southwestern territories, their cities bustling with life yet always casting a wary eye toward the east. Together, the two peoples forged an alliance that stood the test of time, their shared history of cooperation against familiar foes binding them in mutual respect and loyalty.

The elves were a different story.

Once noble and wise, the elven nation fractured ages ago. Those who still held to goodness were scattered, their influence diminished, and they were powerless to stand against the rising tides of evil. Now isolated in remote corners of Asheros, they were but shadows of their former selves, their magic waning. In contrast, those who had forsaken the light became dark elves, their bodies twisted and corrupted by ancient, evil magic. Their betrayal, which had occurred long before Ordi, Verdun, or even their father drew breath, was now the stuff of legend and horror. It had been a turning point, a moment when the very balance of the world shifted toward darkness.

For as long as Ordi could remember, the alliance between humans and dwarves was constant, a steady foundation of peace amid the chaos. Yet the ever-present threat of the Dark Lord and the uneasy reminder of the elves' betrayal loomed over them. Ordi grew up knowing only the friendship between dwarves and humans, but in the back of his mind, there was always a sense of unease—a tension that whispered of a world on the brink of collapse.

Now, as they ventured closer to the Fringe, that unease gnawed at Ordi's soul. Beyond the familiar borders lay a land where the dead walked, where darkness stretched its fingers ever closer, and where ancient betrayals had yet to meet their reckoning.

By midday, the trio decided to rest their ponies and eat lunch. They found a serene clearing off the road with a small stream at the far end from which the ponies could drink. Mira took advantage of the stop, drinking deeply from the stream and then lazily stretching out in the warm sun. The sun hung high, shining brilliantly without a single cloud. It was comfortably warm, not quite hot, making the day pleasant for travel. The trees, still barren from the harsh winter, would soon begin to bud with the promise of spring. Despite the frequent stops to "fix" or adjust something, the day felt almost idyllic.

Ordi and Verdun sat down with their backs to the stream, facing the road. In these parts, any travelers they might encounter would most likely be fellow dwarves traveling between Kamrar and Iron Forge, a mining camp in the Iron Mountains. Thus far, they had encountered no one. Truthfully, fewer people were on the roads this time of year; travel generally picked up later in the spring and summer months.

Verdun pulled out some dried salted pork and handed Ordi a piece. They bit into the jerky, eating in comfortable silence and watching the trees sway gently in the breeze. Ordi was the first to break the silence. "It is so peaceful here, but I fear something dark is brewing. The calm before the storm; this beautiful weather conceals what we fear is coming. I don't mean to be grim, but this is not your average errand from the King."

Verdun took another bite of his pork, thinking of what Ordi had just said. "Yes, brother. I feel the same. It concerns me why this errand and why the haste. If the rumors are true, we may be in for the battle of our lives."

"This battle may be bigger than even that," Ordi said. "If it is anything like the last time, the darkness swept across most of the lands; it devoured many people." He sighed and finished his jerky. "All right, enough doom and gloom. We must make for Elks Grove before nightfall and hope to find an inn." Elks Grove was a tiny settlement about a half-day's journey from Karadar Tower, so small that it never showed up on any maps.

The two gathered their ponies, which were casually grazing on the grasses nearby. Verdun double-checked his saddle, tied his boots, and adjusted his tunic before throwing his leg over the saddle and grabbing the reins. His sword fell to the side, so he tightened the belt and nudged his pony forward. He followed Ordi out of the clearing and back onto the path. Seeing them set out, Mira jumped up and chased after them.

Along the way, they mainly passed farms, with fields stretching off to the northern and southern horizons. Most of the land within a few days' journey from Kamrar was farmland, as the soil here—closer to the mountain—was fertile. As they traveled, the tranquility of the farmland provided a picturesque backdrop for their journey, though the weight of their mission lingered in Ordi's mind.

"Ordi, tell me what you've been up to since serving the King," Verdun asked as they rode along, finally making good time.

"Eh, honestly, it's mostly tedious work. I've been doing a lot of restoring the library after Master Galen died. I got called out south of Kamrar to help some nomads a few weeks ago. I found some of the Dark Lord's runes in a cave by a makeshift altar. Someone is either messing around or trying to do something evil. What worries me is how someone could know this. It makes me wonder if we have a spy in the area or if someone is trying to scare the locals. I don't know what to make of it. The runes were hastily drawn, but the person knew the pattern. It was designed to corrupt the primary water source for Kamrar." Ordi paused for a moment as they rode on.

"I assume you destroyed it," Verdun asked.

"Yes. Mira kept a mental image of the runes, and we traced them safely in my den. Dark magic, brother, it has me worried."

"It is frightening. So what now?"

"That is why I went to Talamar. The cover story was to help students, but I tried to research and inquire about the runes further. Unfortunately, no one was able to help. It almost felt like they were holding something back. I couldn't quite place my finger on it, though. I told our King, and he is interested, but this quest is a higher priority now. I'll be asked to do more research when we get home," Ordi continued. Silence surrounded the three as they traveled through the afternoon.

Evening came before the pair reached Elks Grove, and the chill caused the ponies to slow down a bit. Urging them to push on, they came up over a small hill that overlooked the village below. "Less than 200 yards, Bill. Let's push on, and then we'll rest," Ordi said. "Verdun, tell me what you have been dealing with."

"I wish I had captivating stories, Ordi. But the life of a warrior is boring—drills and patrols. When I am dispatched, it is usually a political issue that needs to be resolved, and I act as an arbitrator," Verdun noted as they approached the town.

"The two instances for me were the most exciting times. Now I am just spending time in the library," Ordi recalled.

The three crossed the town limits and set their eyes on the inn in the middle of the village. They reached the doors of the stable, handed the reins to the stable master, and paid the fee for the night. They exchanged thanks and headed into the inn.

The inn's atmosphere was as dark as its dimly lit room, with a single bar positioned in the middle and tables scattered around. Only two grimy windows allowed sparse, dusty beams of outside light to penetrate the interior, their glass panes smudged with years of neglect. Ordi guessed it was a slow night, as only a few tables were occupied, and a single bartender tended to the meager crowd.

The clientele mainly comprised dwarves, with a few humans scattered about, making Ordi and Verdun feel quite at home. On the other hand, Mira hesitated upon entry, her nose wrinkling at the bar's lack of cleanliness. The patrons engaged in muted conversations, telling jokes or reminiscing.

Their laughter and voices created a low hum that filled the room.

The only source of warmth, a small fire burning in a hearth set into the exterior wall opposite the door, provided a feeble cocoon of heat against the night's chill. The floorboards creaked with every step, and the smell of stale beer and old wood permeated the air. Ordi noticed cobwebs clinging to the corners of the ceiling and dust layering the surfaces of unused tables.

Despite its lack of cleanliness, the inn exuded a certain rustic charm—a refuge for weary travelers seeking solace and companionship for the night. Ordi and Verdun found a vacant table near the fire, its warmth a welcome comfort after their day's travel. Mira reluctantly followed, eyeing the surroundings warily as they settled in and awaited the bartender's approach.

"Have a seat wherever you like. Ale for both? Anything for the, uh…" The bartender hesitated, unsure what to call Mira.

"Mira, that is her name. She is my companion and will eat whatever meat you have on hand," Ordi said.

"Yes, ale for us, and if you have any bread and cheese, that would be appreciated. Any smoked meat, by chance?" Verdun answered the bartender's original question.

"Aye! We have all that. Sit and relax; I'll bring it out in a moment. Name's Mitch, by the way." He was a tall man with a scraggly beard and thinning gray hair on the top of his head. Ordi figured he owned the establishment. Mitch met them at the table, placing two full pints of ale in front of them, the foam rolling over the sides.

"So, what brings you two to Elks Grove?" Mitch asked, his curiosity piqued.

"Business of the king. We will also need a place to stay for the night," Ordi replied, keeping his response vague. He didn't want to delve into their purpose for traveling. A mage, a warrior, and a posh hound traveling together often turned heads, especially since mages were typically seen only when battles were on the horizon. It was rumored that mages were becoming rare, which was why they were seldom seen, and people would start to fear the worst when one passed through. Ordi hid his insignia and traveled like any dwarf who wanted to go unnoticed. The rumors would continue, though, despite how Ordi dressed. He couldn't help but notice those in the inn with them as they sat. Among the patrons, an elderly dwarf with a long, braided beard sat in a corner, nursing a pint of ale. His face was etched with deep lines from years of mining, and his muscular arms bore the scars of countless battles. He sat alone, quietly humming an old dwarven tune, lost in memories of days gone by.

At another table, a pair of boisterous human traders occupied the space. They were dressed in rugged travel clothes, their boots caked with dust from the road. One wore a vibrant red scarf wrapped around his neck, and his laughter echoed through the room as he recounted tales of successful trades and near misses. His companion, a burly man with a thick mustache, joined in with hearty laughs, slapping the table in amusement.

Near the bar, a young dwarven couple shared a quiet moment, their heads close together as they whispered. The woman had thick, brown hair that gleamed in the dim light, and her eyes sparkled with mischief. The slightly older man had a kind face and a gentle smile. They sipped their drinks, seemingly oblivious to the other patrons, wrapped up in their private world. Though they appeared to keep to themselves, they occasionally turned to Ordi and Verdun, muttering something to themselves.

Lastly, in a shadowy corner, a hooded figure sat alone, his face obscured by the raised hood. The figure's gloved hands occasionally reached for a tankard, taking measured sips. Though the individual was a mystery to the other patrons, an undeniable aura of danger surrounded him. Most gave the hooded figure a wide berth when passing by.

The bartender nodded and proceeded to cut bread and cheese and stack some smoked meat on a platter. He dropped them off. "On the house, for the King!" Mitch said.

"Thank you, sir, but we can certainly pay," Verdun interrupted.

"*If we get free food, don't complain, Ordi!*" Mira said.

"Yes, but it's not how Verdun and I operate. We want to pay if we are able to," Ordi reminded her.

"Nah, it's no big deal. It is the least we can do to serve the king who has done us well," Mitch replied.

The dwarves nodded gratefully at Mitch before he departed to serve other tables. Ordi and Verdun were famished, having had nothing to eat since midday. Without hesitation, they grabbed handfuls of freshly baked bread, the warm aroma bringing a touch of home to their weary souls. They helped themselves to generous portions of succulent meat, the juices dripping onto their plates.

Mira, who didn't need to eat as frequently, settled contentedly by their feet. She closed her eyes, satisfied with her once-daily meal, her presence a comforting constant amid the clatter of the crowded tavern. The warmth and aroma of the hearty food enveloped the trio, providing a brief respite from the trials of their journey.

"Silly dwarves and their constant eating," Mira said.

"Hey now, we have to keep up our hearty lifestyles," Ordi replied.

Ordi and Verdun ate silently for more than ten minutes, their hunger overriding any desire for conversation. They cleared the platter with gusto.

Ordi finally sat back and patted his stomach, a satisfied burp escaping his lips. "Yeah, that hit the spot. It felt like ages since we ate last. Hard work riding a pony and not doing anything else," he said, a hint of amusement in his voice.

Verdun chuckled in agreement, wiping his mouth with the back of his hand. "At least we're set for the night," he replied, leaning back in his chair. He savored the brief respite as he eyed the chair.

He settled back into his chair, which creaked under his weight and startled Mira. "Most definitely. Much needed." He made sure to place all four legs back on the ground for fear of snapping the rear two. Though they had only eaten a few hours ago, dwarves try not to go more than two to three hours without eating something. They take great pride in their stout figures.

They drank their ales and, as they got up to leave, Ordi left two copper coins on the table. "Thank you, Mitch. It was delightful! About those rooms."

"Yes, master dwarf, take the keys and head upstairs and down the hall. The last two doors are on the left," Mitch said, tossing a key to Ordi before proceeding to clean up a spilled beer.

The three began to ascend the stairs and move down the dimly lit hallway. Cleanliness was not high on the owner's list, as dust bunnies collected where the floors met the walls. The walls were dark and dingy, with grime and muck accumulating on the sparse hallway furniture. Tables with lamps dotted the area, along with an alcove containing a small bookshelf, all covered in years of neglect. Mira nearly tiptoed, trying to keep her fur clean and looking distinctly unimpressed with the accommodations.

"Gross. I can't believe you expect me to stay here," Mira said, sticking her tongue out.

"It's only one night. It's better than the stables," Ordi replied.

They reached their rooms and bid each other good night, planning to wake at first light and continue their journey to the Fringe lands.

Ordi entered his room, with Mira following behind. The thin light from the hall pierced the darkness, casting long shadows. Ordi walked to the fireplace, lowered his staff, and released a small fireball into the wood pile. The fire ignited, casting a warm glow and illuminating the dark, dingy room. He swept his staff across the floor, clearing a spot for Mira to lie down. She gave Ordi a disgruntled look, clearly displeased with the state of their lodgings.

"What? It's not perfect, but it will work for one night," Ordi said as he continued preparing the room.

Mold crept up the south wall, and the window was caked with dirt and dust, blocking any exterior light and preventing Ordi from looking out. The bed in the center of the room was no better. *"No wonder this place was cheap,"* Ordi muttered to Mira. He grabbed a pillow and tapped his staff against it. The dirt and grime disappeared. He placed it near the fireplace for Mira to sleep on.

"Cheap isn't always better," Mira thought as she tiptoed across the floor.

"Ey, but it is the only available place to stay. This, or we sleep on the road."

"I may consider the road next time," Mira said. Ordi laughed.

He tapped his staff against the bedding, and the dust vanished instantly. Crawling into the center, he sat cross-legged, holding his staff with his left hand, and drifted into a deep meditation while Mira curled up near the fire.

Meditation was a technique taught to mages at the Academy, designed to focus on drawing energy into themselves without releasing it. This practice proved more beneficial for mages than simple sleep while questing. As he meditated, the energy flowed into Ordi, repairing the day's aches and pooling energy to be dispersed the following day.

While meditating, Ordi thought of his training and how he could tap into the arcane magic for various spells. He envisioned sitting on a hillside, looking out over a valley. The sunset bathed the landscape in warm hues, and a gentle summer breeze moved softly through his hair and beard. Suddenly, his vision went dark. Drawing in breath after breath, he focused on the energy transfer.

His envisioned hillside was now saturated in darkness, with no visible features. The sky overhead was pitch black, devoid of stars. Ordi's face twitched, and sweat pooled on his brow. From the left, a figure approached—blacker than the surrounding darkness. Despite the pitch blackness, Ordi could make out the outline of the hooded figure, its presence more ominous than anything he had encountered before.

Before he spoke, the figure flicked his wrist and bound Ordi to the spot. "Ordi, I see you are all grown up. Yet, you have no idea of the power you claim to wield. You pathetic mages with your little school. Do you think you know the power in this world? You know nothing. And with your ignorance, the downfall of your people comes. I will eradicate this world of your filth and build an empire of powerful necromancers and wizards who know the true power deep in this world. I am coming for you." His voice dripped with malice, and as his words echoed in the void, he disappeared, taking the darkness with him.

Ordi jolted out of his meditation, nearly falling to the floor and startling Mira. "It's okay," he reassured her, though his voice trembled. He was drenched in sweat, his body shaking from the encounter. "Who was that?" he whispered, trying to steady his racing heart. Mira pooled arcane magic and channeled it to Ordi, allowing his body to draw upon the source.

"*Ordi, what is wrong?*" Mira asked.

"*I don't know. He appeared to me again.*"

"*Again?*"

"*Yes. Mocking me this time. He spoke to me,*" Ordi said.

"*That is concerning,*" Mira stated.

Ordi was now lost in thought. Indeed, this couldn't be the exact figure that had appeared to him during his trials at the academy. The instructors had never covered anything like this. How could someone appear during meditation?

Was this some telepathic energy? Was it dark magic? What did he mean by their ignorance of magic? Ordi's mind was a whirlwind of questions, each more troubling than the last. *Why was he being targeted? Did this have something to do with the vision outside the castle? Was this the same person who had meddled with the altar?* Ordi thought. *No, that was preposterous.*

He had always believed that his instructors were the most accomplished mages of their time, celebrated by both kingdoms as protectors. The mages were responsible for defeating the Dark Lord centuries ago.... or is that what we were led to believe?

"*They speak of ancient magic, Ordi—one where necromancers can walk between realms. I only briefly recall this from when you sorted Master Galen's works,*" Mira stated calmly.

"Yes, I recall that. It's dark magic, whatever it is. We have too many questions and no answers at the moment," Ordi replied.

Too many were left without answers, and now Ordi feared for the outcome of their journey. What was going to happen? Was another war on the horizon? Could the people of Asheros endure another conflict? One thought troubled him deeply—the realization of how little he knew.

He understood now that the academy could only impart so much knowledge to students; the rest required initiative and a thirst for deeper understanding. While some students excelled at this, others were content with learning a few skills to take back to their towns. But Ordi knew now that contentment was not enough in a world with such dark forces.

Ordi lay down, calming himself and drifting into a deep meditation once more. This time, without any further occurrences. Mira returned to her spot after channeling some more arcane magic to Ordi. Morning came quickly; however, the sun barely pierced the dirty window. The fire in the fireplace had gone out, and Ordi awoke from his meditation. Refreshed as much as possible, he left his room with Mira and walked over to Verdun's door. Knocking twice with his staff, dust flying with each hit, Verdun responded with a good morning. "Want to grab some food before heading out?" Ordi asked.

"AYE. I'm starving, and this room wasn't the most pleasant stay," Verdun replied as he continued to brush the dust from his tunic. "I won't miss this place. How did you manage to stay clean?" He looked more filthy now than when they had departed the night before.

"I uh…magic…" Ordi chuckled, "I fear we'll have far worse stays in the coming months. More about that on the road. Let us get clear of this town and any potential ears," Ordi said.

"Well, will you cast some of that magic to clean me up?" Verdun asked.

Chuckling, Ordi said, "No." He turned and walked down the hall. Verdun gestured as he walked away from him.

Entering the bar, the three saw a female waitress presiding over it this morning, greeting the group as they sat down. "We have eggs, bread, cheese, and hot tea this morning. Will that be okay?" the waitress asked.

"Yes, one for each of us," Ordi replied.

Verdun couldn't help but notice Ordi's unsettled demeanor as they waited for their meal. "So, what happened? Why are you so spooked this morning?" Verdun asked.

Ordi hesitated, glancing around the bar. "I don't want to talk about it here. There are too many ears that could be listening. Something happened last night. I am deeply troubled by it."

The food arrived lukewarm, and despite the quality, they ate to fill their stomachs. Mira had her share of chewy eggs, which were not up to her standards but good enough. After their meal, they left the dirty inn and walked to the stable. A young boy was helping the stable master and fetched the two ponies. Ordi thanked the stable master and left a few extra gold coins. "The stable master was the only thing worth paying in this town. I'm not certain we wouldn't have been more comfortable sleeping with the ponies," Ordi said. Both laughed at the thought.

They saddled up their ponies, and Verdun once again tightened everything down, double- and triple-checking his knots. They mounted and started down the path, heading toward the city gates and passing into the open country. Mira ran ahead and around the two ponies as they progressed. The road was vast and empty on this fine spring morning. The sun was shining brightly, and a warm breeze from the south added to the pleasantness of the day. They set off eastward and slightly south again for just a few days until they reached the Fringe.

The day unfolded without any usual signs of life. The road was deserted, and the fields were devoid of wildlife. It was as if the entire world had frozen in time, leaving only Ordi, Verdun, Mira, and their two ponies to navigate the unsettling stillness. This eerie quietness lent a surreal quality to their journey, underscoring the unusual nature of their surroundings.

"So, Ordi, tell me, brother…what bothers you?" Verdun asked, breaking the silence.

Ordi hesitated momentarily before speaking, his voice tinged with lingering unease. "Last night, while meditating, a hidden figure appeared. I do not know how… He entered my vision, turning everything black. He bound me to my spot and spoke to me. He told me we were ignorant and had no idea about the magic we meddled in. He said we would all be destroyed. Then he disappeared. I was snapped back into my room, covered in sweat and distraught."

Verdun frowned. "Well…this isn't the first time he's appeared. Who is it? What do you think it means?"

"It is either Xerxes or a servant of his… but what would he want with me? I am merely a mage… It could be my magic, but that doesn't make sense either! I do not know what it means, but something sinister and evil is brewing in the east, in the dead lands. As we traveled, I felt a depletion of magic. In some areas, the magic seems less than it should be. It almost feels like it is being drawn somewhere… to someone," Ordi responded.

At that moment, fear seized Ordi—fear of the stories he had read coming true, of the Dark Lord's return. The thought of what could come to pass was a heavy burden on his mind. He had pored over the stories, dissected them, and understood the devastation that Xerxes wrought. But one story eluded him, one that was never clearly written: the rise of the Dark Lord. No historian could explain why or how he amassed such power. The only records that survived were of the Great War and its aftermath.

The journey continued, but the conversation was devoid of joy. Lunch was a brief interlude, and the journey pressed on until they reached their next stop. The ruins of Agnar, a human fortress from the Great War, now long abandoned, would provide shelter tonight for the dwarves. They dismounted, tied their ponies to a dead tree inside the fortress, and set up camp. A small fire crackled as they cooked the fish they had caught earlier in the day, but the atmosphere was far from cheerful.

Mira was exhausted as well, not caring to eat much other than a few bites of fish and some jerky. She curled up next to the fire and fell fast asleep. Ordi and Verdun sat silently, the crackling fire providing the only sound as they pondered the ominous events and what lay ahead.

"Rest up; we must depart at dawn," Ordi said as he rolled out his sleeping bag. Verdun nodded, too tired to speak. He laid his head down and fell asleep instantly. Ordi, however, remained by the fire a while longer. He poked the hot coals with a stick and threw another log on to keep warm. His mind wandered back to the unsettling meditation from the night before. Fear again gripped him as he pondered the dark figure's words. The stars shone brightly in the night sky, and Ordi took in their beauty, finding a momentary solace in their distant light as he finally drifted off into a light sleep.

Before dawn broke, Ordi was awake again. He let Verdun sleep a bit longer and quietly began saddling up the ponies. Mira awoke with Ordi and headed out to hunt for a morning meal.

As dawn broke, Verdun stirred and stretched. "Thanks for getting the ponies ready... breakfast first?" he asked, rubbing the sleep from his eyes.

"Yes, eggs are all we have. The bread is stale now," Ordi replied. The two ate quickly, the simple meal enough to sustain them for the road ahead. When they finished eating, Mira appeared to have had a successful hunt. She nodded her approval, and with the ponies ready, they departed Agnar just as the sun breached the horizon.

Day three of their journey from Kamrar to the Fringe was uneventful. Heading south, they passed a few farms and tiny villages, their numbers dwindling as they neared the borderlands. The people they encountered were a mix of dwarves and humans, living sparse and humble lives. A few children waved as they rode past, offering a fleeting moment of normalcy and hope. The terrain was rugged and unforgiving, with rocky outcrops and dense, tangled undergrowth slowing their progress. Yet, the sense of impending doom weighed heavily on their hearts. The closer they got to the Fringe, the more they encountered the remnants of villages and homesteads, now ghostly husks bearing the scars of recent raids. The air was thick with the scent of decay and the lingering despair of those who had once called these lands home.

The open road stretched ahead, with the land gradually becoming more rugged and untamed. Despite the lack of incidents, a lingering sense of unease from Ordi's vision hung over their journey like a dark cloud. They pressed on, driven by both urgency and the distant promise of finding allies and answers in the Fringe.

"*I sense something uneasy. This area may be untouched physically by the darkness, but it is in the air. The magic here is tainted,*" Mira told Ordi.

"*Yes, I sensed that too. The arcane is off. The elemental magic is unusual as well. It is hard to say what the culprit is. Never have I felt the channels do this,*" Ordi replied. Coming over a small hill, they noticed a town in the distance. "Verdun, there is Ashton; we start our investigation there."

"Ey. Let's rest tonight and start looking around in the morning," Verdun replied.

They reached the village of Ashton towards the end of the third day. The Fringe would be a mere half-day's journey tomorrow. They came to what appeared to be the inn and proceeded to enter. They found the bartender and requested the Lord of the town.

"Aye, I can summon him, but he'll ask who requests his presence at this hour," the bartender said. Ordi informed him and noted the urgency behind the request.

The dwarves waited and drank ale while the Lord was summoned, and Mira remained patiently at Ordi's feet. The bar door creaked as a beaten and worn man stepped inside, his boots heavy against the wooden floor. His once-tall frame was now slightly hunched, and his shoulders slumped under the weight of past battles. Once styled and kept, his hair was now unkempt and matted, a testament to the harshness of his life. His face, lined with deep wrinkles, bore signs of many battles and sleepless nights. His armor was battered, bruised, dented, and scratched from countless blows. His sword, once a shining beacon of hope, now hung limply at his side, its once-sharp edge dulled from many fights. Despite his weariness, the hero's eyes still held fierce determination, a sense of purpose that refused to be extinguished by the trials he had faced. He scanned the room with a watchful eye, seeking refuge from his journey and a moment of peace before the next battle.

The ragged man approached Ordi and Verdun. "I hear you requested to talk with me. Is this about the attacks on our people?"

Ordi spoke first. "Yes. We come on behalf of King Telophap. We have been sent to gather information on incidents occurring near the Fringe. I didn't catch your name."

"Lord Cedric," he replied. Sitting down, he was handed an ale by the bartender. Thanking him, he asked, "What does the King of the Dwarves care about us out here? He is too busy shut up in his mountain to pay us attention."

"There is no need for petty bickering," Ordi said quickly. "We received scattered messages about what has happened here, and the King desires to know more. He has sent Verdun and me to investigate."

Scoffing at Ordi's words, Cedric responded, "Well… you tell the King we are undermanned. We have no weapons, and with the farms burning, the food rations are dwindling. The enemy is not pressing full force but attacking at random. Small groups are getting bolder with each attack due to the feeble resistance we muster."

Pondering Cedric's words, Verdun said, "We have heard rumors that the enemy is rising. Our scouts couldn't tell us much more than that. We have not witnessed any battle marks on our way.

Cedric interrupted Verdun. "You are right, master dwarf. You will have to go further east and somewhat south. They are only crossing so far into our territory. Mostly just past Decaywold, they have targeted only farms and a few small villages. They seem to be getting bolder with each raid."

Ordi spoke next. "Can you take us there tomorrow? We want to see it reported to the king. I am confident he will send a caravan of supplies and troops. Would you happen to have a messenger fox out here? We can pen a note to the king and get an answer back quickly. Have you been in contact with King Leifric?"

Leaning forward in his chair, Cedric nodded. "Yes, we have a few foxes. We can arrange for one to leave immediately. No, I have not heard from him in some time. Again, another king locked away safely in his castle with armies around him. These folk are restless and scared, and truthfully…" He leaned closer. "They are not fond of either king; neither has shown much dedication to assisting with this new evil. EY! What is it going to gain me by complaining? It is late. Write your note and get some rest. We have a busy day tomorrow."

Cedric rose. His heavy boots echoed through the bar as he departed. The door slammed shut behind him, and Ordi looked at Verdun. "Well, it appears we have some tension here. We must be delicate. Though we are still in the kingdom of Telophap, people out here are distressed." Ordi quickly wrote his note, passing it to the bartender. The two rose from the table and proceeded to the room set aside for them, with Mira trotting behind Ordi.

"Humans always seem grumpy when you show up." Mira said.

The night passed quickly, resulting in little rest for Ordi and Verdun. They met early in the morning in the bar with Cedric. "Follow me; your ponies are ready." The two dwarves and Mira followed Cedric out of the tavern and onto the street. The sun rose, casting a golden glow over the village, and the air was cool and crisp. There was little to no sign of life in the small outcrop village, adding an eerie stillness to the morning.

The four made their way out of the village and onto the eastward road. The journey was quiet, the only sounds being the clopping of hooves and the occasional rustle of leaves in the breeze. After about an hour's trek, they came across the first burnt and destroyed farmstead.

As they approached, Mira ventured onto the blackened grass, sniffing around and investigating the scene. It only took a moment before the images were relayed to Ordi. He shuddered as the vivid scenes flashed in his mind: hordes of goblins ransacking the home, pulling apart beams and furniture, and setting the crops ablaze. The destruction was thorough, leaving nothing but charred remains behind.

Cedric gestured to the ruins. "This has been happening more frequently. Small groups of goblins loot and destroy everything they touch. They strike swiftly and disappear before we can muster a defense."

Ordi felt a chill run down his spine. The images from Mira were so vivid, so brutal. "We need to find their hideouts and stop them at the source. Reporting this to King Telophap is crucial, but we must also take immediate action here."

Verdun nodded, his face grim. "We should scout further east and maybe south. They might have left more tracks or clues."

Cedric agreed. "We'll need to be quick and cautious. The goblins are cunning and won't hesitate to attack if they spot us."

After examining the farmstead, they mounted their ponies and continued their journey. The tension was palpable as each scanned the surroundings for any movement. As they traveled, the landscape grew increasingly desolate, with more charred fields and ruined homes bearing testament to the relentless assaults.

Mira remained vigilant, her keen senses alerting the group to potential danger. The sense of urgency drove them forward, determined to uncover the source of the attacks and bring an end to the terror plaguing the land.

"Ordi, the land feels broken. There is something wrong here." Mira spoke.

"Ey, I feel it too."

Their conversation was interrupted by Cedric. "Goblins came through here maybe three weeks ago. Luckily, no one was home. The farms and crops were destroyed. We intercepted the pack of goblins and slaughtered them later that night. This, and many others, are recent. All happened within the last few months. We had a long stint of peace and no issues, but suddenly, raids started, and people are now fearful. Further along, we'll see where the dark elves came and killed an old farmer and his wife. They stayed in the house for three days before we ever caught wind. They were fierce to fight against, and their talents with magic made it almost impossible." He continued riding, heading eastward. They arrived at the homestead that the elves had invaded. Half the upstairs floor was missing, and there were scorch marks all over the side of the home.

"Do you have any mages or paladins out here?" Ordi asked.

"We have one mage who travels among the villages and one paladin that accompanies him," Cedric answered.

The air grew still. A creaking sound echoed from within the house.

"Something is here, Ordi!" Mira screamed as she assumed a defensive stance.

"Brace yourselves. Something is here!" Ordi steadied himself with his staff.

A chilling war cry pierced the air without warning, and a horde of goblins descended upon them from the ruins of the house. Their grotesque faces twisted in malevolent glee as they brandished jagged weapons, their eyes gleaming with bloodlust.

"Ambush!" Ordi shouted, barely drawing his sword in time to deflect a blow aimed at his head. Verdun, quicker on his feet, raised his shield just as a goblin's blade clanged against it with a force that reverberated through his arm.

Mira sprang into action, her growl a feral warning. She lunged at the nearest goblin, her powerful jaws snapping shut around its neck. With a violent shake, she tossed the lifeless body aside, blood dripping from her jaws. The goblins were only a few feet tall and were easy targets for her as she tore through the rushing mob.

The goblins kept coming, an endless tide of ferocity. Ordi raised his staff, summoning a powerful gust of wind that knocked several goblins off their feet, sending them sprawling into the jagged rocks. He followed it with a burst of flame, the intense heat scorching the ground and incinerating any goblins caught within its reach.

Verdun fought beside him, his shield a battering ram against the onslaught. He drove his sword through a goblin's chest, the creature's scream cut short as it crumpled to the ground.

Cedric struggled to keep up. His age slowed him, but his eyes burned with the fierce determination of a warrior who had seen many battles. A goblin lunged at him, its rusted dagger poised for a lethal strike. With a grunt of effort, Cedric swung his rusty sword, a deep, visceral growl escaping his lips. The goblin's head flew from its shoulders, rolling away as its body fell.

Despite their efforts, the horde was relentless. Goblins swarmed around Cedric, sensing his vulnerability. Ordi saw his friend falter, a goblin blade slashing across Cedric's arm, blood gushing forth.

"Cedric! Hold on!" Ordi shouted, hacking through the goblins blocking his path. He raised his staff, conjuring a barrier of shimmering light around Cedric, protecting him from further attacks.

Sensing the danger, Mira bounded over and tore into the goblins surrounding Cedric. Her claws raked through flesh, and her teeth snapped at limbs. She emitted a guttural snarl, her fur bristling with magical energy, and suddenly unleashed a wave of force that sent goblins flying, bones snapping upon impact.

With a roar, Ordi extended his arms, channeling his inner power. The air around him swirled with elemental fury. He summoned a vortex of wind and fire, the combined elements forming a cyclone that tore through the ranks of the goblins. Screams filled the air as the raging inferno engulfed the creatures, their bodies reduced to ashes.

Verdun, driven by a desperate need to reach Cedric, fought off the remaining goblins with a series of rapid, precise strikes, each blow landing with lethal accuracy. His sword flashed in the dim light, a silver arc cutting through the gloom, each impact sending bone and steel jarring. He moved with almost supernatural speed, a blur of motion, his stout body twisting as he launched himself toward a goblin, the blade slicing upwards with a sickening wet sound, severing the goblin in half and sending a spray of blood and gore across the floor as more goblins rushed toward him, their crude weapons raised. He did not hesitate, his breath coming in ragged gasps, as he continued to parry the crude, wild swings with flicks of his wrist, turning their attacks aside before delivering his own devastating jabs and slashes, each move fluid and deadly, the sharp clang of metal on metal echoing in the confined space.

Cedric, though injured, did not fall. He lifted his sword once more, summoning a well of strength, and struck down a goblin that had dared to breach Ordi's protective barrier.

Ordi's eyes glowed with arcane energy as he called forth a final spell. Slamming his staff into the ground, he released a pulse of pure magic. The ground beneath the goblins erupted with earth and stone, swallowing them in a deadly embrace. Mira added her power to the mix, her eyes glowing as she channeled the earth herself. Roots and vines burst forth, wrapping around the legs of the goblins and dragging them down into the hungry earth.

The goblins shrieked in terror and rage, but Ordi's and Mira's combined might was unstoppable. Within moments, the horde was either destroyed or fleeing for their lives, their cries echoing through the darkening wilderness.

Finally, the battlefield fell silent. Ordi, breathing heavily, surveyed the scene. Bodies of goblins lay strewn across the blood-soaked ground.

Rushing to Cedric's side, Ordi lowered his hand to check the depth of Cedric's wound. "You're going to pull through," Ordi said, his voice filled with relief. "We'll heal you."

Verdun quickly tore strips of cloth from his tunic, fashioning a makeshift bandage. "You did well for an old man," he told Cedric, a slight chuckle in his comment.

Cedric managed a weary smile, his bloodied hand reaching up to grip Verdun's shoulder. "I'm not done yet," he rasped. "I have a fight or two left."

In the battle's aftermath, Mira summoned a gentle, healing light to channel through Cedric's wounds. The gashes began to close, and the bleeding slowed. "Rest for a night. We'll keep watch."

"I'll keep watch tonight. I am rested enough, Ordi. By the way, I am surprised by how Verdun fought. He was incredible. He has truly improved, and his quick thinking with the bandage. Let him know you are proud of him," Mira said.

"If you think you're up to it, I won't object to you keeping the first watch. I am not a fan of telling Verdun I am proud of him," Ordi replied as they prepared to camp for the night.

"Stop being stingy and just do it." Mira said.

Mira stood vigilant afterward, scanning the horizon for threats.

Ordi walked over to Verdun, "Uh, Verdun. I'm proud of you. You fought brilliantly out there today. You have really progressed as a warrior."

"Really, you mean that? Well thank you Ordi. That means a lot." Verdun said. "I appreciate it, but I'm tired. Good night."

The night passed, and morning came with no further issues. The sun rose as they gathered their gear and secured their perimeter. The four prepared to continue their journey eastward. Mira led the way, her keen senses alerting her to signs of danger.

They continued their trip through the farmsteads, and the same scene repeated. All along the borderlands, the farms were destroyed or abandoned. The sun was now high overhead; it was midday. The trio and Mira sat down for a quick lunch.

"The fox was dispatched last night and should reach Kamrar tomorrow. That is the fastest way we can get word to King Telophap. What about King Leifric? What does he request?" Cedric asked, gripping his arm where the wound was healing. Mira had applied some arcane healing, but it was slow. The pain would remain for a long time.

"We have not heard from him yet. We've got an emissary dispatched to speak with and take counsel from the humans," Verdun said. The three finished lunch quickly and mounted. They proceeded south a short distance, examining the continued stretch of destruction left by the attacks. They made a wide circle and headed back west to Ashton. The entire time, Mira kept relaying images back to Ordi. This was a typical trait for a posh hound: standing somewhere and uncovering recent past events. Their visions into the past could only extend a week or so, but it was enough for Ordi to see the elves' and goblins' movements and patterns.

"The land is broken, but I do not sense any more danger. It could have been a rogue pack of goblins yesterday," Mira said to Ordi as they continued their journey.

They arrived just before nightfall in Ashton. Cedric did not speak again until they reached the town. "Will your king send supplies and reinforcements? Are you departing tomorrow?" Exhaustion was evident in his voice. The day's battle had been intense and had shaken him to his core.

"Yes to both. We do not want to abandon the outer cities to these creatures. Verdun and I will depart for Kamrar first thing in the morning," Ordi responded resolutely.

Cedric reached out with his good arm to shake their hands. "Thank you both. I hope we truly get the help you have promised."

"We will do our best to ensure the people out here are not forgotten," Ordi said as he grabbed his hand.

Verdun likewise said, "You are welcome. Be vigilant, and we will come."

Cedric's mood softened as he displayed a moment of appreciation. Ordi, Verdun, and Mira entered the tavern again, seeking what rest they could muster. Settling down in the room, Mira curled up by the small fire. Ordi quickly fell asleep but tossed and turned throughout the night, weary and haunted by vivid dreams.

Morning came, and Ordi stirred, sore from riding and the battle before but determined to move. He rose from bed, threw on his tunic, and met Verdun. The three departed without eating breakfast and hurriedly left Ashton, returning to Kamrar.

The first day on the road was a hard push. There was no time to stop and linger. They ate their food while riding and paused only to water their ponies. They rode into the night before stopping to make camp, their goal to return to Kamrar within two days and report to the king.

They rose before the sun and set out. The second day was overcast—a chilly day in early April with a drizzle that refused to cease. Ordi and Verdun moved along safely, though they knew they would be delayed as the road softened with the rain, forming mud puddles.

Mira was unhappy with the constant rain and the lack of breaks, and their ponies were equally displeased, slowing further. *"This is not what I had in mind for a return trip. I suppose you don't care one way or the other, do you, pony?"*

The pony neighed in response, and the group carried on. After a while, Ordi decided it was enough rain to stop. They found a canopy that offered some cover from the downpour and set up for lunch. Continuing with haste, they finished and attempted to dry off their ponies before heading back on the path.

By mid-afternoon, the rain had ceased, but the clouds remained. The chill had lessened, but there was little relief. The journey continued, and they arrived late on the second night in Kamrar.

Upon entering the city through the main gates, Ordi and Verdun announced their arrival home. They were quickly ushered into the throne room, which was filled with dwarves who made up the ruling council. A few dwarves from other kingdoms were present to discuss the matters at hand. Ordi and Verdun approached the king, bowed, and proceeded to give their report. They informed the council of the current state of the farms on the Fringe and described their day with Cedric.

"Your Highness, the situation on the Fringe is dire," Ordi began. "Cedric described the accounts of attacks by dark elves and goblins. They have become bolder and are driving deeper into our territory each week."

The king leaned forward, his eyes narrowing. "And what of the provisions in Ashton?"

"They dwindled, Your Highness," Verdun interjected, his voice unwavering. "Cedric informed us that their mage and paladin are stretched thin, constantly fighting along the

Fringe. Ashton is running desperately low on supplies. Goblins even ambushed us during our travels."

The crowd of advisors reacted immediately. Their discussions rose in volume, escalating into heated debates about the best course of action. Concern etched itself across every face.

One council member shouted, "We must act swiftly. The enemy cannot be allowed to gain more ground!"

Ordi nodded in agreement, his face grimly set. "We sent a message via a messenger fox explaining the dire situation. Cedric fears that Ashton may not withstand much longer without immediate reinforcement." The urgency of the situation felt like a weight pressing down on them.

The king sighed heavily, his brow furrowed with deep concern. "Yes, the fox arrived," he confirmed gravely. "The report is why we summoned this council today. The humans will arrive tomorrow, and we can discuss our strategy in greater depth. It pains me to think of the times we live in. For almost 400 years, peace has been our companion. For 400 years, we believed the Dark Lord was destroyed and his followers scattered to the winds. I fear these attacks are not mere chance. They may be the harbingers of something far more sinister."

A heavy silence fell upon the room. Each dwarf present absorbed the gravity of the situation. The king's words gripped their hearts with icy foreboding, and fear crept into their minds like a chilling mist, shrouding their thoughts in uncertainty.

"Through his research, Ordi informed me that this is how it began last time," the king continued, his voice laden with sorrow as he relived the distant past. "Small, precise attacks with what the enemy considered expendable troops fractured us through stealth and surprise. It weakened the elves most of all, leaving them fragile and vulnerable. And now, none can predict what fate awaits the dwarves and men if this resurgence truly marks the return of the Dark Lord."

The weight of his words hung in the air. Only the heavy breaths of those gathered could be heard. Finally, one council member stepped forward. "Your Majesty, what course of action do you propose?"

"We must strengthen our defenses and reinforce Ashton and the surrounding towns without delay," the king declared with resolve. "We cannot permit any further losses. Additionally, we must gather more intelligence on the enemy's movements and strategies."

Verdun stepped forward. "Your Majesty, Ordi and I are prepared to return to the front lines. We can assist in the defense and gather the necessary information."

The king nodded approvingly, a glimmer of gratitude in his eyes. "Your dedication is commendable. But rest tonight. A long road lies ahead of us all, and tomorrow, we will organize further with our human allies."

As the room emptied, Ordi and Verdun remained with the king. "Ordi, Verdun, there is great fear within these halls, and it undoubtedly echoes across the land," the king said. "We must not let these rumors or your reports shake our subjects. These attacks hint at deeper malice, and I believe we shall uncover some answers tomorrow."

With those final words, the king dismissed Ordi and Verdun. As they departed the chambers, they carried the weight of the king's charge upon their shoulders.

"I don't think the king sees the urgency we do," Verdun remarked as they left.

"It may seem that way, but we have much to discuss. The king has many considerations now, and with the Men's involvement, we may have the answers we seek. I do not believe he will forsake the people out on the Fringe. We do not need to press the matter. Let us see what the next few days bring," Ordi replied.

Outside the throne room, Mira paced impatiently, uninterested in joining Ordi and Verdun for their brief respite. Once they reached their homes, they collapsed into their beds, exhausted from their journey yet resolute in facing the challenges ahead.

"It is about time. I was getting bored," Mira smirked at Ordi.

"The king is debating enforcements. It's just the usual meeting stuff to work through. Let's go," Ordi replied calmly.

The night was short. A message from the king arrived before dawn broke. A knock on Ordi's door could be heard. A moment later, the knock turned into constant pounding.

Aimlia woke Ordi. "Ordi, go to the door; someone is there." Ordi stirred and rose from bed. Groggy and half asleep, with sand in his eyes, he stumbled over the furniture. He gathered himself and went to the door.

Upon opening the door, a petite young dwarf appeared, nervous, as this may have been one of his first assignments. "Master Ordi, sir," he stammered. "The king has requested your presence immediately." With that, he turned and ran off to the next stop, across the street to Verdun's house.

Chapter 6 The Meeting

Ordi stood dazed as he watched the small dwarf run off to his next errand. Mira trotted up to watch the young dwarf scamper away. Ordi rubbed his eyes to clear the sleep after a long night. He returned to the house, shutting the door with Mira behind him. He balled up his fist and threw a fireball into the fireplace, igniting a small fire to warm the room and provide light. He woke Aimlia and informed her that the king had summoned him. She hastened to prepare a quick breakfast without saying anything.

He entered the bathroom and, looking into the mirror, saw a face that he hardly recognized. The years had not been kind to Ordi, drawing dark circles under his eyes, sprinkling gray in his beard, and thinning his hair. He remembered his youthful face—no scars or marks, no gray, and a full head of hair. He sighed, wondering where the time had gone. Splashing water on his face to wake up further, he dressed in formal mage garments. He selected black trousers, a loose black shirt, and a robe that draped over his shoulders and closed across his chest. The robes were the elegant part of the outfit, a vibrant purple that contrasted well with the black underclothes. Across the back, the King's symbol of a lion rampant and roaring was stitched to signify that he was in the King's court. The cloak was enchanted with minor gems in the fastenings, allowing him to be more precise with his spells and deadly when needed. Wearing the cloak provided a unique advantage, as it gave Ordi a stronger connection to the arcane magic in the world. Each mage cloak was distinct in that only the sole bearer of the garment received the enhancement of power. Of course, these were standard enhancements found elsewhere in the dwarven empire, as dwarves were exceptionally skilled enchanters.

"I hope to be home in time for dinner, my love," Ordi said. "You need not worry about making my lunch today."

After dressing, Ordi kissed Aimlia and told her he would return later. He always worried that he might be summoned for a quest that would take him away for an extended period. After yesterday, he did not know what to expect. For today, he hoped to be home before supper. Sometimes, these meetings ran long into the night.

He leaned in to kiss her. "I know, but I always worry you'll be hungry. Here," she handed him a small sack. "I packed your favorite cookies for the meeting." A sparkle appeared in her eyes. Ordi knew that she always looked out for him. He always kept his interests at the forefront of her mind.

However, he did not fear going hungry because the King always provided sufficient food and drink. Walking to the door, he grabbed his staff, a symbol given upon promotion to the King's coterie. The staff was enhanced to connect more deeply with the arcane power. He had room for crystals to be embedded, but only one had been placed. The staff stored magic for later use. When Ordi had put on his full royal garb, he felt the arcane power pulse through his body. He knew casting any spell would not take much effort, and he smiled at the satisfaction.

The two embraced once more, sharing their lives, which had always brought Ordi happiness. "You are my anchor. I would not be the mage I am today without you." He kissed her again. "I love you, Aimlia. Hopefully, this meeting is quick, and I can return to my library work."

"Here, you forgot this." She handed him his journal. The leather cover wrapped around parchment was something Ordi had only recently started keeping. It was hard to categorize the history of magic. He noted anything unusual he found and each unique spell that he came across.

"Thanks, dear. As always, I would be lost without you," Ordi said as he slid the journal into his jacket pocket. "Mira will stay here today. I hate to make her sit through another one of these meetings. She can play with the kids."

"Oh, the kids will love that!" Aimlia replied.

She smiled as he held her hand for a long moment, staring into her eyes. He kissed her once more and turned to leave. He hurried out the door and onto the road towards the king's keep. The robe flowed behind him despite the stillness of the air around him. The symbol of the King was always visible when Ordi left his home.

He had been wearing the King's sign for almost three years, and not a day passed that Ordi didn't think about the honor bestowed upon him. He was fortunate to be able to channel arcane magic because not every dwarf possessed his unique ability. His selection to the academy had been unique as well. He was the only dwarf in his class, alongside a human named Sabastian and an elf named Askra. Sabastian continued his training to become a paladin, skilled in light magic and the ability to wield a sword. Askra specialized as a druid and was the only elf Ordi had ever met. She didn't talk much to him, but Sabastian and Ordi became quick friends.

They passed the trials the same week and went their respective ways to serve their kingdoms.

Over the past few years, Ordi had lost contact with Sabastian and assumed he was busy serving his king. Ordi's workload kept him from visiting Talamar often, as King Telophap had him running everywhere, investigating minor skirmishes and random incidents. None amounted to anything significant, but the king insisted they be looked into. Ordi, being a Kingsman, did as he was instructed. With little time for his family, Ordi cherished every moment he spent with Aimlia and his children. He hoped he wouldn't have to leave again soon.

He had spent countless hours in the library sorting and organizing works and rejuvenating the ancient shelves. He ran a few errands for the King, such as handling a dispute between miners and lords between Kamrar and Peakforge. The miners wanted higher wages, while the lords of Peakforge were reluctant to pay. He resolved the issue and moved on to the next task. He was dispatched to address a dry spring with whispers of dark magic, and he recently traveled with Verdun. The load never lightened, and Ordi had a feeling in his stomach that it would only get worse.

Ordi made his way towards the throne room, the weight of King Telophap's summons heavy on his mind. Arriving at the massive wooden doors, Ordi took a deep breath and gathered his resolve before pushing them open.

As he stepped inside, the chamber was alive with muted conversations, the light from the grand chandeliers casting a warm glow over the assembly. A long table dominated the center of the room, with an array of chairs packed closely together, leaving just enough space for Ordi to slip into his designated seat.

The human king, Leifric, sat at the head of the table next to King Telophap. The two rulers were deep in conversation, their faces a mix of concern and contemplation. Behind them stood aides and scribes, furiously taking notes and whispering, ready to support their leaders' needs. Servants moved efficiently around the room, ensuring that drinks and food were always within reach.

Accompanying King Leifric was his entire royal council, a group of ten influential men who radiated authority. Among them was the dean of the academy, Master Stow, whom Ordi recognized immediately. Ordi gave him a respectful nod, which Master Stow returned with a slight smile, acknowledging the mage's presence.

Sitting near the middle of the table, Ordi was positioned somewhat apart from the main conversation between the two kings and their senior advisers. From his vantage point, he could observe the array of emotions etched on the faces around him—concern, determination, and the heavy anticipation of the discussion.

"Good to see you, lad," Alistair Blackwood whispered. He patted Ordi on the shoulder as he took a seat. Alistair was the senior mage at the academy. Born a human with incredible power, he excelled at his position, and upon the retirement of Master Stow, Alistair would assume control of the academy. His knowledge was unmatched when it came to ancient magic and spellcasting.

The atmosphere in the throne room was tense but focused as murmurs of the current plight swirled through the air. Ordi glanced around, taking in the sight of various dignitaries and high-ranking officials, each aware of the gathering's importance. This was no ordinary meeting; it was a convergence of minds and powers coming together to address their realms' dire situation.

King Telophap, known for his commanding presence, raised a hand to call for silence. The room gradually quieted, the subtle hum of voices fading into a respectful hush. All eyes turned to the two kings, awaiting the start of a critical discourse.

"It's good to see you as well, Master. I'm glad you're here," Ordi whispered.

King Telophap began to speak, his voice resonating throughout the throne room. "Ladies and gentlemen, dwarves and men, we welcome King Leifric and his company to our halls! It is surely good to see you all here. I only wish it had been under better circumstances. There is a growing crisis that must be addressed before doom spills forth upon us."

The room's buzz faded as the king's words captured everyone's attention. "I will let Master Ordi explain this briefly, but mind you, this is something that both dwarves and men must fight together. If the elves were worth anything, we would have involved them too... but they are so scattered and leaderless now that they are quite useless."

A soft chuckle erupted around the room, breaking the tension momentarily. King Telophap gestured with his arms to quiet the room. "It is unfortunate about their state, though. They were once a mighty people, ruling the lands and sacrificing much to destroy the evil in the land... an evil that has seemingly returned."

The king's expression grew more solemn. "Master Ordi, are you ready?" King Telophap asked, turning his attention to the senior mage.

Ordi was not prepared to speak, nor had he brought any notes from his previous journey. Though he was unprepared, he was equipped to work under pressure. Clearing his throat, he said, "Yes, Your Majesty." Ordi stood and looked around. Every eye in the room fell on him at that moment.

"Verdun and I were sent recently to investigate the goblin raids on the Fringe. We journeyed to Ashton and explored the area north of Decaywold." He tried to keep his voice and language polished. The patience demonstrated was impressive, Ordi thought as he continued.

"We met with townsfolk and examined the farmsteads there. Goblins destroyed many, and elves had pillaged and ransacked the area. In one instance, we were ambushed by goblins, but we survived. Uh…" He trailed off for a moment. "The attacks are becoming more frequent and moving closer to the larger villages. Lord Cedric requested support, troops, and food." At this, the room's noise picked up. People around the tables started to whisper to each other. The whispers grew louder, and small debates began to take place.

The King raised his hand, and the room silenced again. "I believe what Master Ordi is saying is that our enemy is on the move once more. It has been years since we've had any attacks like this, and it deeply concerns me."

A gentleman next to the king began speaking, "Your Majesty. We cannot possibly take this as truth." He wore all black, which was uncustomary for an advisor to the King.

His jet-black hair was slicked back to his shoulders. His face was stern, showing no emotions.

"Clive," the king responded, "we must take these accounts seriously. Ordi is one of my most trusted mages. He would never stretch the truth." At this, Clive subsided, though the expression on his face never changed. No emotions ever crossed it. "Ordi, please continue," the king said.

"Thank you, Your Majesty. Uh. Where was I? Yes… We noted the farms and areas attacked and sent a fox back with our notes. We believe the attacks require further investigation and that a small caravan of supplies must be sent."

"Who is going to provide the supplies for this caravan?" one of the advisors yelled. Others chimed in, asking the same question.

Clive leaned in and whispered something to the king. The two conversed for a moment as arguments erupted in the throne room. The expression never changed on Clive's face as Ordi began to study and observe the new advisor to the king. A long moment passed; then he sat back in his seat, and his black eyes met Ordi's. The two held the stare for a moment until Ordi looked away, disturbed by the intensity of his glare.

King Leifric, who had been listening the entire time, rose and said, "We have supplies to help, but they are in Talamar. However, the journey will take longer for us to reach Ashton and those areas. We must get something there sooner to assist those in need before our supplies arrive."

"What about troops?" someone else yelled.

"We can send a small unit of troops with our supplies," King Leifric said calmly. "We have plenty of troops not doing much at the moment. This will be a good exercise for them. I can send a fox today, and they can be dispatched from Fort Marrel."

The council started to agree with this. For Ordi, it felt like the right thing to do, but Clive spoke as the room appeared settled on the issue. "My Lords, this is not a simple matter of food and soldiers. We must deeply consider if we want to help those living in such dangerous areas."

Ordi could sense something in that last statement but could not pick up on the tone. Clive continued speaking, "If you want my opinion, Your Majesty," he spoke directly to King Telophap, "we should refrain from sending supplies and troops." At this, the room broke out in disagreement.

"How can we ignore the pleas of our people?" someone yelled.

"Who are you to provide such ridiculous counsel?" another asked. The accusations grew, and people stood and yelled, pointing at each other, changing topics, and naming other issues. Clive sat with no emotion, his eyes fixed on Ordi. The two connected again, and Ordi sensed something wrong that he could not quite explain.

Ordi had known of Clive, but this seemed uncharacteristic of him. He was usually a reasonable advisor.

"To all who object, what resources would you send to help with this caravan?" As Clive asked, the room grew silent. "We must be mindful of the times we live in. Food is not as readily available, and we may have troops, but we must be prepared for the enemy. To please everyone here, this is my proposal." Anticipation grew strong in the room. "We move our food stores to Fort Marrel." Yells and cursing erupted in the room. After a few minutes, it settled down, allowing Clive to speak again. "As I was saying, we move our food stores and our available troops to Marrel, and from there, we can decide where to send them next."

The conversation broke out again, with each person talking to their neighbors and the kings talking to each other. Ordi sat and watched as the room continued to buzz, confused by the suggestions and recommendations on what to do next. Hours passed, and no one proposed anything better, yet the conversations continued. Ordi grew tired, as minimal discussion had anything to do with him. He looked to see Verdun talking to the two kings about troop movements.

Time passed. King Telophap raised his hand again. "Gentlemen, the night is closing in, and many of us are weary from all the talk. Let us continue this tomorrow. An ancient relic was brought to my attention. Master Alistair will tell you more tomorrow. You are all dismissed."

With that, the room emptied, and Ordi headed home. He entered the house, and the savory smell of beef on the fire made his mouth water.

"Daddy's home!" With that announcement, his kids and Mira came racing towards him as they always did, jumping into his arms. He embraced them tightly.

"Hi, honey," Aimlia said, coming around the corner and drying a dish in her hands. "How was your meeting?"

"Eh, unproductive. We could not decide what to do about sending aid to the Fringe. Nothing was decided. I fear I will be sent with a relief caravan."

"Oh, Ordi." Aimlia embraced him, holding as tightly as she could. "I know our service is to the king, but I can't bear it when you leave us."

"I know. Nothing is certain yet. We meet again at first light tomorrow." He held her in his arms, looking into her deep blue eyes. He kissed her once more, reminding her of his love for her.

Dinner passed, and bedtime for the kids came and went. Ordi took this moment to tuck each of the children into bed, reading a bedtime story to each and waiting until they drifted off to sleep.

Ordi found himself sitting in his chair, thinking about what could occur in the coming weeks if he were dispatched. While his name only popped up a few times today, he knew the King would want him in the thick of any action. This deeply concerned him, as he would rather be with his family than off in a war somewhere.

"You won't solve the world's problems tonight, Ordi. Come in and get some rest," Aimlia said from the doorway.

"You're right. I am no good unrested." He retired into the house with Mira walking beside him. *"You'll come with me tomorrow. I may need you."*

"*I am always willing to serve,*" she replied.

The following day, Ordi woke before everyone else and dressed quickly. Since the meeting was set before dawn, he left with Mira as soon as he was ready. They entered the King's chambers again and found themselves in the midst of continued conversations. Food was brought in and set before everyone, but yesterday's discussions distracted everyone from it. Ordi sat down and grabbed a plate of food as Mira sat behind him. King Telophap rose from his chair and demanded that the room settle down.

"Yesterday, we had many suggestions about what to do. We worked late into the night, and I think we reached an agreement. While we will make that proposal in a moment, I also want to discuss the relics. I noted that Master Alistair will tell you about them and hopes to inform us all." The King paused to let the room grasp the weight of the day ahead.

"The Dwarves and Humans have decided to send food to Fort Marrel, along with troops. This will enable them to aid the East if needed. We'll decide later on the amount to be sent, but we've agreed on this now." He waited to see if anyone would protest. However, no one dared offer any.

He beckoned to Master Alistair. "Master Alistair will guide us on some history and the importance of these lost relics. Like many of you, I am not well-versed in this story. We should listen closely to what he says."

At this, Master Stow murmured to himself about the obscurity of the relics.

Master Alistair rose from his chair next to Ordi. He stepped forward. "Yes, Your Majesty." His voice was steady and clear as he addressed the assembly. "I bid you all the warmest welcome that can be expected on this day. Rumors are running rampant, and I venture to say that many may be aware of an ancient enemy stirring in the east. A darkness we once conquered has arisen from the dust and ashes. Not much is written about Xerxes, but I want to provide as much history as possible."

The room fell silent, every ear attuned to Alistair's words.

"You may know him through history as the Dark Lord, sometimes referred to as the Fallen One; he is, in fact, King Xerxes. At one time, he was a great king, ruling over the eastern and southern provinces for decades. Peace and tranquility were his specialty. He had an unnaturally long life; while a man can be expected to live to 120, he was still strong at 160 years old. He was powerful in arcane magic and, unbeknownst to many, in dark magic. Some say he channeled arcane power to extend his longevity."

Alistair paced slightly as he continued, "As our chronicles show, around the year 45 BFO, before the Fallen One, he started to slip into darkness. Some say it was the madness of old age; others suggest he meddled in necromancy. It is hard to pinpoint what exactly happened. He became corrupt with the magic that had served him for so long, lashing out at his allies, seeking new territories, and laying waste to the land."

He paused momentarily to drink water before continuing, "Then, a great battle left the elves scattered and the humans and dwarves in disarray. It took almost 100 years to rebuild what was destroyed, and some lands have not fully healed after 400 years. We do not have a record of what transpired after the last battle. We assume Xerxes perished as we laid siege to his camp. Some suggest that he was betrayed by someone in his inner circle, someone seeking power."

Alistair paused to take another big gulp of water, allowing the information to sink in. Resuming, he said, "We never discovered his body, but the tent he occupied was destroyed. The darkness lifted after this battle, leading to six months of silence from what we now call the Deadlands. Peace came to all, and the hordes of goblins and trolls disappeared. Today, we have word of new movements and armies amassing again in the Deadlands. We've already witnessed dark elves and goblins ransacking farms along the fringe."

Master Alistair grew more assertive. "These minor Fringe attacks, while devastating to the families affected, have been nothing more than minor outbursts. Something to get our attention… or to distract us…"

Alistair let his final words hang in the air, the weight of their meaning pressing down on everyone present. The room remained silent, deep in thought.

Before Alistair could continue, the heavy doors of the throne room flew open with force. Before them stood an elf—tall and slender, with dark olive skin and jet-black hair pulled into a ponytail. He entered the room with an air of authority and began speaking immediately.

"I am Druid Nimue Leafwhisper. We have never met. I come bearing news for all. I tried to arrive yesterday but was delayed. I came urgently to discuss something we have been observing. This man," he said, pointing to Alistair, "is correct in what he says. His history coincides with the records we elves preserved in our libraries. We face a familiar enemy who has grown far more powerful over the past 400 years. He can raise the dead and perform magic unlike anything I have seen. He calls upon mercenaries from the north and far east, drawing hordes of goblins and dark elves to wage war once again."

A sigh escaped Nimue's lips, and his voice grew more grave. "But I fear he is too strong for us. Centuries ago, the elves would have formed a formidable defense, but we are now a broken people. Very few of us still possess magic, and our soldiers are no more. Our time in this land is waning. However, I have been sent here to provide what aid I can. Has anyone heard of the missing relics?"

"I thought Master Alistair was going to tell us about them before you interrupted," someone called out.

A murmur spread through the room, and Master Stow scoffed. "Those are just myths, nothing more. Truth be told… what good will they do against this enemy? They are merely a few items that would benefit a handful of individuals. We would need an entire army of these 'relics' for them to make a difference. So, what now?"

Nimue responded promptly, "A myth? Heavens, no, good sir. They are not a mere myth but are real. Can they help us? I cannot answer that, but we need all the help we can get now. They may be lost to time, but we elves know our history. We once possessed some of these relics, as you call them, but they are Otthroite Gems. At the time of high sorcery ages ago, they were crafted to aid those who led the respective studies of magic. One could say they were a gift from the gods. Those who possessed them could wield great power."

The room fell into rapt silence again. "These relics were infused into armor and weapons used by the best sorcerers and paladins during the Fallen One's last campaign. They were made with the final remaining Otthroite Gems and were sealed as eternal stones. This had never been done before, as these stones were previously only bound to their wearers during the owner's lifetime. The men who wore these relics sought to rid the world of all evil after the Fallen One's defeat and have not been seen since. These items will aid us in our struggle, unlocking ancient magic and spells and enhancing our ability to perform complex magic."

Nimue paused his speech and paced around the room. "We know many gems were used to make two sets of armor. One gem was bound to a tome, and the other went to a staff for the druid. Eryndor Dawnstrike last held the missing Druid Tome and staff, the mage Elwynn Starweaver's staff, and the paladin Arcturus Lightbringer's plate armor. To our understanding, these items could be scattered throughout Asheros, and some perhaps reside in the forgotten isles south of The Last Outpost in the Lost Hope Sea, where they were last seen. Our last record comes from the close of the Great War, as we were driving out the Fallen One in the south. Reports say the heroes went north to purge the lands further, but unfortunately, nothing else is known.

"Sounds like a fool's errand," someone interrupted Nimue.

"Perhaps. But what if you are wrong, sir? What if we rediscover them and help turn the tide in the war that will inevitably come?" Nimue replied. The room began to whisper again. Men turned to their neighbors, made comments, and laughed. A few kept a severe demeanor and sought answers.

"The tale of them going south may be a fool's errand, Master Elf," Alistair spoke, his voice rising above the low rumblings of the room. "The Dragons were the last to return these relics to the dwarves. We do not know more than that, and I am sure it will be dangerous to seek them as war rages around us." Alistair's remark left the room speechless, the gravity of his revelation sinking in.

King Leifric asked, "How do we find these relics? Where do we even begin to look? They are lost to history, as you say."

"Yes, lost, but not forgotten. We have some records of their last whereabouts. We will follow these trails and hope to find them. These items are the only hope we have," Nimue spoke.

"What good will they do when we face massive armies?" Clive chimed in.

"These items, while small in your eyes, can serve the two armies immensely. A druid and mage with these items can call upon ancient magic and release spells that haven't been spoken in centuries. They will be a force to be reckoned with on the battlefield.

"The paladin's armor will make the bearer powerful and fast. It enhances his strength and allows him to call upon light magic for healing and defense. Druids have deep elemental power that allows the world to bend around them. The gems allow the druid to draw upon and harness each power into a single gem for devastating effects. The mage… well, the mage is the deadliest of all. If channeled right, their power gives them access beyond that of paladin and druid. He would be almost unstoppable on the battlefield." Nimue said. "This journey will not be easy. We will need to make haste as the trail has long gone cold. I have a word for an old fortress in Witherwood that could have some clues." He continued, "We do not have time to wait. I am ready to go right now!" He finished and stood.

The two kings sat speechless, staring at the elf. The whole room had fallen silent. No one dared to make a noise. King Leifric broke the silence, "I can see we are all grappling with what has been spoken. If we may, let us pause for food. We could all take a few moments to digest while figuring out everything we just heard." He stretched his arms across the table, gesturing towards everyone.

Ordi waited to take this all in. He had a few notes written down, trying to keep up with all the changing topics. As the heavy oak doors creaked open, a troupe of dwarven and human servants paraded into the grand hall, each bearing platters laden with an abundant feast. The aroma of spiced meats and fresh-baked bread mingled with the smoke of the torches, creating a heady, mouth-watering scent that filled the air. Platters overflowed with roasted boar, glazed to a glistening perfection with honey; alongside them, rich stews bubbled in bowls crafted from the finest dwarven stonework, fragrant with herbs and earthy root vegetables.

Golden loaves of bread, still warm from the oven, emitted a comforting warmth, while bottles of ale, fermented to a fine clarity by the skillful hands of dwarven brewers, promised to satisfy even the stoutest thirsts. Fresh honeyed fruits and jewels of the harvest added color to the long wooden tables set for the gathering as the feast was laid out.

The room broke into numerous conversations as many around the tables grabbed food. The discussions continued for over an hour as servants came and went, bringing hot food and removing empty plates.

Ordi had a plate full of food; he turned to Mira, *"What do you think about all this? You've been quiet."*

She lay at his feet, going unnoticed for most of the morning, *"I am trying to process these Otthroite gems and their importance, if they have any. This elf seems like he knows something, but I am wary. And I grow more wary of Clive. He is up to something."*

Ordi stuffed his mouth full of boar before speaking again to Mira. *"I think we need to keep an eye on Clive. He seems off; he has too much power as a new advisor. I am curious where this conversation with the elf will end up."* He handed Mira a plate of roasted boar for her to eat as the room filled with conversation and food. Ordi had written everything down in his journal, as he had only noted the legendary gems once before. He needed to research them further when he had the opportunity.

"I think we may be sent to look for these missing gems, Ordi," Mira informed him.

"Maybe, but I do not think the King wants me to go out on such a foolish quest," Ordi replied.

The room continued to buzz as advisors took notes and discussed the previous two days' events with those gathered nearby.

King Leifric raised his hands to officiate today's meeting. It was time to resume, "If what you say is true, what do you require? And for what it is worth…" he paused, "Where is your starting point?"

"We have word that the last known location for the Druid's tome was with the Gray Elves, and their last known dwelling place was in Witherwood to the east. Since they were more nomadic, they may have ventured elsewhere. Some have pointed further north to the Unknown Lands. The elves were entrusted with the tome, which is hard to decipher. There are two stories: one claiming the gems stayed together and another pointing out that they split."

"Master Nimue, I think the gems went north instead of south," Master Alistair interjected.

"That may be. I have heard your tale as well. I can start exploring the northern regions since I am already here. Could I request a small group to accompany me?" Nimue asked.

The room once again erupted. "How can we send folk with you and to Marrel?" one yelled. "You ask a lot from us, Elf!" another said.

"I am not asking much," Nimue replied, calming his voice. "I am simply asking for a few volunteers to assist on my quest."

Clive leaned over to King Telophap and whispered something. Clive stood, "I think it is wise to send our best with you, Nimue. Sir, may I suggest Ordi and Verdun for the task?"

Ordi was shocked to hear his name mentioned. He had been half paying attention because he didn't think this would ever involve him. It was suggested that he accompany this strange Druid on this odd quest.

"Aye…." Telophap said, acknowledging Clive's suggestion. "I think we can manage that. Ordi, Verdun, see to it. Get provisions to sustain you. Thrain Frostbeard, I want you to accompany them as well. This brotherhood will go with you, Master Nimue. May the Almighty be with you on this quest."

King Leifric said, "I would like to send our paladin Roland Volton with you as well. I see it as fitting for men to accompany you on this quest. The evil will come for us all, and men intend to do our part." Ordi remembered Roland from when they encountered that witch. It would be nice to work with him again. It had been a long while since he had served with him on that brief mission.

"If that is all, we have much to do. Let's get to it!" King Leifric dismissed the meeting. Ordi rose with Mira behind him and exited the chamber.

The three dwarves met the paladin outside the room. Ordi embraced Roland, "It is great to see you, brother."

"Great to see you again, Master Ordi," the paladin replied.

Nimue followed out, "We need to make haste. I want to leave quickly."

"We need to tell our families and pack before departing. Can we leave at first light?" Ordi asked.

"No, master dwarf. One hour," Nimue spoke as he and Roland walked away from the dwarves. "ONE HOUR!" he yelled over his shoulder.

"One hour," Verdun mocked Nimue as the two left. "One hour… I can't even pack food in one hour."

"You have an eating problem," Mira said.

"It's a good thing he can't hear you." Ordi told Mira.

"Take your time, brother. Say our goodbyes, and we'll leave when we are ready," Ordi replied. Thrain started to walk away as well.

The two turned and made haste toward their homes. It was late afternoon; Aimlia should be busy preparing dinner, Ordi thought as he opened his front door. "Aye, love," Ordi hollered down the hall. The smell of another delicious dinner filled Ordi's nose. He would hate to miss tonight's meal. "How long until dinner is ready?"

"It's ready now, dear?" he heard her reply as she made her way to the front of the house. He hurried into the kitchen as she fetched a plate for him. "It is good having you home for dinner."

"I must leave again," Ordi said, disappointed. "The king has ordered a mission. I do not know how long this will take me. Verdun and Thrain are going, and it is all because of this elf who showed up."

"An elf!? From where?" she asked, a shiver of anger in her voice.

"I don't know. He just showed up. I think, personally, it's nonsense—a bunch of fairy tales. He wants us to find lost relics, missing gems. They have been legends for centuries. But an elf thinks he knows where the druid's tome is," Ordi explained.

"Oy! Wow. Oh, Ordi, I can't bear watching you leave again. The kids will be devastated," Aimlia cried softly. The tears rolled down her face. She turned away, not wanting him to see her like this.

He hugged her. "I know, dear. I wish I could be here, but the king's orders. It is easy for Verdun to pick up and leave; he doesn't have a wife. I will return, my love."

"How long?" she asked desperately.

I don't know. Our trek may take us far north into unknown lands. I can't say if it will be a month or more. This is a unique quest." He fumbled through his explanation. "I don't want to scare you, but we don't know what obstacles we will face. I would hope to say we'll be back in a few weeks, but I do not want to lie."

She broke down sobbing. "Hurry back, love," Aimlia said, wiping away her tears.

"I will. Let us enjoy this meal before I leave."

The two ate in silence, holding each other's hands.

After the meal, Ordi stood up and said, "I do not have much time. I must pack and meet the others at the stables as soon as possible." Ordi explained, "Can you prepare some dried meat and bread for me to take?"

"Yes, dear." She hurried off to prepare food for Ordi while he gathered clothes in the bedroom. He knew he could not take much. He was more concerned about the space for food. He grabbed a few tunics, trousers, leather belts, and socks. If anything, socks were key; he could deal with a dirty or wet shirt, but wet socks were the worst.

He would ensure his traveling robes were embedded with the same stones as his King's robes to fine-tune his magic. He placed his bag next to his staff, grabbed his longsword from the closet, and wrapped the belt around his waist.

Aimlia returned to the room. "You'll have to ration your food, my love. I know you love to eat. But if you are gone for a long period, try to space this out for a while." There was a hint of humor in her voice.

"I will, love. We can hunt and scavenge along the way."

"Be safe, be aware. Return to us." She kissed his cheek. "I'll let the children know when they get home."

"Aye. Thank you, dear. I shall return," Ordi said as he threw the satchel over his shoulder and grabbed the drawstring bag and his staff. He gave Aimlia one final tight hug and a long, passionate kiss.

He proceeded out into the road carved between dwellings in Kamrar, with Mira trotting behind. Seeing Verdun leave his home, he nodded to him.

Verdun and Ordi met Thrain and headed toward the main gates just a moment later. Thrain was an older mage, having served the court for twenty-five years. He was entirely gray in his beard and had thick gray and black hair on his head. Wearing the same robes as Ordi, he was not much distinguished from other mages, save for the length of his beard and an old crag in his nose from where it had been broken decades ago. It was customary for dwarf men to wear beards, but not all did. Depending on the job, having long facial hair would not be wise. Thrain did not often speak to Ordi, nor Ordi to him. In the three years Ordi served the court, this was the first time they had been assigned together on any quest.

"I trust you've brought your finest skills for this, Ordi. I hear good things about you, but if what that elf says is true… I wouldn't mind getting my hands on those mage relics,"

Thrain said as they passed through the main gates and into the warm sunlight.

Ordi sensed a degree of greed and selfish ambition behind Thrain's words. He saw how these relics could drive someone to greed. The idea of more power was always welcome, especially since the world's climate appeared to oppose it. The trio met Nimue and Roland, who had their horses prepared. The stable boy was busy preparing three ponies for the dwarves to take. Bill was once again assigned to ride Ordi.

Ordi walked over to Bill and gave him a nice long rub down his neck. Bill shook his head in approval. He tightened the saddle and secured his bags to the side of Ordi. Grabbing the saddle horn, Ordi hoisted himself up and flung his leg over. He sat gently on the beast, grabbing the reins. He nudged Bill out of the stable behind Verdun and Thrain, who were also exiting.

"We have a two-and-a-half-day journey to Karadar Tower. We will begin our search there. Let us hope our trip goes unnoticed," Nimue spoke as he urged his horse forward. The Brotherhood proceeded out of the stables and onto the main road out of Kamrar, making their way southeast along the path.

Chapter 7 Karadar Tower

The Brotherhood rode east out of Kamrar on the first day of their journey. Their intended first stop was Karadar Tower, another day and a half ride away, barring any unforeseen issues. The dirt path that Ordi and Verdun had recently traveled south to Ashton was familiar. As they rode north of Icewater Lake, they aimed to traverse the rolling hills by the end of the first day. The air was crisp as a gentle breeze blew off the lake.

"Nimue, what do you expect from us?" Thrain asked.

"I am not sure yet; there is a lot that I can't foresee about this quest," he replied.

Nimue rode at the front of the pack, his demeanor stoic and focused. He spoke no further, maintaining a constant pace that kept his horse moving steadily along. Behind him, the ponies, slower in speed, trailed, with Mira keeping a steady pace between the two groups. The path wound through a verdant landscape, with patches of wildflowers dotted along the roadside and the occasional rustle of small animals in the underbrush. The scent of pine and damp earth filled the air, evoking a sense of nature's resilience despite the looming threats.

The party halted for food as the sun remained high overhead, indicating it was past midday. Nimue slowed his horse and dismounted into a small clearing shaded by a group of majestic oak trees. The gentle babble of a nearby stream added a serene sound to their brief respite. Birds chirped softly from the branches, and a light breeze rustled the leaves, providing a momentary escape from their urgent mission.

"It is time to eat and rest," Nimue announced, dismounting gracefully. "We should not spend too much time lingering. We are in a race against time."

Although they had not yet reached the rolling hills, this shaded haven offered a brief reprieve. Allowing their ponies and horses to drink from the cool, clear stream, they sat down and unpacked their lunches. Each party member had brought enough provisions for two days, though they knew the journey would be longer. They would hunt and forage for food, a skill that came naturally to the dwarves, especially when traveling long distances. Ordi and Verdun managed to bring extra dried meats for snacking.

Ordi unwrapped a bundle of dried meat and bread. Verdun followed suit while Thrain checked their surroundings for any signs of danger. Roland sat on a fallen log, eyes scanning the tree line, ever vigilant. While they were not far from Kamrar, the need to be cautious was important. The Brotherhood could only guess where the enemy had spies.

"We can't be far enough to worry about enemies yet, could we, Roland?" Verdun asked, taking a bite of meat.

"Perhaps not, Master Dwarf, but my training keeps me always alert, always looking," Roland replied.

The sunlight filtered through the leaves, creating dappled patterns on the clearing. Insects buzzed lazily in the warm air, and occasionally, the distant call of a hawk echoed through the trees. Mira lapped at the stream before trotting back to Ordi, her eyes alert for any subtle movements in the foliage.

"Watch the back trail," Nimue instructed in a low voice. "We cannot afford any surprises."

Verdun nodded and positioned himself to keep an eye on the path, his hand resting on the hilt of his sword. The ponies, now watered, grazed on the lush grass near the stream, their occasional whinnies blending with the natural sounds of the forest.

As the Brotherhood ate, they shared a few words, each lost in their thoughts about the journey ahead and the unknown challenges they would face. The scent of pine and damp earth mingled with the aroma of their simple meal, grounding them in the present while their minds grappled with the uncertain future.

"Mira, I want you to stay vigilant as we go, occasionally heading up the path to see what we may encounter. Ignore the others," Ordi said.

"I can easily ignore them. I will run ahead and inform you of what is coming," Mira replied.

The crops had not yet been planted as spring was still fresh. Ordi thought farmers would be out here within a few short weeks with their mules tilling the ground and planting seeds. "Nimue, what's your plan? Do you have anything to go on other than a few ancient stories?" Ordi asked, anxious for an answer to write down in his journal.

Nimue looked around at the gathered group as they ate. "Master Ordi, I feel you may still be a skeptic, yet you are also wise. There is much to tell, and in time, I will disclose all I know." He took a deep breath, momentarily irritated by the question, then slowed his breathing to relax and rejuvenate.

"We Elves have a long-recorded history for our relics. Older records, unfortunately, have been destroyed or lost to time. The relics we seek were made long ago by the gods. They forged them from their magic and hid them away in their creation. Dwarves were the first to find them as they mined the mountains. The relics were seen as great treasures before the dwarves truly understood their purpose. There are no records of when that knowledge came, but we know the mages were informed long ago, some say by the dragons." Nimue paused for a moment. Ordi took a moment to write down a few notes, ensuring he captured what he could about these mysterious relics.

At first, the humans, elves, and dwarves were peaceful. The humans were given the armor because they were a noble race with many well-trained paladins. They saw the need to defend the weak and heal the sick. The armor was a gift to enhance and empower both fighters and healers. It was light yet impenetrable and could draw upon the world's magic to enhance the person wearing it. The user could move as no man could, leaping great distances and running faster than animals while never tiring. The paladin armor was a true gift from the gods, and only one set was ever crafted. It was intended for the one who would don the armor to wear for the rest of their life.

Nimue took a drink from his waterskin. "The other items we elves received. We were superior in understanding magic, and it was a long time before the dwarves ever realized they held the ability to channel. The dwarves focused more on mining and making money than on using gems and relics. Our primary focus is the Otthroite gems."

Ordi and Verdun listened intently. Although the story of their peoples' discoveries was familiar, hearing it from Nimue's perspective brought new understanding.

"While we kept good records, much has been destroyed. Yet, for 400 years, we have roamed this world looking for a future... but it appears our time is closing," Nimue continued, a hint of sadness in his voice.

"But enough of that... the task at hand," Nimue's tone shifted. "We do not have much. We know there are runes at the Karadar Tower. They were studied long ago, but nothing came of that. I also want to see if we can find the tribe of Gray Elves who claim knowledge of the druid's tome. It is said that they hold a piece of the mystery of lost time."

"Why don't we have enough time? What is our urgency?" Thrain asked, irritated.

"Time is relative, master dwarf. We do not know how much we have left before the enemy moves. Rumors speak of a great evil stirring in the Deadlands. Someone or something is sending these forces against your homesteads. If we can retrieve the relics, we may be able to stop the evil before it spreads," Nimue replied, disregarding the annoyed Thrain. The group nodded. They finished their meal, packed their supplies, and prepared to continue eastward.

Ordi watched Nimue to see if he would add anything to the story. After a few moments of silence, Ordi said, "So, we have some runes that need to be translated or read again? And these may not even exist anymore. Personally, I feel like this is a fool's errand. But by the direction of the king, I will see it to the end."

"It will not be a fool's errand, master dwarf. We may spend a considerable amount of time going from place to place. Time, though, is something we do not seem to have much of. So, we must make haste while we can," Nimue replied with slight disgust in his voice.

The conversation died as the Brotherhood finished eating. Each member was lost in their thoughts. Once they finished their meal, they began saddling up their horses and ponies. As Ordi worked, he noticed the brush in the distance shaking slightly. Though he couldn't see anything, it didn't mean nothing was there in the tall grass. Ordi knew that kobolds, tiny, greedy creatures, stalked these parts.

"Mira, do you sense that?" Ordi asked.

"I can't sense anything. It could be the wind," Mira replied as she continued to stare at the brush, daring it to move again.

Kobolds were known to prey upon travelers and steal their goods in plain sight. It was said they possessed some magic capable of eliciting nightmares to keep travelers away from their territory. They weren't strong but were certainly a nuisance. Ordi noted the shaking grass but decided not to dwell on it as he threw his leg over the saddle and nudged Bill back onto the road.

The afternoon went on. The Brotherhood traveled north of Icewater Lake, then further eastward. The landscape was peaceful, filled with rustling leaves, the distant croaking of frogs near the water's edge, and the sweet scent of wildflowers. Past the trees, the fields stretched onward, patiently waiting for farmers to plant crops. The sun began to set, casting a warm orange glow across the land, signaling the onset of twilight. As the golden hues painted the horizon, the air grew cooler, and the Brotherhood decided it was time to find a place to camp for the night.

They moved about fifty yards off the road, choosing a campsite near towering oaks. The ancient trees provided shelter, their branches interlacing to form a natural canopy. A small, bubbling river nearby added a soothing background melody, further enhancing the sense of tranquility. As they set up their tents, the air was thick with the earthy smell of the forest floor, mingled with a faint pungent odor of distant farm animals.

Once their tents were secured, Thrain set to building the evening fire. The group gathered around the warm flames to relax. The crackling fire cast dancing shadows on the faces of the Brotherhood as they ate a light meal. The night deepened, and the chirps of crickets filled the air, mingling with the gentle rush of the river. Out of the corner of his eye, Ordi saw the grass shake again, this time more pronounced and harder to ignore. Casually strolling over, he kicked the grass aside with his boots but found nothing but the earth beneath.

"Mira, here it is again…the grass shaking. I think it may be the Kobolds," Ordi said.

Mira trotted over. *"I can prowl around and see what I come up with."* She hunched low to the ground and started sniffing around.

Returning to the campfire, he realized his food pouch was missing. "Hey! Did anyone grab my pouch? I had it sitting right here, and now it's gone," Ordi called out, frustration evident as he began to search the immediate area. Mira immediately raced back to the group.

"Could have been kobolds... those pesky little bastards," Thrain muttered, anger rising.

Verdun got up to help, his eyes scanning the surroundings. "I think we are being watched or followed. There are faint lights over in the distance, near the foot of that hill."

The lights vanished as the other members joined him, the darkness swallowing any trace of illumination. "I don't see anything. Could have just been tricks of your eyes," Roland suggested. They stared into the murky distance briefly before returning to the campfire. As they turned around, realization struck—they discovered that all their food pouches were missing. Thankfully, not all the food was gone.

"Blimey! Those damn kobolds tricked us. Those weren't lights; it was a ruse. Their sorcery got the better of you, Verdun," Roland grumbled, his voice tinged with frustration.

The party murmured their hatred of the kobolds, feeling that the mischievous creatures had outsmarted them. They readied their sleeping bags, each man sensing the weight of the day's travels and the impending uncertainties.

"I will kill the first little bastard kobold! AH! I am going to bed before my anger boils over," Thrain said. "Good night, all." He crawled into a tent, got into his sleeping bag, and pulled the cover over his head.

"Good night," the others echoed.

They retreated to their tents, trying to sleep despite the increasingly chilly wind that blew steadily and caused the fire to die quickly if left unattended.

Ordi and Mira retired to their tent, where she curled up next to his legs. Ordi laid his head down, and within minutes, he drifted into a deep sleep, slipping into a vivid dream that felt eerily real. He stood before a dark, deserted castle, its drawbridge hanging broken with chains shattered from previous battles. Scorch marks marred the walls, and the keep door was blown wide open, revealing an interior cloaked in darkness. This was the human capital of Talamar, but it looked like an echo of its former self, abandoned and ravaged by conflict.

As Ordi drew closer to the castle, an overwhelming sense of dread washed over him. The sky was dark and stormy, lightning bolts illuminating the castle's ruined towers and turrets. The wind howled through the broken windows and shattered walls, creating eerie whistling sounds that seemed to taunt him, whispering secrets and despair.

As he entered the main hall, Ordi's heart raced with fear. The room was filled with shadows that moved and shifted independently, as if alive. Suddenly, he heard a low growling sound and saw a pair of glowing red eyes appear in the darkness. Horror struck him as he realized he was not alone. Gripping his staff tightly, he prepared to fight, but the shadows closed around him, enveloping him in suffocating darkness. Ordi smashed his staff against the ground to send out arcane energy, but it felt like he was fighting an invisible enemy—his magic had no effect. The sounds of claws scrabbling on stone and the snarling of an unseen beast echoed in his ears, but he could not locate it.

As he fought, Ordi felt as if each step was challenged, weighing more than the previous one. Bolts of arcane energy shot from his staff, smashing into the walls around him, but hitting nothing. The shadows grew thicker and more oppressive, and his breathing became loud, echoing in the silence until it was all he could hear. Suddenly, the darkness lifted, and he stood in a vast, empty chamber. The walls were lined with piles of skulls and bones, and a single torch burned dimly on the far wall. As he approached the torch, a chill ran down his spine. The flame flickered and danced, casting eerie shadows.

Ordi gasped in horror as he saw the ghostly image of a figure standing across the room, clad in black robes that concealed his face. The blackness of the robes made him appear as a void, as if he were melting into nothingness. He stood tall, his presence commanding and ominous, demanding all to bow before him. Ordi tried to turn and run, but his legs refused to move. He was frozen in place, staring at the apparition. Suddenly, the figure moved—slowly at first, then faster and faster—until it charged toward him at full speed. A hand of bone stretched out from the robes, fragments of old flesh dripping from the bones and grasping at the air where Ordi stood.

Ordi woke up in a cold sweat, heart pounding. He knew the memory of the blasted castle and the ghostly figure would haunt him for a long time.

Panting and sweating, Ordi looked down at his hands, noting their slight tremble. He rubbed them against his pants in an attempt to calm himself. Exiting his tent, careful not to wake Mira, the cold night air bit at his face, cooling his sweat. He fetched a few pieces of wood and stirred the coals, causing the fire to reignite. He pumped a small flame from his palm to increase the fire's size. Its warmth enveloped him as it grew. The night around him was eerily quiet and dark, with no birds singing or animals making noise. Only Mira's snoring could be heard.

He sat by the fire for a few more minutes, absorbing the warmth, and then returned to his tent to try and sleep again. It felt as if no sooner had his head hit the pillow than the sun broke the horizon.

As morning dawned, the Brotherhood prepared to continue their journey. Each man silently grappled with the remnants of his nightmares, the oppressive memories of the night clinging to their consciousness. The chilly wind that had blown through the camp during the night had subsided, leaving the air crisp but still. They packed their tents, saddled their mounts, and resumed their eastward trek toward Karadar Tower.

No one spoke, but their faces revealed everything Ordi needed to know about the previous night. "Nightmares?" he asked.

They all nodded. "I don't think I've ever experienced anything so real. It was like a glimpse into the future. Ruined landscapes, trolls and goblins running freely, fires burning… Ugh. Horrific," Thrain said. The others shared similar dreams of barren landscapes and ruined cities, with bodies piled up everywhere.

Roland spoke next. "I think there may be some similarities. Mine was of Talamar in ruin. Blood scattered everywhere, but I didn't see many bodies. Mine had people as slaves, working and building new quarters for the vile to live in. The tower of the Order of Light was destroyed. That was where I was trained. We fell. We have no hope." His voice trailed off. The dream brought to reality the consequences of their failure.

"My dream was just me holding the king's dead body in my arms as goblins charged toward me. Kamrar had fallen," Verdun said, rubbing his hands on his leg. "I feel like I can't get the blood off my hands."

"You don't have blood on your hands, Verdun," Ordi said.

"I know… It just feels so real."

"If it makes you feel better, tell everyone I slept great," Mira replied, strolling alongside Ordi.

"Not now," Ordi scolded her.

The smell of fear and death lingered in the air. It is known that the kobolds can inflict lucid dreams, but these felt like they were the product of a darker, more sinister power. Could the Dark Lord be influencing magical creatures? But why so far from the Deadlands? Are the kobolds agents of evil? Thoughts stirred in Ordi's mind.

"We cannot waste time. They were dreams and nothing more. We must continue moving. Let's go," Nimue said. "We should reach Karadar Tower if we skip lunch and travel at night."

The dread built in the group as the day progressed. Each kept a watchful eye on their surroundings, jumping whenever something made a sound. Yet nothing happened except the hot sun beating down on the company on a spring day. They ate as they walked and watered the ponies when needed. By nightfall, the Brotherhood could see the Forest of Witherwood rising in the distance, which meant the tower would be close. They approached under cover of night and proceeded toward the tower, which sat some distance from the road at the forest's edge.

"This tower once belonged to an enormous castle that has been demolished. The elves once roamed these lands long before the God War and many years before the Dark Lord. All that is left is this tower…but we may find some of the runes with ancient writing. That is what we seek." Nimue stated as they approached. "I hope to find the Grey Elves tomorrow if possible."

The group entered the vast area around the single-standing tower. The ruins were overgrown with grass and moss, and the stones looked more like small hills now than once-polished silver stone. In the center rose a tower no more than 40 feet high, with stones missing throughout, indicating an unstable foundation. The wind howled through the small remnants, bringing a slight chill to the night. Ordi grasped his tunic a little tighter and began looking at the ground. It was slightly damp from a quick shower that had passed through before the Brotherhood's arrival.

"Verdun and Roland, start pulling back that moss and see if you can find anything on the stones beneath. It may be faint, but we should be able to make out what they say," Nimue said as he bent down to pull back some of the leafage.

The air was filled with the earthy scent of wet foliage, and the light from their torches cast long shadows across the stones and trees around them. Ordi bent down and tried to grab a handful of moss. As he pulled, it slipped through his fingers, causing him to fall right on his backside. The rest of the Brotherhood laughed as he grumbled and dusted himself off.

Mira yelped loudly. *"Thank you for that. I needed a laugh!"*

Ordi scowled at her. *"Yeah, you're welcome."*

"Nothing like a little tumble to lighten the mood, huh?" Verdun chuckled.

Ordi, cheeks flushed with embarrassment and determination, returned to his knees. He tried the moss again, this time ripping it off with a vengeance. The moss came free, but it revealed only a smooth stone underneath. Undeterred, the group continued their efforts, diligently pulling back the moss and attempting to uncover any ancient inscriptions. Mira was busy pawing away at the moss, diligently searching with the rest of the crew.

As they worked, the sounds of the night enveloped them —the rustling leaves, the distant hoot of an owl, and animals scurrying in the nearby woods. The torches flickered, casting an almost mystical glow on the ancient stones. Each stone they uncovered seemed to tell its own story, even if only through its texture and age.

"There is nothing so far, and with no moon now, the darkness makes it hard to see. I say we pitch camp," Verdun whined. He was right, though, Ordi thought. The night yielded no results, and they were exhausted after a full day's journey. The camp was made, and a small fire was kindled as they crawled into their tents and fell asleep.

As the first light of dawn began to penetrate the darkness, the Brotherhood remained deep in slumber, each man troubled by the remnants of his nightmares from the previous night. The air was crisp and still, the fire reduced to a few glowing embers. The quiet of the pre-dawn hours was interrupted only by the occasional rustling of leaves and the gentle babble of the nearby river.

As Nimue had hoped, the Gray Elves had arrived during the night. They stood silently among the trees, their presence so subtle that it went unnoticed by the sleeping men. Their leader, an elf with striking long, silver hair that cascaded past his shoulders and piercing blue eyes that seemed to hold the wisdom of centuries, watched over the camp. His expression was one of calm authority, a serene yet commanding presence that radiated strength and tranquility. He wore intricately crafted armor that blended seamlessly with the natural surroundings, adorned with symbols of ancient elven lore.

Just as dawn approached, Ordi was the first to stir, the vivid nightmare still fresh in his mind. He sat up slowly, rubbing his eyes and trying to shake off the lingering unease. The cold air bit at his skin, and he shivered slightly as he reached for his cloak. As he emerged from his tent, he noticed the stillness of the camp and the eerie silence that hung in the air. Mira stretched deeply and followed him out. Her senses were alert, knowing something was different.

As the rest of the Brotherhood began to awaken, they, too, felt the strange stillness. Verdun and Roland stretched and yawned, shaking off the remnants of sleep. Nimue, always alert, sensed something amiss almost immediately. His sharp eyes scanned the camp's perimeter, and it wasn't long before he spotted the silent figures standing among the trees.

"We are not alone," Nimue said softly, alerting the others.

The Brotherhood turned to see the Gray Elves emerging from the shadows, their leader stepping forward with graceful authority. The elves wore garments that blended seamlessly with the forest, making them nearly invisible in the dim light.

Nimue approached the leader with a respectful bow. "I am Nimue Leafwhisper. I have been dispatched to Kamrar to find the missing gems. My people suspected that you would know where the missing Tome may reside. My apologies for not seeking you out sooner; we only just arrived last night." Nimue bowed as he finished.

The leader of the Gray Elves inclined his head slightly. "I am Elandor. We are familiar with your quest; word spreads among the allies as you speak. You can thank the Gnomes for that."

Mira approached Elandor as he spoke, examining him cautiously and taking in the scene around her. *"He is a great ally, Ordi."*

"I know," Ordi responded.

Elandor was taken aback by the Posh Hound as she joined the group. "The relics and gems you seek are legendary, but our knowledge is limited. The Dragons were charged with protecting these gems and relics. They have long held their secrets close, even from us."

Nimue's face showed signs of both relief and disappointment. "I had come to that conclusion. But I have heard two sides; one points to the dragons, the other suggests that they were kept elsewhere." While the two elves exchanged information, Ordi wrote down the details.

Elandor shook his head. "It is quite possible. We did not have much interaction with the world during that period. The

Dragons are elusive; their paths are hidden. They reveal themselves only to those they deem worthy. However, Karadar Tower holds ancient runes that may provide clues. It is a place of power and mystery."

Nimue nodded thoughtfully. "We will start here. Any guidance you can offer us on reaching the Dragons would be invaluable."

Elandor's gaze swept over the group, his eyes settling on each member of the Brotherhood. "May your journey be guided by the wisdom of the ancients. We will offer what support we can." He handed Nimue a small, intricately carved wooden amulet. "This will serve as a token of our support. Show it to those who may question your intent."

Nimue accepted the amulet with a bow. "Thank you, Elandor. Your assistance is greatly appreciated."

The morning wore on as the elves disappeared back into the dense forest. The Brotherhood quickly got back to work. The old fortress was scattered throughout the area, leaving hundreds of stones that needed to be examined. After a quick meal, Ordi ventured into the small opening of the tower.

"Verdun set those traps again for small animals. We will need something to eat later on," Ordi called out from the tower.

"I can do that," Verdun said as he quickly set the two traps outside the camp.

The tower was primarily dark and had a damp feel in the air. There was nothing to it except a spiral staircase with missing steps throughout its ascent to the ceiling. Behind the foot of the staircase, Ordi moved to see if anything was left. His step was hollow, and as he looked down, he saw no sign of a trapdoor resembling a latch. He was standing on stone, but as he jumped, he heard the hollow noise again below him. He must have been standing on a hidden door disguised to look like stone. Out of sight and hidden away, this had to be something!

"Come, everyone!! Take a look at this!" Ordi yelled, but his voice was swallowed up in the tower, and all he heard was the nipping wind outside. He moved to the entrance, squeezed through, and yelled again, "Hey! Come here, I think I found something."

Mira ran over to join him. *"What is it?"*

The Brotherhood quickly gathered around Ordi, their interest piqued by his excited shouts. Nimue, Verdun, and Roland joined him at the tower's entrance.

The party met each other's gaze, curiosity and determination flickering in their eyes.. As they approached the tower's opening, they began discussing the discovery, their minds racing with possibilities. The air was thick with anticipation, and each member of the Brotherhood was keenly aware that they stood on the brink of a significant discovery.

"What is it, Ordi?" Thrain asked, walking up to him.

Ordi felt a sense of worry, though. "I don't know exactly, but there is something off about this tower. Here, let me show you." Ordi directed the group through the narrow opening and into the larger center of the tower. Once everyone was in, he continued to show them what he had found. "Behind the staircase, there appears to be a trapdoor. But I do not see any latches or hinges, and it looks just like the rest of the stone floor."

The party looked puzzled, but Nimue was familiar with this. "This is ancient magic that we elves use to uncover secrets. This must be where they hid the runes or perhaps some information we seek. But this magic is dangerous and sometimes unpredictable. I would advise everyone but Ordi to leave. He and I will work on removing the spell and opening the door." Everyone left, trying to keep their distance while still able to see. Nimue looked at Ordi. "What kind of disenchanted magic have you worked with?"

"Eh, not much, honestly. Most of what I was taught focused on arcane magic used for either shield protection or attack. I was not good at disenchanting; it was not a topic often discussed at the academy or during my apprenticeship," Ordi responded.

Nimue's expression was disgruntled. "Did they teach you anything? What a waste of a school if you never learned how to disenchant."

"I know a few spells, but I'm not certain they will do any good," Ordi said, readying himself with his staff over the floor where the hidden door was. "Aperi nunc ostium," he yelled. In that instant, an explosion erupted, sending both Ordi and Nimue flying back against the walls, away from the door. The explosion's force could be felt outside as the others were knocked backward from the tower.

"OUCH!" Ordi yelled, the pain reverberating between his eyes. Standing slowly, he noticed Nimue beginning to stir. "Nimue, I am sorry… I had no—"

He was cut off. "Of course, you had no idea what would happen," Nimue said sharply. "But neither did I," he added, his tone softening with sympathy. "These spells are old—

possibly older than even us druids. These doors appear sealed with a specific hold that only a certain word or phrase can open." Nimue sat down next to the door, staring intently at the floor. He took a deep breath. "I do not know," he said, his voice laced with defeat.

"Well, what do we know? Could it be the name of the fort? It could possibly be simply locked by interchanging spells?" Ordi wondered. A few minutes later, he exclaimed, "Could it be the name of one of the gods?"

"Highly unlikely. And before attempting more spells, let me think in silence for a moment," Nimue said. The two sat in silence for a while. Nimue hadn't moved in hours. Ordi paced quietly behind, sometimes pondering to himself and other times speaking aloud, but each time he was silenced by Nimue or ignored. "I don't want to attempt any more spells for fear of the door shutting itself permanently. That is a safety mechanism built in. So many failed attempts will render the door locked until the original mage comes by. And that… seems out of the question." The two remained seated in silence for a while longer.

Outside, the party sat and waited. The air grew cooler as the sun began to set. A gentle breeze finally blew in, stripping the humidity from the air. In the distance, animals could be heard, and even farther off, the howling of a wolf. As night crept in, the surrounding forest came alive with all different types of nocturnal animals. There was little to discuss as the party was exhausted from searching for stones and waiting on Ordi and Nimue. Mira found this a good time to run off for an evening hunt.

"*I am going to hunt, Ordi,*" Mira said.

"*Eh, try to find something big enough for everyone,*" Ordi chuckled.

After the sun had set, it was a while longer before Ordi peeked his head out the door. "Eh! Get a fire going, you lazy sacks. Don't waste the night away! And what about dinner?" Ordi's tone sounded irritated as he pulled his head back in.

"Well, he's right; let's not waste more time throwing stones around. Roland, get the fire going. Thrain, help gather firewood. I'll start working on dinner," Verdun declared.

The party went about their duties. Roland used his magic to conjure a fire while Thrain gathered wood to fuel it. Verdun retrieved and prepared two small rabbits that had stumbled into their trap that day. It wasn't much meat, but they also had some potatoes to cook. Soon, the fire was roaring, and the rabbits were strung on a stick, roasting over the flames. The smell of roasting meat made everyone's mouths water.

It didn't take long to roast the thin rabbits. Verdun set to work breaking up the portions and handing plates to everyone. Ordi and Nimue joined them, and they all ate in silence. Though the meal was simple with small portions, the fire's warmth and the comfort of their comrades' company made it more enjoyable.

Once dinner was complete, and although no one was entirely satisfied, they cleaned their plates and put them away. Fresh logs were tossed onto the fire, which roared high into the air, providing warmth to all sitting around it. The flickering light cast long shadows, and the crackling sounds of the fire filled the night air. The night was alive with insects and frogs adding to the sounds of the fire. Calmness settled over the Brotherhood.

Ordi resumed his time in the tower near a contemplative Nimue. Both sat in silence, staring at the trapdoor. "You said it could be an ancient spell that seals this door, right?" Ordi asked.

"Yes, and I am not even sure about that. Unfortunately for the elves, magic has diminished more and more with each passing year. We are not as strong as we once were.

"I may know a spell…but I am uncertain if it will work. We discussed it only briefly during my time at the academy. I remember the magic and can call upon the spell's process. It is much more involved than a simple incantation, and I ultimately don't know if it will work," Ordi said.

Nimue took a step back. "At least wait until I get outside and away from the tower. I do not want to have another ricochet like earlier." Nimue departed the tower and yelled at the group to stand back. As she left, Mira returned to the camp, dragging a small deer behind her.

"Great! We actually have a bountiful dinner tonight!" Verdun yelled as Mira brought the carcass forward.

Verdun hurried over to retrieve the dear and began preparing the meat.

"You would eat twice," Mira said.

"Finally, a good meal, thanks, Mira," Thrain said, patting her head.

"My pleasure." She replied.

It wasn't long before Verdun had the meat cooking over the fire, ready for everyone to eat their second dinner.

In the tower, Ordi cleared his mind, focused his energy, and channeled the power of the elements to perform an ancient spell known as "Ornistek's Sigilbreaker." He began tracing intricate patterns with his fingertips, forming complex glyphs that hung suspended before him. Instantly, sweat began to bead on his forehead. A soft, ethereal glow emanated from the glyphs with each passing movement. The air crackled with energy as Ordi summoned the forces necessary to break the seal. Drawing upon the wisdom gained from his extensive studies, he finally uttered the words he hoped would unlock the door. The words resonated with power, vibrating like a distant echo as he called upon the energy of the ancient spell.

As Ordi extended his hands toward the locked trapdoor, his palms glowed with a pulsating blue light. Wisps of mystical energy gently flowed from his fingertips, swirling around the edges of the door's lock. The ancient spell had taken effect, weakening the magic holding the seal. With intense focus, Ordi increased the flow of his magical energy, pouring his strength into the spell. The air crackled with raw power as shimmering energy waves enveloped the trapdoor, resonating with the ancient magic that bound it.

As the energy surged, the seal on the trapdoor started to weaken. Faint cracks formed along the edges of the lock, yielding to the power of Ordi's spell. The ancient magic that had kept the door locked for centuries trembled under the overwhelming force of the incantation; each crack was a sign of the imminent breakthrough.

With a final surge of power, Ordi gave a commanding shout, directing his magic to shatter the weakened seal. A brilliant flash of white arcane light erupted from his fingertips, engulfing the lock of the trapdoor. The sound of cracking and snapping filled the air as the ancient magic gave way. The light surged around Ordi and filled the entire tower, spilling into the night. Those outside stood in sheer wonder at the intensity of what was taking place.

As the light faded, the trapdoor creaked open, releasing a cloud of dust and revealing the hidden chamber beneath. Ordi's spell had successfully broken the ancient seal, granting access to the long-forgotten secrets that lay within.

He collapsed on the floor, drenched in sweat and breathing heavily. Pressed against the far wall, Nimue stared in silence before a huge smile crept across her face. "YOU DID IT! I haven't seen magic like that in ages!"

"Eh. I don't know what came over me. I started to recall a single spell, but it felt like the world opened its energy and poured it into me," Ordi finished as the rest of the Brotherhood stormed into the small room.

Nimue watched and said, "Let us descend to the chamber and see what we find." He descended the old wooden ladder. Over the years, nails had popped out, causing the boards to warp and become loose, making each footfall uncertain. The ladder was short, only about seven feet high. As Nimue reached the bottom, he dropped to the floor. Coughing from the dust that had been stirred up, he called out to Ordi, "Come on down. I need light."

Ordi carefully worked his way down the ladder and reached the floor of the hidden chamber below. Mira remained behind outside, not a fan of ladders. Raising his staff, Ordi willed its tip to illuminate, slowly at first but growing brighter with each passing second. Soon, the room was bathed in light, and Ordi could make out the small chamber where he now stood. Above, the Brotherhood maintained their vigil, ready to assist at a moment's notice.

The chamber was modest in size, its stone walls damp and layered with centuries of dust and cobwebs. Nothing was in the room except a small, worn desk with an old wooden chair and some parchment scattered across its surface. The air was thick with the musty scent of forgotten history.

Ordi and Nimue stood in the middle of the room, their eyes fixed on the desk, hopeful it held some long-forgotten secret. Ordi reached out and gently picked up one of the small stacks of parchment, his fingers leaving clean streaks in the dust covering it.

"There isn't much written here, just small notes about the old fortress," Ordi said, his voice tinged with disappointment and a deep-seated curiosity that refused to be quenched.

Nimue leaned closer, examining the parchment over Ordi's shoulder. "These notes might still hold some value. Sometimes, even the smallest clue can lead to a greater discovery."

Ordi nodded, carefully flipping through the pages. The notes detailed mundane aspects of the fortress's upkeep, records of supplies, and brief mentions of its inhabitants' daily routines. While none seemed immediately significant, Ordi felt there had to be more hidden within this chamber or elsewhere in the fortress.

"We need to examine every inch of this place," Nimue said, his eyes scanning the chamber for other signs of hidden compartments or clues. "There must be more here than meets the eye."

Ordi began to inspect the desk methodically, feeling for false bottoms or hidden drawers, while Nimue paced around the room, tapping on the stone walls and listening for hollow sounds.

The small chamber seemed to hold its secrets tightly, but Ordi and Nimue were determined. The air tingled with the promise of discovery, and despite the initial disappointment, their resolve grew stronger.

Nimue grabbed the other small stack of parchment and flipped through the pages. After about a minute, he slammed them to the ground and, with fury, screamed, "HOW COULD THEY! This fortress was said to house the Druid's relics for a time. This was the last fortress of the Elves, but these notes state that in the final days, they moved the relics north."

Anger swirled around Nimue, his eyes blazing with frustration. He attempted to calm himself, but it was no use. "I don't know… I think you were right, Ordi; these relics seem to be more like fairytales these days. I may have exaggerated my faith in them… placing too much importance on them. But I must hold to the truth. They are out there somewhere." He paused to think for a moment. He grabbed another piece of parchment. "This piece says they were put into a caravan and sent north to the Unknown Regions to be kept safe. It leads me to think the Dragons have or had them at one point. This is dated weeks before this fortress fell in the great battle. I was told there were secrets here, but we have no further information as this happened 400 years ago."

Breathing heavily, Nimue's hands gripped a cold, hard wood of an old chair. With a shout of frustration, he heaved it against the far wall. It shattered on impact, wood splintering and scattering across the floor. As if to release his pent-up rage, he conjured a fireball and hurled it at the broken remnants. The former chair erupted in a flash of fire, the flames licking the stone walls and filling the chamber with sudden, intense heat.

Ordi watched in silence, the glow of the flames casting long shadows on the walls. The weight of their discovery and the reality of the relics' elusive nature weighed heavily on him. "Feel better?" he asked. Nimue's outburst had a sobering effect, reminding them of the difficulties ahead on the treacherous journey to the Unknown Regions, the potential confrontation with the Dragons, and the mystery of the secrets hidden in the fortress. These were the challenges that lay before them.

Taking a deep breath, Nimue replied, "Yes. We can't give up, Ordi," his voice steady despite the turbulence of the situation. "This information, though limited, is still a lead. We know the relics were moved north, and the Dragons may have them. It's more than we had before."

Ordi took a deep breath, the fire in his eyes slowly dimming. "You're right. We can't let this setback deter us. We have to continue the search. The fate of our world may depend on it."

The two stood in the flickering light of the burning chair. "Is everything all right down there? We have dear meat if you are hungry," asked Verdun. He was standing at the entrance, the light casting his silhouette against the darkness outside.

"Eh, maybe... I don't know yet. Nimue thinks the relics have moved," Ordi replied.

"Kriff... really?" Verdun asked.

"Yes, Master Dwarf, the relics have moved north. This means we must decide to either give up this chase or pursue a 400-year-old legend," Nimue said as he walked toward the ladder.

"Well, come and eat," Verdun gestured for the two to join the party.

Ordi and Nimue climbed the short ladder, emerging into the darkness. The light from Ordi's staff illuminated the tower room but slowly faded. The magic dissipated as Ordi neglected the spell. Soon, darkness engulfed them as they made their way to the entrance. The rest of the Brotherhood sat around the fire, conversing.

"The room was empty. There was nothing but some old scrolls and a message. So, we have a decision to make: either we go forth and continue our search for the missing relics, or we head back with our tails between our legs. I know this hasn't been strenuous yet, but the message states that if we go north, we will continue into the Unknown Regions, where mystery awaits us. There is no further message, but I know my people will leave signs and markings pointing to the destination. However, after this time, I am uncertain if I can discern anything visible. I vote we head north and continue our search," Nimue finished, eyeing the men around the campfire. He grabbed a chunk of meat and began to eat.

No one spoke for a while as they all pondered what they wanted to do. Verdun spoke first, breaking the silence. "I know the King commissioned us to do this. I don't know what help they will be against The Fallen One and his armies, but I am willing to seek any advantage we can find. We cannot linger long. We do not know how much time we have before the world implodes."

"My only question is… where could these items all be located? We could travel the world and not find them all or only one," Thrain said.

"Yes, it will be a challenge," Nimue quickly replied. "I gathered that all the articles are relatively close or near each other. Where one is, the rest should be. I cannot guarantee this to be true or provide an appropriate timeline. I should look for some markings on the scrolls as we travel. My people do not like to go north because of the horrors said to reside there, and that could be where these items are found."

"Well, we should get moving. How much time do you reckon we have left before the Fallen One moves?" Roland asked.

"Ey, maybe no more than a few months. It's hard to say; the scouts couldn't get reliable information. We know from the raids that goblins and elves are increasing, but we don't know at what rate. The faster we act, the better it will be for everyone," Ordi explained.

Once Nimue and Ordi finished eating, they packed their bags in the dead of night, the urgency of their mission driving them to waste no time. The air was cool, and the night was cloaked in heavy silence as they loaded their ponies and prepared to set out. The narrow dirt path ahead seemed almost foreboding under the moonlight.

"We are entering Witherwood, an old forest not often traveled. Be wary of your surroundings and watch your step. It's hard to say what lives in this forest," Nimue advised, his voice calm but firm.

Nimue led his horse to the front of the pack. "We make for Witherfort," he announced. "A three-day journey. We need to be swift and careful. My people no longer watch these woods." The group moved as one, stepping onto the narrow dirt path and into the dense, shadowy embrace of Witherwood. The ancient trees loomed overhead, their branches knotted and twisted, obscuring the moon's pale light. The forest floor was a tangled mess of roots and fallen leaves, making every step hazardous.

As they ventured deeper, the sounds of the night enveloped them—the distant hoot of an owl, the rustling of small creatures scurrying through the underbrush, and the occasional snap of a twig breaking underfoot. Verdun attempted to take a deep breath, but the air was thick with the scent of damp earth and decaying foliage.

His eyes scanned the darkness for any signs of movement. "Stay close and keep your weapons ready," he whispered, his voice barely audible over the forest's whispers.

Ordi's mind raced with thoughts of the journey ahead. Witherfort was their next destination, shrouded in history and mystery. The path through Witherwood was fraught with danger, but it was a risk they had to take. The relics were their only hope, and every step north brought them closer to uncovering the ancient secrets that could save their world.

Chapter 8 The Witherwood Forest

The Brotherhood carried on late into the night. After leaving Karadar Tower, they progressed only a short distance before realizing how uncontrollably tired they had become.

Ordi yelled out, "Kriff! What in the world! Ten minutes ago, I was wonderful, but now, I can't keep my eyes open!"

Drowsiness settled over them as they struggled to keep their eyes open and focused on their ponies. Ordi fought the tiredness and attempted to meditate but was unsuccessful. A moment later, his eyes closed, and his hand slipped from the reins. He slumped over and fell off Bill hitting the ground hard.

The group halted their mounts, and Roland commented, "Yes, I, too, am exhausted. It must be this forest. There is something heavy here. The magic seems to be unbalanced. I feel very little connection to the arcane rivers. I, uh…." His voice trailed off as he fell off his horse and onto the ground, not moving. Ordi had fallen deeply asleep, and it wasn't long before the rest collapsed to the ground. The ponies and horses lowered themselves into a deep sleep as well. Mira, not faring any better, collapsed next to Ordi.

Drifting into a deep sleep, they dreamt again. Instead of separate dreams, they awoke together under a moonless night. Unfamiliar surroundings greeted them as they discovered a colossal hedge wall encircling them, reaching into the sky and blocking all light. Entangled in a sinister labyrinth, skeletal tree branches twisted into an impenetrable maze, tightening their grip as the party moved forward. The air was heavy with a foul stillness that clung to their skin, while malevolent mist formed obscure, grotesque beast shapes that swayed gently.

"Seems more of a scare tactic than an actual threat," Verdun remarked, swiping his sword through the mist to no effect.

As they ventured deeper, the leaves beneath their feet crunched ominously, and it felt as if this place plotted their betrayal. Ordi raised his staff to draw light, but the tip only flickered.

Ordi tried to reach deeper into the arcane channel and found it almost nonexistent. "I can't seem to gather any magic. We are on our own here." Without warning, a massive gust of wind blew against them, and the trees shifted position, closing off the path they had been walking. The wind settled, and a new path emerged with alternate routes for the Brotherhood.

"What kind of place is this? This is not the forest we just entered; this forest is alive. It has a presence that saps magic from the earth…I've never felt anything like it!" Thrain exclaimed. "I can't channel magic nor feel any connection to the elements. It's like I am naked in here."

"Ordi, my connection to the arcane feels weird. This is very odd. This is not of this world," Mira said.

"It's unusual. I have never felt this before. Stay vigilant," he replied. He pushed his mind deeper, finding the arcane magic. It was distance, suppressed under a cloak of darkness. *"You need to go deeper, the arcane is masked."* It took a moment, but Mira responded, "*I think I have it."* In that moment, Mira appeared to radiate power, pulsating through her vibrant fur.

The group chuckled at Thrain's comment. But as they pressed forward, the very walls of the maze seemed to shift and writhe, the pathways twisting and contorting into impossible configurations. The trees themselves whispered with cruel laughter, as if mocking the trapped brotherhood. Darkness engulfed them as the laughter increased.

The trees shifted again, exposing an open circle with a black figure in the middle. "You pathetic wizards think you can stop me? I am only beginning. Go ahead, find your precious little gems. They will do nothing to impede me. Your kingdoms will be crushed. The time is coming soon for the world to burn!"

Mira jumped in front of the group, and the air around her snapped and crackled with electricity. She lashed out toward the figure standing there, connecting with it. The Brotherhood watched in amazement.

The mysterious figure vanished with a hideous laugh.

"What in the world! Ordi, was that the figure?" Verdun asked. In a snap, the group woke to the chill of the night, all lying scattered on the ground. Their ponies started to stir, and Mira finally woke, too. "Ordi…what was that? Was that the Xerxes?" Verdun asked, brushing himself clean of the dirt and leaves. The air moved steadily, keeping the group chilled —no animals about nor birds in the trees. Everything was silent.

"I don't know, but it appears to be. Same darkness, same condescending tone. I think it might be Xerxes. He was the only mage powerful enough to wield such power. I have no idea how he is doing this; how can someone mimic such vivid dreams that feel real? How does he keep intercepting my dreams?" Ordi said, perplexed.

"This is ancient magic, older than the elves. We have only heard of it in stories, but this…dates back to the God Wars of old before man, dwarves, and elves. A wielder is strong in the dark arts if he can conjure this. From a distance, he can pinpoint our location and elicit a dreamlike state where he appears to us. This type of magic is dark, and the elves want nothing to do with it. The enemy moves and does not wait for us. We must make haste and ride on," Nimue explained.

"Why? He said these relics are worthless and will do nothing to hinder him," Thrain stated. The group murmured in agreement.

"You are more than welcome to leave," Nimue said harshly. "I know it appears to be a fool's errand. But at this stage, we do not have any options left. No other people. No one. We are alone…and our small armies can't possibly withstand the power of the Xerxes. The world is doomed if that dream was any indicator of his power. His darkness will cover all the lands. If you are with me, we shall go north with haste and attempt what seems to be impossible."

The Brotherhood was only partially convinced that the relics would accomplish anything, their grumblings echoing softly as they prepped their ponies for the journey north. However, their progression was slow, as ponies were known more for their sturdiness than for their speed. The dwarves favored them because they were stout and reliable but dismounting and running might have been faster in this situation.

As the morning began to break, the light from the east cracking the horizon was obscured by the dense, dark forest. The changing colors of the sky could only be glimpsed through the few breaks in the canopy. The Brotherhood pressed on, tired and weary from the previous day's adventure.

Traveling north, the air was cool under the trees' cover, but the eerie weight of the forest hung heavily over them. The ancient trees' branches intertwined, creating a tangled passage that seemed to close in around them. Shadows danced at the edges of their vision, amplifying their sense of unease. The twisted path drew memories of the night before; caught in the labyrinth, the forest offered no rest from the constant threat of evil.

They ate as they rode, the simple meals doing little to lift their spirits. The ponies trudged forward; their hooves muffled by the soft forest floor. Little was spoken among the members. Each was lost in their thoughts as they followed the narrow path to their next destination.

Ordi, feeling the weight of their journey, tried to shake off the drowsiness from the forest's enchantment. He glanced at Nimue, whose keen eyes scanned the surroundings, ever watchful for any signs of danger. Verdun and Roland rode in silent contemplation. Mira walked alongside Roland for a while, silently observing him. She turned her attention to Thrain, who remained isolated, not paying attention to anyone or offering much in conversation.

"Ordi, there is something off about Thrain. It could be nothing but keep an eye on him." Mira said.

"I've sensed that too. I think he's just greedy. Nothing more. But we shouldn't let our assumptions go to our heads." Ordi replied.

The dense foliage and intertwined branches overhead seemed to whisper secrets of the past, as if the forest remembered the ancient battles and lost relics they sought. Every rustle of leaves, every scurrying creature heightened their senses, keeping them on edge.

Despite their weariness, the Brotherhood's shared resolve kept them moving.

"We knew that by pledging ourselves to this quest, we would face unknown trials. A great evil is awakening in the world, and many of the old paths are unsafe," Nimue said as they continued riding.

"That is all well and fine, Master Elf, but there seems to be something stalking us," Thrain grunted in response. "But it is the will of my King. I will see it through until my end comes."

"I have seen many evils in my time with the Order of the Light, but this is different. This is new yet ancient. I can't describe it," Roland said.

"Ancient, yes," said Ordi. "I feel Xerxes somehow influences events and will continue to show up randomly."

"That is a possibility, Ordi," Nimue replied. "Nevertheless, we must continue until our end comes." The Brotherhood agreed.

The promise of the relics and their hope for their world's salvation spurred them onward. Each member understood the stakes—they weren't just searching for ancient artifacts; they were on a mission to reclaim power that could turn the tide against the encroaching darkness. Despite this, they still had concerns.

As they rode deeper into Witherwood, the forest's enchantment seemed to fade, replaced by an ominous stillness. The path narrowed, and the trees grew even thicker, their gnarled roots forming obstacles that made the journey treacherous. The hours stretched on, with the only indication of time passing being the faint light breaking through the canopy above. They knew that turning back was not an option; their only way was into the unknown, where the relics awaited. Despite the forest's oppressive weight and the uncertainty of their journey, the Brotherhood's bond and unwavering resolve gave them the strength to continue.

Verdun finally broke the silence. "Ey, Ordi! Why don't you tell them the story of the fire pixie?" He chuckled, the first hint of light-heartedness in hours. Intrigued by this statement, the rest of the group turned their curious eyes to Ordi, encouraging him to share the tale.

"Seriously? I am not too fond of that story. It makes me look like a fool," Ordi protested, though a small smile tugged at the corners of his mouth.

"It'll be fine. The group needs a good laugh," Verdun insisted, his laughter infectious.

"Fine… well," Ordi hesitated but began, "The fire pixie is this little pest that lives in caves. In Kamrar, there are thousands of them. They love the darkness and usually do not bother dwarves unless they are in the mines. They love to torment the miners but are usually harmless. They are maybe six to eight inches tall and can breathe out a little puff of fire.

That is usually what they do to miners: throw a tiny fire at them."

The group listened intently; their curiosity piqued.

"So, one day, Verdun and I had an errand to run, and he thought it would be okay to take a shortcut through one of the old mines. The route was not commonly used but occasionally provided a means to save time for those in a hurry. We decided to take this route. As we were returning to Father, something jumped up and smoked my butt. The damn thing leaped out of nowhere and torched me! I jumped and yelled so loudly that others came running down the old road, thinking I was in trouble."

Ordi paused, the memory of his embarrassment clear on his face, but he continued with a grin. "The fairy is so small it can't do any harm, just a minor burn if it reaches your skin. When the others reached us, they discovered it was me, not a child in trouble. They all laughed, realizing it was just a fire pixie causing a fuss. Not my best day. Damn, pixies are pests and do no good…especially in the mines."

The group erupted into laughter, the tension of their journey momentarily forgotten.

"Ah, I needed a good chuckle, Ordi. Thank you for that. Anyone else got any good stories?" Thrain asked.

Roland had been silent, pondering whether he should disclose anything. Finally, he spoke up. "I have a story. It's not funny, but it helped shape me as a paladin. It was during one of my first missions early in my career, maybe twenty years ago. I grew up in the Order of Light, which is devoted to serving the kingdom as paladins. I was trained from birth in how to use arcane magic and fight. Once we graduate, we are dispatched throughout the kingdom to help protect towns and areas."

The Brotherhood listened intently as Roland continued. "My job was to travel eastward to the Last Outpost. This was a small fortress on the border of the Talamar kingdom and the Creeping Death. There had been whispers of minor skirmishes along the fringe, and small villages had been wiped off the map, pillaged, and destroyed as the darkness started creeping westward. This phenomenon is not new but has been dormant in the South for a while now. So, they dispatched me and other seasoned veterans to the Outpost for a six-month mission. We arrived and were informed that it had been weeks since any movement had been detected. The commander was alert but sure that the goblins had been driven back and were no longer a threat."

He paused to adjust himself on his saddle, the steady movement of the Brotherhood continuing north to their next destination. Taking a deep breath, Roland continued, "The days led to weeks, and the weeks to months. Nothing happened. Most of us grew bored with this assignment, feeling we would be of better use elsewhere. One week before we were to leave and head home, it was late at night when the first building caught fire. The flames were massive and quickly spread to other buildings. We raced out of our tents half asleep, unaware of what was happening. I grabbed my shield and sword as a horde of goblins broke through the gate and charged towards us. They slaughtered everyone in their path and kept pressing on."

Roland's voice grew somber. "We formed a small wall, the four of us. We called upon the arcane magic, but they were too fast. They blasted into us with such ferocity that we couldn't stand against them. My comrades were slaughtered. I only managed to survive because a building collapsed over me, providing shelter from the goblins. I fled into the night during the battle, running as fast as I could away from the fires and goblins."

Roland paused, his voice wavering with emotion. "I came back to Talamar broken and torn. I was the only one to survive and was branded a coward by many. It pains me to retell it, as it took me years to regain most of my dignity." His voice broke at the end, the memories weighing heavily on him.

The Brotherhood rode silently for a while, the gravity of Roland's story sinking in. The forest around them seemed to echo the somber mood, the shadows deepening as they pressed on.

Riding next to Roland, Nimue placed a reassuring hand on his shoulder. "Surviving such a battle doesn't make you a coward, Roland. It makes you resilient. You've lived to continue the fight, to protect those who can't protect themselves. That's what truly matters."

Ordi nodded in agreement. "We're lucky to have you with us, Roland. Your experience, your strength—they're invaluable to this quest."

The rest of the Brotherhood murmured their agreement. As they continued north, Roland's tale weighed on them. Yet, it also strengthened their resolve, uniting them further in their pursuit of the relics and the hope they carried for their world.

"Wow, that is some story, lad," Thrain said. "I had heard about that battle but never knew much more than that the goblins sacked the fort."

The Brotherhood moved forward in silence for a while. Each pondered whether they should say anything but ultimately abandoned the notion of continuing the conversation. Roland's discussion of the sacking of the Last Output revealed what was brewing in the Dead Lands. Something sinister was there and about to move against the free people. The troubling thought was when it would happen. How long until the Fallen One amasses enough troops to lay siege to the people? Will he pick off the small communities first or march toward the capital cities? How much time did they have? These thoughts and more swirled through the Brotherhood as they rode swiftly northward to Witherfort.

The day grew to a close, and they were now just a short ride from the old fort. They decided to rest, having had only one previous break during the day to quickly eat and care for the animals. They made camp and had a fire roaring in minutes, but the flames did not seem to penetrate the darkness of Witherwood—a forest known for its uncertain inhabitants and sinister past. Once home to the elves before the battle with the Fallen One, it was now said to be home to goblins and other evil creatures. The darkness felt like it enveloped the men as they attempted to cook dinner and eat. With each breath, the darkness crept in closer. Stalking the Brotherhood through the underbrush was a foul creature, a Hellhound.

Pounding came on the door as King Leifric enjoyed a deep sleep. He jolted upright, throwing the heavy blanket off. It was early morning, and the sun was rising. The fire had died, and the room had grown cold. The knock came again.

"Yes, yes, I heard you," the king replied. He grabbed his royal robes and opened the door. Guards snapped immediately to attention outside.

"Sorry to disturb you so early, my lord, but we have urgent news that needs to be discussed. Your councilmen are waiting for you," a young man said. The king had only seen him once before and could not recall his name.

"Very well. Let's be off." With that, the two walked down the hall to the small gathering room the king used for such occasions. Three of the king's five advisors were sitting, waiting for him. "I hope you haven't had to wait long. What is this news that must be shared before dawn?"

"My lord, we have reports from the Fringe. It has become hostile, and many living there now refer to it as the Creeping Death. The land seems to be dying—the trees, grass, everything. No animal will set foot on it. The soil itself seems to be discolored," spoke the first councilman, Dillon. He was a short, stocky man, advanced in age, with a gravity that matched his years of service. His hair was a salt-and-pepper mix, thinning at the crown but still framing his face, which bore the deep lines of experience and wisdom.

Dillon had been with the king for years, one of his most trusted advisors. His eyes, sharp and piercing despite his age, held a solemn intensity as he delivered his report. Clad in rich but understated robes, his presence commanded respect in the council chamber. He was known for his unwavering loyalty and keen insight, qualities that had earned him his position at the king's side.

"Any word from the dwarves? We have known about the Fringe for some time; waking me for this seems pointless," the king said, a little irritated.

"No, my lord. We have more," another one of the councilmen, Shawn, said. "We have reports of farms being ransacked and burned, and many who live out there have fled back to the towns. Many are coming here. We currently have a reported death toll of 24 people: 18 men and six women. Thankfully, no children have been on the list; they seem to have fled with their mothers when the attacks started."

"Attacks?" Leifric asked.

The room fell silent. The councilmen exchanged wary glances; the severity of the situation clear in their expressions. The transformation of the Fringe into what was now ominously called the Creeping Death was a dire development that demanded immediate attention.

"Yes, my lord. Most who live east of the Bloodwold have experienced these attacks, primarily from goblins and a few dark elves. They seem to be testing us to see what kind of resistance they will encounter. We have not dispatched any of our forces but know of those displaced due to the attacks," Shawn continued.

"So we have 24 dead as of how long ago?" the king asked.

"Two days, my lord," Dillon stated. "This is the closest estimate, as the attacks have slowed, primarily due to many fleeing. These are simple farmers and country folk, many of whom are older and have no desire to fight again."

The room grew silent as everyone watched King Leifric ponder his course of action. Should he dispatch one unit of troops? Five? Ten? Should he go out to these displaced people himself? The questions swirled in his mind, demanding careful consideration. After fifteen minutes of silence, the king finally spoke.

"We should not move any forces now. We do not know what the Fallen One is planning or where he has his spies. Rumor has it they are within our very kingdoms. Shawn, do you still have that special task unit at your command?"

Shawn, a tall and dedicated man with a scar running down his left cheek—a mark of his many battles—stepped forward. Clad in practical, battle-worn armor, he exuded an air of unwavering competence. His eyes met the king's with a steady gaze. "Yes, my lord. They have been restless, and we could use them for whatever you see fit."

"Let's gather them together and send them east. Have them wear normal attire and work through the small villages and farmsteads. Do not let anyone outside this room know. They are to travel light, not to stir up rumors. Have them armed, of course, and they should be able to disperse any threat they encounter," Leifric commanded.

The council members nodded in agreement, understanding the need for discretion. Shawn bowed slightly. "As you command, my lord. I will prepare them immediately and ensure their mission remains discreet."

King Leifric's decision, though cautious, was met with approval. The task unit would gather intelligence and protect the people without drawing unwanted attention. The king's strategic mind turned to the task ahead, knowing the subtlety of their actions could mean the difference between gaining the upper hand and falling prey to the Fallen One's unknown machinations.

As the room began to buzz with quiet conversation and further planning, Dillon, the king's trusted advisor, stepped beside him. "A prudent decision, my lord. The task unit will serve us well."

Leifric nodded, his eyes reflecting the weight of leadership. "We must tread carefully, Dillon. Our people's safety and our kingdom's future depend on our vigilance."

The council continued to forge its plans, and each member committed to the king's vision. Once tense with uncertainty, the room now thrummed with purpose and resolve.

The others agreed, and the meeting was concluded. The king returned to his cold room, the chill a stark contrast to the warmth of the council chamber. He opened his flint case and struck it, sending a spark into the fire pit. The small flame cast flickering shadows as he lit the fuel in his fireplace. Within a few minutes, a warm fire crackled, filling the room with a comforting glow.

King Leifric settled into his lounge chair; the weight of recent discussions heavy on his mind. The pressing malice of the emerging threat needed to be addressed, but at what cost? His thoughts drifted to the historical scroll detailing the previous war. The Note of Sorrow, they called it—a scattered tapestry of memories and fragmented records of what took place. Many details were lost to history, with only unreliable stories passed down through generations remaining.

Leifric recalled a small fragment of the beginning of the battle when the Fallen One began his siege on the lands. Villages and cities in the east were decimated, claimed by the Fallen One's dark power, and his once-great kingdom was swallowed in corruption. He moved west, destroying everything in his path until he met the resistance that rose against him. The king gazed into the fire, the flames dancing and casting shapes on the walls. Is this happening again? Or are these merely remnants of a past long forgotten?

The weight of responsibility pressed heavily on Leifric's shoulders. The fate of his kingdom hung in the balance, a precarious situation. Uncertainty gnawed at him—would his actions be enough to protect his people from a threat that history barely recorded? The king's thoughts flickered through the possibilities, plans, and hopes for the coming months.

As the fire crackled and the warmth seeped into his bones, King Leifric's eyelids grew heavy. He pondered the outcome of the next few months, his mind swirling with scattered thoughts and concerns. Slowly, he drifted off to sleep, the burden of leadership following him into dreams.

In his sleep, the king's visions were filled with images of battlefields and the faces of his people. The whispers of ancient prophecies echoed through his mind. He stood amidst the ruins of a once-great city, witnessing the devastation that had befallen his ancestors. The Fallen One's shadow loomed large, a reminder of the darkness that threatened to engulf them again.

But amidst the darkness, Leifric saw glimmers of hope—brave warriors rising to defend their lands, the light of their courage piercing through the gloom. He saw the Brotherhood's journey to find the relics, their determination unwavering despite the challenges ahead. In these visions, the king found a renewed sense of purpose.

As dawn approached and the first light of morning filtered through the window, King Leifric stirred. His sleep had been fitful, but his resolve was unwavering. The path ahead was dangerous, but he was determined to guide his people through the trials to come. Rising from his chair, Leifric went to the window, gazing at the awakening kingdom. The fire behind him continued to burn, its warmth a symbol of the flickering hope that remained.

<div align="center">~~~</div>

The beast in the woods prowled in a large circle around the party sitting by the fire, careful not to make a noise as it advanced slowly. The fire continued to diminish, no matter how much wood was thrown into it, and the night seemed to absorb any light the flames produced, causing them to appear almost greyish. Seeing this grey flame amid the darkness was an odd sight. Ordi attempted to draw upon fire from his staff but met the same result. A sudden chill came over the Brotherhood as they stood in defensive mode, waiting for something to strike.

A deep, sinister breathing could be heard beyond the circle; it felt like it was coming from all directions and none simultaneously. Ordi turned to call upon the arcane magic but felt little give as he drew upon the river of magic. There was simply nothing; the flow of magic to him had ceased. Ordi knew this would not be good.

The Brotherhood stood together, with Roland at the forefront. He drew his sword and tightened the straps on his breastplate. The group readied their weapons but felt no connection to the arcane magic. It would have to be a physical fight with whatever was stalking them. The fire behind them gave off an eerie, almost grey light and no heat, as if the warmth was being sucked out of the area.

A snort echoed just beyond the clearing, and deep red eyes appeared, glowing menacingly. The Brotherhood knew instantly what was there: a hellhound. Straight from the underworld, it was one of the most dangerous and rare beasts conjured by their enemy. The beast circled them, gauging its prey. Roland stomped hard with his right leg, hoping to startle the creature, but it merely snorted. It took a few steps closer, eyeing the men huddled together, searching for the weakest link.

Roland raised his sword and charged before the beast could advance, swinging downward at the hound's neck. His blade connected but couldn't pierce the thick hide. The hound snapped at Roland, narrowly missing his left knee. It swiped a paw toward him in the same motion, catching him in the chest. Though his plate armor held, the force knocked him to the ground. Mira moved to protect Roland, casting an arcane shield to keep the hellhound from attacking.

Nimue, Verdun, and Thrain quickly moved to flank the beast. Nimue attempted to distract it with agile movements to its left, while Verdun went for the right. Thrain, with his sword, aimed straight for the head. The beast, however, was quicker than expected. It dodged their coordinated strike, its eyes glowing with evil intelligence.

Ordi watched in growing horror as the hellhound launched itself at Thrain, claws extended. Thrain barely managed to fend off the attack with his sword, deflecting the claws but not the brute force of the impact. He tried to conjure a small shield from arcane magic but couldn't act quickly enough. He stumbled back, giving the beast an opening. Seeing this, Ordi's heart pounded, and he frantically tried to recall any spell that might work. There was simply no magic for him to draw upon.

The hellhound's attention returned to Roland, who had regained his footing. Trembling, Roland faced the beast again. "We need to weaken it somehow!" he shouted, dodging another fierce swipe.

Sensing the desperation of the situation, Mira moved swiftly to Ordi's side. She began to channel the arcane magic back out of the hound, redirecting it to Ordi. Sensing the shift in the magical flow, the hound turned its glowing red eyes towards Mira, growling menacingly. It lunged at her with a vicious snap of its jaws, but Mira deftly dodged and used her agility to maneuver behind the hound, knocking it over a large stump.

Unfazed by the demonic dog's attempts to attack, Mira continued to strip it of the arcane mana it had drained from the area. The process was slow and difficult. She channeled the magic to Ordi, who turned to unleash a brilliant display of white arcane energy that came crashing down upon the hellhound. Sharp, jagged rocks formed from the energy cascaded down, penetrating the beast's hide, one slicing quickly through its neck.

The beast whirled in pain, thrashing violently as another blast of arcane energy came crashing down, this time piercing its head. The hellhound let out a gurgling howl, its fiery eyes flickering and dimming as it collapsed. The beast's body began to decay, its dark essence seeping into the ground it had tainted.

The bright shards of arcane magic evaporated into the earth, and the fire returned to life. Its warmth and light dispelled the eerie chill that had settled over the clearing. The night returned to what was perceived as usual, and the oppressive darkness lifted.

"I am sorry, everyone. I have failed you," Roland said, glancing down as he nursed his sore chest.

"No worries, Roland. These bastards are hard to kill, almost impossible. I only faced mimics of them, and we never knew they could drain arcane mana from the surrounding air," Ordi said, exhausted. He sat down on a log near the fire and warmed himself. "A sword rarely penetrates the skin due to the nature of their origins. Being beasts from the underworld, they are almost indestructible. I got lucky only because of Mira here." He reached down and petted her head. Mira barked in response.

Everyone decided it was time to attempt to sleep. Though most of the night had passed, they sought a few hours of rest. It was a restless night for them as dawn came quickly. They left their tents and broke down camp swiftly, not even bothering to prepare breakfast. They ate leftover food from the previous meal as they started their journey north again.

The Brotherhood proceeded through the day, pausing only briefly to give water to their animals. The morning and afternoon were uneventful, and the forest views remained constant. Occasionally, a pond or a small clearing would appear, but for the most part, the forest offered little to see and minimal sunlight to guide them. The path continued north without deviations, and the Brotherhood witnessed no wildlife. By mid-afternoon, the forest finally gave way to a large clearing.

On the opposite side, an old fortress stood in decay. Half of the south wall lay in ruins, while other parts appeared distressed. "I do not know what secrets are held here, but I believe we can find something that will lead us to the relics," Nimue stated as he crossed the clearing.

Large stones scattered across the ground indicated that a previous wall or portion of the fortress had been destroyed or possibly exploded in a violent event. These remnants lay haphazardly, their sheer size and weight suggesting the formidable construction that the fortress once boasted. The Brotherhood advanced cautiously toward the ruined buildings.

The door at the entrance had been violently torn off its hinges, lying fragmented on the ground amidst the encroaching flora. An eerie, pale mist crept out of the building, winding around their ankles like tendrils of some ghostly presence. The atmosphere was thick with an almost tangible malevolence, making each breath feel heavy. It was reminiscent of a scene from a nightmare; the men's nerves were taut, every shadow and sound putting them on edge, ready for something to leap out from the gloom and attack.

Moving with deliberate caution, they stepped through the yawning doorway. Ordi raised his staff, the tip bursting into a gentle yet penetrating light that cut through the mist and dimness. The illumination revealed stone walls covered in creeping vines and patches of moss, indicative of long abandonment. Verdun followed closely behind, his sword drawn and eyes darting to every corner of the room. Nimue led the party inward, his expression one of grim determination.

Ordi's staff cast long shadows that danced across the room as they moved, the shifting light giving the fortress an almost eerie animation. In the glow, they could see more clearly the extent of the damage and decay. The floor beneath them was made of ancient stone slabs, slick and uneven from centuries of wear and weather. Despite this, their steady steps echoed faintly in the expansive square room, revealing the emptiness surrounding them.

The building stood only one story high, making it less imposing but no less filled with the weight of history. Time reduced its grandeur to ruins, yet the echoes of its past lingered palpably. Tables, now pushed against the walls, were laden with old parchments. These were relics of a bygone era, used for recording during the war with the Fallen One. The edges of the parchments were frayed and brittle. The ink had faded to near illegibility by the relentless hand of time.

Nimue moved towards a table, carefully lifting a piece of parchment as if the slightest motion could cause it to disintegrate. His fingers traced the remnants of the ancient script, trying to grasp the wisdom and strategies lost to history. The room, heavy with the dust of ages and the silence of abandonment, felt like a tomb. Every element spoke of defeat, of a fortified place that had once been a bastion now reduced to a memorial of its fall.

Nearby, Verdun's eyes were sharp, scanning for any threats lurking in the shadows. He knew the dangers that ruins like these could hide. Ordi's light revealed scattered remnants of elven craftsmanship—a broken spear here, a shattered helmet there—each piece telling its fragment of a tragic story.

There was an old bookshelf with rolled-up scrolls stacked high. Nimue moved towards it and grabbed a scroll. He opened it gently and began to read. He threw it down to the ground and grabbed another. Nimue went through almost all the scrolls before pausing at one.

The Brotherhood stood silently in the room, which was a ruin yet a remnant of their people's struggle and sorrow. Nimue's voice broke the silence.

He read it out loud: "The Fallen One has captured the forest. We have lost so many, and our defenses will not hold. I am writing this as we flee north. We have taken what we could, including what armor we have. We have the Suit of the Paladin because the former owner fell in battle. The Druid's Tome was sent along with it. We have taken the Otthroite gems. Find us among the dragons in the north… That is it. That is all written, but it is enough for us to know what to do now."

"I still feel like we are chasing a ghost. Find us among the dragons… what dragons? We have no dragons in the world," Roland stated.

"Ah, but there are stories, Master Paladin," Nimue began, his voice tinged with reverence and sadness. "Centuries ago, we elves used to have deep relationships with some of the dragons. These were not just creatures of fire and scale but beings of profound intelligence and magic. Before the God War, the elves and dragons were close companions, sharing knowledge, wisdom, and even the skies."

"Dragons… they are as mysterious as Posh Hounds," Mira told Ordi.

"I am curious what Nimue has to say on this," Ordi replied.

He paused; his eyes distant as if recalling the golden age of those alliances. "We learned from their ancient wisdom, and they benefited from our insights into the world of men and lesser beings. Our ancestors rode on the backs of these majestic creatures, soaring above the lands and uniting our strengths against common threats."

"We have little written record of them," Nimue said slowly, shaking his head. "Much of our shared history was lost during the subsequent cataclysms and conflicts. Foreseeing the chaos of the gods' war, the dragons chose to distance themselves. They went north and secluded themselves from the rest of the world, a wise but sad decision. They have shrouded themselves in a deep, misty veil, a mystical barrier to conceal themselves from the prying eyes of others."

Nimue stressed, his voice lowering as though confiding a sacred truth. "Some possess ancient magic and have immense knowledge of the ancient world, knowledge passed down from time immemorial."

He leaned closer, his expression grave. "They did this not out of cowardice but to protect the delicate balance of their existence and ours. They chose to allow men, elves, and dwarves to live their lives free of dragon interference. They did not want to entangle themselves in the affairs of what they considered lower lifeforms, not out of disdain, but out of a profound understanding of their nature and ours."

Nimue's eyes glowed with the fire of legend as he spoke. "The dragons believed that our fates were our own to forge, that our destinies should not be shaped by their immense power and wisdom. To them, our struggles, wars, triumphs, and failures were the crucible through which we would either elevate ourselves or fall."

"But now," he sighed heavily, "the tides of destiny bring us northward toward these ancient beings. Perhaps it is time for their seclusion to end and for the ancient alliances to be rekindled. If the relics we seek are among them, it will take more than our strength—it will require humility and respect to earn their trust again."

The group stood there staring blankly. "I feel like you withhold information from us and only allow us to know specific things at certain times. You now bring up these dragons? What else are you not telling us? I feel like we are running blind, and these gems are gone. Are we looking for something for the greater good, or are we just looking for something for yourself? What is your desire to even help fight against the Fallen…" Roland was cut off.

"ENOUGH!" Nimue shouted. "I have not spent my entire life in ruin and despair seeking these gems only to be talked down to by a mere paladin." As Nimue spoke, Roland tightened his grip on his hammer. "Yes, there is vast knowledge the elves carry. But this mystery is perplexing, and it is hard to decipher what to say and when. I am learning as we go. I can only inform you fully when the entire picture is unraveled."

Mira sat patiently, waiting and listening. *"Tensions run high, Ordi. I know Nimue means well, but bickering will not help us."*

She hadn't spoken in a while, Ordi reflected, caught off guard by her sudden intrusive thought. *"I know. But we seem to be at the mercy of Nimue at the moment. I think our ignorance doesn't help either."*

The party murmured to themselves. Roland loosened his grip without others noticing. Ordi spoke up, "We cannot let ourselves argue like this. We have all been charged with this task. If our kings think it is essential, we must see it through. I vote we move north into the vial and see what we discover. We cannot waste time; we must make haste."

He was suddenly interrupted by the intrusion of a fox breaking into their standing circle. The creature was striking in appearance, exuding an air of mystique and elegance that captured everyone's attention.

The fox moved with extraordinary grace, its paws hardly making a sound against the forest floor. It tilted its head slightly as if sensing the moment's urgency and then sat on its haunches within the group, waiting patiently for someone to acknowledge the message it bore.

The fox's fur was a vibrant, fiery orange, glowing like embers in the evening light. Its coat was thick and lush, each hair glistening as if woven from silken threads. A patch of snowy white fur stretched from the underside of its slender muzzle down to its chest, contrasting beautifully with the flaming red of its upper body. The tip of its bushy tail was also dipped in white, twitching with playful curiosity.

Its eyes were the most captivating feature, a piercing emerald green that seemed to see straight into one's soul. They sparkled with intelligence and appeared almost otherworldly, holding the forest's secrets within their depths. The fox's ears were perked up attentively, their insides a soft pink, listening to the rustling of the leaves and the whispers of the wind.

Tied to its back was a small, rolled-up note attached with a thin leather string that blended seamlessly with its fur. A delicate pouch hung at its side, subtly embroidered with ancient symbols, hinting at enchantments or messages of great importance.

The fox moved with extraordinary grace, its paws hardly making a sound against the forest floor. It tilted its head slightly as if understanding the gravity of the moment and then sat on its haunches within the circle of men, waiting patiently for someone to read the message it bore.

Ordi bent down to grab the note as the fox sat beside him, its knowing eyes following his every move. He gently untied the dusty scroll from the fox's back and unrolled it carefully, revealing lines of handwritten script. Clearing his throat, he read it aloud for all to hear.

"Attention, Brotherhood, your assistance is needed immediately in Kamrar. We fear the darkness is spreading beyond our control and request Thrain and Roland return to help support our borders. Make haste; in the pouch, you'll find two hearthstones. Use them immediately."

Ordi then withdrew two small, round stones from the pouch, each etched with ancient glyphs that seemed to pulse faintly with magical energy. With a solemn expression, he passed the stones to Thrain and Roland. "We must make haste, gentlemen; the war is brewing faster than expected."

Thrain's face tightened with frustration as he took the stone from Ordi's hand, his eyes burning with anger and urgency. "I want that stuff, Ordi. I want the staff and cloak and anything else that you find. I am the senior mage to the king—and they are rightfully mine!" he demanded, his voice edged with greed and entitlement. Without waiting for a response, he thumbed the stone in his hand, and his form shimmered before disappearing entirely.

Roland turned towards Ordi and Nimue, giving a quick wave. "Best of luck to you. Make haste and find what you can. Who knows what or who dwells beyond the vial?" His form then flickered, and he vanished just as Thrain had.

The sudden departure of their companions left a palpable silence in the air. Nimue stared at the empty patch of grass where Thrain and Roland had stood moments before. "Well, that was interesting," he remarked dryly. "We cannot lose time; we must travel nonstop. It is dark, and we cannot waste any more moments. Can your companion scout ahead for us?"

"Ey, she can," Ordi replied with a nod. Turning to the fox, he spoke in a gentle yet commanding tone of dismissal. *"Mira, run ahead and see what you find. Keep your senses alert for dangers; who knows what lies north of this old fort."*

Mira, the beautiful hound, nodded with almost human understanding. Her sleek, shiny silver coat caught the fading light, making her an ethereal figure against the darkening forest. With a quick, graceful leap, she sprinted north, her movements fluid and elegant, disappearing into the shadows with barely a sound.

Strapping on their gear, the three saddled up and started north as fast as their beasts could carry them. The forest around them became a shadowy maze as the night grew darker.

Ordi glanced over at Nimue as they rode. "Mira will find a path for us."

Nimue nodded; his expression determined. "Good. We need to keep moving."

"I am not a fan of constant moving. What little rest we do have is threatened by something. I can't wait for my warm bed again. But if we must keep moving, I am able." "Let us move," Verdun said. The three companions departed from the broken fortress and trudged north into the dense forest of Witherfort.

Chapter 9 The Origins

c. 1050 years ago

Alaric Stormrider, a man once known for his courage and strength, now paced along the castle's corridor in Talmar. The air was brisk this evening as a storm brewed on the horizon—a constant aspect of the world these days. Since Alaric began his purge of the lands, darkness had swept behind, calling forth storms of unimaginable strength. The storm outside mirrored the turmoil within his soul.

He had an inkling to change his name; Alaric no longer felt familiar. He barely recognized the face staring back each time he glanced at his reflection. Magic distorted his features, twisting them into something unholy. His once-clear eyes had blackened, turning into inky voids that reflected no light. The veins on his face appeared darker and thicker, creeping tendrils of corruption, while his hair turned jet black and grew long, flowing down in wild, untamed waves. The use of dark magic took its toll, leaving an indelible mark upon him.

The man he once was—Alaric Stormrider, Defender of the West and Keeper of Talmar—was dead. His first death had been necessary, though. By sacrificing his old self, Alaric saw the need to purge the land of filth and bring forth his new empire. His thirst for power and domination was the catalyst for his dive into darkness. Yet, it did not appear as dark magic to Alaric; it was merely magic done right.

He moved purposefully through the dimly lit corridor, his footsteps echoing like distant thunderclaps. The walls were lined with ancient tapestries and portraits of past rulers, now barely visible in the flickering torchlight. Each step forward brought him closer to his goal—an empire built on the ruins of the old world.

In his mind, there was no longer any conflict, no hesitation. The lines between right and wrong had blurred, and he stood firmly on the side of what he believed to be true justice. The old Alaric had fought for others; the new Alaric demanded their submission.

He reached the end of the corridor and pushed open the heavy wooden doors, stepping into the council chamber where his loyal followers awaited. They were a motley crew—mercenaries, dark mages, and those who found new purpose under Alaric's rule. They rose as he entered, their eyes filled with fear and admiration.

"Sit," Alaric commanded, his voice a deep, resonant growl. "We have much to discuss."

As they took their seats, Alaric walked to the head of the table, his blackened eyes scanning each face in the room. "Our plans progress, but the Reapers remain a threat. We must hasten our efforts to eliminate them. The darkness we bring is not our enemy; it is our ally. Embrace it fully, and it will support us."

His words were met with nods and murmurs of agreement. The council had learned to trust his vision, no matter how twisted it seemed.

"In the coming days, the storms will grow stronger," Alaric continued. "They are not mere weather phenomena. They are manifestations of our will, our power. Use them to your advantage. Crush any resistance, and remember, we are not just fighting for a new empire but for a new way of life."

As he spoke, lightning crackled in the distance, illuminating the room. The faces around the table took on an eerie glow, shadows dancing in their eyes.

Alaric's transformation was nearly complete. Where once stood a man of honor and courage, now stood a figure of dark power and relentless ambition. The world had yet to see the full extent of his wrath, but one thing was certain—Alaric, or whatever name he would choose next, was far from finished.

He took a deep breath and felt the surge of dark magic within him, sustaining and empowering him. His path was irreversible, but it was the only path that made sense to him. Alaric Stormrider may have died, but from his ashes rose a new ruler, one who would reshape the world as he saw fit.

"Dismissed," he said, turning away from the table and walking back toward the corridor as the wooden doors closed behind him. The storm outside intensified, a harbinger of chaos and transformation.

He walked outside, standing on the highest precipice of the castle wall.

"My Lord," a voice resonated in his mind. *"The fortress is complete, and the time has come for you to claim your rightful throne."* This voice, Nyx, a constant enigma, had been with Alaric for as long as he could remember.

Nyx, a figure shrouded in mystery, never revealed his origins or why he had chosen Alaric. As Alaric delved deeper into his magical studies and explored his roots as a grand mage, he found a voice that guided him toward his destiny. Today, Nyx revealed the completion of his fortress in the Eastern lands beyond the Bloodwold. How Nyx had this information before Alaric was a mystery; in fact, much of what Nyx shared was new or cryptic to Alaric.

"My Lord, your former name, Alaric, is now irrelevant. Embrace your true identity: Lord Xerxes Voidbringer." As soon as Nyx spoke, he vanished from Alaric's mind, leaving a trail of unanswered questions.

Alaric thought as he paced along the tower overlooking the field, *"He comes and goes as he pleases, but Xerxes does have an authoritative sound."*

The elves had laid siege to his palace days before, which had failed miserably for them. Their bodies lay scattered across the field as ravens and hawks devoured their rotting flesh. The image once would have given Xerxes chills, but today, it resembled what must be done. Years ago, Nyx had informed him of the conspiracy by the dwarves, elves, and princes aimed at removing him from power, and he would have none of it. Thankfully, Nyx was there with him to show him the path to increase his draw upon arcane magic and how to wield it in a deadly fashion. Xerxes made quick work of the small rebellion, but it forced everyone into this long, drawn-out war. Xerxes would finish it…and finish it soon. Upon completing his new fortress in the lands beyond the East, he would have enough orcs and goblins to destroy the Western people.

As Alaric contemplated his dark thoughts, a servant approached, bowing respectfully. "My Lord Alaric," the servant began, but he was cut off before he could speak further.

"Address me as Lord Xerxes from now on," Xerxes demanded, his voice cold and commanding, leaving no room for argument.

The servant hesitated momentarily, then nodded rapidly. "Uh, sorry, my Lord Xerxes. Your carriage has arrived. They are ready to take you to Blackthorn." He stood quietly, awaiting Xerxes's response with palpable unease.

Xerxes turned to face the servant, his eyes glinting with malice. With a swift, almost casual motion, he extended his hand and muttered an incantation under his breath. Invisible tendrils of dark magic snaked outward, wrapping around the servant's neck like a spider's web tightening around its prey.

The servant's eyes bulged in terror as he clutched at his throat, trying to pull away the unseen force. Blood began seeping through his fingers, trickling down his neck in thin rivulets that quickly turned into torrents. The tendrils of magic tightened further, making his veins burst like overfilled water skins.

"That is for your negligence," Xerxes stated with chilling detachment. The servant's body convulsed violently as the dark magic continued its relentless assault, the sickening sound of bones snapping and flesh tearing filling the corridor. His mouth gaped open in a silent scream, blood pouring out in ghastly gushes, pooling at his feet.

Xerxes watched impassively; eyes filled with detached curiosity as the servant's life drained away. The servant's body finally crumpled to the floor, a lifeless heap in a spreading pool of blood. The air was thick with the coppery scent of death.

Other servants, hearing the commotion, rushed forward to retrieve and dispose of the body. Their faces were pale with fear, but they meticulously avoided faltering in their duties. Xerxes paid little attention to the frantic activity around him, stepping over the corpse without a second glance. His dispassion was as dark as the magic he commanded.

With methodical precision, Xerxes walked down to the front gate. He moved with grim purpose, stepping into the awaiting carriage. The carriage itself was an imposing sight, with blackened wood and iron reinforcements drawn by a team of shadowy steeds that seemed almost spectral in the dim light of the evening.

As the carriage jolted forward, beginning its journey to Blackthorn, Xerxes settled into his seat. The destination was as dark and twisted as his soul—a barren wasteland of mountains and forgotten ruins. Blackthorn had been built over an abandoned city, a once-mighty fortress believed to have been the last stronghold of the gods during their final war.

The landscape outside the carriage window grew increasingly desolate, once verdant lands giving way to craggy rocks and twisted, leafless trees. Blackthorn was a place where the echoes of the past whispered through the wind, a land steeped in mystery and foreboding. Here, Xerxes would seek to consolidate his power and draw on the ancient magics buried beneath the gods' ruins.

Xerxes's thoughts drifted to the legends of Blackthorn. The tales spoke of ancient artifacts and powerful relics hidden within the fortress's depths. If he could unearth such forgotten treasures, they would grant him unparalleled power, cementing his dominion over the lands.

The carriage rumbled along the rough ground, the silence inside punctuated only by the occasional creak of the wooden frame and the rhythmic clopping of the horses' hooves. Xerxes's mind was a maelstrom of plans and schemes, each more ambitious than the last.

He clenched his fist, feeling the dark magic surge through his veins. The power was intoxicating, filling him with a sense of invincibility. The man once known as Alaric Stormrider was no more. In his place stood a figure of fear and domination who would stop at nothing to reshape the world in his image.

As Blackthorn loomed on the horizon, its silhouette jagged and imposing against the stormy sky, Xerxes felt a thrill of anticipation. The dark citadel awaited him, a fortress where he would command the storms and darkness to carve out an empire of his making.

The winds howled as they approached the gates of Blackthorn, the ancient iron creaking open to admit their dark lord. Xerxes stepped out of the carriage, his eyes sweeping over the desolate landscape. This was his realm now, a kingdom of shadows and power.

He took a deep breath, savoring the cold, sharp air. "Let the world tremble," he murmured to himself, a cruel smile on his lips. "For Lord Xerxes has arrived."

~~~

The journey was uneventful, as Xerxes had intended. His forces pushed north on the path to Kamrar. Xerxes knew there was no resistance after the small contingent of elves failed a week ago in another attack on him. They were clever, trying to infiltrate and assassinate his staff, but Nyx warned him about their plan. He discovered the traitor and publicly executed him. That night, the force of elves charged at his keep and were quickly slaughtered. Xerxes laughed, feeling the victory was too easy. The world put up no resistance to his forces. He thought there could at least be more trouble with the dwarves, but so far, they had burrowed themselves into the mountains and sealed the door. That wouldn't last forever. The carriage pulled up to the main gate, and Xerxes climbed out.

Awaiting him was a tall, slender man with plain and bland features who resembled more a cross between an elf and a man than anything else. His skin was fair but unremarkable, his eyes a dull shade of brown, and his hair a lackluster chestnut color. Nothing about him stood out, yet his intelligence was unmatched when it came to understanding strategic military movements. General Malachai did not show any facial expressions or even acknowledge Xerxes as he climbed out. "What news of the battles?" Xerxes asked.

"The dwarves remain barricaded in their fortress at Kamrar, my Lord. The humans flee north to join them. We have occupied Lorelend and Ymrat and hold the Greenhills. I have instructed my troops to remain there. As we look to take Witherwood from the elves, we will advance from the Northeast. The dwarves are clever but cannot stay in their caves for long. There is no hope in the west to win, and I will order the siege less than three months before we take Kamrar." Malachai spoke in a dull, unexcited voice.

"Wonderful. This is the finish I have sought for a while. We will break the West and destroy those who oppose our rule. I will gladly be merciful to those who accept us, but only as slaves. Any word on finding gems?"

"None yet, my Lord. My forces have been instructed to watch for them, as we know the dwarves mine them and have used them in the past, but they are rare these days. The world has not seen the use of gems in an age." Malachai replied as they continued along the dirt path. The air was stale, carrying the faint scent of damp earth and decay. The sky overhead was a roiling mass of dark clouds, with small flashes of lightning illuminating the distant horizon. Their steps echoed faintly against the cobblestones as they advanced through the formal courtyard of the once-mighty fortress.

Whispers of ancient spirits floated through the air, remnants of a battle that had scarred the land irrevocably. The gods had descended, fought among themselves, and enslaved humankind to do their bidding. Millions were lost, and great fortresses like Blackthorn were constructed amidst the ruins. Now, this shadowy realm had transformed into the seat of Xerxes's dark power.

"Let us go to my chambers. I have a new spell I have been working on that lets me look through the world at potential threats," Xerxes said, gesturing toward the massive iron-bound doors. They heaved open with a groan, revealing the grand hall beyond. The cavernous space was lit by flickering torches, casting long, eerie shadows on the stone walls adorned with faded tapestries depicting forgotten victories.

Ascending the spiral staircase, they reached one of the highest towers, where Xerxes resided. The room was dominated by a large wooden table strewn with old parchments—some containing ancient maps of the world, others inscribed with arcane spells. Xerxes and Malachai seated themselves on either side.

Xerxes began to chant, his voice low and resonant, weaving the spell's words with practiced precision. "Darkened whispers, shadows deep, grant me vision, secrets reap. Through the veil of night unseen, grant me eyes where foes convene." As he spoke, the room seemed to dissolve around them. The walls melted away, and they were thrust out, hurtling across the lands as their surroundings blurred into a tempest of colors and shapes.

They landed in the darkness of what appeared to be a cave, suspended in mid-air. Their eyes slowly adjusted to the dim light, and though invisible and inaudible to those in the cave, they could see and hear everything before them. A few yards ahead, dwarves hung on platforms, tirelessly mining at the rock. The sound of pickaxes striking stone filled the air, and the occasional grunt of exertion echoed through the cavern.

As they moved downward, they found a lone dwarf distinct from the others. He was chipping away at a vein of gold when he came across a pale-looking rock. Xerxes's heart quickened—he knew immediately what it was—an Otthroite Gem.

While a single gem might not pose a substantial threat, the potential of a few could be troublesome against Xerxes's dominion. He knew well the power such gems could grant an enchanter. But did the dwarves understand their true value? Were there any mages left who could harness such power to challenge him? Xerxes withdrew the spell, and they abruptly returned to his chamber, the sudden transition leaving a sense of foreboding in the air.

"Skat! That discovery is not good," Xerxes spat, his expression darkening.

"My Lord, if I may," Malachai interjected cautiously. Xerxes waved a hand, granting permission. "We cannot predict the exact timing of that gem's discovery. It could belong to the distant past or might be yet to come. However, we can certainly plan accordingly and prepare for any eventualities."

Xerxes sat back, folding his arms, his eyes fixed on the flickering shadows cast by the torches. The dim light concealed the fear gnawing at him from Malachai. "Yes, let us plan accordingly. Do not hesitate to advance against the dwarves. They could unravel our entire strategy and wreak havoc on our plans. If needed, we can summon additional troops to bolster our efforts. You may go."

Malachai stood and bowed deeply before taking his leave. As the door closed behind him, the darkness enveloped Xerxes, leaving him alone with his thoughts. The vision disturbed him more than he cared to admit. Sometimes, the spell perfectly pinpointed troop movements and offered him a strategic edge. Now, it seemed to reveal an uncertain future.

Xerxes began to sift through the parchments spread across the table, uncovering one that lay partially concealed. This was the Voidbringer, the spell he had meticulously crafted to summon Xul'Zaroth, the Corruptor. Xul, as Xerxes understood him, was the god banished centuries ago for attempting to corrupt his sibling's creations.

The plan was clear to Xerxes: bring Xul'Zaroth back and offer him the world he deserved. The other gods abandoned their creations, leaving mortals to fend for themselves. In Xerxes's eyes, they were cowards, undeserving of their divine status. But could anyone truly bargain with a god, especially one whose very nature was bent on destruction and corruption? Xerxes's ambitions were boundless, but the path was fraught with peril.

The Voidbringer spell was still in its infancy, with only a few lines completed. Xerxes guessed it would take over a hundred incantations to achieve its full potential. He had scoured countless ancient texts and scrolls, searching for the fragments of knowledge needed to complete the spell. The task was overwhelming.

The thought of the dwarves uncovering something to aid in their war against him made Xerxes sick with worry. He felt a surge of unease as he tried to reconcile the vision with his plans.

"I told you it would be okay," a familiar voice echoed in his mind. Nyx had returned, attempting to reassure him. *"The dwarves do not know what they have with that gem. What you saw has not even come to pass. We need to advance the siege and lay waste to Kamrar."* Nyx always had a way to either irritate or comfort him. Today, however, her words brought a measure of relief.

"How do I know you are right?" Xerxes asked aloud, knowing Nyx could hear him either way.

"I know things beyond what you can grasp, little one. It is me that you are trying to free. I am that god imprisoned. Unfortunately, I cannot help you with the spell I slumber due to the enchantments my siblings placed upon me. They restricted my ability to convey magic, but after centuries of imprisonment, I have managed to free part of my mind," Nyx replied.

Now, it all made sense to Xerxes. He had been conversing with Xul, or at least a fragment of Xul, the entire time. His thoughts raced with thousands of questions, each more pressing than the last.

"What do I do now?" he asked, his voice tinged with desperation.

"Wait, you impatient git. Humans are always eager to rush into things without contemplating consequences. Let the future unfold, and I will make you like me," Xul said.

And just like that, Xul was gone again as quickly as he appeared. Xerxes felt the weight of exhaustion crash over him. The spells and the intense mental dialogue with Xul had drained him. His body ached, and his mind was weary. He needed rest—rest to gather his strength for the battles that lay ahead.

As he lay down, the flickering light of the torches cast ominous shadows on the walls, and the cold stone of the tower offered little comfort. But a dark resolve burned in his heart, an unyielding determination to see his vision through to the end. Xerxes knew the path ahead would be fraught with challenges, but he would stop at nothing to achieve his dark ambitions.

As sleep finally claimed him, the storm outside raged on, symbolizing the turmoil within and the chaos yet to come.

~~~

Xerxes noted that Xul had not come to visit for over twenty years. The absence of the malevolent deity's voice was both a relief and a source of growing frustration. Those two decades had seen his empire falter and his ambitions wane. The battles that once seemed so promising were now stalled. Humans managed to recapture Talamar, their old bastion of hope, and in a bitter act of defiance, they executed General Malachai.

Xerxes had exhausted his troops, sending wave after wave against the unyielding forces of his enemies. Now, with his armies crippled and their morale in shambles, he resorted to corrupting the elves from the north. Luring them in and capturing them was a relatively simple task, but the corruption process was arduous and time-consuming. The purity of the elves resisted his dark magic, requiring prolonged exposure to the essence of darkness that flowed through him.

The replacements for Malachai proved futile. None could match his strategic brilliance, and they tended to be killed as the humans, encouraged by the recapture of Talamar, gathered strength and marched on his lands.

Xerxes stood at the edge of his deteriorating fortress, overlooking the bleak landscape that had once been the center of his dark empire. The sky, perpetually clouded, cast everything in dull, lifeless gray. Lightning flashed occasionally, a grim reminder of the constant storms that plagued his realm, once sources of his power but now symbols of his failing grip over the land.

He heavily questioned what Xul had told him all those years ago about being patient. Patience, it seemed, brought him nothing but stagnation and defeat. The prophetic words of the dark god now felt like a cruel jest. Xerxes's attempts to capture the dwarves' stronghold at Kamrar had failed miserably. He had been driven back, forced to retreat eastward, losing precious territory and resources.

The weight of his failures hung heavily on him, a suffocating cloak of despair. He paced the worn marble floors of his crumbling throne room, barely lit by flickering torches that failed to chase away the encroaching shadows. Every corner of the fortress seemed to echo with the whispers of defeat, the voices of his fallen soldiers, and his enemies' mocking laughter.

His mind wandered back to countless battles lost, the bloodshed and sacrifice—all in vain. The once grand vision of an empire ruled by darkness seemed to disappear, eroded by time and relentless resistance. Once a mask of unwavering resolve, Xerxes's face now showed lines of doubt and exhaustion.

In the gloom, he reflected on his choices. The dark magic that promised so much now felt like a chain around his neck, tightening with each defeat. The promise of power and dominion instead brought ruin and isolation. Once teeming with life and activity, the fortress was now a desolate husk, reflecting his diminishing influence.

As he continued to pace, his thoughts drifted to the humans. Their resilience was maddening. Each time he struck them down, they seemed to rise again, stronger and more determined. And the elves—corrupting them took far longer than he had anticipated. Their innate purity and connection to ancient, benevolent magic resisted his every effort.

Xerxes approached the grand, weathered map of the realms hanging on the wall. His eyes traced the borders, marking each lost territory with bitterness. Kamrar, a name that still stung from his strategic blunder, was circled in red. He had underestimated their tenacity, and it had cost him dearly.

He looked out through the cracked window of the tower, the once-mighty citadel of Blackthorn now a decaying ruin. The cold wind howled through the broken panes, bringing with it the scent of earth and rain. He sighed a deep, weary sigh and glanced at the few loyalists standing silent and vigilant in the room's shadows.

"What now, my lord?" one asked tentatively, breaking the heavy silence.

"What now?" Xerxes echoed, his voice hollow. "Now, we hold what we have. We must solidify our defenses and continue to corrupt anyone we can. The humans are gathering strength, but they are not indestructible."

He paused, feeling the weight of his words. He needed a plan, a new strategy. Twenty years had dulled his once fiery ambition, leaving him a shadow of his former self. Within that shadow, a flicker of determination still burned.

"The dark god promised us power," Xerxes continued, speaking more to himself than his audience. "But we must seize it with our own hands. We can no longer afford to wait for prophecies to unfold."

Xerxes walked to his throne, settling into the cold, hard seat, his mind deep in contemplation. The plan to summon Xul'Zaroth, to bring forth the Voidbringer, seemed an almost impossible feat now. But he had to shift his focus. The world would not bow easily, but he would not yield to despair.

As he sat there, the dark whispers began to fill his mind again, urging him to embrace the shadows and draw strength from the deepest wells of his power. He closed his eyes, focusing on the darkness within, feeling its cold tendrils wrap around his heart. He would find a way—somehow, he would reclaim his lost glory.

Little did he know that just beyond the walls of Blackthorn, forces were gathering, alliances were being forged, and his name was being whispered as the ultimate challenge to overcome. The world had not forgotten Alaric Stormrider, even if Xerxes had.

"Do you miss me?" a familiar voice echoed in his mind, as cold and insidious as ever. Xul, the eternal darkness who had promised so much, was back.

With a renewed, albeit weary, resolve, Xerxes stood from his throne, his silhouette framed against the dim light of the torches. He would rebuild his power, step by step. The path was unclear, fraught with danger and uncertainty. But he was Xerxes, the dark lord of Blackthorn, and he would not be trounced.

He stepped into the corridor, his presence still commanding, and began issuing new orders. The fortress stirred with a strained energy, a flicker of hope amidst the overwhelming darkness.

"Prepare the defenses," he commanded, his voice echoing through the stone halls. "We will retake the East and prepare for the final assault. This war is not over; I will see it to the end."

As his loyalists moved to execute his orders, Xerxes gazed out at the stormy horizon, the seeds of a new plan beginning to take root. The world would tremble once more under his dark dominion. Yet as lightning split the sky, he knew that the greatest battles still lay ahead, and only the strongest would prevail.

He had once been a force that no one could match, but now it felt like he could not win a single battle. Why had the tides of war changed? What had he done wrong? He paced around, searching for answers. None were to be found.

In the stillness, he heard Nyx's faint whisper once more. *"Patience, little one. The game is far from over."* It was both a comfort and a torment, a reminder that his struggle was seen, but the results were yet to come.

"Where the hell have you been?" Xerxes spat back mentally, his frustration boiling over. *"I am nearly destroyed! My forces were ruined, and I have lost almost everything. They have driven me back over the Eastern barrier."*

"You must learn to play the long game if you want to serve with me," Xul's voice intoned, both soothing and menacing. *"I can make you a god... but first, you must die."*

"Die? Again!" Xerxes's mind reeled at the suggestion, a mix of outrage and desperation.

"You never really died the first time. But yes, you must die. Allow the humans to capture you; I will care for the rest.

In time, you will be reborn as a god like me," Xul's words slithered through his thoughts, planting both dread and hope.

The idea of another death at the hands of humans was utterly humiliating. Xerxes's pride and ambition clashed violently with Xul's demands. While he would allow himself to be captured, he vowed it would not be without a final, fierce struggle.

The final days of Blackthorn began to unfold like a tragic epic. The humans, dwarves, and elves united and laid a relentless siege upon the fortress. Xerxes watched from his tower as the formidable alliance, fueled by years of suffering, closed in on his stronghold.

Night after sleepless night, he orchestrated desperate maneuvers, sending out his dark elves and what remained of his human and goblin forces. But the enemy was unyielding, and their numbers and resolve overwhelmed him. Ballistae and trebuchets rained destruction upon the walls of Blackthorn, and each impact felt like a nail in the coffin of his reign.

The air inside the fortress was thick with fear and the stench of impending doom. His remaining loyalists fought valiantly, each knowing they faced certain death. The corridors echoed with the clash of steel and the screams of the dying. Though he was an embodiment of darkness, Xerxes felt a pang of regret for those who followed him into this abyss.

In the heart of the fortress, Xerxes prepared for his final stand. He donned his dark armor, its surface etched with runes of power, and took up his staff, the symbol of his malevolent dominion. He moved through the shadowed halls, rallying his remaining warriors and preparing the traps and defenses that would make the enemy pay dearly for each step they took within Blackthorn.

"You think you can destroy me?" he whispered to the encroaching shadows of his enemies. His low growl carried the weight of his destructive will. "I am the darkness that will never die."

But as the siege engines battered the gates and the walls began to crumble, Xerxes knew the end was near. He felt the vibrations of the final charge, a shockwave reverberating through the very bones of the castle. With grim determination, he awaited the inevitable breach.

When the gates finally fell, a torrent of human, dwarven, and elven warriors rushed in, their battle cries filled with righteous fury. Xerxes unleashed his dark magic, carving through the ranks of his enemies with spells that turned men to ashes and sent bolts of energy crackling across the battlefield.

Each step backward he took was calculated. He led them deeper into the fortress, drawing them into traps where ambushes decimated their ranks. But his forces also dwindled rapidly; the sheer number of invaders was an unending tide.

The battle climaxed in the final chamber, the grand hall where Xerxes once planned his conquests. The stone walls that had witnessed countless schemes and strategies now bore the scars of the relentless attack. Blood stained the floors, and the acrid smell of smoke filled the air.

Xerxes was a whirlwind of dark energy, his eyes burning with an unnatural light. He took down warrior after warrior, but his strength failed, and wounds began to mar his once-imposing form. He knew the end was close.

He remembered Xul's words as he fought, echoing through his mind like a death knell. He had to die to be reborn. The thought gave him a twisted comfort amidst the chaos.

Finally, surrounded and outnumbered, Xerxes faced the commanders of the allied forces. His eyes met theirs, a blend of hatred, defiance, and dark promise flashing in his gaze. With one last thunderous incantation, he summoned a final wave of dark magic that erupted from the ground, blasting his enemies and collapsing the roof.

In the ensuing chaos, the forces of light swarmed over him. Swords, axes, and arcane energy met his flesh, and he fell to his knees, the invincibility of the dark lord shattered. The killing blow came swiftly, a blade driven through his heart, and with it, the darkness that had held Blackthorn in its grip for so long began to dissipate.

Xerxes's lifeless body collapsed in the ruins of his fortress. The battle was over; Blackthorn had fallen. However, little did the victorious forces know that this was part of Xerxes's final gambit. Although they had killed him, he laid the groundwork for a rebirth that none could foresee.

His essence, empowered by his pact with Xul, seeped into the ground, bypassing the mortal plane and entering a realm of shadows. There, in the heart of the void, a metamorphosis began. Xul's dark power enveloped his spirit, reshaping it and preparing it for a return.

The humans, dwarves, and elves celebrated their victory, unaware of the ticking clock of their doom. Xerxes's transformation continued in the netherworld. When he emerged again, it would be not as a broken mortal but as something more—a god of darkness reborn, ready to reclaim the world that had defied him.

In the depths of the shadow realm, Xerxes's eyes flickered open, glowing with an unearthly light. Xul's voice whispered through the void, a promise of power and vengeance.

"You have done well, little one. Rise now and take your place among the gods. The world shall tremble once more."

In the profound silence of the ethereal night, a new dawn of shadow took shape, heralding the inevitable return of Xerxes, now reborn with even greater and more malevolent power.

Chapter 10 The Gnomes

It is said long ago that dragons and dragon lords ruled the regions in the north. The stories told were passed down by the descendants of those who lived and rode the dragons. Unfortunately, those people have all but died out in the world. What remains now are hermits and nomads, claiming a heritage of something passed into legend. Even the elf's deep bond with the once-mighty race has vanished.

The Brotherhood rode north into the unknown region, turning their attention northeast. The forest remained dense, and the overgrown path extended north past Witherfort. Ordi, along with his companions, advanced swiftly.

They entered a denser part of the forest. The air grew thick, almost suffocating, as towering ancient trees closed in around them. Ordi couldn't shake the feeling that the trees were watching them. The limbs of the trees here looked odd, hanging over the overgrown path like grotesque sentinels. Their bark was dark, almost black, and the veins on the leaves were equally stark, a precursor to something unnatural.

Ordi had heard stories that the northern Witherwood was cursed, but travelers never came here, and the tales remained just that—tales. Yet, surrounded by the eerie silence and looming darkness, those stories now felt uncomfortably real.

A presence lingered in the air, which Ordi found hard to describe. It felt darker and more sinister than anything he had ever encountered before. The sensation sent shivers down his spine, and the hairs on the back of his neck stood on end. Even in his dreams, where he encountered many dark figures, none commanded this evil power. The presence felt almost otherworldly, deeply connected to the disease that seemed to afflict the trees but also distinctly separate, as if it existed on another plane of reality.

As they progressed along the path, the oppressive weight of the sinister force pressed harder on Ordi. Each step felt heavier, and the air grew colder and more hostile. He glanced at his companions, their faces etched with similar concerns. Mira had joined them with little to report. From what she could determine, the path continued north. No traces of animals were noted.

Verdun, breaking the silence, spoke up. "Apart from these wicked trees and the chilling breeze, the forest seems unchanged since we left the fort." Nimue nodded in agreement. Their shared understanding of the situation was evident in their expressions.

"What do you sense, Master Ordi?" Nimue finally asked.

"There is something here, Ordi. I feel an unusual stream of arcane energy flowing through," Mira told Ordi.

"It's hard to explain; it's a power unlike any in this world. Unlike any I've ever encountered. It feels like it does not belong here." Ordi struggled to put into words the pressure, like a weight on his mind, but whenever he tried to analyze it, it vanished. It was fluid, almost like a mist. Whenever Ordi reached out to the channel, it moved around, acting as though it were conscious and aware of his attempts. While Ordi was not a dark arcane user, he had experience connecting to the darkness of the world, countering spells, and understanding how magic flowed through the corrupted.

The dark arcane was simply there, a form of magic that drew its power from shadows and the world's dark forces. It was a power that mages could channel and use worldwide, wielding it for good or ill. But this presence felt isolated within the forest yet flowed in and out of the woods.

"Do not dwell on my thoughts; I see the world differently than you do, Verdun. Nimue, perhaps you, too, since you only deal with elemental forces. This feels off and dangerous. I'll keep my mind and senses open, but I do not think we are alone, a feeling that has become common on this trip," Ordi continued.

"There is a darkness here that I have never felt before," Mira said. She stopped walking and placed her ear on the ground. *"This magic shouldn't be here."* She started walking again.

"I feel the same; it's as if it has been corrupted or ruined somehow. It doesn't feel right when I try to use it. Let us be wary about it," Ordi replied.

The leaves rustled overhead in a rhythmic manner, pulsing like the steady beat of a heart. The uncanny cadence lent an eerie life to the forest, as if the trees were sentient beings, watching and waiting. Despite the constant movement, the breeze did little to stir the heavy, muggy air that clung to the forest. The dense canopy above trapped the humidity, blanketing the travelers in a suffocating embrace that stifled any hope of relief.

The oppressive heat and humidity caused sweat to pour from Ordi's brow, rolling down his face in rivulets. He constantly wiped away the moisture with a small handkerchief, which soon became soaked and gritty with dirt, rendering it almost useless. His sleeve likewise became saturated, the fabric darkening with relentless perspiration. Each step he took felt more laborious, his clothes sticking uncomfortably to his skin. The high humidity affected the travelers and took a toll on the animals. The usually resilient horses and ponies began to slow, their coats lathered in sweat, and their breathing grew labored. The group was forced to pause more frequently, leading the animals to small, trickling streams to drink and cool off, though the lukewarm water offered little solace.

    As they trudged deeper into the heart of the Witherwood, darkness seemed to cling to Ordi like a predatory shadow, following his every move. It felt like a storm on the brink of breaking, a palpable tension growing heavier with each step they took. This sense of impending doom pressed down on him, making the air feel even thicker and more oppressive.

    Despite their determination to press on, the need for rest became unavoidable. They found a small clearing and sat down to catch their breath and attempt to dry off. Ordi stared at the towering black trees surrounding them, their twisted limbs seeming to close in, cutting off any semblance of escape. The forest's unnatural stillness was shattered only by their labored breathing and the occasional uneasy shuffle of their horses.

    Ordi sighed heavily, feeling the weight of the humidity pressing down on him. Every part of him ached from the constant strain and the relentless, cloying heat. He ran a hand through his damp hair, slicking it back from his forehead, and took a deep swig from his water skin. The water felt warm and tasted stale, but he drank it eagerly, grateful for any moisture to quench his parched throat.

Nimue gestured, "Come, we have no time to waste." They had half a day's journey before leaving the forest. After about five minutes of walking, they reached a fork in the road. Each way led north but were separate, distinct paths with about five yards dividing them.

"Ordi, Mira, and Verdun, take the path to the right; I will take the left. If we go over an hour and do not meet up, return and meet here. Do not travel for more than an hour, as we cannot waste time." Nimue waited for the dwarves to proceed before he led his horse down the left path.

Verdun and Ordi agreed and proceeded down the right path, with ponies being led behind. "Ordi, remember that Father sent us to Yssrar to pick up that load of fish? We got there, but they sold our batch to another family. We spent the whole evening fishing on the Icewater Lake docks.

"Yeah, Father was so mad he had them all fired. It was funny that they all worked for Father, and he made them dust rocks for three years, all over some fish. Now that I think about it, Father could be petty over the most minor things yet let significant issues go unpunished. He did think it was funny we sat in the cold fishing, thinking it would be our hindquarters if we did not return with the month's lot." Ordi smiled to himself.

Their father was an unconventional dwarf. While he had a large heart, he would get angry over the smallest issues. He commanded power in the financial areas of the Dwarven industry and significantly influenced the King and the traders of the Dwarves. If he wanted someone fired and shoveling pony dung, he would make it happen. "Father has a unique way of handling issues, that's for sure," Ordi replied as the two kept moving in what they thought was north. After only twenty minutes of walking, they made a large circle and ended right back at the fork in the road with no Nimue in sight.

"That's unusual, don't you think, Ordi?" Verdun exclaimed.

"Why would the path bring us back here? Something foul is at play," Mira said..

"Yes, very. It doesn't make sense. The path never curved or changed. It went north the entire time. How in Moriden's world did we end up back here?" Ordi walked around momentarily, examining the paths and realizing they were identical in appearance. "I feel something in the air. Something not sinister but protective. Not a spell that I am aware of, but something deep in the earth. If I were to guess, the path we walked was enchanted, and after a while, it simply returned us here. The other path, though, could be the right one. Nimue has not returned, nor is there any sign of him." Ordi looked down at the ground to seek any tracks or try to make out anything legible in the dirt.

Seeing nothing, he stood, raised his staff, and twisted it high above him. Mouthing the simple spell to illuminate past events, he and Verdun previously witnessed Nimue heading down the path. Beyond a ground squirrel crossing the path, nothing else occurred. Just before he closed the spell, he caught sight of a black wisp building up at the fork and moving down their path before disappearing into the air. The sight gave him chills as he lowered his staff.

Verdun spoke first, "Nimue walked down just after us, and we only saw that ground squirrel. Maybe it's still around here... I am getting hungry!"

Mira jumped at the mention of food. *"I can go fetch the squirrel."*

"No time for food; unfortunately, something is foul here. This forest is dark, and I saw something conjure and proceed down the path we took just before we came back here."

"No time for food? You always spoil the fun, Ordi!" Verdun grumbled as he reached into his pack, pulled out a small ration, and ate. He handed a tiny bit to Ordi, who did the same. Mouth still full, he asked, "You don't think that the spirit or whatever you saw was after us, do you?"

"No, we never had anything happen beyond being routed back here. It could have simply been the defense mechanism that I'm sensing. It could also be something else that we have yet to encounter. The forces of evil do not often show themselves, especially with simple spells. They tend to be harder to detect." Ordi did not hesitate any longer.

"Could this be a defense to hide something, Mira?" Ordi asked.

She paused for a moment, sniffing the air. She walked in front of Verdun and Ordi and stared down the path. *"Maybe. The path went straight. I didn't make it to the fork before returning to you. There is something here, though, not evil, but perhaps neutral."*

They did not speak for a while as they walked and examined the ground. The dirt showed the tracks they expected and nothing else. The air grew heavier, slowing their progress further. In northern Asheros, humidity was never a huge issue, as the summers were not generally that hot. Ordi knew the feeling, though, having spent several years in the south with the humans. Summer was not his favorite. This weight, however, was heavier than he had ever experienced, and within a few moments, the ponies had all stalled, and he and Verdun were dripping with sweat. Pausing, he tried to grab his flask, but as he looked down, it felt like his pouch was always out of reach. Every time he tried to grab it, his belt would drop away. Verdun laughed as Ordi struggled to get his water, then unexpectedly passed out. Ordi couldn't turn around. He could not get his feet to cooperate; they wanted to go in opposite directions, forcing him to the ground. The ponies slumped down, passing out too. Ordi's last thought was that humidity doesn't do this, but magic does. They were led right into a defensive ward that could be their doom. Before blacking out, he attempted to utter a quick spell in hopes of regaining strength quickly.

 Ordi forced his eyes open as best he could. His head throbbed from the pressure of the spell he encountered. He could see his cloak and staff across from where he sat, his hands tied behind his back. Blinking against the dim light, he found himself lying on a soft bed of moss inside a small, stone-walled chamber. He glanced around, his vision slowly clearing. He saw Verdun, Nimue, and Mira still passed out, with their gear piled neatly next to Ordi's. This did not seem malicious but more protective by whoever took them captive. Ordi tried to draw upon his magic, but the connection was faint due to the poison he had inhaled. It would be some time before he could recover, and sleep would be the best method.

Not sensing any immediate dangers, he drifted back off to sleep.

Ordi was uncertain if afternoon had passed into night. Time in the forest was hard to distinguish, either dark and gloomy during the day or almost impenetrable at night. Outside, the fires around the camp were constantly burning, and the captives could smell food as they stirred. Verdun panicked as he realized his arms were tired and his sword was missing. Nimue expected to be tied up and muttered to himself, "These cords are not tight, but they are hard to get off." Ordi slept while the two tried to break free. Nimue whispered, "Ordi! Are you awake? Verdun? Mira?"

"I'm up. Trying to break these cords, too," Verdun replied. Mira stirred and realized what was happening. She walked behind Verdun and started gnawing on the cords to free his hands.

Ordi did not stir; his sleep led him to meditation as he fought to remove the poison from his lungs. When he came to, he could give Verdun a potion, but the poison had a nasty effect on arcane users. During the meditation, Ordi was aware of his surroundings, even when Verdun called out, but he ignored them. He reached out to sense the area outside the room and saw a handful of Gnomes working on various tasks. Some were cooking; others discussed something while pointing to the tent where the three were kept, while others were engaged in different jobs. As he spirit-walked through the camp, he noticed an unusual figure among the Gnomes, one he couldn't quite make out. It was as if their arcane had acted as a buffer against Ordi, preventing him from sensing them. As Ordi drew closer, the cloud grew denser, and suddenly, a laughing face appeared and disappeared quickly. The cloud became an impenetrable wall, and Ordi moved on. He returned to the building and back into his body just as a Gnome was about to enter the room.

The door creaked open, and a small figure entered. The gnome was no taller than Ordi's waist, with a bushy red beard and bright, curious eyes. He wore practical, earth-toned clothing, and a small lantern warmed the room.

"Ah, you're awake!" the gnome chirped. "I am Glemm, and welcome to the city of Gloomhollow. We found you in the forest, unconscious. You were lucky we came across you when we did." As Glemm spoke, he waved a wand, and the ropes that bound the party fell. Mira had only begun to free Verdun. "We do not usually encounter travelers who wander by, well... now that I think about it, we seldom get travelers to these parts anymore. Dark times these days. They say the Dark Lord is at work again in the world, and all sorts of foul beasts are moving down from the north—scary business." He shuddered once he finished.

Ordi, Verdun, and Nimue exchanged glances. Verdun spoke first, his voice cautious but respectful. "Thank you for your kindness, Glemm. But who are you, and why did you help us?"

Glemm's smile was genuine and disarming. "We gnomes are hospitable folk. We couldn't just leave you there. Dark magic was trying to kill you three—nasty business. Besides, we know of your quest. Word has reached our lands that the heroes of the age seek again: the lost gems. The gem-infused armor is vital to you and all the lands. We gnomes do not forget that our history is more profound than the elves'.

We sit and watch, gather and discuss, and interfere with none. Come, follow." He got up and departed from the stone room.

As Glemm led them through the labyrinthine tunnels of Gloomhollow, the party marveled at the intricate stonework and the ingenious machinery that powered the gnomes' various contraptions. The underground city was bustling with activity, its inhabitants moving about with purpose and energy. Ordi was surprised that the main chamber he sensed was not as large as he had thought. His arcane connection did not provide a complete sense of what lay beyond the doors.

"Yes, a mystery to me as well," Mira said, interpreting Ordi's thoughts.

As they continued, he noticed a hooded figure rising from a corner and slowly began to follow, keeping their distance. Ordi could make out a whimsical shape, but the long cloak kept many secrets. Ordi knew they were there; his connection to the arcane told him that much, but that obscuring aura still protected the figure from his perception.

Glemm kept talking the entire time Ordi focused on the mysterious figure behind them. "We've been preparing for dark times," Glemm explained as they passed a group of gnomes working on a large mechanical device. "Shadows are stirring in the west; we must be ready. Don't mind that little shadow, Ordi. He is simply a young gnome in training. He's trying to go unnoticed, but I see he failed his task today." Glemm chuckled to himself.

Ordi's curiosity got the better of him. "You mentioned our quest. How do you know about gems and armor? It was said to be lost lore, and that no one knows anything."

"Our ancestors dealt with the dragons and entrusted them with knowledge about the relics when the downfall of Xerxes took place. We do not know why the dwarves turned to them, maybe as a neutral party?" Glemm replied. "We believe the relics hold the key to restoring balance to the world. After Xerxes was defeated, the gems were no longer sought after during the Golden Age of Magic. They were said to be no longer useful to the powerful mages who ruled during that time. Magic was stronger after the fall as no one desired to corrupt it and bend it to darkness. When the councils disbanded their armies, the armor and gems of the heroes who wore them disappeared into history and legend. It is said the gems were turned over to the dwarves, and they turned to the dragons for assistance, but that is all we know."

Nimue was impressed; he had finally filled in the pieces to his story. "Master Glemm, how much of this is fable? Our people know some legends, but you have all the missing pieces."

"No legend, my son, all truth. I know because I was there. We Gnomes live thousands of years because we do not meddle in the doings of the big people." Glemm chuckled. Nimue looked dumbfounded and had to be nudged by Ordi to keep walking. Ordi, though, still kept one ear attuned to the shadowy figure that pursued them. As Glemm continued talking about the inner workings of the Gnome empire, Ordi suddenly lost track of the pursuer. He attempted to quest out again but was quickly overwhelmed by the presence of gnomes who surrounded them and walked with them.

As they continued, they were introduced to various gnome elders and leaders, each expressing their support and offering assistance.

"Here is Elder Wulfric; he oversees our day-to-day activities in preserving our knowledge," Glemm said as the group approached the elder gnome. His long grey hair framed his aged yet kind face. He stood discussing something with a young gnome who had been sent off on an errand.

"Yes, Master Ordi and Master Nimue. It is an honor to meet you," Wulfric said ecstatically. "Oh, what do we have here?" He looked directly at Mira as she approached. "A posh hound! Oh, my lanta!"

"This is Mira," Ordi attempted to introduce them.

"Yes, I am quite aware of her name. Gnomes and posh hounds have an ancient connection, but we have not seen any for an age!" Wulfric said as he placed his hand on her head. "I see you will play a big part in this story yet. Oh, what a joyous day! But I must be off." He smiled and nodded before hurrying away.

"He didn't say anything to me," Verdun said in a disgruntled voice.

"Well, to be fair, you are just a sword on this journey," Ordi laughed. Verdun punched him in the shoulder.

The group continued the tour. It was clear that the gnomes of Gloomhollow were allies worth having. In the city's heart, the group was introduced to a lively figure who stood out even among the gnomes.

"Greetings, travelers!" Thalin said with a theatrical bow. "I am Thalin, a humble bard and teller of tales. I've been staying with the gnomes, sharing stories and songs. I hear you are on a noble quest to save the world!" he shouted, and the gnomes cheered. "I would be honored if I could come along and record your quest. That is, after all, what bards do. I can provide a handy sword and swift magic in tight situations while ensuring there is never a dull moment on our journey." Thalin was a bard of elven descent, his slender frame and pointed ears marking him as such. He wore a colorful tunic and carried a lute strapped to his back.

The party looked at each other. Ordi said, "Ey, I suppose you can join us, Thalin. I'm not keen on whether we're up for constant tunes, but an extra sword is always welcome."

Laughing heartily, Thalin jumped off his box and greeted the party by giving each of them a big hug. His enthusiasm felt out of place among the three weary travelers but was nonetheless welcome. "Tonight, we FEAST!" Thalin belted out, eliciting more cheers from the gnomes.

He led the large crowd to the dining hall. The smell of roasted pork and boiled potatoes filled the air, causing the travelers to drool instantly. Ordi didn't realize how hungry he was and how long it had been since they last ate. They proceeded into the grand hall, where thousands of gnomes gathered, already consuming food. They sat at a small table at the head of the room, as was customary for Glemm. The gnomes enjoyed their food and fellowship, having a feast daily, but today they were honored by their friends who would be setting off at first light.

The hall filled with chatter and laughter, and the weary travelers settled down to the meal. Food came forth: an endless supply of meats, sweet bread, and various sides. The brothers ate for hours, stuffing themselves beyond all normal limits. The conversations ranged from the background and history of the world to theology and the fundamentals of magic. For once, the brothers felt rested and restored. Their spirits were lifted by the graciousness of the gnomes and the hospitality they showed. The crowds came and went, continuously conversing with the travelers and seeking their thoughts on the patterns of the world. While the food was filling and the conversations enjoyable, the time soon came for rest. Ordi knew they would need a good night's sleep before setting out again. As the evening wore down and the party thinned out, Glemm approached the brothers with a tiny, petite gnome, her blonde hair shorter than that of the others. Yet, her appearance commanded respect as she displayed beauty and intelligence.

"Gentlemen, thank you for agreeing to stay. As you prepare to withdraw and head to your rooms, I want to introduce my daughter, Glallbi. She is our chief mage who specializes in elemental arcane magic. She has personally requested, and I insist that she accompany you on this quest. We Gnomes do not often engage in the world's affairs, but this matter requires a change of heart. We may even take up arms to help remove the evil before the end."

Her voice was soft when she spoke. "I do not want to be a hindrance, Ordi. Your talents are known far and wide, but this quest is extremely dangerous. I want to offer my services, such as they are, to assist in acquiring the gems," Glallbi said.

"Your services are most welcomed, Glallbi, daughter of Glemm," Ordi replied. "This quest has not been for the faint of heart, and I urge caution in your decision to join us.

Glemm, you know what she is asking. This is not just for the gems; it will lead to war sooner or later. Verdun and I have witnessed the Fringe and the Creeping Death advance across the land. Half of our party was summoned back not even a week ago to assist with armies approaching from the west. We have lost towns and people and will most likely return to fight. We would appreciate Glallbi's presence, and you know as well as we do the danger that lies before us." Ordi sat back and folded his arms.

"Yes, I am aware of the dangers. As I mentioned, our armies have been preparing to assist you, but we are stubborn. If Glallbi goes with you, that may be the spark we need to support you with soldiers and wizards." Glemm spoke, "Brothers, I know your hesitation because she is my daughter, but she is our chief mage and beyond my fatherly control. She has decided to assist you, and I honor that. The hour is late; I insist we retire to our quarters for the evening. Follow me, and I will show you where you will stay. There will be a sending-off in the morning as you prepare to depart."

Glemm led Ordi, Verdun, and Nimue out of the dining hall and up a short ramp. The crowds had disappeared as the Gnomes began retiring for the night. The brothers finally realized how tired they truly were. Exhaustion washed over them, and their steps became a struggle as they reached their rooms. Ordi walked in and dropped onto his bed, passing out and falling into a deep sleep.

While Ordi slept, he transitioned to meditation to give his body the best chance of rest and recovery. He drifted off and found himself sitting on a grassy plain overlooking the valley of mountains outside Kamrar. The air was calm as Ordi constructed his vision for meditation. The sun setting beyond the mountains cast long shadows in the valley below. A cloudless sky warmed Ordi as he sat, observing the birds flying above. He pondered the words of the Gnomes and the path that lay before them. The gems were indeed important, but would they be enough? Would they even help? There were so few that the armor sets would only be worn by select warriors: a druid, a mage, and a paladin. Would it be Verdun, Nimue, and himself? Did he deserve them? These thoughts crept in and out of his mind as he sat.

The air grew sharp with a chill that came from nowhere. The wind gusts picked up, and Ordi transferred to another location. Instead of overlooking his peaceful valley, he stood on a jagged cliff facing the Dark Lord. The air howled around Ordi, sounding like the wails of tormented souls. The sky above transformed from a beautiful blue to a swirling vortex of darkness, pierced only by occasional flashes of eerie green lightning. Below, the once thriving lands of men, dwarves, and elves lay in ruin, a grim testament to the Dark Lord's evil power. The ground trembled as he confronted Ordi, his figure towering and wreathed in black flames that cast a hellish glow around him. He laughed, taunting Ordi, holding him hostage to witness the destruction below them. The lands that Ordi knew and loved were reduced to rubble.

"Ah, Ordi," the Dark Lord hissed, his voice dripping with contempt. "The last, pathetic hope of these pitiful races. Look around you. See the fate that awaits those who dare oppose me. Do you think finding these precious little gems will save you? I have fought them before. They are nothing to me now. I have grown more powerful and knowledgeable than you realize. After abandoning you, the gods selected me to rule over this land." With a wave of his hand, the Dark Lord conjured a vision. Ordi's heart sank as he saw the horrors unfold. The once-proud human cities were now charred husks, their inhabitants either slain or shackled in chains. Dwarven fortresses, renowned for their impenetrable walls, lay in ruins, their defenders lying lifeless among the rubble. The entire mountain system was crushed and reduced to debris. Elven forests, once vibrant with life, were now twisted and blackened, their beauty forever marred. Xerxes's laughter echoed through the air, chilling Ordi to his very core. "Weak," he sneered. "All of them, weak. Just like you, Ordi. You cannot stop what is to come."

Ordi clenched his staff and felt the weight of despair pressing down on him. He had faced many challenges, but the sheer scale of the devastation before him was overwhelming. He tried to speak, tried to stand, tried to do something, anything! Yet, he could utter no spell. Magic was absent from him. The Dark Lord stepped closer, his presence suffocating, his eyes boring into Ordi's soul. "You think your magic can save them?" the Dark Lord taunted. "You are but a speck of dust in the wind, a fleeting whisper in the storm of my wrath." The vision shifted once more.

Ordi next witnessed his brother's death on the battlefield. Verdun, in his paladin armor, lay crushed, his body lifeless. The rest of those who fought alongside Ordi lay scattered across the embattlement. The only movement was the air blowing over a few small, scattered flames. Xerxes's power was immense, and his cruelty boundless. He stood with Ordi. "See what I will do. I will crush you and your friends. There is no hope, no victory for you. Even in surrendering, I will crush you."

Ordi finally managed to push out a word of defiance. "No!"

"No?" Xerxes laughed. "You know nothing of the power in this world or of the gods. Do you think you can stand before me? I have been resurrected by Xul, god of the universe. I will dominate this plane, and all creation will be rebuilt as I desire."

"You may be back, but you have no idea what you fight for. You are alone, unloved. You seek domination for what? To feel appreciated? I know you, Xerxes. You are powerful, but we will fight, and if we perish, so be it. But we will not go down without the greatest battle this world has ever witnessed." Ordi finally managed to stand and speak. He stood in front of Xerxes, who towered over him. The dark power radiated from him, consuming Ordi. The green lightning intensified overhead. The darkness grew thick, closing in on the two of them.

Xerxes laughed, "You think love will save you? You are delusional. I will crush you and your people. Pathetic. Why do I even waste my time trying to discourage you?" The Dark Lord appeared bored now. "Well, know this, dwarf: I am coming like fire and storm. I will sweep across this planet and consume everything in my path. It has already begun…" With that, he vanished, leaving Ordi alone again, overlooking the mountain range at Kamrar. He dropped to the ground, exhausted and trembling.

He awoke from his meditation, sweating and shaking. Unsure of what to do next, he lay there staring at the ceiling in his room. After a few minutes, Ordi moved, grabbed his staff and cloak, and reached for the door to the great hall. He left Mira to sleep and did not want to disturb her.

"I see your dreams, Ordi. I know he stalks you," she said before Ordi could leave.

"I didn't realize you could. I wanted you to rest. But yes, he sought me again. I do not know what to do. There is very little knowledge about dealing with this. Even talking to Verdun won't help." Ordi stood perplexed at the whole situation.

"I know, but sometimes just talking about it can help the rest of the party understand what you are going through. Let Verdun and Nimue know. I'm going back to sleep." Mira stretched back out as Ordi departed.

No gnomes were walking, as it was late into the night. He walked a few yards to where Verdun was staying and lightly tapped on his door with the bottom of his staff. It took a few more raps on the door before Ordi heard Verdun start to stir.

After another minute, the door opened, with Verdun standing there looking disheveled. "What is it, Ordi? It's late!"

"Verdun, I had another vision. The Dark Lord spoke to me; he gave me a vision of the future. The world is in ruin, and everyone is dead or enslaved," Ordi blurted out quickly.

Verdun, tired and trying to make sense of what Ordi said, replied, "Ey, again, huh? Well, do you think it is merely to try and scare you? Or perhaps this is what awaits us if we fail?"

"No, he even said the gems are worthless."

"Oy… Well, we need to finish this quest. The Gnomes seem to know what they're doing. Maybe he's frightened of them?"

Ordi pondered that for a moment. "Yes, perhaps. I don't know at this point. But we need to be wary; I fear the agents of the Dark Lord will be more vigilant on our quest now. Sorry to wake you. I needed to discuss this immediately."

Verdun replied, "No worries, brother. Get what sleep you can. We leave in a few hours."

With that, the two brothers returned to their rooms and fell asleep. Morning came quickly for Ordi, who had only a few hours of sleep after the vision with Xerxes. He reached into his bag and grabbed a red phial. "I hate drinking this sludge. But I need energy." He popped the cork and chugged the contents. The thick paste, stiff to push down, tasted like garbage, making Ordi gag. Instantly, he felt his body respond, and a pulse of energy surged through him. The energy potion, like others, tasted foul and was used sparingly, but it always had results for the user. Ordi washed his face quickly and dressed. The Gnomes had laundered his gear overnight, carefully washing his cloak and vest. He grabbed his bag and left the room after making the bed. He made his way past the dining hall, grabbing some breakfast meat and sweet bread. He walked down the long hall to where they were to meet Glemm.

A large crowd was already gathered to send off the brotherhood on the second leg of their journey. Ordi and Mira joined Thanlin, Verdun, Nimue, and Glemm in front of the crowd. Glemm welcomed them personally and announced to the crowd.

"Fellow Chroniclers, welcome!" The Gnomes gave their appreciative applause. "We have waited for these days for many years, always looking and waiting to see if the Dark Lord would return. As he has, we now assist those on the quest to defeat him and return him to the void!" More cheers erupted from the crowd.

Glemm continued, "As these heroes prepare to leave, we want to ensure they depart with the gifts that will equip them best." A Gnome walked forward, carrying various items. Glemm turned to Nimue, "Nimue, here we have some of our finest shin plates, light and flexible. You will never know you are wearing them. They will connect you deeper into Asheros and the elements." Turning to Verdun, he said, "For you, a soldier of the highest rank, a new breastplate made of our finest steel. Another item that is light to wear but will protect you in the toughest of battles." Turning to Ordi, he said, "Ordi, a mage of mages, we give you the Gnomes' bracers. Wear these, and your fortitude will increase, and the power you draw from the arcane channels will be great!" He smiled and accepted their thanks. "These will aid you in your quest," Glemm said. "And take this map." He handed it to Nimue. "It will guide you through the Valley of Dusk and help you avoid more dangerous areas."

Ordi, Verdun, and Nimue thanked the Gnomes for their generosity and prepared to leave Gloomhollow. They knew their journey would be dangerous, but they felt bolstered by the support of their new allies.

"May your path be clear and your journey swift," Glemm said as they departed. "And remember, you will always have friends in Gloomhollow."

Thalin yelled out, "A song to be sent off with!" He sang as the travelers gathered their items and walked to the door.

"Farewell, my friends, until we meet again; our paths may part, but our spirits remain. With songs in our hearts and tales to unfold, may fortune and joy in your journeys be told."

"Through the mountains and the meadows, across the river's flow, we'll carry the light within us, no matter where we go. Every end's a beginning; every farewell, a new start, with the music of our friendship always in our hearts."

Ordi, rolling his eyes, bade the Gnomes farewell and climbed out of the hole in the tree that led down to Gloomhollow.

"Mira, what do your senses say about our path?" Ordi asked.

She paused for a few moments. *"I think we have a choice. We must face the dragons and the gatekeeper."* She turned to face the path. *"The road is difficult, but we may have luck on our side from here. But I am still unsure about that."*

"Let's make our way north then. If the gnomes did their job, the gatekeeper will expect us," Ordi replied. "Our journey takes us north. From there, we hope to encounter the gatekeeper and the dragons. As Nimue always says, 'let's make haste.'" With that, the group departed Gloomhollow. Ordi, Mira, Verdun, Nimue, Thalin, Glallbi, and the ponies advanced northeast to the Valley of Dusk.

Chapter 11 The Journey North

The party continued out of Witherwood. The path widened past a single-file dirt road. The forest ended atop a small hill. Rolling fields stretched as far as the eye could see. The peaks of the Red Mountains loomed in the distance. The fields before them appeared uninhabited, and they would be able to see anyone approaching. As the group trudged on, Ordi spoke to break the silence, "Let us keep a steady pace. We should reach the Northern Gap in three days, with another few days to the Valley. If we remain consistent, we can camp at the Northern Seeing Tower tonight—or what is left of it."

The group, bound by their shared mission, quietly acknowledged what Ordi had said. They maintained a steady pace throughout the morning, and little was spoken among the travelers. The weather in the north was slightly brisker than the summer heat south of Witherwood. The company welcomed the cooler temperatures, making the journey across the fields easier. Glallbi rode a pony next to Ordi to ensure she kept up with the group's steady pace. While ambitious, she was shorter in stature and found it difficult to keep up. Thanlin, on horseback, stayed in the middle of the pack, playing his flute lightly to provide a subtle hint of music in the air without overpowering the others.

Glallbi shared what the Gnomes knew about the gems, and Nimue rode up to listen. "My father spoke of the essential aspects of what the Gnomes know, but I have spent much of my life researching the gems," Glallbi said. "I'm sure Nimue has shared his extensive knowledge as well, and truthfully, perhaps only a few aspects could be discussed further." She smiled at Nimue. "The great Dwarven empire of Unrar uncovered the gems centuries ago. Long before Xerxes sought power, the mages used them to bind into their gear through Infusion. They performed a powerful spell that would bind a part of themselves into the gem, equipping it into whatever they wore to enhance their power. We do not know how many spells were created; mages usually kept that secret," she exclaimed. "We know some were quite creative, granting the bonded mage enhanced elemental control or the ability to fly. From my research, though, the last gems maintained a soul bond, which breaks part of the mage's soul to grant them longevity. The idea is that when part of the soul entered the gem, the gem's magical essence extended the wearer's life due to the direct connection to the Arcane Source. From what we know, it's a painful process, and we have only a few documented instances in magical history where the mage completed the spell. Only one or two spell books that the Gnomes know of still exist, but we do not know where they are now." Glallbi's explanation prompted Ordi to think deeply about what could be achieved once they found the gems.

What else could they do? Could he fly? He smirked at the thought. Could he extend his life? Dig back into deep-forgotten magic? His thoughts wandered as Glallbi kept talking. "…But now those gems are worth more than the wealth of the dwarves and men combined."

"I'm intrigued by all of this. Mages seriously could fly with these gems?" Ordi asked.

"Well, yes. I suppose. But there are spells and a process to make it work with the right Otthroite gem," Glallbi explained.

After Glallbi spoke about the gems, silence ensued for a while. The hills rolled by, and the forest began to disappear behind them as they continued traveling. Midday approached, and Nimue signaled for them to stop and take a break. A small pond broke the rolling meadows, and they stopped to water the animals and rest. The Gnomes provided many supplies, including food. The party ate well while the animals grazed. Though the sun was overhead, the air was relaxed and the breeze gentle, bringing a much-needed break from the chaotic weather of the forest they had left behind. In the distance, they could see a lone hill with a small tower built to shelter them for the night. Reviewing the map, Ordi examined the path closely; once they departed the tower the next day, they would head due east to the Northern Gap into the Valley. If they followed that path, they would reach the Valley of Dusk and turn northeast to the Pass of Ferrus. While obstacles could delay them, they expected the journey to take another five to six days before they reached the gatekeeper. Mira noted some dangers but did not specify what they would face. He called out to her, "Mira, what lies beyond the tower?"

While she was chewing on some meat, she replied, "*Trolls.*" And left it at that.

Ordi was shocked, but given what they had gone through, trolls probably wouldn't be unexpected this close to the mountains. They were driven out of Kamrar centuries ago and were rarely seen near Dwarven territory. Mira continued to eat, paying no attention to anyone or anything. The rest of the party finished eating and returned to the saddles of horses and ponies. Ordi threw his leg over Bill, the pony, and nudged him forward. The group set off once again, crossing the small stream of water. The day drew on, and the party inched closer to the tower with almost no change in scenery. Boredom crept in, and Verdun broke the silence, saying, "Ordi, remember when we used to hunt cave moles and ride them?"

Ordi, taking a drink of water, spit it out to the group's laughter. Thalin, who had quit playing his flute, was intrigued by the story. "Oh Ordi, do tell, my lad!"

"Eh, we were kids and did it growing up, as did all young lads. It was almost a rite of passage that became a game to play when bored. We would go down into the closed mines and seek them out. They were hard to find, so that was half the challenge. Fat, hairy mountain moles were difficult to distinguish from rock. We carried sticks to poke around to see if we could feel one. Verdun found one, jumped on it, and rode it down the tunnel and into the open air. The mole was able to kick him free and sent him flying into a thorn bush. It was the funniest thing we saw while doing it. Needless to say, the elders found out we had gone down to the old mines without permission. They punished us and banned us from coming within 20 yards of any entrance." The group was laughing as Ordi finished his story.

"Dwarfs are an interesting race," Thalin said as he finished laughing. "I could not imagine going down to hunt for moles to ride them." The group continued to laugh for a few more minutes. As the chatter and laughter settled, the group neared the tower, and the landscape shifted slightly. More brush was present, and the ground became a little rockier. Ordi, leading the pack, paused his pony and gestured for the others to stop.

"Well, would you look at that?" Ordi pointed down to the ground a few yards in front of him. In front of the brotherhood were massive footprints imprinted into the ground, moving from the west to the east and beyond.

Nimue jumped off his horse to examine the footprints more closely. "These are not fresh, maybe a few days old. There is some grass growing in them. I do not think it is anything to worry about but be wary; the closer we are to the mountains in the north, the likelier we will see trolls." He saddled back up, and the group rode on. Each paused momentarily to look at the massive footprints.

The Northern Seeing Eye Tower loomed ahead, its ancient stones etched with luminous runes that pulsed faintly in the dying light. The tower had long been abandoned and stood as a testament to times past. The Dwarves used the northern tower in Unrar to watch for enemies approaching the East. As Unrar was abandoned, so was the tower. The Dwarves duplicated the structure for Kamrar by building the Central Seeing Tower, now primarily used as a meeting place between the Dwarves and Men. Few inhabitants traveled north of Witherwood Forest, let alone back into Unrar. When the last riches were mined, the Dwarves packed up and left. Kamrar held more promise for the Dwarves, with some moving south and picking up mining jobs while others moved elsewhere in Asheros. As they drew closer, the decrepit tower appeared to be little more than a shell of what it once was. "My father's father was once stationed here in his early years, before they came to Kamrar," Ordi said as they climbed the staircase to the plateau. They crossed through a series of short halls that opened into a grander hall. "Let's make camp here; we can use the old fireplace for heat and light," Ordi pointed to the north wall.

Ordi found Nimue pacing around the room, studying the runes and relics etched into the walls. His fingers traced the intricate designs. His long, silver hair caught the setting sun's light, giving him an ethereal glow. "These markings... They speak of times before even the oldest of our kind remember," he murmured, his voice filled with reverent wonder. His sharp green eyes examined each symbol with the practiced gaze of someone who had spent centuries studying the ancient arts. "The Dwarves' knowledge here runs deeper than even the Elves!" He stepped back in shock.

"Ancient reminders of a magic that even I have yet to fully grasp," Ordi replied, his voice steady but tinged with curiosity. He could feel the power within the tower calling to his burgeoning abilities. The stone was cool to his gentle touch. He felt the magic seep into his fingertips, a strange sensation that was both comforting and overwhelming. Memories of his grandfather flashed through his mind, his voice speaking of old spells and the perils of misused magic. His grandfather had passed away so long ago… yet the power in these walls brought him back to life before Ordi. "How can these ruins have so much power? The mage council never speaks of them or any landmarks."

"We should remain vigilant," Verdun interjected, breaking the moment of reverence. "This place may be ancient, but danger often lurks in such places." Ever the watchful guardian, he glanced around, his senses on high alert. He gripped his sword harder. As he did, he reached out and grabbed an old, dusty amulet from the table and began to examine it. Holding it, he felt an odd power pulse through him, making him feel more vigorous and alert. He had never experienced this power surge before, and without anyone noticing, he pocketed the amulet, hoping he could someday be viewed as equal to his brother. This amulet, he thought, could even give him an edge. While he loved his brother, he had always lived in the shadow of Ordi's accomplishments.

The group moved forward cautiously, their collective breath visible in the cold air. Thalin, the Bard, trailed behind, humming a light-hearted tune that juxtaposed with the grim setting. He pulled out his flute and began to play. Ordi shuddered. The song attempted to lift their spirits, but the melody was somber.

"Thalin, I appreciate the song, but let's stick to the humming," Verdun finally said. After a moment, the bard lowered his flute and kept it in his hand as the group continued moving. His colorful cloak fluttered as he turned around, the many patches and trinkets sewn into it jangling softly.

"This place gives me the shivers," Glallbi said with a shudder. The young gnome's eyes were wide. Her red hair, tied back in a messy bun, contrasted sharply with her pale, freckled skin. She moved with a slight bounce, her energy infectious even in dire situations. "How about that fire, Ordi?" She turned and cast a small flame into the dusty old fireplace, igniting the old wood into a roaring fire. Within minutes, the room was flooded with warmth and light.

Verdun, his tone a mixture of respect and warning, replied, "This room is a remnant of a time long past, filled with memories and whispers of ancient power." He glanced at Ordi, the unspoken understanding between them clear. Both knew the weight of the legacy carried by these old places. "It is odd that Grandfather never spoke of this place. I wonder what else was done here before or after the Dwarves abandoned it."

Nimue continued to walk around the room, examining the runes and flipping through old scrolls. "There is indeed a deep magic here, but it is not the building itself. The building sits upon a channel of pure arcane energy, like a deep river, slow and steady but mighty. I cannot pinpoint its origins, but it is older than any channel I have ever felt. That could be why the tower was built here. There may be significance to this place from before the end of this war."

"I sense it too," Ordi muttered, gripping his staff tighter. The pervasive hum of ancient magic thrummed beneath the surface as if the ground below the tower was alive. It was unusual for Ordi, something he had never experienced even while working in what was considered the magic center of Asheros in Talamar. "Either way, we're staying here for the night. The tower will provide shelter from whatever wanders these plains at night. The fire will keep us warm." Ordi started to unfold his sleeping bag, as did the others.

"What do you think we'll find in the gap?" Glallbi asked as she sat close to the fire, her eyes reflecting the dancing flames.

"It is not so much the gap that I worry about as the Valley of Dusk and the Pass of Ferrus. Those are places we dwarves care not to enter and know little about," Ordi replied. He stretched his hands towards the fire, feeling the warmth seep into his fingers. "But we must prepare for the unexpected. The gap has always been a place shrouded in mystery."

Thalin took out his flute, playing a soft, soothing melody that harmonized with the crackling of the fire. The sound was peaceful, and their minds drifted toward sleep. As Thalin continued to play, the group huddled under their blankets, letting the fire's warmth and the soft melody of Thalin's flute lull them to sleep. Ordi felt the fatigue of the journey finally catch up to him. His eyelids grew heavy as he considered their upcoming trials and challenges. He was confident in their strength and doubted none, but a fear lingered in his mind. Uneasy thoughts pressed at him, and the presence of Mira did little to assuage the fear that sat within him, reminding him to be vigilant that something unexpected might take place. As he wrestled with this fear, he patted Mira's head softly and drifted off to sleep, listening to the sweet, slow melody of Thalin's flute.

Once the group had fallen asleep, Thalin recited a spell over them to ensnare them in a deep sleep. He then turned and played another melody on his flute; a dark and dense tone rang out. A spirit walked forth from the shadows.

"You have done well, Thalin. The plan shall proceed as normal. Take care not to show them any hints of your motive. Ordi is smart, but you can handle him when the time comes," the spirit said.

"Yes, master. He is smart, but I have been studying him, and I believe I see his weaknesses," Thalin replied.

"Don't underestimate him. He is a dangerous foe."

"The gnomes did not suspect anything either. They assumed I was a bard looking for adventure." Thalin said.

"You have deceived them well, now that we are past them, you focus on Ordi. You're betrayal to them must come only when you find the gems. I want those in my hands. Do not fail me," the spirit said.

"I will not. I will report back once I have the gems," Thalin said. A moment later, the spirit disappeared.

The rest of the night passed uneventfully, and the first light of dawn bathed the mountains in a soft, golden glow. Ordi woke to find Verdun watching over the group, his breath forming small clouds as it hit the frigid air. The fire had died early, waking Verdun from his deep sleep.

"Morning," Verdun greeted Ordi with a slight nod. "We should get moving soon." In this early morning, he had been thinking deeply about the new power he felt coursing through him. He had no idea how to access it or what to do, and he contemplated even asking Ordi about it. He did not want to alarm him or start a fight, but the time would come when he would have to reveal his new finding.

Ordi nodded back, sharing a silent understanding. "Let's wake the others." He stirred and rolled out of the bag, throwing a small flame into the fireplace, causing the embers to spit out new flames. The warmth was welcomed again into the large room. The rest of the group began stirring as Ordi and Verdun woke each person up. They proceeded to eat a quick breakfast and pack their belongings. It was not long before they exited the old Tower and began the day's journey east.

The group set out again, and the terrain grew steeper and more challenging with each step. They left the easy grassy plains for rocky, broken ground. The path narrowed, and they occasionally clung to the rocky walls to avoid slipping into the abyss below. The uncertain ground would sometimes give way, dropping into deep chasms. The biting wind howled relentlessly, forcing them to brace against its icy onslaught. They drew their cloaks closer, but even that did little to prevent the wind from reaching their bones.

Hours into their arduous journey, they came across an ancient rope bridge spanning a deep chasm. The bridge looked fragile; its surface cracked and weathered over time. Yet, even amid the relentless wind, the bridge did not sway; it was held firm.

"We cross one at a time," Verdun yelled, eyeing the structure warily. His voice was almost lost to the wind. "No sudden movements." While the bridge appeared to be steady, it was old and unpredictable.

"I'll go first," Ordi volunteered, gripping his staff tightly. He stepped onto the bridge carefully, feeling the wood shift slightly under his weight. Each step was measured and deliberate. He drew in some magic, making himself slightly lighter than a moment before, not wanting to put unnecessary stress on the bridge. As he reached the middle of the bridge, Ordi felt a sudden gust of wind that almost caused him to lose his balance. He steadied himself, heart pounding, and continued until he was safely on the other side.

A slow creak, then a groan, then another creak, then a thud. The sounds of the bridge echoed in the air as the party crossed. Each step a deliberate weight on the old wood, as it strained under their weight. Glallbi, light as a feather, seemed to float across, her steps barely making a sound. Thalin waited until last, carefully placing each foot on the worn wood, the silence a heavy weight in the air. The Bard moved with a confident step, until the sound of splintering wood pierced the quiet, and the ground disappeared beneath him. He was falling—the wind rushed past his face, the rough rope tearing at his hands as he grabbed for purchase, his legs flailing desperately, his mind filled with a cold terror. Ordi shouted and his power lashed out in a burst of light, but it was too late and Thalin was violently pulled back and forth in the air, swinging like a broken doll.

Thalin screamed out, "WHAT ARE YOU DOING, ORDI?" Ordi steadied himself and attempted the spell again. The wind made it difficult, pushing and pulling the arcane wherever it desired. The second spell yanked Thalin off the bridge, sending him hurtling through the air of the brotherhood, making him land on the dirt path with a loud thud. He reached for his pouch, ensuring that his flute was not broken. "Well, that was not fun. I do NOT advise it again." He laughed as he struggled to get up and dust himself off.

As they moved away from the bridge, Thalin pulled out his flute and played a joyful melody to keep the company in high spirits. There was a small amount of magic behind the playing that would influence those who heard his music. Thalin continued to play a series of songs. The group continued their walk, their spirits lifting. They pushed forward until they reached a plateau that offered a brief respite. They stood at the edge, looking out over a breathtaking landscape of snow-capped peaks and deep valleys, the vast expanse a reminder of the beauty and danger of their journey.

"Let's take a moment to rest," Nimue suggested, lowering his staff. "The path ahead will require all our strength." As they sat down, Verdun handed out rations, a mixture of dried fruits, nuts, and jerky. "Eat up. We need to keep our energy up."

As the group ate and rested, they took in the serene beauty of their surroundings. The snow-dusted peaks shimmered in the sunlight, starkly contrasting with the dark, mysterious gap ahead. After their brief rest, they resumed their journey, descending from the plateau and heading towards the Northern Gap. The sense of anticipation grew with each step as they walked into the unknown. Mapmakers had vaguely described the area, and the maps constantly contradicted each other. For hundreds of years, no one had ventured this far north; some said there was an impassable chasm, while others noted the rugged land to traverse. The terrain thus far had been rough, with random points in the ground crumbling away. The great chasm, or gap, loomed ahead based on the description of the land. The air grew colder as they neared where they assumed the gap would be. A heavy breeze blowing in from the east discouraged them from advancing. Finally, they found the massive chasm.

The wind whistled through the rocks with an eerie moan. The shadows lengthened, casting a dark and foreboding atmosphere. The massive gap stretched out before them, seemingly swallowing all light, as jagged rock rose high into the sky on the opposite side. They appeared to have reached a dead end. Verdun plopped down on the ground, armor clanking. Mira stood next to Ordi as the two stared out into the abyss of the gap. Suddenly, Verdun jumped up from his spot. Ordi ran up, yelling, "VERDUN!" He reached the edge and could hear laughter.

"Down here, it looks like there is a path that we can follow." Laughing, Verdun landed about five feet down on a platform with a descending path.

Disturbed by Verdun's actions, the rest of the group hopped down to accompany him on the ledge below. They left their animals above, free to return home or wander as they wished. They stripped them of the riding gear and equipment. This journey was now to be completed on foot. The group descended into the gap, their steps slow and deliberate. The chasm's walls rose above them, blocking the sun and casting long shadows that danced in the dim light.

"There is magic in the part that is ancient, deeper than anything I've felt. Ordi, it feels like this is from the Gods," Mira said.

"I sense that too. It is profound. The Arcane is almost so crisp you can taste it," Ordi said.

Ordi led the way, his staff glowing softly, casting a comforting light on the darkened path. "The air here... it's different," he murmured. "Heavy with the presence of ages gone by. It feels like the Tower, the magic running deep into the earth."

Verdun could feel it, too, the weight of ancient magic pressing down on them. It was both exhilarating and intimidating, a reminder of the power hidden in this sacred place. He kept silent about his newfound gift—if it was even that, Verdun thought.

As they traveled deeper into the gap, the walls closed in, and the path narrowed until they had to walk single file. The silence was almost deafening, broken only by their footsteps echoing off the stone walls. They came across an ancient carving on the wall, the intricate designs depicting scenes of dragons and dwarves, of battles and peace. Ordi paused, running his fingers over the symbols. "These carvings... tell a story," he said softly. "A story of power and wisdom, of a time when dragons and dwarves lived in harmony."

"Looks like we're not the first to walk this path," Thalin said, gaping. "And we won't be the last."

The group continued, moving deeper into the gap. The air grew colder, and the sense of magic intensified. Ordi could feel the energy pulsing from the walls. The path they descended slowly began to close around them into a tunnel like a cave. They proceeded to walk through, slowly descending with each step. They finally reached a large open chamber, its vast expanse dimly lit by glowing fungi that lined the walls. Stalactites hung from the ceiling, their shapes creating a natural cathedral of stone and light. Glallbi, who had been quiet for most of the time, finally spoke up, "This magic is incredible! I feel so connected, deeper than ever before."

An ancient altar stood in the center of the chamber, its surface encrusted with dust and grime. Nimue approached and wiped the top, revealing engraved runes that glowed faintly with an otherworldly light. "We've reached a place of great significance," Nimue said, his voice filled with awe. "A place where the veil between the past and present is thin."

Ordi reached out, his fingers skimming the surface of the altar. A surge of energy shot through him, filling him with visions of a time long gone. Dragons soared through the sky, their scales glinting in the sun, and dwarves crafted wonders in the heart of the mountains. The image spun, and he found himself pulled out of the world. He floated in darkness, watching his world below; it was being… created. Three massive angelic beings hovered over the world, each taking a role in creation. One paused what they were doing and turned to look at Ordi, hovering near him. He winked and went back to work. Ordi was shot forward in time, back to the ancient room. "Did you see it, Nimue? Did you experience a time walk?" Ordi asked.

"Yes, of sorts. I was looking into the future, witnessing great destruction if we failed our quest. The Dark Lord sweeps over this land and consumes all, including the dragons. Everyone and everything is destroyed. The land is covered in blackness, and the foul beings of the planet walk freely." Silence held the group for a long moment. No one spoke; no one moved.

Glallbi spoke up, "Have you experienced these visions before?"

"Yes. A few times, Ordi mostly," Verdun said.

"Anytime we encounter visions, it is always death and destruction. Something is warning us of what may come if we fail this quest," Ordi said. "We encounter these ancient places and leave with more questions. This altar resembles the one Mira and I destroyed a while back. The writing here is older. Why here? Perhaps it has something to do with the dragons?"

"The dragons are a mysterious group, even for the gnomes. We try to chronicle some of their knowledge, but few have ventured that far north. Nimue may be able to explain some of the older relics in the world," Glallbi said.

Nimue took a deep breath. "I don't know what this place is or why it is here. We Elves could answer many questions, but I have none for this place."

Ordi paused. "Even the tower from the other night has no record save for defense and trade. There is much in the world that we do not understand. How much history was lost in the last great war?" The room continued to remain quiet for a time. "We cannot linger; time quickly escapes us. We need to get to the Pass soon." Ordi knew there were secrets in the world. His vision had him transfixed on what was taking place here and now. Why did he go to the past and see what he assumed was Moriden? Why had Nimue gone to the future to see the desolation? Was this a sign from the gods? Ordi gathered his gear and walked to the opposite side of the room. The door appeared to be the exit, but where it led was the next question that needed answering.

The rest nodded in agreement with Ordi, grabbed their bags, and followed. Nimue looked back at the altar and bowed. Something ancient and magical had occurred here; for them to stumble upon this was no accident. Nimue's understanding of the world and everything in it changed daily. The door led to a narrow tunnel that descended as they walked. They walked for a long time until the path opened into a massive cavern. The walls glowed with bioluminescent fungi, casting a soft, ethereal light over the entire space. In the cavern's center lay a pool of clear water, its surface reflecting the glowing walls like a mirror. The water was crystal clear, but its depth was hard to gauge, as it appeared to drop endlessly into the earth below. The group walked along a narrow path on the right side of the cavern and stared at the pool next to them. Walking alongside Ordi, who had been quiet during their descent, Mira finally spoke to him. "The magic you have been feeling, I feel too. It is ancient—greater than what the Gnomes or Elves could even understand. It is hard to trace the origins, but I saw your vision, Ordi. I witnessed the gods of old as they forged the world. They poured their magic upon this land and enriched the earth with a power that has been dormant for ages. I think this is what we are feeling. As we descend further into the unknown territories, that magic deepens and becomes more alive. I do not know what it means, though." The two walked ahead of the group as they continued to pass through the enormous cavern.

"Mira, what do the Posh Hounds know about ancient magic?" Ordi finally asked.

"Nothing more than the Gnomes, sadly. We are not a collected group that shares knowledge like the people of this world. We are beasts that run free. We are born with a connection to the arcane channels, and my bond has taught me how to use that connection deeply. I can access knowledge of the world, but it is limited to what I can see and sense. Glallbi appears to be well-versed in the basics, but in *time, we will learn more about your visions and what else exists in this realm for us,"* Mira responded. Her pace quickened slightly as they reached a narrow part of the path, and she moved ahead of Ordi. *"I will trot ahead and see what I can find. I can see well enough in the dark."* With that, she was gone again.

The path opened out, and they reached the other side of the lake. Here, carvings on the wall and signs of ancient visitors were visible. They discovered tools and remnants of a long-forgotten campsite or village. Glallbi was astonished by the discovery. "Do you think this means what I think it means?" she asked. She traced her fingers along a scene depicting a dwarf and dragon standing next to each other as if they were brothers or comrades.

Ordi nodded. "I think there was once an alliance between the peoples and the dragons. We have our tales, but they are from a time long forgotten. We always thought they were fairy tales when we were growing up."

Laughing, Verdun responded, "Mom would always tell us about dwarves riding dragons. I thought it was funny. How could we even ride a dragon?" He pulled back an old tarp, revealing rusty swords and shields. "It appears those who came here were once warriors or at least had some sense to defend themselves." He picked up a sword and held it for a moment. "This is an old sword. I can't date it, but it is from an age long past. We no longer use this metal, as it is scarce and hard to find. But it is sturdy and has a good blade, even though it is rusted."

They kept moving, not pausing long to read the writing on the walls. They had to make it through this cave and reach the end, hopefully finding everyone on the other side of the chasm or somewhere in the Valley of Dusk. Exiting the massive cavern, the path twisted eastward and began to ascend. They climbed at a steady pace. Ordi's staff gave off just enough light, but the perpetual darkness wore on them. Finally, they all saw a glimmer of light. Thalin pulled out his flute and started to play another joyful tune. Everyone welcomed the exit into the fresh air.

Mira trotted back to Ordi, "I have found a path; we have made it through the Gap. The Valley is just at the bottom of this hill." Mira pointed behind her. Down the path was a wide walkway with a large rock wall on either side. While the Valley itself was enormous, there was only one path—the one that lay before the group. "I have bad news: darkness swarms the Valley, and the Dark Lord is expanding his reach. We have trouble ahead of us."

Chapter 12 The Pass of Ferrus

The terrain did not favor the brotherhood. The ground was rocky and challenging to traverse, seemingly mocking their every step. Sharp stones jutted from the earth, and the uneven surface made every step a calculated decision. As night set in, the sky grew dark, and clouds gathered, threatening rain. The wind howled between the cliffs, sounding like a lament from ancient times.

"I'll light my staff, but we either make camp or take it slow and push as far as we can," Ordi said. Its glow cut through the encroaching darkness, casting long shadows on the rocky path ahead. Flecks of light danced off the wet stones, creating an eerie, almost magical ambiance. The Gap had been a unique experience, uncovering ancient relics; Ordi was concerned about what Mira had meant by trouble. It had unsettled him. They faced unusual elements on their journey, but was the Dark Lord playing with them? Was he moving troops north to attack? Recruiting more forces, seeking the evils of the world? The group continued along a thin ledge, with a rock wall shooting up into the sky, a deep drop-off to their right. They moved in single file, with Nimue bringing up the rear to ensure everyone made it through safely.

The group advanced carefully, each step deliberate as they navigated the narrow pathway. The thin, crisp air amplified every sound, from the crunch of their boots to the howling wind that whipped through the passes with chilling ferocity. Ordi could feel the ancient magic permeating the air, a constant reminder of the power hidden within the Northern Gap.

"Ordi," Nimue yelled. "What do you see ahead? A storm is coming, and we must find shelter soon."

The howling wind picked up, blasting them with icy cold as the rain began to *fall. "Mira, stay close to the rocks. The ledge is getting narrow,"* Ordi urged, his voice barely audible over the wind's roar.

"I'm trying. The wind is not fun, nor is this ledge easy. We must find shelter soon. This storm is coming quickly," Mira said.

As they trudged slowly along the narrow ledge, the sheer drop to their right grew more menacing with each step. The rock wall on their left was jagged and unyielding, scraping their armor and clothes. Each step was deliberate, their senses heightened by the precariousness of their position. Ordi could feel the tension in the group. Verdun's foot slipped, sending a cascade of stones tumbling into the abyss, causing everyone to freeze momentarily. "Drat!"

"Careful, Verdun!" Ordi yelled over the howling wind.

"No kidding! Actually, I may fall next time," Verdun said.

"Go for it then," Ordi replied.

They heard the stones clattering far below before being swallowed by the darkness. As the rain intensified, the ledge grew more perilous. Cold droplets stung their faces, and the wind threatened to knock them off balance. Ordi's staff flickered, the light struggling against the elements. Below, the abyss resonated with an endless hollow growl, adding to the sense of impending doom.

"The storm is getting worse. We need to find shelter!" Verdun shouted over the gale.

A few steps further, Ordi spotted a small alcove in the rock wall. "There! It's not much, but it'll shield us for now," he pointed.

"YES, let's make camp here tonight," Verdun shouted, flinging his pack off his back.

"Good idea," Nimue said. The party responded by unpacking. The alcove would be too small for tents, so a small fire and sleeping bags would suffice for the night.

The group cautiously approached the alcove, grateful for the scant protection. They huddled inside, their bodies pressed against the cold stone. The narrow space forced them into close quarters. A small fire did not bring much warmth to the group. The night was entirely quiet on the border of the Valley of Dusk. No other signs of life appeared, and the travelers slept as peacefully as they could, welcoming the softer ground beneath their backs. They wrapped themselves in their cloaks. Ordi took the first watch, his eyes scanning the dark horizon for any signs of danger. The chaotic pattern of rain hitting the ground became a soothing backdrop, blending with the occasional rustle of the leaves.

"The storm will not be letting up soon," Mira said.

"I'm glad we found this little spot to camp. It would be miserable out there," Ordi replied. The two sat watching the storm roar through.

After what felt like hours of pelting rain and gusting winds, they finally made it through the rocky terrain of the Gap. Before them, the land expanded and opened up. The ground grew soft with dirt. Scattered trees and vegetation ahead created a more hospitable environment. As morning came, they broke camp and continued traveling. The sun shone overhead but provided little heat. The air was cool as they proceeded into the Valley; on the far sides, they could see mountain ranges; the southern peaks were the Deadlands, a place they had no desire to visit, while the northern peaks led to the Unknown Lands, which the Dwarves often referred to as the "Red Barrier." That was their destination, but they had to reach the Pass of Ferrus to cross the peaks.

As the day became more enjoyable, Thalin pulled out his flute and played a joyful tune. He paused between notes and sang, "In the Valley of Dusk where the shadows play, we march together, come what may. We journey beneath the twilight sky with brave hearts and spirits high." He continued playing his flute, pausing again for the chorus: "Oh, the winds, they sing our tale, of heroes bold who shall not fail. Our hopes and dreams will see us through the mist and twilight's hue." The group united in their purpose, continued walking under the warm autumn sunlight, traveled through the valley, and spoke little except for Thalin's melodies, which kept them moving.

As the day went on, the weather did not change. Thalin ceased playing and grew weary from the continuous traveling. The afternoon wore on, feeling like it would never end. The travelers noticed that the wind had stopped blowing, and the day settled into an unusual darkness. The sun was hidden, and no stars shone through. Darkness swirled around them; something was coming. The group, though weary, was ready for whatever shadows were about to descend upon them.

Roland rode east on his stallion, followed by an army of humans and dwarves, warriors and mages. Since returning to Talamar, he had been in charge of this as Verdun traveled with Ordi north. Roland, being a suitable paladin and leader, had the opportunity to prove himself. Reports poured in that dark forces were sweeping west and threatening Ashton and potentially significant cities. The vast plains north of Decaywold stretched out, awaiting the bloodshed of war. The grass swayed under a fierce wind, beneath a sky choked with dark, roiling clouds. Roland ordered his troops to halt as he surveyed the lands before them. Approaching them were the grotesque forms of goblins and the sinister silhouettes of dark elves, their eyes glinting with evil intent.

The air was thick with an unnatural chill as the goblins and dark elves continued their advance. The dwarves and humans remained quiet. There was no movement. No one spoke. They stood there, their tension palpable, awaiting the oncoming battle. They outnumbered the Dark Lord's forces and noticed it was a tiny fragment—like a small gnat on a summer afternoon that you squish. Next to Roland, Thrain's pony trotted up. "Looks like a small force, but those elves will trouble us. Our scouts had said their numbers were twice as many. I'm curious to know where they went."

"We need to dispatch a group to deal with them. This battle will be hard enough. The Fallen One has tricks up his sleeve. We must be vigilant today," Roland replied. They sat on their mounts, watching and waiting as the charging horde approached. Their twisted forms moved with a feral grace, and their weapons shimmered with dark enchantments. Whispered chants of dark magic echoed across the plains, heightening the tension. Roland raised his sword, imbued with arcane runes that glowed faintly in the gloomy light. "Hold the line, defenders of Asheros! Today, we fight to send a message to the Dark Lord that the world stands united against him. Do not cower in fear; do not back down. Stand and fight, men! Stand and FIGHT!" He bellowed, his voice carrying back among the ranks, offering reassurance to the warriors and comforting those who had never seen battle before.

Thrain gathered a group of mages before him as the creatures approached and instructed them on the upcoming battle. "Use your area damage spells. Bring down as many as possible. The goblins are easily dealt with, but the elves resist magic more. Try not to engage them one-on-one." The thunder of the goblins grew louder as they approached. "MAGES!" Thrain yelled, "READY!" With that, the small group of mages that Thrain had gathered let loose fireballs and ice shards. They soared over the gap between the two parties.

As the fire and ice came crashing down, Roland completed the incantation to protect himself and those around him: "By the arcane forces, be shielded from darkness!" He raised his sword and yelled, "TO DEATH!" Those around Roland shouted and charged forth to meet the goblins in a clash of swords and magic. The battle began with a thunderous roar. Roland led the troops, his blade slicing through the first wave of goblins with a burst of arcane energy. Each strike released a blinding flash of light, banishing the shadows that clung to their grotesque forms.

Thrain unleashed a barrage of ice projectiles, skewering goblins and freezing dark elves in their tracks. "Embrace the biting cold of the ancient north!" he cried, his staff glowing with icy power. The two armies clashed in a vicious confrontation. Goblins excelled at slaughtering the warriors, while overwhelmed mages struggled to stem the relentless tide. The mages couldn't keep up with the fearless goblins pressing into the ranks of warriors. They were mindless thralls, paving the way for the elves who attacked from behind, casting dark sigils in the air.

A cascade of dark fire and shadow bolts rained toward Roland and his allies. "Protective wards, now!" Roland commanded, raising his hand to conjure a shimmering barrier of arcane light. The dark magic splashed against it, sparks flying as opposing forces collided. Thrain, drawing from his deep well of magic, enhanced the barrier with frosty runes, strengthening their line of defense. "Thrain, I need you to do something about those goblins. They are wiping out the entire front line."

Thrain aimed his staff and sent shards of ice into the attacking goblins, piercing their thin flesh. Dropping the handful that had closed in on him, he stepped back a few yards to clear some space to work. He created a thick barrier of ice that was tall enough to prevent the goblins from jumping over. He finished and raised himself on a small platform above the wall.

"Yes, sir!" Thrain reinforced the rune spell to withstand the onslaught of dark magic used by the elves. They wore no armor other than robes to enhance their abilities. They would fall quickly to a blade but reaching them was challenging.

The elves kept their distance, their dark sigils held prominently in the sky above. Before them, waves continued to clash, sword against armor. By the hundreds, goblins swarmed into the armies of dwarves and men, slaying recklessly as they charged before meeting their demise. Thrain finally elevated onto the platform of ice overlooking the battlefield. Carnage was everywhere, and wounded allies were trying to flee. They were jumped upon by goblins looking for a quick kill. The troops held their ground, but the small, agile goblins continued to sweep through the ranks. Thrain cast a protective charm over his troops to shield them from the wide area damage spells he was preparing to cast. As soon as the charm was in place, Thrain proceeded to unleash spells upon the goblins. Goblins were small and quick, dodging the ice shards that fell. It was almost impossible to kill many this way. He shifted to direct ice shard spells, hurling them at goblins as he could, taking down many before they reached the troops.

Suddenly, Thrain heard screams from behind. Elf assassins, using concealment spells, crept through the lines, deep into the ranks of humans and mages. They sliced down the unsuspecting with deadly force. Their daggers were quick, and the elves were silent in their approach. An elemental dwarf mage screamed, "TO THE REAR! We're being attacked from both sides!" The troops in the middle split their attention; some pulled back while others remained fixed on the goblins.

"Roland!" Thrain yelled, "We have shadow elves in the rear!"

"Summon the paladins!" Roland responded. He had withheld the paladins from the battle as a failsafe. He did not want to use them, but he had no choice. As he requested, Thrain summoned a massive white beam in the sky to call the paladins. Minutes later, the paladins rode in, sweeping through the assassins and cutting them down quickly. The arrival of the paladins brought renewed energy to the troops. They gathered and stormed forward, clashing against the goblins and defeating them swiftly. The dark elves were not the only troops remaining, for they had been concealing one more surprise from the Dark Lord: orcs.

In the distance, the banter of a human fire mage could be heard: "Feel my cleansing fire, you scum!" He lashed out with incinerating flames at a large group of goblins. Thrain chuckled to himself as the tide slowly turned. The paladins reached the middle of the oncoming forces. Thrain stood beside Roland as they prepared to deal with the orcs. They were larger, had thicker skin, and were more difficult to kill, but they were also dumb. They possessed raw power but were uncoordinated and rarely followed orders. The paladins charged after the orcs who stood between them and the elves. The elves unleashed burning dark fire, raining it down and engulfing the paladins and their horses. The fire was like tar; it stuck to the target and burned continuously. The paladins attempted to extinguish it using their own arcane magic. The charging front erupted in brilliant white light as arcane energy swirled around them, peeling off the black tar. Most paladins rode through, but a few were not so lucky. The tar struck true, burning through the neck of one and killing the rider.

"It burns! It's eating my plate!" were screamed as the tar killed paladins who were unfortunate.

The paladins made quick work of the orcs as the mages launched a cascade of fire and ice from behind, raining down upon them. The elves remained fixed, continuously dropping black fire into the ranks of warriors behind the paladins. As the riders approached the elves, they stepped aside, revealing their champion.

Emerging from the chaos was a towering figure clad in black armor – the Dark Lord's General, an elf of immense power, wielding dual scimitars that crackled with dark energy. The black plate armor shimmered with the appearance of lightning. He towered over the others as he advanced towards the paladins on horseback. He raised his scimitars and lashed out, quickly slashing through the paladins' armor, dropping two who came charging. The others veered off, concerned about this new foe. Roland noticed the new enemy dispatching his comrades with alarming ease. Even their arcane magic failed to save them against his immense dark power. He sliced through the last of them, their bodies falling around him. Laughing, he turned his attention to Roland. "Ah, Roland, the failed paladin. Your powers are weak, old man. I will crush you."

Roland stood before the General of the Dark Lord's armies. "Vorath." He spat on the ground. "I heard he recruited you and twisted you to his will. Pathetic." Roland smashed his sword and shield together and drew a protective sigil in the air. He tapped into the holy arcane and lashed out, then jumped towards Vorath, swinging his sword down.

Their blades met with a thunderous clash, sparks flying as light and darkness collided. Vorath's scimitars moved with lethal grace. Roland parried and countered with precision, each strike imbued with arcane might. Vorath's laughter was cold and mocking. "Is this the best the Light's champion can muster?"

Roland responded with a flurry of attacks, his movements a blur. "The light will always prevail!" He struck with an overhand blow, releasing a wave of searing light. The General hissed, deflecting the attack with a shield of dark energy. Drawing upon the surrounding shadows, he summoned roots of darkness that lashed out at Roland. "Fall to your knees, paladin!"

Roland dodged and weaved, his sword cutting through the tendrils. He grasped the air with his free hand, summoning a sphere of arcane fire that he hurled at the General. "I will never bow," Roland grunted as he continued to call for more power in his attacks.

The blast struck the General, but he quickly shrugged it off, his eyes burning with intense hatred. "Impressive, but futile." He closed the gap with uncanny speed, landing a glancing blow across Roland's chest.

Roland staggered, blood seeping from the wound. He gritted his teeth, refusing to fall. "I will not yield!" he roared, mustering his strength for another attack. Thrain, from behind, chanted a spell to send healing frost toward Roland. "Hold fast, my friend!"

Sensing his moment, the General summoned all his dark power, his scimitars crackling with destructive energy. "This ends now!" He launched into a devastating assault, his blades a blur of lethal strikes. Roland parried desperately, but Vorath's ferocity overwhelmed him. Taking advantage of an opening, Vorath drove a scimitar deep into Roland's abdomen. Roland gasped, his sword and shield falling from his grasp as he collapsed to his knees.

The battlefield seemed to freeze at that moment. Thrain's eyes widened in horror. "Roland, no!"

The General leaned closer, his breath cold and deathly. "And thus, the light fades into darkness," he whispered, withdrawing his blade. Roland fell, his body hitting the ground with a resounding thud. Thrain unleashed a furious storm of ice, driving the General back momentarily. Vorath laughed and walked away, turning his attention to reinforcing the struggling army; he unleashed a brilliant display of black magic, raining down fury upon the remaining dwarves and humans.

The defenders of Kamrar, witnessing their leader's fall, were momentarily shocked. Thrain's tears mingled with the frost on his beard. "For Roland! He shouted for the light!"

Arcane mages and warriors, inspired by Roland's sacrifice, rallied with fierce determination. The clash renewed with greater intensity, driven by the hope that Roland's spirit still watched over them. Thrain stood protectively over Roland's body as the battle waged on, a frosty barrier encasing them both. "The battle is not over, my friend. Your sacrifice will not be in vain," he murmured. Their renewed vigor was not enough. Their lines began to break. Overwhelmed by goblins and elves, the paladins faltered.

The elves amplified the black fire, and Vorath continued to sweep across the lands. The soldiers continued to fall. Roland's lifeless body lay encased in ice as Thrain desperately tried to protect him. An elf walked over and raised his wrist, breaking the ice wall. "Coward," the elf spat.

Thrain raged angrily and lashed out with ice shards, sending them directly at the elf. The elf dissolved into black mist as the shards flew past. He reappeared again, throwing a ball of black magic toward Thrain. Dissolving the blast with ice, he turned and slammed his staff into the ground, sending out a shockwave of ice. The elf was momentarily knocked off his feet and lunged toward Thrain. He was swift with his response, casting another frost blast that hit the elf in the face. The ice finally did its job, driving deep cuts into the elf's flesh. The dark elf staggered back and attempted to recover but tripped and impaled himself on a sword from a fallen enemy. His body sagged after a moment.

Thrain breathed a sigh of relief. He looked out upon the battlefield. Vollrath was off in the distance, slaughtering the remaining warriors. All around him lay the bodies of the fallen, mixed between the Dark Lord's forces and the forces of Light. Thrain sobbed, knowing a fight that should have easily been won was lost. A significant number of their troops were gone. And Vorath and his elves continued westward.

The darkness was overwhelming. Thalin's tune shifted from an upbeat, joy-filled melody to something darker and grittier. It was subtle, but Ordi noticed. He couldn't understand why Thalin's music had changed as the darkness closed in, but the transformation seemed to encourage the encroaching shadows. Then, abruptly, the music stopped. The darkness thickened, swallowing the path and preventing the adventurers from seeing more than a few feet ahead. Ordi lit his staff, casting a soft glow around them.

"Seems unusual, Thalin. Did your playing change the environment?" Ordi asked, his voice tinged with unease.

Taken off guard, Thalin replied, "Me? No! How could I?" His response carried a hint of defensiveness, perhaps even guilt. Though Thalin had stopped playing, the darkness lingered. As they shuffled along, their progress was slow and uncertain; the only sound was the soft crunch of their footsteps as they zigzagged between trees and cliffs.

Ordi turned to Mira, *"Do you sense anything? I feel nothing, and the arcane channel feels off here."*

Mira pricked her ears, straining to catch any sound. *"No, nothing dangerous. What I encountered was closer to the Pass. We have a day's journey, but this darkness is unnerving."* Their footsteps seemed drowned out in the deadly silence that engulfed them. A thick, cold wind blew directly from the west, cutting through their cloaks and chilling them to the bone. The blast lasted only a moment, then silence enveloped them once again. *"Something is brewing, but I do not know what."*

"Let's camp here, though I do not know where 'here' is," Nimue finally said. They halted and began unpacking. Ordi walked over and planted his staff in the middle of the clearing. Its light flared up, revealing their surroundings.

"Glallbi, you and Thrain fetch some firewood. Ordi, do we have any food left? We may need to see what we can gather," Nimue instructed, gathering sticks to start a fire.

"I'll check," Ordi said as he rummaged through the bags.

After a while, everyone returned except Thrain, who had told Glallbi he wanted to search deeper into the forest. Glallbi lit a small torch for each to carry, attempting to penetrate the impenetrable darkness. Ordi found some last pieces of dry meat for their evening dinner. They sat, talking about the oddities of their journey and how evil found them at every turn. Mira still did not tell Ordi what she had encountered as she lay by the campfire and fell asleep for the night. This unsettled him as the conversation continued to reflect on their journey so far.

"I wish we had more time to spend at that altar we discovered in those caverns. What wonders and mysteries could we find? Why is it there, who built it, and how long ago? Glallbi kept talking about the cavern. She desired to visit after this whole mess is over. Her people valued knowledge and found ways to preserve it.

Nimue wanted a moment of silence after Glallbi finished talking. "We do not know much about the Pass of Ferrus, but we know the dragons are unpredictable. They were once great allies, but that was ages ago. I do not know how they will react if they see us. They have secluded themselves from the rest of the world. In many cases, their existence is pure myth, as they have not been seen since the god wars." Nimue took a long drink of water. "Ordi, did you say that Mira encountered the gatekeeper?"

"She did say that. Though, I am not sure what a gatekeeper is."

"The Gatekeeper was the mage entrusted to protect and guard the dragons. They requested a mage to place a barrier around their lands so no one could enter or leave except through him. They say he is ageless, but we think he found ways to prolong his life, or the dragons have bewitched him. The dragons come from a time when magic was much different, wilder, and more powerful than it is today. It is relatively tame and restricted these days. The gatekeeper may have been the last to benefit from such ancient magic." As Nimue spoke, the rain started to sprinkle overhead. The silence of the valley was haunting. Even the rain falling made an eerie sound as it connected with the dirt around them. The rain remained a steady drizzle for the rest of the evening, causing the group to disconnect and turn in for the night. They pitched their tents and proceeded to call it a night.

Morning came with no change to the weather or darkness. They awoke to a steady drizzle of rain in the darkness, which further dampened their mood. Even Thrain failed to uplift them with a tune at breakfast. They packed up, and Ordi, carrying the staff to light the way, proceeded to head westward down the path. The trees reached ominously towards the sky, yet neither sun nor star could be seen—just utter darkness. "Ordi, this is not natural," Verdun said as he came alongside him.

"I know. Something more significant is happening than mere darkness in this valley. My gut tells me Xerxes is on the move. We do not have time to waste, though I feel a great tragedy is about to befall our lands."

Verdun said no more. They kept walking through the morning. The silence weighed heavily again, each footfall dampened by the atmosphere. As the day wore on, it became difficult to tell the passage of time. The path below turned to rock, and the trees began to thin out. The ground started sloping upwards. The valley was ending, and the Pass of Ferrus was nearing. As they ascended, the darkness began to lift as the grayness of day broke through. Within a few minutes, the darkness gave way to a cloudy, cool day. Ordi looked back down the path and saw no shadow or darkness; the valley looked pleasant and peaceful. He could hear birds chirping as the valley appeared alive, causing him to wonder what they had just experienced. He extinguished his staff's light as they continued through the rocky terrain. They finally approached the Pass. The Peaks towered high, providing a gap large enough for the party of five to pass side by side, with Mira in the front. The ground leveled out, stretching forth into the land beyond. At the end of the plateau sat a large hut with smoke rising from the chimney.

"I believe this is what we are looking for," Ordi said, pointing towards the hut. The brotherhood moved forward cautiously, unaware of what awaited them inside. They reached the door, which had a large metal knocker in the middle. Ordi reached up, grabbed it, and dropped it hard against the door. No response and no noise could be heard from within. They waited a moment, and Ordi knocked again. Still, no answer.

"Maybe no one is home?" Thalin said half-jokingly. They hesitated, not knowing what to do next. For a third time, Ordi knocked. Finally, movement was heard inside the hut—a shuffling towards the door, accompanied by a groggy voice coming from within.

"What do you want?"

"We are here to speak to the dragons," Ordi called out.

Silence awaited them once again. Minutes passed as they waited outside. Finally, the door unlocked, and there stood an ancient wizard. His skin was wrinkled, and his hair was white as snow. He wore old, ragged robes that were torn and hung off his frail body. "You folk have come to the wrong place," he finally said as he considered the group before him.

Chapter 13 The Dragons

Ordi stood shocked by what this frail man was saying.

"Turn back now. It would be best if you were not here," he repeated. "Why did you come to bother me? What could you possibly want?" He stopped ranting when he noticed Glallbi standing in the back of the group. "A Gnome? Why?" His tone changed abruptly from a warning to deep-seated curiosity.

Glallbi, trembling with fear, said, "I...uh…sorry, master mage."

She was cut off: "Gnomes are not allowed to talk to me," the old man barked.

Nimue spoke up, "She is a companion who has come to assist us on our quest. Sir, I beg your pardon. We are unsure of your name. We have heard of the legends but nothing further. I am Nimue, a Druid from Greenhills. Our leader, Ordi, is a master mage. His brother Verdun, a warrior, and our newest companion, Thrain, a bard, joined us as we left the Gnomes." Nimue bowed low as he greeted the Gatekeeper.

Hesitation crossed over the old man's face—uncertainty showed upon the weary travelers. After a moment, he spoke again, "I am Arcadius Shadowmend. I am known as the Gatekeeper. The Council of Mages appointed me over a century ago. I have been the protector of the dragons since." As he spoke, his figure appeared to fill out, as if life returned to his body. The holes in his robes fixed themselves, and his messy hair straightened, appearing smooth and kept. "Why do you travel to these lands? They are forsaken. The dragons want nothing to do with the world; they have retreated to live their days alone and unbothered," he continued.

"Lord Arcadius, if I may?" Ordi started. Arcadius nodded. "We have an urgent quest that led us here. I can provide some elements, but Glallbi is far more knowledgeable about the situation and the urgency behind our quest."

"Pah, she disgusts me. I do not care to hear the lies of the Gnomes," Arcadius said.

When talked about, Glallbi wanted to disappear; she did not like confrontation. She could solve her problems through conversations or fireballs. Facing the age-old hatred of the ancient mages was painful. She had only read stories of the problems her elders dealt with when the mages were in power. "I understand your issue, my Lord, but the times of both our people are long past. We do not have time to waste over petty arguments."

The elder mage's face dissolved of emotion. "Yes, you are right. My apologies. It has been over 1,000 years since I have spoken to Gnomes. Please tell me of your quest."

With that, Glallbi did what she did best: discuss history. "I am sure you know of the Otthroite gems, which are what we seek. The gnomes have long foreseen the day when they will be needed again. Our only mishap is that we cannot trace them. The elves have some knowledge, but even they fail to know the depths of the gems' journey. When we heard of Ordi and Nimue's quest, I offered my assistance to join them, and we have since journeyed this far north. After some time, we are here with you, my Lord." Nimue and Ordi filled in the earlier parts of the quest, finally giving the ancient mage the whole picture.

He did not seem shocked by the story. "Yes, I gathered it would be only a matter of time before someone came looking for those pesky things. We hated them; they were always a burden to equip someone's armor, and many abused and broke them for personal power. The gems were not well-liked in my time. Why are you so desperately seeking them now?" he asked.

"We

"We were told they would assist us in our battle against Xerxes, that we could use them to enhance our arcane magic," Ordi spoke as he stumbled over his words. Usually, he could be assertive, but now he could not think of a definite reason to chase down the gems.

"Bah…" Arcadius spat. "Those gems are cursed. I do not know who put you up to this ridiculous quest."

"It was brought to our attention by Nimue," Ordi continued. "We have always heard of them, but there is little information on how they could help us. The stories say that the one who uses a gem will gain additional powers and be able to connect to the arcane channels, unlike those without the gems."

"Yes, they do that. But the gems can be dangerous in the wrong hands. Those of us on the council of mages were not in support. We saw the raw power they brought and how they could corrupt wizards. We placed restrictions on them and closely watched who had them and how they were used," Arcadius replied.

"We could use all the help we can get against Xerxes," Verdun said, speaking for the first time.

"Who's Xerxes?" Arcadius asked. "Never mind… I am sure he is another corrupt wizard. We dealt with enough of those in my day. You'll have to pardon me. I have not spoken to anyone in so long."

"Xerxes is the Dark Lord. He was corrupted over 500 years ago, and we thought he died in battle then. Rumor has it that he is back, brought forth from the dead by dark magic," Nimue said.

Arcadius chuckled, "Oh, if you had been around during my time. We fought against so many dark wizards and evil. It would seem that about every year, someone would try to overthrow the council of mages."

Unsettled, Ordi asked, "Why so much evil?"

"The gems, of course!" Arcadius said sharply. "Bah. I think your mission is foolish. But either way, if you want to speak with the dragons, you must pass a trial. This was set forth long ago, and no one has ever attempted it. This trial is the Guardian Monolith. It would be best if you faced this challenge collectively. You will either pass as a team or fail as a team. This determines if you are worthy to speak with the dragons. Each of you will be tested and pushed both mentally and physically." He waved his wand, and a portal appeared before them. "Enter the portal. When you complete the task, you will be brought back here."

Each member of the Brotherhood stepped into the portal, teleporting into a new realm. The environment changed from a rocky mountain pass to a dense ancient forest. The trees were thick and full of magic, towering over them. A path lay before them, the task ahead unknown. Ordi led the way down the path, and it was not long before the trees gave way to a vast stone archway covered with luminescent vines. As they approached, they noticed a pulsating ethereal energy coming from the archway's center. They approached cautiously as the weight of centuries-old magic pressed upon them.

"This is the Monolith. From here, do we wait or walk through?" Ordi asked. Mira walked closely to Ordi and responded to his question.

"We walk through."

"Mira says to go through." Ordi took the first step, but it wasn't a portal. It was merely the entrance to the trial. The ancient forest appeared thicker on the other side. The dry and dusty ground began to shift and give off a dark, swirling mist. The mist was thick and alive, pulling each member away onto their isolated path. Ordi found himself alone with Mira in a narrow corridor, the darkness creeping around him. He illuminated his staff. The light flickered as it struggled against an unseen force. Mira paced back and forth, trying to discern if something was approaching them.

"Darkness moves. Something approaches. Why is it always darkness?" Mira asked.

"Good question, I wish it weren't," Ordi replied.

A shadowy figure emerged, mocking whispers filling the air. "You can't protect them," it hissed. Mira buried her head in her paws at the sound. "Your decisions will lead them to ruin," it continued to taunt. Images of Ordi's past failures and potential future disasters appeared before him. As the images flashed by, each more horrifying than the last, Ordi's heart pounded faster.

Ordi tightened his grip on his staff. "I have failed many times. I have won many times. My success is not dependent on my past failures, but on whether or not I get back up." As he spoke, Mira drew upon the arcane channel and pushed it toward Ordi for strength. The shadows darkened and shifted, revealing more images of destruction and ruin. A world laid to waste, as if this were reality and not a possibility. As the images continued, those he loved were shown spread out on the ground, unmoving, as goblins and orcs ransacked towns and villages. Death and fire lay before Ordi.

"Do you see what I have caused? It has already begun. Death will sweep the lands, and your pathetic attempts to save the world will fail. I have the power of gods on my side. You are a weak mage. You and your little pet will die at my hands." Mira was helpless. She could hear the voice and see the shadow, but could not figure out where she might land a strike. She tried connecting to Ordi, but that was even more difficult with the immense darkness swirling around them.

"Enough! I will not fail my companions." He smashed his staff into the ground, casting an incredibly bright arcane light that swallowed the darkness. Mira smiled as she watched the shadows retreat.

Ordi and Mira passed the test.

Nimue stood among a thick jungle patch, shooting vines in every direction. Alive and mischievous, they lashed out to cut and tear at his skin. From the vines, a dark shadowy figure emerged. Taunting him, the figure said, "Nimue, the last of a broken house. You will fail your companions just as you have failed your people." The vines crept in as he spoke, wrapping themselves around Nimue, restricting and confining him.

Pain swept through his body as the vines tightened around him. Thorns sprouted, piercing his flesh. "My people died because they broke their vows to the gods. I did not fail them. I kept my vow to serve until my last breath." Air escaped his lungs as the vines closed tighter. "I…will…not…break…"

He reached deep into the earth, healing the tormented vines and soothing their anguish. Suddenly, the vine's pressure lessened. They released their grip and freed Nimue.

Nimue passed his test.

Verdun found himself in a stone arena. He was clad in full plate armor and wielding a two-handed battle axe. Towering over him was a beast unlike anything he had faced before. The beast growled at him, "Verdun, you have failed to protect your companions. Your failure will result in death for everyone."

"I will fight to the death to defend the people of Asheros!" Verdun yelled as he charged the beast. He swung the axe high in the air, but the beast blocked the incoming strike. The creature raised its left arm and swiped down, crashing into Verdun. His body crumbled to the earth. He regained his composure, struggling to stand after the massive blow. He swung his axe back and forth to fix his grip. Instead of charging again, he waited for the next blow to come. He blocked with the blade of his axe and forced it upwards, slicing the arm of the beast off.

The beast roared with pain and anger and charged Verdun once again. With the axe weighing heavy in his hands, Verdun lunged at the creature's knees, embedding the axe into the left knee, slicking through, and bringing the beast down. He stood victorious as he swung the axe down on the neck, slicing deep and killing the beast.

Verdun passed his test.

Glallbi was alone in a dark room. The air was dusty, and ageless silt covered the tables. On the opposite side of the room was a single bookshelf with one book. Only a sliver of light came through a broken window, yet Glallbi could not determine where or when she was. An empty room with one book; was it based on intelligence? Or was this a test of arrogance? Unsure of what she would face, she walked over to the shelf and carefully picked up the book.

Healing for Beginning Mages: A Lost Art

The title was unusual, as healing was not considered a focus for mages, and Glallbi recalled no records of mages having the ability to heal. She opened the book and thumbed through the frail pages. Written on old parchment, the ancient pages cracked and broke as she turned them. Trying to be delicate, she read the spells and attempted to understand how they could be practical.

As she finished the spell on healing broken bones, a white mist pulled off the pages and swirled into a great shape before her. Materializing before her was an old female apparition, shorter than she and from a time long forgotten. "Oh, I see you have found my book, dear," she spoke. "My name is Gladius. How may I help you?"

Glallbi froze for a few moments, trying to decipher what was happening. "I…uh…don't know." She was struggling to comprehend the spirit before her. "I have so many questions. Am I limited in time or questions?"

"Time? Time does not affect the dead, young lady. You may converse with me for as long as you wish. But remember, the more time you spend here, the more risk you place upon your companions. So I advise you to use your time wisely," Gladius replied.

"OK, first, how can you talk to me? You are dead! The dead are not known to speak with the living," Glallbi was trying to find the right way to phrase her question.

Chuckling, Gladius said, "Oh dear. You have so much to learn. First, let me say this: Your companions will be faced with unimaginable evil in the months to come. They will be tested from outside the group as well as from within. The world is breaking, and you four—five if you include Mira—are the only hope to save it. The gems are important, but each will find their strength, or they will break. You, Glallbi, are unbalanced."

"How do you know my name?" Glallbi interrupted.

"I know much about you. You are a weak fire mage, so you were brought here. Each challenge is designed to push the person to their breaking point, but we felt it was better for you to change your path entirely. The book that you hold is your key now. We are stripping you of your destructive arcane powers and rebuilding you with a power that has not been seen in this world in over 1000 years. You, Glallbi, will be able to heal your companions. You can enchant them with spells to enhance them before battle, and while they fight, you will channel to them and boost their health and agility, keeping them fighting for longer. But be wary; this will wear on you, and you'll need to rest and drink water often."

"So, I have to learn how to heal?"

"Oh no, dear. When you leave here, it will already be imprinted into your soul. Just like using fire, you'll wield light as the Paladins do, but you'll use it for others while they use it for themselves. It will feel natural in some respects, but we want you to take this book and continue to read and explore the depths of your new power." As she spoke, her apparition became fainter, slowly fading into the darkness. "Before I go, beware of the one who claims to care." With that warning, she was gone. Glallbi was alone in the dark room again.

Glallbi passed the test.

Thalin awoke in a vast, empty grassy field that stretched for eternity. "Hello!" he shouted, but there was no answer; not even the wind responded. The sky overhead was a dark grey, hovering on the brink of a late-evening storm that never seemed to come. Thalin knew a basic amount of magic, but his true talent was music. He found great passion in playing and entertaining people. He could influence emotions around him simply by playing and channeling some magic. Standing alone in the field, he did not know what trial he would face or what to do to prove his worth.

He waited for hours, alternating between playing and listening. The blades of tall grass stood still as the clouds above slowly crept by. After a short song, he looked up and noticed a figure in the distance approaching him. Tall and dark, the figure glided towards Thalin. "Hello, Thalin, bard. I have been watching you and waiting for this opportunity," the figure said.

"Who are you?"

"It is irrelevant who I am at the moment. What is relevant is the task you have been created to perform. See, Thalin, we all have a purpose in this life. You will soon discover why you were made. I tell you this not as a suggestion but primarily to make you aware. You will betray your companions, and you will kill Ordi. That is your duty." The figure spoke with such harshness that Thalin was taken aback. Betray? Kill?

How could this be, he thought. "Why are you telling me this?"

"Oh, the gatekeeper had some pathetic little trial to test your will, but I wanted to come and break you. Before it was completed, I intercepted this trial personally and ensured my spirit was here to speak with you. Was it odd that nothing happened? No wind, no people, nothing. You waited for me," he laughed. "As I said, you will kill Ordi. That is your purpose. That is why I made you." He laughed again.

"Made me? Are you a god?"

"You could say something like that. I have power over life, death, and some types of people made in this world. When you complete the task, come to Ashton, and you'll learn more. Do not speak of this; you will not remember much of it by design." The figure turned and glided away.

Thalin passed the test.

The group met once again on the plateau before the Gatekeeper. Arcadius smiled as he saw the adventurers before him. "You have been tested on various attributes and strengths. I hope you have been changed for the better. But before you move on, you must face one more challenge. This quest may not be something you would expect, and it may appear simple on the surface, but deep down, if done correctly, it will bind you more than anything battle will." With that, he disappeared again, and the Brotherhood found themselves in a dark underground cavern.

"Just like home!" Verdun chirped as they started down the corridor. They quickly found themselves in an immense chamber with a massive forge at the center. The anvils were aglow with molten metals, and the gears were churning with use. The air was heavy with the heat of the lava and the rhythmic pounding of the forge. Before them stood an immense spirit.

In a booming voice, he said, "I am Morgrim. I am the worker of this forge, tasked with challenging those seeking unity and fellowship. You have been brought here for one final task. You will forge an artifact that will embody your combined strengths. When the task is completed successfully, I will duplicate the artifact so each member has their own. You will be tested in teamwork, trust, and fortitude. You may begin."

Nimue gathered them around. "We each have a unique talent that we will need to use here. I can use my elemental connections on the crystals, but we'll need more mined. Verdun and Ordi, you can handle that. Thalin, you'll need to play everything you can so we can find the right frequency for the crystals to light up and ensure they are bound properly. Glallbi, can you heat the crystals to initiate the binding?"

Glallbi hesitated momentarily. "My fire was removed; they changed my entire ability to use arcane magic. I heal now." Silence befell the group. "Ordi can heat them, but I need to find a role to play."

Nimue pondered for a while, trying to move the puzzle pieces around. Ordi spoke up, "Glallbi, you can heal? How?"

"The vision in my trial was slightly detailed, telling me I needed to change. It is my destiny to be the one that keeps this group alive. I have this book." She held up a dusty old tome. "I think I can find some work from an alchemy perspective. I know how to mix some potions. This room is laid out for a purpose with everything we have. I don't think it's just binding some crystals together. We have more here that we must consider. Let us gather our pieces and see how this puzzle works."

"Good. We will play a role. Let us get to work," Ordi said. The party broke up, each to their tasks. Verdun and Ordi walked over, picked up the axes, and chipped away at the rock. "Wow, this is a hard surface. It may take a while," Ordi said. He took another swing, and the pick hit the rock with a loud bang, but nothing chipped off. Verdun and Ordi continued to strike the wall.

Thalin played scales on his flute, trying to find the pitch or range that would be perfect for lighting up the crystals. These rocks were unique and required different elements to activate their essence. Alchemy primarily used them to store potions and bind elements together. They were less potent than Otthroite Gems, making them less valuable but more common, as they were plentiful worldwide. The Brotherhood was familiar with them, knowing the essential elements and how they worked together. Glallbi started to gather the herbs and minerals crucial to the process, sorting through and picking out the good from the bad. She discarded what would not be used and kept what she wanted, sorting the herbs by type to ensure she could hand them to Ordi and Nimue when needed.

Thalin continued playing. While it pleased the group as they worked, it was frustrating for him as the correct notes continued to elude him. The swings from Ordi and Verdun continued while Nimue sorted through the gems. Mira found herself bored, walked over to Ordi, and rested. "Don't swing so hard. You are wasting your strength. Swing gently; that is the trick to the puzzle. You'll find greater rewards."

Ordi heard Mira and stepped back. Wiping the sweat off his brow, he swung gently and noticed a massive chunk knock itself off the wall. Astonished, he made a few more swings, and the rocks broke apart. Verdun mimicked the softer swings. They had knocked off a good amount of rock and started sorting through, looking for crystals that might have fallen with it.

As the group gathered the materials, Thalin focused on the range of notes that might bind the material together and finally found the correct range. Playing through a handful of notes, the crystals lit up brilliantly as they harmonized. Now that Thalin had completed his task, it was time to combine the elements and channel the power through the crystal. They each poured a part of themselves into retrieving and preparing the artifact.

They carried the components to the great forge while Morgrim watched silently. Nimue started to infuse elemental essences into the materials, his hands glowing with power. Thalin played a specific melody, orchestrating the materials' energies. Ordi stood at the center, casting protective spells and stabilizing the process. He began the binding process by gently heating the crystals before placing them in the forge. Glallbi ensured the correct alchemical reactions took place, her knowledge guiding each step. Verdun operated the giant bellows, controlling the temperatures with precision.

"Careful with this essence, Nimue," Glallbi instructed, "It is quite unstable."

Verdun strained his muscles as he worked the bellows, the forge's heat intense. "Keep the rhythm, Thalin," he called out, sweat pouring down his face. Thalin responded with a lively, rhythmic tune, his music providing a steady beat. Everyone was tired from the heat pressing in, the delicate process of adding so much to the crystals was straining them.

Ordi's spellcasting surrounded everyone, and white and red sparks flashed through the crystals. Nimue kept honing in on the binding process. "I think we're almost there now," Ordi exclaimed as Mira poured more strength into him. The group worked together perfectly, each adding parts of themselves to the artifact to ensure the task was completed correctly. As the pieces came together, Thalin stumbled, his flute interrupted by a cough. He dropped it to the ground and fell, clutching his throat.

"Water," he sputtered.

Mira raced to grab a water flask and brought it to Ordi. He withdrew the flask and placed it at Thalin's mouth. Coughing through the drops of water, Thalin finally managed to drink some before passing out. The heat of the furnace had overwhelmed him. Morgrim stood silent, watching as Glallbi started casting arcane light spells. The movements and spells came naturally. Each spell was more brilliant as the light pulsated from her hands into Thalin's body.

Ordi rolled him onto his back and propped his head up using his pack. The light in the crystals dimmed and finally extinguished. The music had ceased, causing the binding to pause.

"What do we do now?" Verdun asked.

"We wait for him to recover. It appears he has heat exhaustion," Glallbi said. "Morgrim, what can we do next?"

Silence. Morgrim said nothing and did not flinch at the question. Instead, he stood watching, waiting for the group to finish their task. Ordi fanned Thalin while he lay sprawled on the floor. The group sat for a long while before anyone spoke. "How long will he be out?" Verdun asked.

After a few minutes, Thalin stirred, coughing and sputtering, and sat up. He wiped the sweat off his face and groaned. "What a trip! How long was I out? All I remember is getting hot and then blackness."

"By my estimations, you were unconscious for a brief moment. The stones have grown cold now. We need you to start playing and Ordi to reignite them before placing them back in the forge," Nimue stated.

After a few more minutes, Thalin regained his strength. The group got back to work. Thalin played while Ordi continued to produce magic to heat the stones. Nimue performed the bonding of the elements. Verdun continued to fan the flames of the forge, all in perfect sync with each other. A short time later, the crystals were complete. They glowed with a brilliant snowy blue, powered by each person's essence. Each contributed to the work: Verdun's strength, Ordi's fortitude, Nimue's elemental embrace, Glallbi with her knowledge, and Mira with her ancient connection to arcane magic. Each contribution would make this crystal a binding agent for the group, ensuring they would uphold their oaths. As they marveled at the blue mist, they failed to see the black streak swirling in the middle.

They brought the crystal to Morgrim and handed it to him. "We have completed the task," Ordi said.

He took the crystal and examined it. He flipped it over in his hands, looking at every angle. Each time he moved it, the thin black mist was elusive, making him think he saw something odd. "You have poured yourselves into this. You are successful." He walked over to his table and set down the crystal. He raised his hands, and a booming sound rattled the caverns. He grabbed a set of crystals and handed each person one identical to the original. "Keep these close. They are special and will assist you before the end."

With that, the brotherhood returned to before Arcadius. "Well done, travelers. You have completed all my tasks successfully. Let me lead you to the dragons. They are an ancient race, and only a few are left. They prefer to live their days unbothered, and the older ones rarely come out anymore." He sighed. "They used to rule the land, swooping in to assist us when we desperately needed them. Then, one day, they decided their time was over. They fled north and requested a mage to ensure trouble stayed away. They have not spoken to anyone since. Follow me."

Arcadius led them down a rocky path toward a rock wall. As they approached the smooth face of the mountain, he waved his hand over the surface, and a doorway appeared. He beckoned the brotherhood to follow him as he stepped into it.

It was a completely different world on the other side of the door. The ground was scorched red from the ash of volcanoes in the distance, and the air was thick with brimstone, creating a hazy appearance for the travelers. Ordi marveled at this world that had been sealed up for so long. Before them was a vast plateau with mountains peeking up throughout the land. A river could be seen at the bottom of the path before them. Miles off to the northwest, a dragon could be seen flying toward them while another circled on the peaks.

Arcadius waved for the dragon to come before them, and after a few moments, it descended, landing before Arcadius and bowing its head in respect. Typhomir stood as a testament to the primal power of ancient dragons, his presence commanding both respect and fear among all who beheld him. His sinewy form stretched to a formidable length of about thirty-five feet, every inch of his body exuding strength and raw ferocity. His scales, the color of molten lava, shifted from deep crimson to burning ember hues, shimmering like hot coals in dim light.

His eyes were slits of pure molten gold, smoking with an inner fire that betrayed his ancient wisdom and cunning. Each of his four limbs ended in deadly, razor-sharp talons capable of tearing through the most formidable armor. Though not vast, his wings were broad and robust, their membranes streaked with dark veins and glowing faintly at the edges with the same fiery hue as his scales. Typhomir's head was crowned with imposing, backward-curving horns, their blackened tips starkly contrasting with his vibrant body. A fanged maw stretched across his face, capable of a terrifyingly wide grin, revealing rows of serrated teeth glistening with anticipation.

A thicker, almost armor-like layer of scales protected his chest and underbelly, each interlocking perfectly to shield vital areas. His long, whip-like tail tapered to a jagged, spiked tip, ready to lash out with bone-cracking force. Typhomir exuded heat, and the air around him seemed to waver and distort, as if standing too close to a roaring bonfire. When he spoke, his voice was a rumbling, deep, and resonant inferno, carrying the promise of ancient knowledge and unyielding tyranny. "Why have you crossed the barrier, Arcadius? We do not wish to speak with outsiders." Typhomir was dreadful and appeared to be building up wrath against the group standing before him.

Despite his size, Typhomir's movements are fluid and graceful, each step calculated and deliberate, like a coiled spring ready to unleash its stored energy. His very presence reminds the people that power need not be colossal to be utterly terrifying.

"In all my time serving the dragons, none have dared to bother you. These adventurers seek your counsel and assistance. They say evil is mounting in the world and seek the lost gems," Arcadius replied, not intimidated by the dragon.

Snorting, "Gems, eh?" Typhomir looked at each of them individually, daring any of them to flinch. "Why the gems?

We know where they are. We are sworn to protect that secret; obviously, it has been lost to you folk." He hissed the last sentence. "I care not about dealing with the world. The elder dragons care even less." He started turning to leave.

"Wait!" Ordi shouted. "I know we are ants to you, and what happens in the South is of no consequence to you, but the power that Xerxes has could spill into your lands, slaughtering everything."

The dragon laughed. "You think we fear some petty mortals?"

"Not any human, but one said to have risen from the dead—a great sorcerer. He commands legions of troops and seeks to destroy everything. He is bent on conquest, wielding great magic the likes of which we have never witnessed." Nimue tried to soothe the dragon. "We know that the dragons have no desire to help, and we are not here asking for it. We want to know where the gems were moved. Our records have been destroyed over the years."

The dragon swooped into the air and landed again with a loud crash. The impact sent rocks and dust into the air, forcing the brotherhood to cough. Arcadius looked on without flinching. The dragon took off again and flew off into the distance, landing by a tree.

The Flameward Tree stands as a natural wonder. Its fiery red canopy blazes brilliantly against the sky, giving the illusion of perpetual flames dancing at its peak. Despite its vibrant and fiery appearance, the tree is impervious to the destructive force of fire. The underside of its leaves, contrasting sharply, is a dark charred hue as if ancient embers have burnished it. The trunk is thick and robust, covered in bark with an intricate pattern resembling cooled lava—smooth yet rugged. Its roots spread deep and wide, drawing strength from the earth and anchoring it firmly in place. Mystics say it draws on the elemental energies of fire and earth, making it both a guardian and a symbol of indestructibility in the forest. The tree produced a scroll, which Typhomir took and read. He flew back high and landed with a loud thud, sending more dust and debris into the air.

"Fine. I can show you where they are if you think the trials Arcadius sent you through were nothing. I know what guards the gems." He snorted again, smoke pouring out of his nose. "I will tell you, but we want nothing to do with that evil."

"My Lord," Verdun said. "We have come a long distance and have traversed the land to speak with you. We know the evils of this world and will fight whatever we have to retrieve the gems."

Typhomir laughed again. "You can't kill that which is already dead."

Chapter 14 Caverns of Unrar

Typhomir's laughter echoed throughout the land as he soared into the air. It seemed like he would fly away and abandon them for a while. His words rang in the adventurers' ears, *"You can't kill that which is already dead."* After he spoke, he flew up into the sky and appeared to have abandoned them. Arcadius scowled at the dragon as he flew away. "Damn, dragons are good for nothing. I've been protecting them for a century, and they can't return a single favor." As he finished, he turned, raised his staff, and sent a massive fireball after the dragon. The ball dissolved before it reached Typhomir, but he saw the angry wizard's attempt. He swooped back around and came hurtling towards the group tremendously fast.

He hovered just above Arcadius, his chest glowing a fiery red as he gathered his power. A torrent of fire and smoke erupted from him, aimed at Arcadius, who swiftly raised a shield to deflect the attack. The shield held, but the heat was so intense that everyone except Arcadius was forced to step back. Arcadius retaliated with a brilliant white blast from his staff, but the dragon's thick armor absorbed the attack.

Before a second blast could be unleashed, Typhomir dropped to the ground, his laughter echoing in the cavern. "Oh, Arcadius, you old fool. You love to put on a show. But I am old, and I do not have the strength to rattle these newcomers." The dragon's laughter was so thunderous that it left the Brotherhood bewildered. Just moments ago, he had promised to talk to them, and now he was trying to provoke a fight with the wizard. Ordi couldn't help but wonder what was going on.

"What are you going on about, dragon?" Ordi demanded.

"Master dwarf," bellowed Typhomir, "You have no right to speak to a dragon like that. But if you must know, Arcadius and I never get travelers here anymore; I think it has been almost 900 years since the last person visited." He lowered himself to his belly and placed his head level with the group. "We get bored out here, and there is only so much we can do to stay active. Flying, sure, but we rarely have to spew fire anymore."

"What can you tell us about the gems?" Nimue asked. Ordi nudged him hard at the question. "What?" he demanded.

"Oh right, the gems. You small folk are impatient." He hesitated for a moment. "Yes, the gems. Well, I do not know, honestly. They say the gems were taken to Unrar to be kept there. But I believe the dwarves abandoned that place, correct?" Typhomir continued.

"We have not been there in ages," Verdun confirmed.

"Now there lies the problem. The gems could still be there, locked deep within the mountain, or they could have been taken elsewhere. We were entrusted with keeping them safe, and at the time, Unrar was the best fortress in the land. We held them here for a while, but dragons are not good guardians of precious items. We tend to be greedy and hoard them away, letting them get lost among our treasures. We kept the gems here for a long time, but the dwarves came and had them moved again and mentioned Unrar," Typhomir continued to explain.

They exchanged confused looks. "It seems like no one knows where the gems reside. We've been chasing these things for weeks, and it seems the goal keeps moving away from us. I feel our entire journey has been a waste of time," Verdun whined.

"Waste? No, Master Dwarf. Not a waste, at least not in my eyes. If done correctly, the gems may be helpful, but your task is beyond the mere gems now. You are out to uncover the ancient magic of the gods. That is the true purpose of seeking the gems. That is why you came to inquire from us. We know some of these magical strains and have an assortment of scrolls that can help you uncover more spells from ages past. We may be limited in number, the Elder Drakes; we no longer mingle with the blue or black drakes. They are wilder, more vicious, and more challenging to communicate with. The red or fire drakes, or whatever you want to call us, are more concerned with preserving history and knowledge. The other dragons only care for themselves. They are younger than us and do not know the ancient times as we do." He stood up. "Follow me. I will show you the scrolls. We can discuss the gems more." He walked away as the ground thundered with each step, and his eyes, gleaming with fiery wisdom, invited them to follow and learn.

Everyone followed the massive dragon as he stormed away. His pace was quicker than the rest, but he always stayed within a reasonable distance. The twilight sky began to burn a deep orange as the setting sun cast long shadows over the rugged landscape. Verdun leaned over to Ordi and whispered, "Do you trust this dragon?"

Mira followed behind Ordi. He responded, "I do not think we have a choice. He seems to be a little absent-minded or just plain bored. I do not know what dragons do all day."

Mira perked up at what Ordi said. *"Dragons tend to sleep a lot. They rarely come out unless it is to hunt, maybe once or twice a year."*

"Interesting. Never thought of that," Ordi replied to Mira. "Mira says they generally sleep. Beyond that, it's hard to say. Either way, we have come this far. We need to figure out where to go next." They traveled for a short while before coming to a river and a large hall built into a stone wall.

"Welcome to Eldraenor. The library of the world. Centuries ago, this was a great city that housed all the information regarding magic and the world. They say the gods would even come to dwell here for periods. But it has fallen vacant; no one comes to visit anymore. I don't even think people remember it is here." He stopped speaking and sat back on his hind legs. He shouted something in the dragon's tongue.

Typhomir's enormous form began to shimmer and shift. The air around him crackled with raw magic. His scales seemed to melt into his body, their fiery hue fading into a deep, rich tan. Within moments, he stood before the adventurers not as a dragon but as a tall, powerful-looking human. He towered over the rest as he walked towards them. His skin had a faint, almost imperceptible glow, hinting at the fiery essence still burning within him. His hair, a cascade of dark auburn locks streaked with glimmers of gold and ember, fell just past his broad shoulders, giving him a wild, regal appearance. Typhomir's eyes remained unchanged, the same molten gold burning with intense wisdom and ancient knowledge.

When he looked at you, it felt like he could see straight into your soul, assessing, understanding, and commanding all at once. His features were chiseled and sharp, with high cheekbones and a strong jawline, radiating an aura of indomitable will. His nose was straight, and his lips, although capable of curving into a warm yet intimidating smile, often rested in a thoughtful, almost brooding line. Dressed in simple yet finely crafted clothing befitting an enigmatic traveler, Typhomir wore a dark leather tunic with intricate dragon-scale patterns embossed into the fabric. His trousers were made of the same material, sturdy but flexible, allowing for fluid movement. Across his shoulders, he draped a cloak of deep crimson, the same shade as his dragon scales, its edges embroidered with ancient runes that seemed to shimmer in the light.

Nothing could have prepared them for this transformation. The party stood mesmerized. When Typhomir spoke, his voice was a melodic blend of deep, resonant tones, somehow carrying the strength of a roar within a gentle human cadence. "You act like you have never seen a dragon transfigure before. How else do you think we can enter buildings like this?" He laughed with the same deep, bellowing sound as when he was a dragon. "Follow me."

He pushed on the large stone doors and entered the old, dark building. The chamber was bathed in a dim, eerie glow from crystals embedded in the walls. Ancient scrolls and tomes filled the towering shelves, the air thick with the scent of parchment and mystery.

Nimue's breath caught in her throat, "This place is incredible."

Typhomir turned his head. "Legends speak of powerful magics hidden in this library. Some say the magic could even summon the gods of old. But I have no idea about that; I rarely visit this place myself as I have little need for the spells here. Be my guest and seek out what you need for the journey ahead." He blew into his hand and cast it out into the room, lighting the torches that spanned the massive library.

The group fanned out and started to examine the scrolls. Glallbi was drawn to a dark recess of the room. The scrolls here were covered in thick layers of dust from centuries of neglect. She delicately picked up a scroll, its edges brittle with age. Unrolling it carefully, she caught glimpses of incantations and symbols that were unfamiliar yet tantalizing. The scroll held spells for levitating and moving objects simply by a wrist flick.

The scrolls contained spells that did not require wands or staffs, which was unconventional for mages. It was almost as if the magic was controlled solely by the wizard. She found more scrolls on elemental magic and many other topics, such as how to conjure food and water. She was stunned by the vast wealth of knowledge and thought she could spend years here.

Ordi and Verdun walked down the center aisle, looking up and down the shelves. There appeared to be an order to the scrolls, but it was not by magic types as one would expect. They were arranged from the most accessible and straightforward to perform to the more complex magic at the back of the library. "Typhomir, can we take any of these scrolls? What would we possibly need?" Ordi asked.

"I don't see a problem with that," came Typhomir's deep voice from the front. "There are leather bags on the back table you can use."

Ordi and Verdun began to grab scrolls and quickly read through them. He opened one: *"How to Talk to Animals."* He put it back gently and continued to open the scrolls. So far, nothing exciting had caught his attention. He reached up and grabbed another dusty scroll: *"How to Speak to the Dead."* "Hey, Verdun, look at this one."

"How to Speak to the Dead? That's a creepy title." Verdun grabbed another: *"How to Tame a Werewolf."* "These are unusual spells." They kept looking, pulling one after another off the shelves and placing them back. They moved toward the back and saw the table that Typhomir had described earlier. But the hall stretched on. It would take them hours or days to find anything remotely close to what they wanted.

"Verdun, let's split up." Ordi and Mira moved further down while Verdun explored the immediate shelves.

"Ordi, I sense a set of scrolls near this far wall that may contain something similar to what we are looking for." Mira pointed with her dark paw.

"I sense that too," Ordi said as they moved towards the corner Mira had pointed out. He reached up and grabbed one from the top shelf. He opened it: *"How to infuse gems."* He grabbed another: *"How to bond souls and gems."* The more he took from these shelves, the more spells and information he found on the gems. "I think we found what we need, Mira;

these are exactly what we're looking for." He placed an assortment of scrolls into the leather bag and met back up with Verdun.

Thalin continued to work through scrolls related to music. He found one entitled *"How to anesthetize someone with a flute."* He hesitated, then decided to pocket it. *"This one could come in handy later,"* he thought. The rest of the group was gathering where Arcadius and Typhomir were talking. Thalin was the last to join them. He had no idea why he felt compelled to take the scroll, but something in his mind urged him to do so.

"Master Ordi," Typhomir started, "Did you find what you were seeking?"

"I believe so. We found a good deal regarding the gems and other spells I've never heard of before."

"Good. We must be on our way. I can only hold this form briefly." The party left the library and stepped back into the fresh air. The evening was setting in, and they quickly realized how tired they were.

Arcadius waved his hands. "I think it's growing late, and we do not need to travel further tonight." As he spoke, he waved his wand, and tents appeared. "Let us retire for the night. It would be best for us to rest before tomorrow comes."

The brotherhood agreed and started to unpack their equipment as they entered their tents. Typhomir transformed into a dragon and lay outside the camp to protect it from wandering beasts. It did not take long for everyone to crawl inside and fall asleep.

Morning came as the sun rose over the distant peaks, bathing the riverbanks they camped by in warm light. Nimue was awake before sunrise and sat meditating outside his tent. Ordi was the next to rise, with Mira by his side. It did not take long for the others to wake up. Typhomir and Arcadius were awake and conversed quietly with each other as the others changed clothes and packed up. They used the nearby river to wash their clothes. Ordi dried them with his staff before they were put away. "Young travelers," Typhomir spoke, "We move to the northeast. I will carry you, but I cannot bear you over the mountains. Arcadius will open a small portal for you to travel through the Red Peak. Before reaching Unrar, you will follow the coast for a few days and hopefully experience no setbacks."

They climbed onto Typhomir's back and settled in. Once everyone was secure, he soared high into the air. His wings flapped steadily as he raced north along the mountain range that separated the world from the unknown regions. The last mountain in the range before the ocean towered higher than any other they had passed. He soared at tremendous speed, and it took only a few hours before they reached the base of Red Peak. They dismounted the dragon's back and stood along the shoreline as Arcadius approached.

"You are all bound on a deadly quest. We do not know what lies before you, but you are meddling in ancient magic that this world has not witnessed for ages. Tread carefully wherever you go; trust no one, for the enemy will have agents everywhere," Arcadius warned sternly. He stepped up to the side of the mountain and cast a spell that opened a portal so the heroes could enter the other side of Red Peak. The group bid farewell and thanked Arcadius and Typhomir as they entered the portal.

Finally, along the shoreline, they found themselves on the opposite side of Red Peak. The sky above was hazy and dull, and a cold breeze was coming off the ocean.

The brotherhood crept along for most of the afternoon, rarely speaking, but all were determined to reach their destination. The terrain was unfamiliar to Ordi, and neither Verdun had ever traveled to Unrar. The Dwarves had abandoned this mountain long ago. The day was uneventful. Birds flew overhead, diving periodically into the water to fetch a fish for dinner, paying no attention to the group of travelers that walked past.

They made their way up the path to the long-abandoned city of Unrar. The towering mountain blocked the sun, and shadows loomed around them. The massive doors hung open, the door on the right still hanging by a single hinge. Ordi slipped past the broken doors and into a large entry hall. The rest followed him as he lit his staff to illuminate the chamber. The stone was worn and broken after years of neglect. Fragments of long-forgotten artifacts scattered the floor, crunching under each footstep. They walked through the vestibule and into the great hall of Unrar. The layout resembled Kamrar, a large hall that branched off into various areas for business and personal life for the dwarves. The grand hall encircled the mountain, creating a ring-like structure. The mountain's core housed the government and residential areas, while the outer sections were designated for businesses.

The adventurers cautiously made their way through the abandoned corridors of the ancient dwarven city of Unrar. Shadows danced along the stone walls, and the air was thick with the scent of decay. Ordi's staff flickered with arcane energy, casting a restless glow that illuminated their path. The dwarves generally had a treasury in the lower core designed to house the riches mined out before they were processed. That would be their starting point. As they ventured deeper into the mountain, the atmosphere grew heavier.

Thalin, ever the charismatic bard, kept the group's spirits high as he played softly on his flute. But beneath his charm lay a hidden agenda that would come to fruition soon enough. The group crossed the vast hall as Ordi's staff lit the walls. Beyond their bubble of light, blackness swarmed and filled the cavern. Cave-ins had blocked the old skylights that once brought in natural light, leaving the entire mountain in complete darkness. As the group moved, their footsteps echoed in the chamber, mingling with the moaning of the mountain. The noise was familiar to Ordi and Verdun, who had grown up in the mountains, but it was off-putting to the rest. Ordi led the way down the main corridor that would have led to the mines within the mountain.

"I've never seen anything like this. It is a great wonder of the world, the craftsmanship of the dwarves. Yet, I sense that once this place was abandoned, someone or a group of people placed something here that they didn't want others to know. I think we are close to the gems," Mira said.

The labyrinth of Unrar seemed to grow more confounding the deeper they ventured into the heart of the mountain. The ancient dwarven corridors twisted and turned in unpredictable ways, with each bend revealing new layers of mystery and deception. "These passages are nothing like

Kamrar," Verdun whispered as Ordi waved his staff to dispel the illusions blocking their path.

"It would appear that defensive spells were enacted to confuse or deter us from finding the correct path," Ordi said as he dismissed another illusion. Fake walls and rubble were placed to direct people to the wrong place. If an intruder were unfamiliar with the Dwarven layout, they would have been led out of the great city.

With the last illusion removed, a three-way fork presented itself, and the group found themselves at a critical juncture. Each path looked identical, illuminated only by Ordi's flickering light and the dying glow of ancient wall sconces. There were no markers, no runes, no signs to guide them.

"We're getting lost," Glallbi muttered, worry etched in her voice.

Having been silent since entering the mountain, Nimue said, "The earth has a pulse that seems to draw us forth down the center." The group fell silent as Nimue focused, feeling the ancient energy coursing through the mountain.

His connection to elemental arcane guided them through the twisting passages, but the mountain seemed to resist, shifting around them as if it had its own will. At times, the corridors appeared to stretch unnaturally, the walls bending and warping as if trying to entrap them.

"Ordi or Verdun would be better suited to lead us. I do not trust my feelings about this; the mountain does not like me," Nimue said.

"Let us take the path that appears less traveled," Verdun stated as he moved toward the center of the fork and started down the passage. They followed Verdun's intuition as he led the group. He drew his sword and kept it ready. Ordi followed behind with his staff lit, providing light for the group.

"Mira, what do you sense?" Ordi asked.

"It is hard to say. The mountain does not give up her secrets. I sense something evil in the ground, but no traces of life exist. I do not know what to make of this," Mira responded to Ordi.

As hope began to wane, the wall before them shuddered and crumbled, revealing a hidden passage. Dust and debris filled the air, but the newly revealed path seemed to beckon them forward. "It's as if the mountain itself is guiding us," Thalin commented.

As they pressed on, the environment felt increasingly hostile. The mountain wanted to thwart their quest, trying to lead them in the wrong direction or down false passages. Ordi and Verdun continuously had to reroute and attempt other paths to ensure they were on the right way to the treasury.

The rock began to warp and writhe, taking on an almost sentient malevolence. The adventurers came upon narrow stone bridges that spanned bottomless chasms. The chasms seemed to exhale a freezing breath, sending chills down their spines. The bridges were slick with age and moisture, making each step difficult. Verdun continued to lead on. Behind him, the others moved cautiously, measuring each step, aware that any misstep could spell disaster. A faint howling of wind echoed through the chasms, adding to the sense of impending doom as they navigated the passages.

They moved deeper into the mountain. The walls around them oozed a dark, viscous substance as they descended further. It dripped and pooled on the floor, creating an unsettling sound that echoed through the passageway. Further along, they found greenish-yellow fungi growing on the walls. It emitted a faint light, which was not enough to guide them. They continued to rely on Ordi's staff. As his light washed over the fungi, it retracted back into the wall as if repelled by the staff's glow. In their peripheral vision, they perceived movement; spectral apparitions flitted back and forth through the corridor. They moved with a haunting grace, their faces contorted in silent agony. The spirits paid no attention to the Brotherhood as they glided back and forth, often amid the group traversing the passageway.

Continual turns left them feeling lost and uncertain of their whereabouts. Verdun finally led them to the end of the passage. An old wooden door wedged into the rocky wall stood before them. Verdun grabbed the handle and pushed. The knob broke off, but the door opened. The room was narrow and long, with a row of tables on either side and another door at the end. Laying on the tables were piles of old parchments covered in centuries of dust and grime.

"Hey, come look at this," Ordi called out as he picked up a set of ancient scrolls. The parchments were inscribed with intricately carved runes that seemed to pulse with latent power. "These spells are incredible. I've never seen anything like them. The dragons should have kept these." He placed them carefully in his satchel to research later.

"We have no time; we must keep moving," Nimue said as he passed the tables and approached the door at the end of the room. Passing through the opposite door, they found themselves in a long corridor once again. They continued, but the mountain was not finished testing them. The deeper they ventured, the more treacherous the path became. The dark, viscous substance continued to seep from the walls, giving off a more pungent scent the further they moved. Navigating through a maze of passages, crossing bridges, and marching through rooms and large caverns, they finally made it to the chambers where the wealth of the dwarves was kept.

They pushed open the doors and investigated the rooms. Each room was stripped bare, save for shelves and tables. They continued to examine the entire area around the circumference of the massive mine at the center of Unrar. Ordi pushed open another door and surveyed the room with the light of his staff. A small box in a dark corner caught his eye. He walked over and picked it up, using his robes to dust off the top of the box. Ancient dwarven runes were etched on the lid, describing its contents. He opened the lid, and there lay a single gem. It was plain-looking, with a grey mist swirling within it. As Ordi held his staff close, the mist started to swirl more purposefully, glowing with embedded light. Mira yelped with excitement.

"This is great! But where are the other three?" Mira asked.

"I'm not sure; I think they have to be here in Unrar somewhere," Ordi replied.

Ordi called out to the others, "In here! I found them!" Verdun, Nimue, and Glallbi joined him. "Where's Thalin?"

"I don't know. I thought he was with you," Nimue said.

"No, I don't recall seeing him for a while. I don't even recall hearing his music for some time," Ordi replied. As Ordi finished, they all heard the soft tone of a flute off in the distance, but it was not the normal upbeat rhythm Thalin usually played. This tone was dark and laced with evil intent. Ear-piercing screams could be heard in the distance. Scratching sounds and rocks falling could be heard, and glows of eerie green could be seen massing together. An unnatural cold wind snapped through the room, bringing deep chills to the group. The flute sounds increasingly darkened, bringing forth an unknown enemy.

The sounds of objects being dragged across the floor could be heard as the group prepared to fight whatever crossed the doorway's barrier. Calls rang out from the chambers beyond, encouraging the trespassers to be destroyed.

"Seek the gems, seek death. Seek the gems, seek death. For the adventurer, that is their only fate." The calls were repeated.

The undead, long dormant, had awoken and started their journey to where Ordi and his companions resided. Their grotesque forms emerged from the shadows: skeletal warriors with tattered flesh, spectral beings whose bones glowed with that eerie green light. The dead, of all races, crawled out of their resting places; some wore ancient armor fused into their decaying bodies. Others wielded weapons dripping with dark arcane magic.

"Moriden's beard. What did we awaken?" Verdun asked as dark figures slowly inched toward the room.

Amidst the chaos, an evil laugh echoed through the chamber. Thalin stepped into view with a sinister smile spreading across his face. "Fools!" he hissed, his voice dripping with betrayal. "Did you honestly believe I was here to help you? Keep the joy up by playing my little flute. The gems are mine. I will take them to my master and be greatly rewarded. I shall wield the ancients' power, and you will all perish at my hand. I have three of the four already." He laughed again.

Thalin raised his hand, and the undead responded to his command, surging forward. Some undead unleashed blasts of necrotic energy, corroding everything they touched. Others summoned whirling vortexes of bone and ash, trapping the adventurers in a vortex of darkness.

"Thalin, what have you done?!" Ordi shouted, unleashing a bolt of lightning that narrowly missed the traitorous bard.

Glallbi's eyes filled with tears. "Why, Thalin? We trusted you!" As Glallbi looked on, a loud voice broke over the chaos.

"Thalin! You have been found unworthy. Your bond is broken." The crystal sprang from his pocket and exploded in the air next to him. The shards sliced into his face, cutting deep gouges and causing more anger to spew from him.

Ordi blocked the swings from the undead and thrust the point of his staff toward Thalin. A ball of magic erupted, flying toward the evil bard. He dodged as the arcane sphere collided with a horde of skeletons, blasting bones everywhere. The undead continued to swarm toward the group. As they passed Thalin, the undead moved forth, showering the Brotherhood in a storm of bones and debris. Thalin disappeared into the chaos, slipping into the shadows and escaping the judgment that would have befallen him. Three undead reached Verdun. He raised his sword to slice, but they were quicker. One lashed out, cutting across his shoulder with a rusty blade. The sword, being so old, shattered upon impact.

Glallbi witnessed the attack, and before Verdun could react, she cast a healing spell on the wound. Instantly, the blood dried up, and the skin closed. He looked at her with amazement.

"I didn't think it could be so fast. Take care of them, just don't be reckless," she yelled as she prepared more healing spells.

Verdun lashed out, engaging a multitude of the undead. Swinging away, he drew a horde of skeletons to distract them from Nimue and Ordi. Glallbi continued healing him; every cut and slice healed instantly. She even fortified his agility, increasing his speed and adrenaline.

The undead kept sprouting forth from the ground, their numbers continuing to increase. Ordi smashed his staff down, blasting arcane energy in a radius around the Brotherhood, shattering the skeletons that were close to him. Glallbi continued to cast enchantments on the Brotherhood, ensuring they had the endurance for the fight. Mira channeled directly to Ordi, reinforcing his connections.

Nimue called forth roots to entangle a group of undead as he shouted, "Retreat! This way!" He dropped back down the main hall into the massive, abandoned mine. Verdun protected the retreat as he stood, slashing down skeleton after skeleton. Mira assisted by snapping the arms off those Verdun missed. Glallbi cast healing spells that kept Verdun and Mira safe and healthy. Ordi continued blasting the hordes of undead as they retreated. They carved out enough of a gap to turn and flee down the narrow corridor through the levels of the mine. As they moved, more undead pressed through the ground, grabbing at the fleeing adventurers. The chase was relentless, the undead driven by the malevolent will of Thalin. He created a catastrophic storm by calling forth the dead of Unrar.

"Quickly, this way!" Verdun directed, slashing an arm and pushing it away. Glallbi had enchanted the group with spells that continued to heal and enhance them as they moved through the darkness of the mines.

As they moved, they could hear a dark voice chanting over the wind that blew past them. Thalin continued to recite dark incantations from afar, drawing forth more darkness from Unrar. The walls around the Brotherhood constricted and shook as black vile dripped from the ceiling. The group continued running, dodging hordes of undead seeking to ambush them.

Verdun spotted a heavy door inscribed with ancient runes as they rounded a corner. "In here!" he shouted, shoving it open with all his might.

The adventurers tumbled into the chamber beyond, slamming the door just as the undead reached it. The heavy stone groaned under the weight of the assault but held firm... for now. Breathing heavily, the group could still hear the moans and scrapes from the other side.

"Thalin's betrayal changes everything. We have to be ready for the unknown," Nimue said solemnly. "Do we have any of the gems?"

"We have one. The gem that I found," Ordi said.

"That means he could have the other three," Nimue said.

"I heard him say that," Verdun replied. Each could sense the disappointment in the darkness. The sounds of scraping continued on the other side of the stone.

"How do we get out of here?" Glallbi panted, her eyes darting between her friends and the barricaded door.

Suddenly, the chamber walls began to rumble, revealing a hidden passage in the stone.

"Looks like our only choice," Verdun said, tightening his grip on his sword.

Ordi nodded, casting one last look at the sealed door. "Let's hope this isn't a trap."

"I can't sense anything in the darkness, Ordi," Mira said as she walked through the opening.

With a final glance at each other, the adventurers plunged into the unknown depths of Unrar's heart. The echoes of the undead faded behind them. Their journey was far from over; their trust was shattered, but their determination was unwavering. The darkness enveloped them again as the passage sealed behind them, leaving their fate in unsettling suspense.

Made in the USA
Columbia, SC
11 June 2025